C. J. Greene

MAMBA'S DAUGHTERS

BOOKS BY
DU BOSE HEYWARD

∿∿∿∿∿∿∿∿∿∿∿∿∿∿∿∿∿∿∿∿∿∿∿∿∿

ANGEL

SKYLINES AND HORIZONS

MAMBA'S DAUGHTERS

PORGY: A NOVEL

PORGY: A PLAY IN FOUR ACTS
(WITH DOROTHY HEYWARD)

CAROLINA CHANSONS
(WITH HERVEY ALLEN)

DU BOSE HEYWARD

MAMBA'S DAUGHTERS

A NOVEL OF CHARLESTON

THE LITERARY GUILD
NEW YORK 1929

AUTHOR'S NOTE

Because I believe that regional literature, even though it be avowedly fictional, should be unequivocal in its identification with its locale, I have not hesitated in this novel to apply the correct names to the city, streets, and outlying districts of which I write. Lest this course should lead the reader into confusing the narrative with either history or biography, I desire to stress the fact that the work is purely imaginative and is concerned only with certain social and spiritual values existing in Charleston and its environs. For the purposes of the novel the material has been subjected to an intense synthesis. Thus the phosphate mining camp stands not merely as an exposition of an isolated industry, but as a focal point for the drawing together of a number of mental attitudes and incidents typical of the industrial black belt. With the exception of allusions to people whose correct names are used, and who will be readily recognized, the characters who appear in the book are fictional creations and are not intended as representations of actual characters either living or dead.

DU BOSE HEYWARD.

Charleston, South Carolina,
    October, 1928.

PART I

IT was no mere chance that, during the first decade of the new century, brought Mamba out of the darkness of the underworld into the light of the Wentworths' kitchen. Casual as that event seemed, there is good evidence for the belief that it had its origin in some obscure recess of the woman's mind; or in perhaps some deep and but half comprehended instinct that drove her, against the reasoning of her brain, to embark upon what must have seemed a fantastically hopeless venture. For Mamba had arrived at an age that lay on the downhill side of fifty, and her habitat had always been the waterfront.

The amazing thing is that, having arrived at her decision, she was able to muster the courage necessary to take the step.

In the Charleston of Mamba's day the negro population might have been divided into two general classes: the upper, consisting of those who had white folks, belonged to the negro quality and enjoyed a certain dolorous respectability; and the lower class, members of which had no white folks and were little better than outcasts.

How long Mamba had incubated her amazing plan there is no way of knowing. It is quite certain, however, that she reinforced the initial whisper with a "cunjer" that promised success, and that then, armed only with an enormous and devious experience and a remarkable histrionic talent, she selected her point of attack. But in the last step she showed the genius that was to predestine her to ultimate success.

The Wentworths, as was well known, had been wealthy plantation people before the war. But that fate which arranges the rise and fall of aristocracies had placed the original grant from the

British Crown directly across the line of march to be taken six generations later by General Sherman. The condition of the Wentworths after the army had passed through their plantation was a sustained corroboration of the general's famous definition. Immediately after the war the family had abandoned the charred remnants of what had once been the ancestral home, sold the land to liquidate old debts, and moved to Charleston. There they settled in the little brick dwelling near the Battery that they still occupied when they were elected by Mamba as her point of attack.

At that time there were four members of the family. Mrs. Wentworth was a widow in the early forties, possessed of intelligence, unquenchable industry, and a personal charm that the exigent years were stiffening into a manner almost too rigid for so soft a word. It was so desperately important for her children to hold their place in the society in which they had been born. It was as though, knowing the material odds against her, she dared not give an inch. The boy, St. Julien de Chatigny Wentworth, was now fourteen years of age. He had inherited an ancestral curse in the nickname of Saint, and was at the stage of being torn between a genuine desire for knowledge and the frustrating public-school system of the period. Polly, the girl, was altogether charming. A slender blonde of twelve, she was now in attendance at the Misses Sass's school for young gentlewomen, on Legaré Street, and in accordance with the custom of the old city was just beginning to attend her first dancing-school soirées in the company of her brother. The fourth and by no means the least important member of the family was Maum Netta. She was a small intensely black woman of great delicacy of feeling, and with a sense of social values that was infallible. If she lacked anything that one had a right to expect it was, strangely enough for her race, a sense of humour, and one shrewdly suspected that she had deliberately suppressed this quality as jeopardising the dignity of her position. It is certain that she requited the Wentworths for their protection and love with a loyalty, devotion, and faith that imposed upon the two children an obligation of fulfilment almost as deep as that implicit in the relationship of child to parent.

It will be readily seen that the Wentworths just described presented a highly vulnerable front to the invasion of the Four Hundred planned by Mamba. Had the family been larger and wealthier she could not have gained the attention of the white folks and would probably have been given scant courtesy by the new-time negroes in the kitchen. Here was a family born in the slave-holding tradition of amused and even affectionate tolerance toward the negro once that negro had detached himself from the mass and become identified as an individual. Here, too, in the person of Maum Netta was a gentle and highly competent instructor in the intricate technique that the aged tyro must acquire. True, she knew that the old servant would treat her with well-bred condescension, but, with the true spirit of the social climber, she was prepared to pocket her pride until it could be worn with dignity.

The exact moment of attack was timed to a nicety, and slipped into its place with that appearance of casualness which is the result of infinitely calculated preparation. It was spring in Charleston, and almost overnight the sudden uprush of life from the soil had transformed the town. Wisteria dropped its purple stalactites from the trees and gateposts, and the roses lifted in a foam of colour and perfume over the garden walls. Even the air had a soft velvet on it, like pollen on a petal. It was inconceivable that at such a time hearts could be hardened or harsh words spoken.

The evening was one of unusual excitement in the little brick house. Saint was to escort his sister to her first soirée. Polly was slim and lovely in her white dress with its hand-worked border made after hours by Mrs. Wentworth. But there were no flowers for the début. In all the city of bloom the little brick house was without a garden, its four massive walls crowding the little lot to the limit of its accommodation.

The child was breathless with longing.

"Please, Mother, please; May, and Damaris, and the Hugers all have big gardens. It won't take a minute to run over to Legaré Street and ask for some roses. Saint will go. Won't you, Saint?"

But the mother said: "I am sorry, dear, you can't, you know. We are too poor to have our own, and that is the very reason why we cannot ask. Remember what Landor says, 'You have already paid the highest price for a thing when you have asked for it.'"

"Yes, I know. Horrid, rich old thing. I bet he never wanted anything in his life that he couldn't run to a shop and buy."

Saint put in: "Aw, they have millions and millions of them. It wouldn't be really giving, they wouldn't miss 'em."

"I know, dears, but they will have to be offered. We cannot ask."

Tears then—tragedy in that gay moment of departure; high-strung little nerves jumping from tears to laughter and back again. And a mist in Mrs. Wentworth's eyes, the obstinacy of an idealist in her firm mouth and lifted chin.

And Saint: "Aw, come on. Don't get all messed up over a few flowers."

Maum Netta opened the door from the kitchen into the dining-room where desire and ethics were grappling. "Dere's uh 'oman outside wot say she want fuh see Missie. She ain't berry clean. Maybe Missie better come in de kitchen fuh see um."

The three Wentworths adjourned to the immaculate little kitchen, and there they beheld an incongruous picture. Mamba stood just within the door, and as they entered she dropped a deep courtesy. She was a woman of medium height, frail almost to a point of emaciation. She was not a full-blooded African negro, but her prominent nose, and the coppery cast to her dark skin suggested a strain of American Indian rather than an admixture of white blood in her veins. Her face had reached the point at which it tells nothing of age. As it looked now with its multitudinous wrinkles, it would still look at her death. She smiled a little timidly and revealed a lonely yellow fang in the middle of her lower gum. Then she took a step forward into the full light of the kerosene lamp and looked into the face of the slender blonde girl. From the network of wrinkles the woman's eyes, large and of a peculiar live brown brilliance, looked startlingly out, bright with the fire of indomitable youth. Standing directly before Polly she courtesied again and brought from behind her back a large shower of Dorothy Perkins roses. The stems were wrapped with tinfoil and tied with floss that had been fashioned into a cord with tassels exactly like those displayed in the florists' windows on King Street.

"Ah tink how my Little Missie goin' tuh dance tuh Miss Snowden party to-night, an' Ah say dat de p'utties' lady dere ought fuh hab flower."

She swung her rags about her in another courtesy, and extended the bouquet.

Polly gave a gasp of pleasure and held out her hand to take the flowers. The terrible ogre of ethics again raised its head. If one could not ask a neighbour for roses, could one accept a gift of roses that had undoubtedly been stolen over the wall of the selfsame neighbour?

"I think that we must know where those flowers came from before we take them," Mrs. Wentworth interposed a little weakly.

"Ah gots frien' who gardener on Legaré Street, Miss. He gib me lot ob flower."

Saint cut the Gordian knot: "Take the old flowers and let's go. We'll be late, anyhow, with all this talk." Then, seizing his sister by one arm as she caught the bouquet to her breast with the other, he rushed her to the door, and before Mrs. Wentworth could say anything more, their feet had pattered into silence down the street.

The mother turned and looked at Mamba. There was a moment of silence, then the strange old woman gazed up into her face with her amazing girl's eyes, and smiled her wide single-toothed smile. Mrs. Wentworth threw back her head and laughed. "Where did you come from?" she asked.

"Oh, not so fur. Ah been see Little Missie go by ebery day, an' Ah jes can't wait no longer tuh put dem flower whar day b'longs."

Mrs. Wentworth turned with her hand on the dining-room door knob. "I am sure it was very good of you," she said, "and now you must let Maum Netta give you some supper before you go away. It was so very odd, your coming just to-night."

But was it odd, after all? Was it not rather one of those inevitable happenings that are so often mistaken for coincidences but are in reality the mathematical result of a premise originating in some remote but unswerving human purpose?

★

There was that about the invisible comings and goings of Mamba, after that first night, which tended to confirm Mrs. Wentworth's grave misgivings. It suggested a proficiency that smacked of the professional, like a game of poker or billiards that is almost too expert for a gentleman. She would prowl about the kitchen dooryard as silent and as unswervingly watchful as a neighbourhood cat, and then, without having been seen in the house, she would leave the evidence of a visit there in some gift for Polly or service for a member of the family.

On the morning following the soirée there were fresh roses, with dew still on the petals, heaped on the girl's breakfast plate. Mrs. Wentworth, who was a sharp observer, noticed that they had been torn from the vine. Gardeners on Legaré Street were well trained and were provided with shears. Most certainly she must tell Maum Netta not to allow the woman to return. She was not of the type to be encouraged. But after breakfast, when Mrs. Wentworth repaired to the kitchen, she encountered a new complication.

Maum Netta was seated in unaccustomed ease eating her breakfast and Mamba was just drying the last of the dishes. During the moment that Mrs. Wentworth stood unobserved in the doorway, she was an eavesdropper upon a masterpiece of diplomacy. Mamba was saying: "Tek yo' ease, Mistress Netta, tek yo' ease. Ah knows dishwashin' ain't fuh de quality cullud folks. Attuh yo' done git up, an' comb yo' putty gray hair, an' cook dis fine breakfus, an' 'splain tuh yo' white folks what tuh do all day, yo' ought fuh tek yo' ease an' studdy 'bout yo' frien' Gawd, while some poor-folks nigger like me cleans up attuh yo'."

Maum Netta, with great dignity, expressing itself in a heavy lugubriousness, but already making social concessions:

"Well, it use' tuh be dat-a-way. Dey was always kitchen niggers in de ole days. But t'ings is change' now, t'ings is change'."

Mrs. Wentworth's cool high-bred syllables fell chill across the gathering warmth and requested Maum Netta's presence in the dining-room. When the door was closed she turned to the old negress.

The mistress could have bungled then. A single flat order could have done it. But instinctively she closed with a question, thereby throwing the burden on Maum Netta, and at once rebuking her and re-establishing her integrity.

"I am really provoked, Mauma" (she had not gone as far as that in years); "I was just going to ask that woman to leave the premises, and I find you accepting favours of her. You know we have no money to pay a servant. Now, what am I to do?"

"Ah sorry, Miss. Dat a hahd 'oman tuh say no tuh. See if yo' can find a ole dress or somet'ing an' Ah'll gib it tuh she an' sen' she away."

There was silence in the kitchen, and the tension of impending crisis when Mrs. Wentworth returned with some old clothing thrown over her arm. In a cool, positive tone of finality which dismissed a mutual future and expunged the past, she said:

"Maum Netta will attend to those dishes. Thank you for helping us. Here are some old clothes."

But she got no further. Mamba courtesied almost to the floor, with her rags trailing grotesquely about her. Then she raised a face that was radiant with gratitude. She started talking rapidly while she took the clothes, and her volubility increased as she backed toward the door. Twice Mrs. Wentworth attempted to stem the tide, then gave it up.

"Oh, t'ank yo', Miss. Ah's too t'ankful. Ah's been too 'shame' tuh come roun' yo' an' Little Missie in dese ole rags. Now Ah's goin' be dat clean my own ma wouldn't know me. Now Ah t'ink dat de nex' time Little Missie go to dance she ain't goin' be 'shame' fuh let me go long wid she an' carry she slipper bag."

The queer bobbing figure paused for a moment in the open door; then, with its hand on the knob, raised its head. Out of the meshed wrinkles and folds of skin looked the woman's astounding eyes, audacious and mocking, then for a second in the closing door they caught the mood of the toothless smile and overflowed with laughter.

★

Two days passed and a Sunday came. No sign of Mamba. Mrs. Wentworth dismissed the whole episode as closed. The day was glorious with spring sunshine, and the air was throbbing to the music of St. Michael's chimes. Mamba rounded a corner a block

away from the front door of the Wentworth residence, then
stopped and lingered unobtrusively in a recessed gateway. She could
not keep her feet still while the chimes were playing, and the
shabby, broad toe that extended from beneath the hem of her recently acquired neat gray dress tapped gently on the pavement.
She knew well the rotation of the tunes: "Shall We Gather at the
River?" "There Is a Blessed Home," and the way the music dropped
an octave on a high note where a bell was missing. George Washington Christopher Gadsden, the ancient bell ringer, was a crony
of hers, and she smiled now at the thought of his favourite joke on
the white people in the pews. Yes, there it was, slipped in between
"There Is a Blessed Home" and "Onward, Christian Soldiers":

> "Sistuh Ca'line, Sistuh Ca'line,
> Can't yo' dance the peavine?"

Two lines of the old song that the negroes loved, then on into the
next hymn without missing a beat. He'd be laughing now at his
joke, up there by himself in the steeple.

Suddenly the tune stopped and the bells commenced to toll.
Three minutes now before service. Mamba peered from her retreat,
and an expression of satisfaction overspread her features as the
three Wentworths stepped from their front door and proceeded
decorously toward the calling bells.

In the Wentworth kitchen Maum Netta was washing her dishes
and singing a spiritual in her high, slightly cracked soprano. She
reached for a high note and held it with evident pride. Then
through the open window there entered a melodious contralto note
that met it and rang with it in resonant chord. Maum Netta's eyes
widened with pleasure while she held her note to the limit of her
lung capacity. Then she crossed to the window and looked out.
Mamba was seated immediately below her on the doorstep, and she
met the older woman's gaze with an expression of awe. "My Gawd,

Mauma," she half whispered, "how come nobody ain't nebber tell me yo' kin sing like dat?"

"Cose Ah kin sing." Then slowly the necessity of being firm with this person began to triumph over flattered vanity. "But dat's neider here nor dere. Ah gots orders from Miss Wentworth not fuh leabe yo' come 'roun' here no mo'."

"Cos yo' has, Mauma, cose yo' has. Ain't Ah knows Ah ain't yo' kind ob folks? Ain't Ah knows my place? Now, don't yo' worry none about dat. Ah ain't goin' let dese feet go ober dat do' no matter how hahd dey begs me. But sence all de white folks done gone to church, why can't yo' an' me set here, jes as we is, yo' in yo' place, and me jes in de outdoors, an' sing some tuhgedder. Ah jes been a-wonnerin' if yo' knows 'Light in de Grabeyahd Outshine de Sun!'"

Without waiting to risk further parley, Mamba raised the tune.

> "Light in de grabeyahd outshine de sun,
>   Outshine de sun, outshine de sun,
>   Light in de grabeyahd outshine de sun,
>   Way beyon' de moon.
>
> "My Christian people, hol' out yo' light,
>   Hol' out yo' light, hol' out yo' light,
>   My Christian people, hol' out yo' light,
>   Way beyon' de moon."

Deep, tender, and true, and slurring only a little from the toothless gums, her contralto notes lifted to the window where the older woman stood, and called with that same irresistible quality of youth that shone in the woman's eyes. Mamba was not merely singing for her supper now. The gratification of that mysterious urge that had started her on her adventure hung in the balance. She let the whole force of her longing throb in the mysterious music.

Maum Netta listened for a moment. No negro can resist harmony, and while soprano voices of great beauty are common enough among them, contraltos are rare. Mamba's tone dropped almost into the baritone register, and throbbed there full and true. She commenced to sway slowly from side to side as she sat there on the step. Maum Netta tried the harmony with one light note, and it was as though she had unlocked floodgates, for the spiritual swept irresistibly from her lips. She returned on tiptoe to her dishes, her head thrown back, and her soul going out in that strange communion that comes from merging two separate and imperfect voices into a rare and beautiful common offering. The little kitchen, and the small brick-paved yard rocked to the enchantment of it. The rhythm possessed itself of its creators. In the dining-room the little mahogany clock on the mantel sent its hands spinning on toward noon.

Church was over, and Mrs. Wentworth approached the little brick house chatting with several neighbours.

"I did not know there was a negro church near," one of them remarked. "Why, that singing seems to be right in our block."

"And Sunday too!" contributed a little woman with arched eyebrows and a chronically shocked voice.

Mrs. Wentworth did not like this neighbour, so she said sweetly: "Well, after all, they are spirituals, you know. The negroes evidently still think that Sunday is the Lord's Day." But her defensive attitude wilted suddenly. She was before her own door now, and grim forebodings were upon her. She excused herself hurriedly and entered. A moment later she stood surveying a scene that, while it tempted her to laughter, told her in no uncertain terms that she was in that moment witnessing her own defeat.

Maum Netta sat just inside of the room with her turbaned head nodding back and forth to the measure of the spiritual. The door stood wide open, and upon the step sat Mamba swaying and patting with her large, flat feet and throwing her whole being into the music. But the visitor had not been idle, and therein lay her triumph. Before her on the marble step, fairly sparkling in the sun, were ranged all of the shoes possessed by the family. The last one, a dancing pump of Saint's, was just being given a final polish.

Mrs. Wentworth was obliged to speak a second time before she could make her presence known.

"Maum Netta, have you gone raving crazy?"

Instant silence in the kitchen, and the slow gathering together of faculties in the two before her, like people waking from a daze. What was the use! Mrs. Wentworth re-entered the dining room, closed the door behind her, and gave herself over to impotent laughter.

With the success of the shoe-shining episode, Mamba attained her first definite objective. As a matter of fact, Mrs. Wentworth was predestined for failure in such a situation by reason of her virtues rather than her weaknesses, and where such is the case, a cause is indeed hopeless. Mamba, born of a race that owed its very existence to its understanding of the ruling white, knew just how vulnerable those virtues were, and so she had only to direct her attack against them and bide her time. Her position was now fairly secure. She had only to keep a favour ahead of her victim, leaving upon her the burden of an unrepaid obligation. The Wentworths had no money wherewith to compensate her, and so, in lieu thereof, she must be given food in the kitchen and the outworn and easily recognisable garments of her new mistress. To the neighbourhood, and even in her own eyes, this soon gave her the superficial colouration of a retainer of the aristocracy. Presently, when she was safely out of earshot of Maum Netta, she commenced to refer to the Wentworth household as "my white folks."

Mamba had no regular hours for her comings and goings, but

she had a way of materialising dramatically in the moment of emergency, and she delighted in certain conspicuous services of a social nature. To Polly's great pride she insisted on following her to the soirées and carrying her slipper bag ostentatiously to the dressing-room door. Then, while the dance was in progress, she would play the ladies' maid with the waiting negresses who had come with the wealthy girls from the Battery homes. More than one amazing story of her daughter's talents and her own wealth circled back to Mrs. Wentworth, and were easily traced by her to these below-stairs gatherings at the dances.

Mamba's logic in these cases was simple: what could possibly give her more distinction than to be the maid of a young lady of quality, who was sufficiently distinguished to have a maid! But around the little brick house she was humility personified.

How the old woman must have longed to adopt the head kerchief such as was worn by Maum Netta and was the traditional badge of the house-bred servant! But she was well aware that this would be a fatal presumption. For the present, at least, she must depend on the neat, partly worn clothing of Mrs. Wentworth for her borrowed respectability. As for her head, it was still treated in the astonishing manner common among older negroes who had not been born to the dignity of the kerchief, and whose generation had not yet adopted kink-remover. The wool was divided into a dozen or more equal tufts. Each of these was tightly wrapped with string, commencing at the tip and ending at the scalp; then the collection, resembling rope ends, was drawn together and united in a tight knob on the crown. The general effect was as though an enormous gray tarantula had settled upon the head, and was holding on tightly with outstretched legs. But if Mamba dared not essay the head kerchief, she did the next best thing, and was seldom seen thereafter without her hat.

When the first autumn arrived neighbours were commencing to
identify Mamba as "that new negro of the Wentworths'."

★

Three years passed without a change in the relative positions
of Mamba and her adopted white folks, except that by her
continued association with them she became a copartner in their
fortunes. She received no wages, and this gave her an independence
that she loved. She had a way of dropping out of sight for days
at a time. The Wentworths never speculated as to her private life.
They took her as they found her. But so subtle are the forces that
knit human relationships together that the time arrived without
their realising it when no matter of serious importance could affect
either of the participants in the strange partnership without bearing
upon the destinies of the other.

Fortunes had waned in the little brick house. Polly was
approaching the time when she would graduate from her school.
She could name the English kings forward and backward, speak
French, spell perfectly, and do sums in elementary arithmetic. So
much for what might have been classed as commercial assets with
which to meet the exactions of the Twentieth Century. But from
the gentle and charming old ladies she had absorbed the old Southern
gentlewoman tradition that had lingered on in the disintegrating
old school like rose leaves in a jar. She danced beautifully, and in
her eyes was that unutterable word that men, seeing, answered.
She already had a host of beaux, and the career to which she was
predestined by birth, tradition, and instinct resolved itself in its
particular detail to a matter of selection when the proper time
should arrive. But she must be given an opportunity of appearing
to advantage during the momentous period that would lie between
graduation and marriage.

Saint was a disappointment to every one but Mamba. He had

failed utterly to yield to the standardising process of the public school. He was sensitive and took refuge from humiliating realities in a dream world of his own. The result was absent-mindedness. Teachers told him that he was a fool, and he believed them. A gangling adolescent of seventeen, out of school and not yet at work, practically penniless, with the look of a hurt animal in his eyes, he spent most of his time roaming the waterfront. His acquaintances who caught glimpses of him in those days decided that he was definitely a failure, and potentially a confirmed ne'er-do-well. Not that he was dissipated. It was probably worse. The old town looked with indulgent eyes upon youth in its wild-oats stage. That was something rooted in tradition, understood. Good blood could be counted upon to win through in that reckless period. Fathers and uncles would exchange sly winks that condoned the indiscretions of to-day, while they implied a vanished but far more adventurous youth of their own. "Get it safely over with, then marry and settle down." "Better before than after." "Young blood, young blood." Yes, undoubtedly boys not only would, but *should*, be boys. But Saint was a boy who obviously did not even have the initiative to be one. It was too bad. And poor Kate Wentworth a widow too. The boy felt it rising in the air about him like a tangible wall—a wall against which he could bruise himself cruelly, but from which he could not escape.

Sometimes at the waterfront he would forget. There were sights there that had nothing to do with the personal equation, that were detached from actuality and seemed to invade the territory of dreams. Negroes crossing a dock head single file, with cotton bales on their trucks—a frieze of rhythmic bodies against a blue-green sea horizon. He'd like to catch that so that it could not elude him again; fix it in some medium that he could carry away with him— paint, maybe. But one could not study to paint, one could not study anything until one had passed in algebra. There it stood like a Chinese wall about all knowledge. It had to be mastered before one could go on. Well, he had been born without that kind of a brain. His friends had been more fortunate and were getting ahead. He had been dropped from his classes—the fate of the fool. He was at least logical enough to follow that to its conclusion. But here he was—and what next?

Only Mamba seemed to understand the boy. Days would come when the old woman would grow restive under her straitjacket of respectability, and the two would be discovered by Mrs. Wentworth in a corner of the kitchen yard seated on an empty packing case. Mamba, with her disguise laid aside, and a look of low and humorous cunning on her lined face, would be nodding her gray tarantula up and down while she told a story. Saint was always the listener, laughing his shy, quiet laugh and forgetting himself in the tale.

★

Summer came, and with it a desperate decision on the part of Mrs. Wentworth; a decision that quite unexpectedly resulted in an important step in Mamba's social evolution. That one may know how desperate the situation in the little brick house had become, it is only necessary to say that a cottage was to be hired at the shore, furnished with the Wentworth plate and linen, and that a limited number of "paying guests" were to be permitted to share the sanctity of a Wentworth home.

Mamba decided to accompany the family; Maum Netta went as a matter of course, and at the ferry that was to convey them on the first phase of the journey they were joined by a round-bellied negro who had about him a look of great importance. Upon arriving at their destination this individual was found to possess a reputation for cooking, an enormous white chef's cap, and, to the delight of the two women, an entirely adequate tenor voice.

Mamba was living well now, and she should have been happy. She performed only such light work as suited her fancy. The kitchen was far enough from the house to allow almost constant singing. There was a shady breeze-swept piazza for the hot mornings, and at night the unremitting flow of broad sea winds under the soft summer stars. But that mysterious fire in her spirit would not let her rest. The other negroes tried to laugh her out of her preoccupation, but without avail. Sometimes in the middle of a song she would leave and stand at the piazza rail, gazing over the bay to where the lights of the town created a false illusion of dawn against the west, and her eyes would be filled with a nostalgic longing.

By August Mrs. Wentworth's venture had proved itself to be a distinct success. The house was well filled, and the pleasant uneventful days were yielding a financial profit that promised well for the future. But to Mamba the month was tremendous and memorable, for it brought to that opportunist the epoch-making episode of the judge's teeth.

Judge Harkness had arrived for a rest immediately after the June term of court. It is unlikely that a more distinguished figure had trod the sands of Sullivan's Island since the historic days of General Moultrie. He was tall, and of a commanding presence, and the proper finish was added to his appearance by a well-clipped beard, and pince-nez. Maum Netta placed him socially with the tribute:

"Me an' you, Cook, we talks cullud folks' talk. Miss Wentwort', she talk white folks' talk, but de Jedge, now—he ain't speak nutting but de grammar."

But the judge was too closely allied with the law for Mamba to admit his superiority. She had a way of sucking her tooth with a loud, derisive sound, and she employed this method of expressing her disdain to the kitchen whenever he was discussed. Once she contributed her comment, and with it stripped him to the fundamental weakness of the male.

"Yas, Ah seen um once, a-settin' on he bench wid he long black robe on, sendin' nigger tuh jail, like he been Gawd. But don' yuh fergit, onnerneat' dat black wrapper he gots on two-leg pants same like Cook dere."

Now the cook had acquired a reputation among the negresses of the neighbourhood, and the connotation freighted her remark with outrageous implication. The cook beamed with unctuous satisfaction. Maum Netta pretended at first not to understand, then frowned her disapproval. Mamba, enjoying her own audacity immensely, closed her eyes to narrow slits, and sat there looking darkly mysterious.

This particular August morning was in the midst of one of the hottest spells of the season. From the Wentworth cottage the waves could be seen crawling far up the beach and dissolving into low, monotonous breakers, as though reluctant to release their cooling spray into the close atmosphere. The judge had risen early and gone in for his morning dip. Several guests sat listlessly on the piazza, waiting for breakfast with pre-coffee indifference to life so common in the American home.

Mamba was cleaning a pan of fish in the kitchen when her keen ears caught sudden exclamations of interest from the front of the house. She dropped her pan, and, trailing a suggestion of whiting behind her, ran to the piazza and gazed over the heads of the guests who were gathered at the piazza rail, their coffee for the moment forgotten.

In the shallow surf, not a hundred yards away, a most amazing sight presented itself. The judge was on all fours, roaming back and forth over a section of beach that might have measured twenty-five feet square. The agitated movements of the body, the turning at a given point as though stopped by steel bars, inevitably suggested the caged animal.

"Why, he's gone crazy," one of the women shrilled.

Suddenly the strange performance ceased. The judge got to his feet and started toward the house. As he passed the piazza on his way to the rear entrance, it seemed to the onlookers that his dignity had fallen from him. His figure in its wet bathing suit gave the effect of shrinking away. One hand was held over his face but was unable to conceal the blight of senility that seemed to have settled upon it. In a final blundering rush he gained his room and closed the door behind him.

A babblement of speculation and comment burst forth, but was immediately met by Mrs. Wentworth's instinctive generalship. "The judge seems a little upset," she remarked quietly. "I am sure he will appreciate silence in which to collect himself. Saint, you must go at once and see what you can do for him."

It is unlikely that the shy, self-conscious boy ever experienced a more cruel moment. But there was actual physical propulsion in Mrs. Wentworth's voice that morning, and it seemed visibly to lift the reluctant lad to his feet and thrust him through the dreaded portal.

The guests waited eagerly for Saint's return, but when he came they were doomed to disappointment, for he went straight to the kitchen door and summoned Mamba.

When he had conducted her out into the middle of the road, safely out of earshot of the house, he said:

"What do you think?—the old boy's lost his teeth."

The woman bent double in the silent folding contortion that served her for laughter. The boy continued: "And, as he never wears his glasses in, of course he could not find them. I thought of you right away and told him you'd go down and look for them. That cheered him up a lot. Says he'll give you five dollars if you find them before the next car to town."

Mamba was very serious now. "Yo' ain't forget yo' frien', does yo', Mistuh Saint? Ah'll git right down."

The morning advanced and the heat became intense. There was

no breeze from the sea and the sun was a white dazzle on the broad, flat beach. It would be noon before the judge could get his car to the city, and up to the last moment Mamba could be seen engaged upon her search. Then, almost in the moment of the judge's departure, drama developed at the little station. The unfortunate man left the cottage and hurried toward the tracks with a furtive air. Mamba approached from the beach and was joined at the house by Saint.

"Any luck?" he whispered.

Mamba raised her eyes, and for a moment the boy was puzzled by what he saw there. He got the odd impression that some conflict was taking place behind them, some working of the brain that the old woman wanted to keep to herself. This was not like his friend. She told him things, just as he did her. A question was on his lips. Then suddenly she looked down, and her old body seemed to wilt. Her face quivered slightly and she mopped the moisture from her brow with a corner of her apron.

"No, Ah ain't fin' um," she muttered, "an', Gawd, Ah's hot an' wore out." The hand that held the apron corner trembled.

"Well, he's got to give you something, anyway," the boy asserted with a new note of authority. "Come along quick."

The cars were pulling in when they reached the station. They had no time to lose. Saint touched Judge Harkness on his sleeve, and a face was turned toward him that would have been mirth-provoking had it not been for its pitiful defencelessness.

The authority in the boy's voice was going, and he spoke hurriedly on the last of its ebb: "This old woman has been searching the beach all morning. She did not find—anything. But she's awfully hot and tired and all that."

The man fumbled in his pocket and drew out a two-dollar bill which he handed to Mamba.

"All aboard!" shouted the conductor.

Judge Harkness climbed the steps. The wheels commenced to grind on the sandy tracks. Saint felt his body thrust sharply aside, and a figure leaped past him and on to the platform of the Jim Crow car. Wheels were humming now, and windows sliding past in a blur of glass and faces. Then suddenly Mamba's face and an arm waving to him from a rear window. Dumfounded, he looked into the wide, laughing eyes. Then Mamba smiled that broad, unforgettable, single-toothed smile of hers, that was unlike any one else's that Saint had ever known. A sudden premonition smote the lonely boy and etched the strange picture indelibly into his memory. It was well that he caught it then, for it was more than twenty years before he saw it again on Mamba's face.

Under the pelting heat of the August sun two passengers left the ferry the moment that it landed in the city and, taking opposite sides of the street, set off briskly toward the retail section. One of them was Judge Harkness; the other, Mamba.

Taking the least frequented streets, they cut across the city, the man furtive and ill at ease, the woman smiling the secret smile of a Mona Lisa, while the sun hurled its vertical rays down upon her unprotected head. When they arrived at King Street, with its shop windows and hanging signs, their ways parted. The judge crossed the thoroughfare, hesitated for a moment before an unobtrusive brass plate marked DENTIST, then plunged through a door into welcoming gloom. Mamba continued on her way until she came to a glass case, fastened against the front of a building, that had often engaged her fascinated regard. In it were a number of examples of dental art, and in its centre a complete set of teeth operated by a mechanism that kept them chewing with a slow hypnotising rhythm upon an imaginary cud.

Mamba knew this place by reputation. It was here that her wealthy friends came for their gold teeth. She entered and climbed a flight of stairs to the office. Through an open door she saw a

young man in a dirty white coat sitting in a dentist's chair, reading
a newspaper. She smiled, and the young man raised his eyes, then
threw away his paper and stepped eagerly forward.

"Can I do anything for you, Auntie?" he asked superfluously.

In portentous silence Mamba hoisted her apron up and untied a
large knot in one corner. Then she exhibited to the astonished
gaze of the dentist a dollar bill, eighty-five cents in change, and
a formidable set of teeth, which, upon examination, revealed the
fact that their interstices were filled with sand.

"What do you want me to do with these?" he asked.

"Fit 'em tuh me."

"Were they made for you?"

"Not zactly, but most."

The man handed them back. "Sorry, but you have to get them
made especially for you. Now, for forty dollars——"

Mamba laid her hand on his arm. He stopped speaking and
looked up in surprise. He had not noticed her eyes before. Now
he saw in them an agony of longing that made him hesitate. She
had his hand now, and was fumbling with his fingers, keeping her
eyes on his all the time. She pressed the money into his hand that
still held the teeth, then closed it tightly between both of hers.

The man tried to protest, but Mamba, still holding his hand
closed so that he could not return her possessions, plunged into her
plea. "Here's yo' an' me an' dem teet' an' one dolluh an' eighty-
five cent all right here togedder now. It done tek me ober six
yeah tuh arrange um. Ef we ebber get separate' now, Gawd know
ef it eber happen again. We gots tuh fix 'em somehow, Boss. We
jus' gots tuh!"

"But, Auntie, it's like I told you."

"No, yo' mus' lissen tuh me fust. Ah gots tuh hab 'em fuh
somet'ing p'tic'lar. Now, how's dis? Dere's a fambly Ah knows
whut jus' gots dere pa's lodge insurance, an' dey is all goin' get gol'

teet'. Now yo' go long an' fit me tuh dese an' Ah'll bring 'em all
tuh dis shop. Yo' see ef Ah don't."

The dentist laughed. He could not help it. He was
entirely unconvinced as to the existence of that family. Thin!—
did she think he'd be taken in by that sort of stuff? He stood
looking down at her, and his laughter stopped. Now he felt something about the comic old figure that was not comic at all. A force
was being exerted against him that he could not define but that
somehow stirred his rudimentary imagination. He commenced to
feel that there was something big here, too big for the pitiful
subterfuge that it had employed. Slowly he became aware of the
conviction that some tremendous and forlorn hope hung in the
balance, and that it rested with him whether it should triumph or
fail. Charity. No, not that, somehow. Chivalry, then. Absurd,
for this funny old negro woman. A far glimmer came to him
from a boyhood buried under ugly years of negro dentistry, a
figure in armour, Sir Galahad, or something of that sort. This must
have been the way he used to feel when he went to do those silly
things for women and knew he wasn't going to get anything out
of it. Then at this picture of himself, he laughed outright.

Mamba knew then that she had won. Now she must clinch her
victory. "Gawd bless yo', Boss," she exclaimed. "When, now?"

The transformed young man was smiling down at her. "There's
no saying no to you, is there, Auntie?" Then, after a moment,
"No, not to-day. But come in to-morrow and we'll see."

Mamba started to carry her treasured possession away with her,
but at the door she thought better of it, returned, and handed it to
the dentist. "Yo' look aftuh dese fuh me," she begged. "Dey is
too val'able tuh carry 'bout de street." Then, wagging her head up
and down, while she rolled her eyes mysteriously, she added in a
deep-throated, dramatic whisper: "Yas, suh, yo' mightn't b'leabe
me, but dem quiet teet' whut yo' is holdin' so safe an' purty in yo'

han' come out a mout' what has done sen' plenty ob nigger tuh meet dere Gawd."

The dentist started and looked down again. Against his palm the passive double row of ivories seemed suddenly to become ferocious, almost carnivorous.

When he looked up for further explanations Mamba had gone.

*

Employing the mincing step and decorous bearing that had become almost second nature to her, and that she considered in character in a white folk's nigger, Mamba took her way downtown. When she had travelled for twenty minutes over the scorching pavements she turned from Meeting Street into a narrow lane shadowed by high buildings that led to the Negro Quarter. Instantly a change was noticeable in her manner. She dropped the mincing step for a long, slouching stride, and breathed deeply of the damp coolness that emanated from the lichen-hung wall above her. A long happy sigh escaped her lips, and her eyes narrowed to slits of amused insolence. A waterfront nigger now, and able to hold her own with the best of them.

Wharf smells blew toward her down the narrow alley; sulphurous fumes from the mud flats, fish from the smacks on the beach. The stench of a he-goat filled her nostrils. She sniffed it delightedly and looked about her. Porgy, the crippled beggar, was across the way, his little goat cart drawn up in a cool archway. He was eating his lunch, and he paused to hail her. "Do look at Mamba. War yo' been all dis time, Sistuh?" "Oh, Ah jes been tuh gib my white folks a little outin' tuh de seasho'," she threw back at him. She slipped on a rotting watermelon rind, sprawled flat, and came up smiling. An emaciated cur crept from behind a garbage can and bared his teeth at her. She cursed it with a deep and fluent affection, and it recognised her kinship with a gay bark and a snap at her skirt.

Mamba turned south at East Bay and walked along in the shadow of the tall brick buildings that had once been occupied by the aristocracy but which had long since forgotten their proud heritage and gone black. This was home. Everywhere there was colour, sound. That drab and profound melancholy which settles upon a house of high estate that has fallen into a white slum was conspicuously lacking here. Where a shutter had gone it had been replaced with a new one of parrot green or vermilion. New spots of plaster were daubed with pink or yellow wash, and that particular tint of cerulean made by the negroes by the simple and economical process of dropping washing bluing into their whitewash was splashed lavishly over gateposts and cook-shop fronts. Nor was there in the faces of the people either the sullen resignation or the smouldering rebellion of the white who has fallen to slum life. Here grievances against Fate were forgotten in song. Tomorrow would be time enough to worry. Thefts and loves were casual, frank and gay affairs. The corrosion of hidden sin did not mark the faces, for the consciences that might have been sitting in judgment had not yet been scourged into consciousness. There was only the police. One was caught and had sinned; one escaped and was innocent. How marvellously simple. No wonder that even in the noon heat there were song and laughter in the houses that Mamba passed.

Arriving at a narrow archway between soaring brick structures the old woman entered and presently emerged into a court, flag-paved and cool beneath its surrounding walls. Several women looked up from along the interlacing clotheslines and hailed her. "Well, ef here ain't Mamba. How yo' does, Sistuh?"

"Po'ly," she replied happily, "berry po'ly, t'ank Gawd. Whar Hagar?"

Two of the women tittered, and the one who had spoken to Mamba addressed them sharply: "Shet yo' damn' wutless mout'."

Instantly the visitor's expression changed: "What wrong, she ain't drunk again?"

There was silence. Mamba broke out suddenly in a loud bullying voice that was oddly at variance with the pain in her eyes. "Ah bet Ah goin' hab tuh tek de hide off dat black debbil. Ah can't leabe she fuh a week widout she git drunk."

She strode to an entrance, stamped up a flight of loose steps, and kicked open a door. The embalmed remains of many smells rushed out to greet her. She knew them all, loved them, but above them now floated the peculiarly rank effluvium of drunkenness. She crossed the room to the bed. Upon it a huge negress was sprawled. The arms thrown over the head were muscled like a stevedore's, and there was a strange incongruity between the masculine shoulders rising high on the pillow, and the full, heavy breasts of a woman. The face, dark and broad-featured, showed no effects of dissipation, but seemed singularly childish as it lay there in the oblivion of sleep. Below the chest the body was not ungainly, the swell of the hips scarcely noticeable, and the legs, slender and powerfully thewed, seemed wholly masculine. A creature designed by nature to bear her young, then, single-handed, to wrench their sustenance from a harsh physical environment; an enormous maternity and the muscles of a fighting male bound together, and the face of a simple child set in watch over them. A pre-pioneer type, not versed in the solving of riddles. And here she was in a land of paradox. Glass in the windows; Christ in His little church two blocks down the street; the state liquor dispensary across the way; a policeman on the corner.

Mamba seized the heavy shoulders with her thin fingers and attempted to shake the inert bulk. Then she crossed to the washstand, returned with a pitcher, and dashed a quantity of water into the sleeping face. Slowly the eyes opened, and instantly an observer would have known by them that the two women were mother and daughter.

Mamba flung herself forward as though in an effort to drive her words into the dulled brain: "Yo' dutty houn'. Yo' done promise' me not tuh git drunk while Ah's gone, an' now Ah fin' yo' like dis. Wake up an' tell me—whar's Lissa?"

The woman moved her arm heavily and drew the covers aside, disclosing a sleeping child of perhaps three years of age. Mamba pounced on the little form and carried it to the window. The hot afternoon sun poured its light over the baby's face, and it opened its eyes. There they were again, warm, and of that peculiarly live-brown quality so unlike the eyes of the usual negro, linking the child unmistakably with the other two occupants of the room.

The baby threw its arms around Mamba's neck, and she hid her face against it, muttering softly into its ear, and stroking its skin, which, unlike either that of its mother or grandmother, was of a light bronze hue.

Hagar was up now. She lurched ever so slightly as she crossed to the washstand, filled a dipper with water, and dashed it over herself careless of where it fell. She shivered, but the shock brought her tremendous vitality surging back, waking her drugged nerves, stiffening and co-ordinating her muscles. By the time that she had finished dressing her hands were steady. She was childishly shamefaced and repentant. She said: "Ah sorry, Ma. Ah stay straight 'til las' night. But when Ah teck de clo's tuh de boys on de *Pilot Boy*, dey hab plenty ob licker an' dey done drunk me. But yo' can't say Ah ain't tek good care ob Lissa. Ain't she well an' fat?"

Mamba's voice was scornful: "Ain't yo' shame ob yo'self, aftuh all Ah gib up fuh yo' chile! Here yo' ain't gots nuttin' tuh do, 'cep' meet de steamer an' wash fuh de sailor. Yo' gots yo' own home tuh lib in, and yo' frien' roun' yo', an' yo' gots yo' baby fuh pet

an' handle. An' all Ah ax is dat yo' keep sobuh an' don't git lock up
in jail. T'ink on dat, den 'membuh what Ah's doin' fuh yo' baby so
she kin hab chance in de worl'. Leabe my frien', an' de talk an' all,
an' put up wid de damn' quality w'ite folks." The strident voice
wavered, then rose to a note of protest. "Ah swear tuh Gawd my
belly fair ache from de pure polite. Some time Ah t'ink dat ef it
ain't fuh dat boy, Saint, Ah'd hab tuh gib up tryin' an' tell 'em all
tuh go tuh hell."

Hagar's brain had cleared, and she came back promptly with:
"Well, ef dat's de way yo' feel, yo' can't blame me fuh gittin'
drunk some time. Yo' is talk lot ob talk, but it look tuh me dat
yo' is done lef' yo' w'ite folks now an' is settin' here. Yo' ain't gots
so much tuh growl 'bout."

"Well, Ah's goin' back soon's day gits tuh town."

Hagar's lazy contralto laugh sounded: "Sho yo' is. An' ain't Ah
sobuh now? An' ain't Lissa fine? Whut done is done. Fergit
'bout it."

Several women, hearing the laughter and realising that whatever
scene there might have been was over, came in.

Mamba was lolling back in a wrecked rocking chair with the child
in her arms. She called to one of the new arrivals: "Ah gots some-
t'ing tuh ask yo', Sistuh. How much time Jedge Harkness gib yo'
man de las' time he put um up?"

"De las' time?"

"Sho, de las' time. Ain't yo' 'membuh fuh steal dat butts meat
out de freight car?"

"Oh, dat time! Lemme see—he gib um sixty day."

"Well, den, pull yo' chair up here an' lissen tuh dis."

Then Mamba gave them the story of the judge's teeth.

The room shook with spontaneous African laughter. Hands
slapped backs and thighs. In the court homecoming men were
calling to their women. The sea-damp evening air swept cool

through the open window, and some one near by was cooking cabbage for supper. For the old woman life's tide was at the flood again. Existence had its compensations, after all.

★

Autumn in Charleston. A keen sweet wind travelling over the roofs, causing the leaves on the great trees in the Battery gardens to whisper their valedictories, edging the choppy waves in the bay with white. Residents returning after the long summer in Flat Rock, White Sulphur, Europe. Busy housemaids stripping linen pajamas and nightshirts from the furniture that had been dozing the days away in hot darkness. Rugs going down. Cedar and camphor in the nostrils. Legaré Street and the Battery coming to life again. New people appearing here and there, renting old houses, secretly purchasing antiques, learning to say "gyarden" and "cyar," creating the illusion of indigenousness. Housewives, with an energy that was in itself a fatally alien admission, hustling a Duncan Phyfe table into the hall behind the colonial doorway, and searching for a servant sufficiently antique to appear at home beside the Duncan Phyfe. Very effective, these old negroes, looking as though they had been "born in the family" meeting the guest with a Sheffield card tray. And economical too, for they could be obtained at from five to seven dollars a week, where an inanimate hautboy would have cost several hundred dollars.

When the Wentworths returned to town they found that the large frame house that crowded their lot on the south and which had long remained vacant had been renovated and occupied. Through the open windows came sounds of irresistible energy being applied to obstinate masses, and a loud, clear voice rolling its R's.

Mrs. Wentworth drew on her gloves with an air of resignation. "Come on, Polly," she said, "we might as well have it over with."

"Oh, what's the use, Mother? We are never really going to know them. It's so silly being polite now, then having to snub people later."

"You are forgetting your manners, my dear. Calling on neighbours and making them feel at home in our city is one thing; making friends quite another. Get your gloves, now. This is a formal occasion."

In an upper room of the house next door Mrs. George J. Atkinson paused in the middle of her instructions to an aged negro who was assembling a four-poster. She took the cards that were handed to her by a breathless maid and ran her finger appraisingly over them. This was evidently not reassuring. She looked at them closely and found that they were written in a fine clear hand. "James," she said in her incisive voice, "who are the De Chatigny Wentworths?"

The man looked at her from under grizzled eyebrows. After a moment he said: "Dey is de Wentworths, Miss."

"Is that all you know? The card says that they are the Wentworths."

He hastened to set her straight. "Ah ain't say dat dey is de Wentworths, Miss. Whut Ah say is dat dey is *de* Wentworths." Then, after a pause during which he looked hopefully toward her for some sign of understanding, he added, "Dey lib in de little brick house nex' do'."

"Oh, she's the woman who keeps the summer boarding house and has that silly-looking, long-legged boy."

She turned to the maid with her abrupt, efficient manner.

"Tell her that I am not at home."

But the servant had not reached the door before she was stopped. "Wait a moment. I'll go down. It is just as well to be on speaking terms with one's neighbours. Stay and help James with that bed and come down in five minutes and say that I am wanted on the telephone."

When the maid entered the drawing room with the message, The Wentworths were sitting very erect in their Chinese Chippendale chairs smiling wooden smiles, and Mrs. George J. Atkinson was doing the talking.

"Just imagine," she was saying, "taking boarders all summer. And Mrs. Raymond tells me that you take in fancy sewing too. I must remember that when I have some work to be done. Yes, really, you must let me ask you to help me mark my new linens. What is it, Mary? Oh, the telephone. Yes, in a moment. Oh, must you really go? Well, thank you for calling. Very neighbourly, I'm sure."

In the street Mrs. Wentworth said: "Well, that's done. Let's forget it."

But Polly answered in a hard little voice: "Forget nothing! Talking down to you in that 'My good woman' tone of voice. Be a good Christian and forget if you want to, but I am going to remember."

The day following the Atkinson call the three Wentworths were together in their dining room. They had been discussing the matter, and it was sour on their tongues. Mrs. Wentworth was hatted and gloved for one of her many errands. "Well, there's no use dwelling on the ignorance of other people," she was remarking. "They simply aren't our kind. For me they do not exist. That is all." She turned to depart, then she gave a slight start. A stranger had entered from the kitchen door, and stood silently in the room watching them. "If you are waiting to see Maum Netta she will be in the kitchen presently," she told the negress. "Close the door, please, as you go out."

But the woman advanced toward the little group and stood looking from one to the other with the manner of one who has a thrilling and mysterious secret in her keeping. She was of medium height and weight and had about her an air of eminent, almost assertive impeccability. Her dress was covered by a spotless apron, and upon her head was a white starched cap with a ruffle that shaded her eyes. Her most salient characteristics were a large mouth with firmly compressed lips, and a squareness about the lower face that gave it an expression of grim severity. During a moment of profound silence she stood surveying the group, then slowly and deliberately she smiled, revealing a double row of big masculine teeth.

Saint's voice, long-drawn and incredulous, broke the silence: "Well, I'll be damned!"

The visitor bent double in a paroxysm of silent laughter.

"Mamba!" chorused the room.

Polly came immediately to the point: "Where in the world did you get them, Mamba?"

"A kind gentleman whut lub de nigger gib dem tuh me. Gawd bless um!"

A picture flashed into Saint's mind: hot summer sky, sand, Judge Harkness in full flight, and Mamba swinging aboard the Jim Crow car as it gathered speed. "*Yes*, he did," he said.

Suddenly the spark of understanding leaped around the circle. Maum Netta had entered a moment before, and it brought her up standing, with a look of horrified disapproval. It confounded Mrs. Wentworth with a simultaneous compulsion to laughter and the obligation to be stern. It took Saint and Polly and flung them forward on the table in convulsions of mirth.

Almost immediately Mamba recovered her composure and stood waiting for the laughter to subside. She was not there to be amusing now. Four years had gone into building toward this moment; four years of cajolery, flattery, clowning. That typical gesture, bent double with hands on her stomach, had been given only as an unmistakable revelation of an identity to which she was in the very act of bidding good-bye. She was emerging as a

new entity now. The strange assortment of accessories that had
gone into her make-up: cast-off clothing of Mrs. Wentworth, teeth
of a distinguished jurist, manner sedulously copied from Maum
Netta, apron and cap from God knew where, were losing their
separate identities, merging into the new ego that they were
destined in the future to express.

Finally, while the Wentworths watched, the transformation was
accomplished, the last sense of incongruity departed, and Mamba
stood before them re-created in her own conception of the ideal
toward which she had been striving. In some strange manner she
seemed to dominate the little room in which she had until so recently
come and gone on sufferance. She brought a new, compelling element into the atmosphere that seemed subtly to disturb the ancestral rhythm of thought and action. The room was very quiet.
The abrupt change from hilarity made the silence seem ominous.
Mrs. Wentworth cleared her throat. Polly sat with a blank, mystified stare. Only Saint seemed to have his bearings, and looked up
with a faint smile into the shadowy eyes under the stiff cap ruffle.

When Mamba spoke her voice was low and tense. She must have
thought her speech out with care, for there was no hesitation, no
hedging. She was desperately in earnest. The years of palaver
were over. These white people had given her much, but she had
been careful to pile up the countless little uncompensated tasks
against this day. The balance was in her favour. There need be no
talk about it. Real white folks did not need to bargain. She knew
and they knew. Now for the accounting.

"Ah gots tuh get uh pay job now, Miss Wentworth. Ah gots tuh
get money fuh somet'ing p'tic'lar. An' Ah gots tuh fin' uh white
boss whut kin look attuh my chillen when dey meets dey trouble.
Yo' an' Mauma here, yo' knows Ah ain't a real house-raise' nigger,
but dese new w'ite folks whut comin' tuh Chas'n now, dey ain't

knows de different, an' dey is want ole-time house-raise' nigger whut use' tuh b'long tuh de quality. Ah is axin' yuh now tuh gib me letter an' say Ah is raise' wid yo' fambly."

"But, Mamba! That would be an untruth," exclaimed the dumfounded lady.

The old woman leaned forward and looked into her face:

"Ah gots tuh hab um, Miss. Ah gots tuh."

Mrs. Wentworth studied the figure before her, a strange fragment of human flotsam that had been seized and animated by this transfiguring purpose. How little she really knew of Mamba, after all. Where had she come from? Why had she sought them out?

"Tell me," she said, "why are you doing this?"

"Tain't fuh me, Miss. Ah kin tek care ob Mamba. But time is changin'. Nigger gots tuh git diff'ent kind ob sense now tuh git long. Ah gots daughtuh, an' she gots daughtuh, an' all-two dem female is born fuh trouble. Ah gots tuh be ready when de time come."

"And this granddaughter of yours, how old is she?"

"Yuh 'membuh when Ah fus' come an' bring dem flower fuh Little Missie?"

Her listener nodded.

"Dat when she born."

"Aw go on and give old Mamba the letter," urged Saint.

Polly's eyes were dancing with excitement. "I've got it, Mother," she cried. "We'll get her some recommendations and send her to the Atkinsons. She's pretty hateful, Mamba, but she's rich as all get-out, and she's dying to be thought somebody. Only, if we fix it up for you, you must promise to get everything out of her you can."

"I think that is a disgraceful proposition," said Mrs. Wentworth. "In fact, I am so surprised and shocked that I will leave at once and attend to my business on Broad Street." She opened the door, then turned back for a moment, and the three in the room saw the corners of her mouth twitching irresistibly as she added, "And I want you all to behave properly while I am gone and do not do anything that you would be ashamed of."

She turned to Mamba. "Good-bye, and good luck," she said. "Remember we are old friends, and come and see us sometime."

The old woman gave her one of her looks, so uncanny in their power to convey emotion. The eyes were a little misty, but behind that there was laughter. "Gawd bless yo', Miss," she said a little shakily. Then she whirled her skirts in a courtesy, essayed laughter, and ended by wiping an eye in a corner of her apron.

"Mother's a dear, but she's a 'fraid cat," commented Polly when the door had closed.

"She's a brick," amended Saint as he rummaged for pen, ink, and paper in the secretary. "All right," he said a moment later, "let's go. What's your last name? You've got to have one in a recommendation, you know."

"Whut yo' say dat lady name?"

"Atkinson."

"Now, ain't dat funny. Dat my berry own name. Ain't yo' know my pa use' tuh b'long tuh de Atkinsons? Yes, suh! My ma raise' wid de Wentworth, ain't yo' 'membuh? But my pa raise wid ole Major Atkinson who use tuh own fibe t'ousan' head ob nigger, an' de bigges' plantation on de——" She hesitated for a moment while she weighed the glories of cotton against the importance of rice, decided on the latter, and closed with "Cooper Ribbuh."

*

Behold Maum Mamba! Observe her well, for you have never seen her before. It is the month of November, and the two

Atkinson children are playing among the blowing leaves on the
Battery. They are nice red-cheeked youngsters, and they love their
Mauma. It is true that they love her less when their mother is
about, and she sits with folded hands and solemn face watching
their every move. But for the most part the three of them play
together unobserved. Then Mauma has been known to perform
miracles. Before the children's very eyes she has removed her teeth
and, holding them between thumb and forefinger, has snapped them
playfully at a dandelion or leaf. At times she has even allowed
Jack to wear them to scare the Rutledge children until they have
run screaming to their proper nurses on the benches. Oh, what
fun! She is also content to let her prosy contemporaries have a
complete monopoly on Brer Rabbit and Brer Wolf, while she tells
her charges of glamorous and terrible things that happen in real
life down where the ships come in. Then there are other moments
when they have seen her cast a careful look about to make sure
that she is unobserved, then slip to the street at the garden's edge
and engage in long conversations with certain low hucksters and
fish venders who may be passing. To Jack, who is eight years of
age and precocious, these moments are particularly valuable, for he
has learned that by approaching stealthily he can enrich his vocabu-
lary with words that confound his puerile comrades with their little
hells and damns.

Yes, indeed, Mrs. Atkinson has every reason to feel that fortune
has smiled upon her in sending her Mamba.

"Yes, my dear," she is saying to a friend with whom she is
sitting on the Battery on this particular November afternoon, while
the children play innocently near by and their guardian angel sits
watching them sternly. "Yes, indeed, my dear. We got her
through the most marvellous luck. She belonged to the South
Carolina branch of George's family, you know, and with that fine
old-fashioned loyalty that one encounters all too seldom in these

days, she came and offered herself to us as soon as she heard that we were in town. And she had splendid letters, too, that would have placed her anywhere."

The listener smiles sympathetically. Nothing more is needed. Mrs. Atkinson continues: "Not many of them left now, and what I say is that we should treasure those who are; if for no other purpose but to set an example to the upstart generation of negroes."

"Yes, indeed," as Mrs. Atkinson would say. Patience, application, singleness of purpose have reaped their reward. Behold Maum Mamba on the Battery on this particular November afternoon and say if she has not at last arrived.

PART II

Affairs had gone badly in the little brick house. If, at fourteen, Saint had been a problem to his mother, he was now, at eighteen, her despair. It was not that he was unwilling to work. On the contrary, he hailed each new position that was found for him with shy eagerness. But the habit that had been given to him in school had deepened rather than dissipated when met by the harsher realities of life. The immediate and inexorable array of facts that faced him with each new vocation brought bewilderment to his untrained mind. His thoughts veered from the task of meeting and arranging them, leaped the gap between the bottom and top of the ladder, and solaced him with a fool's paradise of pictured triumphs.

Unfortunately there were only certain occupations that a gentleman could follow in Charleston without sacrifice of family dignity, and if one were handicapped by the lack of a professional training these were reduced to a minimum. One could work in a bank, or one of the bond and real estate offices on Broad Street. One could become a cotton expert, or even a broker in the wholesale district along East Bay. Strange to say, in spite of the unholy stench and overalls, one could seek employment in the great fertilizer factories beyond the city limits. But a gentleman seeking a livelihood in the early nineteen hundreds could not engage in any branch of the retail business without imposing upon his humiliated family the burden of incessant explanation.

Through the intercession of a distant relative, an outdoor clerkship with one of the banks had been obtained for Saint. It had been a fatal beginning. He had approached it with enthusiasm,

43

slightly blurred by his distrust of arithmetic, but genuine nevertheless. Now he could see, after the short period on the street, a
high standing desk in the big banking room, then a roll-top desk
in a small outer office, and finally the directors' room with himself
seated in the massive chair at the end of the table. On the first
day he had stood looking down that alluring perspective until he
had to be spoken to twice by the cashier before he heard. This so
distressed him that he penalised himself by memorising a cotton
warehouse receipt, although he could not make head or tail of the
legal verbiage. His outdoor work took him to the cotton offices on
the wharves, and therein lay his complete undoing, for there were
the ships and the negroes waiting to betray him into long unexplained absences. At the end of the first week his banking career
came to an abrupt end.

Other jobs followed: a swift disillusioning procession of them.
Bewildered and baffled, the boy met them, groped among their
intricate mechanisms, felt them slipping through his hands, and was
powerless to retain them. Finally, on a dark winter morning, he
stood before a door with a panel of ground glass, upon which was
painted in large black letters, PRIVATE. The palms of his hands
were wet and cold, his tongue felt like a withered pea in a dried
pod, and his kneecaps were a quaking jelly. In the distance St.
Michael's chimed and struck eleven. He made a solemn vow to
himself to stick it out for another quarter hour. If he did not
get in then and have it over with, he could not keep his body
there any longer. The last man who had hired him had smiled
over his head at another occupant of the room all the time that he
had talked. He had been sitting where he could not see the other
man, but his back had quivered under the derisive answering smile.
He prayed now that this man would be alone and that he would
not ask him where he had worked before. Fertilizers! This was
about the end of the procession; the last stand. He'd have to get

it, and he'd have to stick it out when he had it. His thoughts touched on his mother and her hope for the success of the interview. A warm, tender wave swept upward from the pit of his stomach and broke in a blinding mist before his eyes. The big, black PRIVATE on the door swam and quivered. Panic! Suppose the door should open now! He dashed his knuckles across his eyes and gritted his teeth.

A low-pitched man's voice had been rumbling monotonously in the room beyond the door that he was watching. Now it stopped. He heard the sound of a chair pushed over a bare floor; then the words: "That will do now. Tell the young man outside that I will see him."

The door with its shaking letters swung inward. A woman passed him and said: "You may see Mr. Raymond now." He set the machinery of his legs in motion, and the woman closed the door behind him.

The room was large and bare. It smelled faintly of phosphates. In its centre a heavy man sat in a swivel chair behind a flat-top desk. Behind rimless spectacles his eyes were keen and appraising.

"So you are Katherine Wentworth's boy," he said in a deep, hearty voice. "I am glad to know you. Knew your father too— boys together—fine, both of them. Got a lot to live up to, Son." He shook hands cordially and waved his guest to a chair at the end of the desk where the light struck his face, and took a good look at him. What he saw was a tall, slender lad with loosely hung arms and legs and a sallow face that flinched away from his look like an open wound under a probe. He saw brown hair with a cowlick over the forehead, and slate-coloured eyes that were too conscious of their own tragic admissions to meet his glance.

Mr. Raymond busied himself deliberately with a silver cigar-cutter and a long, black cigar. He scratched a match, applied it, and blew a funnel of smoke toward the ceiling. He threw a sidelong glance at the boy. Yes, the respite had helped. They could talk now.

"Think you'd like to try the fertiliser business, eh?" There was a twinkle behind his glasses.

"Yes, sir."

"Don't mind starting at the bottom?"

"No, indeed, sir, almost anything. That is, I don't mind doing anything at all."

"That's the proper spirit!" exclaimed the big man. "Now, how'd you like to start just where I did and work up?" The deep voice filled the room with warm vibrations; they entered into the boy's body and started something glowing there. No one had been so understanding before. He felt suddenly that he would like to show this friend what he could do. Perhaps there would be a riot at the factory, all of the other white men gone, and he there alone reasoning with the mob. Or perhaps it would be a fire. He saw himself grown suddenly to splendid stature smashing down a barrier with an axe, manning the hose. He saw the flame leap, gather headway, and roar down the great funnel of a building. Horrors! Mr. Raymond had been talking to him. The big hand slapped the table, and across Saint's vision crashed the words: "What do you say to that?"

What had it been? Saint groped back among the spent words that had scarcely grazed his consciousness. It was no use, they were gone. His benefactor was leaning forward expectantly, waiting for an answer.

"Thank you very much, Mr. Raymond," he said lamely, and wondered wildly what he was being grateful for.

"Good! You accept, then?"

"Yes, indeed, sir."

"Well, we'll start you with five dollars a week. I am going out to the mines myself to-morrow, and I'll take you along. Be here at nine o'clock and bring your grip, so that you won't have to come back for your clothes."

The big man got to his feet and put his hand on the bewildered boy's shoulder. "Started with one myself, ended up with a chain, then came on in here. So you see it can be done," he said, smiling.

In the street Saint stopped and looked up at the window of the room he had left. "Ended up with a chain," he muttered dubiously. "What kind of a chain, I wonder."

*

The next morning found Saint occupying a third of a seat in a dirty little day coach, with a shabby telescope bag tucked behind his legs. The remaining two thirds was snugly filled with the substantial bulk of Mr. Raymond, bulwarked behind an outspread copy of the *News and Courier*. During the half hour of train travel the boy remained in ignorance of their destination and the nature of that chain which apparently represented the goal toward which he was to fight his way.

When they arrived at the little station the paper was folded and stuffed into the man's overcoat pocket, and they climbed into the rear seat of a waiting buckboard. Then the employer turned his attention to the business of the moment. He had a straight man-to-man way of talking to the boy that both put him at ease and held his attention. He watched him closely but kindly, and he drove his ideas in with short, pointed sentences that ended with *"understand?"* It kept his listener's wits on tiptoe. There were no heroic visions now. It developed that he had been engaged as storekeeper in the commissary for the negroes at one of the mining camps. There were other camps, each with its commissary in charge of a storekeeper, and over all of them there was a general manager. One of the storekeepers was destined some day to rise above the others to the managerial position and have the direction of the chain. So there it was at last! Saint experienced a feeling of relief. "In the meantime," the genial voice informed him, "you must watch your stock, send in requisitions for supplies when they run low, and stop a nigger's credit when it runs through his next week's wages. Think you can manage it?"

Out of the bitter past a fear leaped upon the boy. "The money —making change—keeping accounts. Do I have to do that too, Mr. Raymond?" he faltered.

"Oh, that's no bother. Everything's charged, and you won't be hurried. It don't matter how long you keep the niggers waiting."

The road that had approached the mines through the woods now left the trees behind and passed between abandoned fields that had been left to go to broom straw. The brisk January wind changed and veered over the warm brown expanse, roughening its surface like a squall at sea. Presently through the silence of the country there came to Saint a low insistent rumble.

Mr. Raymond pointed: "That's the washer," he explained, "where the rock is cleaned for shipment."

Saint followed the pointing finger with his gaze and saw, far out over the marshes where the river drew a thin S of silver, a great building crouched at the water's edge like an antediluvian monster that had gone down to drink.

Before them the road widened. The ancient negro who was driving drew to one side of the open space and brought his mule to a standstill.

"Well, here we are," said Mr. Raymond.

Saint looked up and saw before him a small clapboarded building with its front gable covered by the false square that always denotes the country store. Across its front ran a low, wide piazza, and upon the piazza three curs and an old negro were dozing in the sun. Behind the little building a wide broom-straw field travelled east until it merged its gold-brown with the silver-brown of the winter marsh, carrying the vision in an uninterrupted flight on to the bright thread of the Ashley River. North, south, and west the little clearing was walled with virgin long-leaf pine. The towering trees swayed gently on their long naked trunks and stopped the shrill cry of the wind down to a grave sustained monotone. Overhead swung a vast empty sky, blue-green over the treetops and almost purple where it dipped behind the warm line of the marsh.

"All out," commanded Mr. Raymond. "Well, how do you like it, Wentworth?"

The boy stood looking about him. His mouth had dropped a little open, giving his face an expression of vacuity, almost stupidity. In a clairvoyant flash he saw himself from outside his being; as his mother would see him, a failure facing this disgraceful surrender, conventionally respectable only because in his penny traffic with negroes he was safely out of sight, and could be spoken of vaguely as being "in phosphates," and he pitied her terribly. He saw himself with the eyes of his employer, and he knew what he was thinking at that moment: that he'd never go any higher; that he would stay here until he rotted down into the very soil of the camp. And yet, deep within him, a frozen core was melting; warm new currents were stirring. Standing there, he almost caught the first faint answers to the passionate questions that his youth had flung against the wind. He turned to his employer and gave a strange answer for a man who presumably had his foot on the bottom round of the commercial ladder. He said: "Thank you, sir. I'll stay. I will be happy here."

*

On a certain frosty January night Mamba sat in her immaculate room in the servants' quarters over the Atkinsons' coach house and took stock of her gains and losses. With the blinds carefully drawn she had allowed herself the luxury of stepping out of character. Her teeth, to which she had never grown accustomed, and which had become symbolic of the innumerable restraints and prohibitions of her servitude, had been cast aside for the solacing stem of her clay pipe. About her the Atkinson air, no longer clean and naked, coiled and eddied intimately in a visible garment of smoke. A familiar gurgling sound rippled the hated quiet of the Atkinson premises. As she sat relaxed in a golden oak rocker with her bare feet thrust from the folds of an old wrapper straight before her upon the spotless bed spread that Mrs. Atkinson was wont to inspect at regular intervals, she gave an impression of physical well-being. But under the veiling fog of smoke her eyes had in them the look of an unsatisfied hunger.

Six years had passed since she had turned her back on the delights of a bland and care-free senility among her own kind and had bound her forces together for her final adventure with life. In the big white house on Church Street her enterprise had been crowned with unqualified success. She had to an amazing degree the racial adaptability that even age cannot stiffen into a set pattern, and in the part that she had played so long and sedulously she was now letter perfect. She was, in fact, more than that, for she lived with that complete immersion in her impersonation that made her for the time being the character itself. With the passing years the old almost unendurable longings had dimmed to a faint nostalgic yearning so far beyond attainment that it was as impersonal as the hunger of some remote acquaintance. The real pang of separation had come two years ago, when it had become necessary for her to leave her quarters with Hagar and Lissa, and live in a room over the Atkinsons' kitchen so that she could be near the children when the master and mistress were away in the evenings. Those first days had been cruel. She had missed the strong talk of the court, the broad, frank humour, the smells, the clashing colours, the curs, goats, buzzards, and tumbling black babies. She had missed her pipe in the long summer dusks with the old men and women who were drifting happily with the days, gossiping and scolding the young negroes to their heart's content. But later her wild longings had found a tame consolation in retrospection. Then she was able to see her compensations. She had a genuine fondness for her white children. She was proud of them. There were moments when she doubted whether she was making a lady of Gwen, but she had at least made a man of Jack, for he could outswear and outfight any boy in the neighbourhood. Yesterday she had seen him meet the neighbourhood bully in the alley beneath her back window, pound him gloriously, and scorch his retreating back with a collection of epithets that would have won the reluctant admiration of Catfish Row. Yes, in spite of Mrs. Atkinson, Jack would do. Now there were food and clothing in abundance. Every week she returned half of her wages to Mrs. Atkinson to put in the bank for her, until now she had a tidy sum awaiting the inevitable emergency. And above and beyond all other considerations, she now had her white folks to stand between Hagar and Lissa and the impersonal justice of the state should evil fortune bring them to that.

But if Mamba had moulded her life according to her plan as far as the big Church Street house was concerned, the same could not have been said of the course of events in the East Bay tenement. Hagar had been in trouble several times. There had been nothing serious; no charges that involved a stay of more than a fortnight, or perhaps a month, at a time in the county jail. But she was getting a bad name with the police.

When Mamba had told Mrs. Wentworth that her motive for seeking permanent white folks of her own was that she had a girl who was born for trouble, she had been as wise as she was prophetic. In the building with Hagar there lived a dozen women who made trouble. In the great honeycomb to the south, as many again. But they had attained the high art of complete invisibility in time of peril. Hagar, on the other hand, with her huge frame and her big wondering child's face, stood dangerously out of the picture. Also the police knew where she could be found. Mamba had given the woman a religion in Lissa. Deep into the simple intelligence she had driven the need to care for the child, to give it a chance. A Saturday night would come when the mercurial spirits of the neighbourhood would leap beyond bounds. There was always a quantity of the peculiarly deadly corn whisky, marked with the seal of the great commonwealth of South Carolina, and known among the negroes as rotgut. Hagar would drink with the rest, and her enormous body, released from its slight control, would become one of the gesticulating, whooping dervishes in the ensuing orgy that inevitably resulted in a riot call.

In the panic the big woman could be counted upon to rush to her room to see if Lissa was safe. The police knew this. A fruitless raid was humiliating to the force. There must be something to show for it at the recorder's court in the morning. All else failing, the officers would stand at the bottom of the steps leading to Hagar's room and whoop for her to come out. At the sound of the summons she would become suddenly cowed. Still a bit dazed by the liquor, dumb and bewildered, she would come down the steps looking like a great child in disgrace. Then some one would go to the Atkinsons' gate and whisper to Mamba, who would come with money and arrange with a neighbour to care for Lissa until Hagar's return.

★

And while Mamba sat in her room on that certain January night dwelling on the past and speculating upon the hazards of the future, in a very different room six blocks away in the black belt Hagar was putting her child to bed. Lissa was a well-grown child for her six years, with a faint colour in her cheeks under the light bronze of her skin. This seemed miraculous to her dark mother, who loved to stroke it with her finger tips. She got the little figure into bed, and sat beside it, singing in her deep contralto which, with her eyes, made up the sum total of her physical heritage from Mamba. It was a week-night, and the court was quiet. Far away on the tracks of the East Shore Terminal a switch engine laboured with a heavy burden. Hagar was singing a sad little lullaby full of minors:

> "Hush, li'l' baby, don' yuh cry,
> Mudder an' fadder born tuh die."

The soft tossing sounds beside her ceased and were followed by the rhythm of faint steady breathing. The mother tiptoed over, dimmed the kerosene lamp, picked up a large bundle of clean wash, stepped out of the room, and closed the door behind her.

Across the street and down the dim perspective of the wharf her gaze travelled and rested on a side-wheel river steamer lying at the pier head. The boat was motionless, but a steam exhaust beside the funnel wheezed and blew a film of mist between her and the frosty stars. Steam was up. An hour now and perhaps the boat would be under way. Her wash was for the fire-room crew, Sam and Abel. She had never seen the men before they had brought the clothes to her. And she did not know the boat. Perhaps it was just touching port for supplies and was going South. She did not trust the men altogether. Her eyes must be kept open; one could not tell about strange river niggers.

When she arrived at the pier head she saw that the fire-room hatch was open—just a square hole flush with the deck. She looked down and saw an iron ladder that descended into flickering orange light and sounds of low laughter. She stooped over the hatch and called:

"Yuh Sam an' Abel. Heah Hagar wid yo' wash."

The laughter stopped and a lazy voice called: "All right, Sistuh, bring um down."

Silence for a moment, then: "No, I ain't gots de time. Come on up an' bring yo' two dollah."

Sam appeared at the bottom of the ladder with his face thrown up toward her. His voice was beguiling. "Aw, come 'long down, Sistuh. Whut mek yo' so onsociable?"

The thought came to Hagar that they might touch at the port regularly and that customers were not to be discouraged. She still felt vague misgivings, but she lowered her heavy bulk through the opening. It was so low between decks that she could not stand upright. The men, who were both shorter than she, laughed openly and good-naturedly at her. This served to allay her suspicions. She chuckled at her own expense, and her teeth sent a white flash across the darkness of her face. Seating herself on an empty box, she said: "Well, dar's yo' cloes."

Abel had not moved when she entered, but continued to sit on the edge of a bunk with a guitar in his lap. He had a round face with a spurious expression of ingenuousness upon it. Now he bent over his instrument and plucked a chord.

Sam said: "Dat's right, go on an' play fuh de comp'ny while Ah git de money." Then, as though on second thought, he lifted a pint flask from behind him and handed it to Hagar. "Go on, Sistuh," he urged, "he'p yo'self."

Abel was picking away steadily now: not a tune, but the intricate improvisation of chords so loved by the negro. The music filled the close space. Before Hagar the red fire box, cut into segments by the black grate bars, grinned like a friendly mouth, and above her the winter stars beyond the hatch showed infinitely remote and pale through the warm light of the fire room. She drew the cork from the flask, and instantly the air was pungent with the rank fumes. She tipped the bottle and took a long pull, then passed it to Abel.

He drank sparingly, returned the flask to Hagar, then took up his playing again. The music beat through the woman in recurrent waves of ecstasy. One broad foot commenced to tap the floor. She lifted the flask, and it seemed as though she would never put it down. Her eyelids dropped slowly, narrowing her eyes to bright slits, then closing them. One might have thought her asleep but for the fact that she remained erect on her box and swayed slowly from the hips with the rhythm of the music.

Through the hatch fell a hail from a passing tug, and the vessel's wash travelled landward under the waiting steamer, lifting it, thrusting it forward, allowing it to settle back, then lifting it again. Across the harmony of the guitar chords rang the bright, certain notes of a ship's bell—seven crystal beads of sound strung with beautiful precision on a thread of music. Sam and Abel exchanged meaning glances, and Sam grimaced the words "Not yet." Overhead a crisp, authoritative step smote the deck, then another, and rapid footsteps dwindled away forward.

Suddenly the shattering blast of a steam whistle filled the night. It stilled the guitar which dropped from Abel's hands. It galvanised the two men into intense activity. They seized Hagar by the arms and hoisted her up until her head struck the ceiling. She opened bewildered eyes and looked blankly about her.

"Step it, Sistuh," Sam commanded. "Dat's de cast-off whistle."

Hagar blinked. Where was she—what was it all about? Her fingers were asleep. They opened slowly and let an empty flask fall to the floor. Sam hustled her up the ladder that eluded her groping hands and feet. Then she was on deck with the cold night air washing over her hot body.

Her conductor gave her a final shove and she was on the wharf. Behind her a negro threw a painter from a bullard, and it fell overboard with a heavy splash. The steamer's rail was commencing to slide past her now, close, where she could still touch it with her extended hand. Sam's face came into her range of vision. He was leaning against the rail, and as she looked at him he threw back his head and laughed. She saw the wide mouth and white teeth. Suddenly a thought was thrown out sharp and clear from the slow moiling in her brain. They were going now. They had tricked her out of the two dollars. The money that she needed for Lissa. Red passion burst deep within her and flooded her body. Her eyes were fixed on the laughing face that was drifting away from her into the night. Across the yard of space that divided them her long arms flashed, and her hands closed on the shoulders of the man. He was wearing a tightly buttoned coat. The stuff balled up in her palms, giving her a firm grip. The face that stared into hers changed ludicrously from laughter to fright. She set her knee against a bullard, and threw her whole weight into a backward heave. The man made a frantic clutch at the rail, but the pull on his shoulders jerked his arms up, and he missed. A second later he lay sprawled upon the wharf with Hagar standing astride of him. Behind them sounded a bright jingle of engine-room bells and the noisy threshing of the paddles. The boat regarded its former fireman with a green and sardonic starboard eye, then gathered speed and was engulfed by the aqueous darkness.

Hagar never nursed a grudge. Always her anger was defensive rather than punitive. Had the man kept his head and made payment of what he owed her it is likely that she would have let the matter drop there. But fatal panic was upon him, and he was smitten with that madness which the gods lay upon those whom they are about to destroy. He scrambled to his feet and attempted to make a dash. A swift, clubbing stroke caught him between the shoulders and hurled him forward against a pile of barrels. He cannoned off at an oblique angle and again tried to bolt, but it was too late. The negro who had cast off the steamer heard the noise and came running. A single lantern hung suspended from the ceiling and only served to make the vast cavern of the shed a place of reeling shadows and elusive half lights. The wharf hand rounded a double tier of barrels and was brought up standing by what he saw.

Hagar had her man in a cul-de-sac between two rows of piled freight. She was not blaspheming like other fighting negresses, nor was she at it with teeth and nails. But there was something strangely, almost grotesquely feminine about her, for she was sobbing loudly and bitterly, and through the sound ran a monotone of two words said over and over, and the words were "two dolluh." Her victim was attempting to speak, but she would not let him, and presently he was so beset that he gave over trying. The watcher saw him emerge from the shadows and balance before the woman. He was small, but quick and wiry. He seemed obsessed with a single idea, to pass the woman and escape into the open. Hagar stood braced across the exit like a Colossus, her arms moving in swift downward strokes from the shoulder as a labourer works with a sledge. The terrified wharf hand saw the man venture too near. A blow took him on the forehead and hurled him back into darkness. "Godamighty!" exclaimed the onlooker, and with eyes showing high lights in the faint lantern glow he turned and raced to give the alarm.

Out of the shadows emerged Sam, driven forward by a single idea—escape. And waiting for him was another fixed and unalterably opposed idea that had possessed itself of the devastating human machine that barred his way. They met, but this time the smaller figure struck, and remained impinged upon the larger one, smashing terribly up at the big sobbing face. Down they went together, striking a pile of boxes that toppled and fell with a crash.

People were coming now, the white watchman swinging his lantern, and men from the boats. They drew together in a little circle and waited.

The bundle that rolled in the shadows lay quiet for a moment, then resolved itself into two individual parts that staggered uncertainly upright. They faced each other, and their breathing sounded above the slap and suck of waves against the bulkhead. Then the man drew himself together and launched himself at the opening in a last desperate attempt. Hagar bent forward and met him with a thrust of the shoulder, her whole tremendous weight flung into the effort. Shock—recoil. The man's body described an arc, struck the planking, and lay where it fell.

The woman's lips moved inaudibly. She bent over the inert body, turned it over, and fumbled laboriously through its pockets. At last she found some bills, opened them, retained two, and returned the remainder with an air of detachment. Then she rose, sighed heavily, drew her arm across her face with an incredibly weary gesture, and started home.

In the tricky lantern light the men saw her coming, a gigantic figure, her massive torso bare to the waist, the great breasts of a woman, and the knotted man's shoulders, blood on her face, and in a dark rivulet between her breasts. No one attempted to stop her. The circle opened as she approached, and with the fixed stare of a somnambulist she passed through, crossed the street, went up to her room, and closed the door behind her.

Twenty minutes later when a policeman came for her she was sitting on the edge of her bed with Lissa pressed to her breast. She was swaying back and forth crooning her lullaby:

"Hush, li'l' baby, don' yo' cry,
Mudder an' fadder born tuh die."

She raised her face and looked at the officer over the laxed form in her arms. Then she rose, placed the child on the bed, and tucked in the covers with meticulous care. Without a word she got a long coat from a hook, slipped it on, and buttoned it over her nakedness. The officer stood patiently in the doorway watching her. He had slipped his gun back into the holster. He had come for her before, and he knew the woman with whom he had to deal. There would be no trouble.

Hagar got several garments from a trunk and bundled them together. Then she returned to the bed and stood looking down at Lissa.

"Come along, Big Un," the officer said not unkindly, "let's get it over with. It don't get no better from waitin'!"

His prisoner bent and pressed her wounded mouth against the smooth cheek of the child. Then she turned obediently and went to the door.

While the policeman stood waiting for her to precede him down the steps, she paused and looked back into the familiar room. It was not until then that the realisation seemed to dawn upon her that this was different from the other departures. From behind the blind veil of the future a faint prescience of some vast disaster flickered its warning. Slowly her eyes filled, and through the tears she looked upon the big, dim room with its familiar disorder, the bed, and the slim form of the child. In the half light of the lowered kerosene lamp she could see the imprint of her farewell kiss showing dark against the light tan of the cheek. She turned and felt her way down the dark stairs with the policeman clumping heavily behind her.

★

There was nothing of the chameleon about George P. Atkinson. His ten years spent in the South had not blurred his Mid-Western outline in the smallest particular. Two years in Virginia had left him guiltless of a broad A, and now he went about the Charleston streets obliviously rolling his R's before him. He refused to attend formal functions because formality bored him. For the same reason he neither played golf nor shot. But he knew cotton-seed oil from the seed to the olive-oil label. He could tell you the Texas cotton crop for 1907, the best market for linters, the advantages of "cold pressing," and the crude-oil market for any given day in the past half year. Every morning he would breakfast at eight o'clock, read the paper for fifteen minutes, walk briskly to his office and say in that snappy tempo with which employers launch a busy day:

"Morning, Johnson. Yesterday's reports ready?" He would have told you that he was a specialist, and, as such, he was not to be despised even by his wife, for the net result to the family was ten thousand a year in a city where many of the socially distinguished families were existing at a shade above life's stark necessities. He might well have been a problem to Mrs. Atkinson in her social ascension, for his ego was strongly marked and assertive, and he showed in raw contrast to the urbane, rather ceremonious, and commercially unambitious men whom he would have met in most of the Charleston drawing rooms in the early nineteen hundreds. But fortunately he asked only to be left at home when she sallied forth on her career, and refused to attend dinners except in his own home. Even on these occasions, Mrs. Atkinson decided that he might have been much worse, for while he said little, she noticed that the men gave him respectful attention when he spoke. He offered cigars and liqueurs to her guests with a natural quiet dignity, insisting on taking them from the butler, and making a little ceremony of passing them himself after they had adjourned to the drawing-room fire. He had the clean-cut "Gibson type" of figure, which was then at the height of its vogue, and he looked well leaning against the Adam mantel. It is true that at times he would break through her restraint and militantly pronounce a spade a spade. But he had mellowed in his fortieth year, and now, at forty-five, did most of his bristling with his close-cropped moustache, no longer giving her the lie when she offset one of his breaks with: "Mr. Atkinson has such a droll sense of humour."

On a murky morning two weeks after Hagar's arrest George P. Atkinson sat with his paper open before him. It was then in the eighth minute of the fifteen allotted to that daily rite, and he had not yet been allowed to commence. He made what he hoped was a decisive effort to dispose of the interruption.

"I can't see it, my dear," he told Mrs. Atkinson. "We go out and hire a woman to work for us. Very good. We pay her adequately. If she is injured in our employ we may be responsible under the Employer's Liability Law, but, in South Carolina, I doubt even that. Not that I would not do the right thing by Mamba. She's a good soul and, white or black, I'm fond of her. But when a disreputable creature of the slums with a police record is dragged in, claimed to be her daughter, and goes to court to take her medicine for setting upon and breaking up a law-abiding negro, I am out. Business is business. Charity is charity. Once in a thousand years justice is even justice. I would be an ass to interfere. I won't. That's final."

"But, George dear, you miss the point. It won't be going out of your way to do it. It's the thing to do. The right sort of people here do look after their negroes. They take pride in it. Most likely you will not be the only one there. You're as apt as not to find a Ravenal, Waring, or Pinckney doing the same thing. The other afternoon at the Saturday Club some of the ladies had the most entertaining stories of scrapes that their husbands had gotten their negroes out of."

"Their negroes! Am I to assume that this person charged with aggravated assault and indecent exposure of the person is my negro?"

"Of course, George. Everybody knows that Mamba's people used to belong to the Atkinsons, and now, since the South Carolina branch of the family has died out, you are in a way the head."

The head of the Atkinson clan balled his paper up in a knot and threw it on the floor, looked his wife in the face, and said rudely: "Bah!" Then he cleared his throat, raised his voice, and deliberately repeated the offensive monosyllable.

It was the secret of Mrs. Atkinson's success that she never lost either her temper or her head. Now, in a voice like a cold douche she said: "You can't bah away an obligation, George, and you know it."

Thirteen minutes of newspaper time gone. Was ever a man so put upon! He snapped: "You know as well as I do that there never was an Atkinson plantation on Cooper River. Why, I asked some of the men at the club about it the other day, and I could see that they were laughing at me."

To many wives this would have meant utter rout, but not to this adroit campaigner. She veered suddenly and took her husband in a most vulnerable spot. "Very well, then," she said, as though the matter were concluded, "be inhuman, and while you are enjoying your pride that justice is being done, imagine your own daughter in desperate trouble with no one to help her, and then perhaps you'll know how poor old Mamba feels."

"Eh, what's that?" exclaimed Atkinson in a startled voice.

"And you don't know the whole story, either. You just read what your hateful paper says. I'll tell you what I'll do. Just let Mamba come in and give you her version of the tragedy; then, if you refuse to help, I'll promise never to say another word about it."

Atkinson emitted a short grunt that was intended to convey scepticism of his wife's promised silence, but she seized it and interpreted it as assent. Opening the pantry door, she summoned Mamba.

The old woman entered with a promptness that suggested pre-arrangement, and advanced until she stood before her master, then waited with bowed head and hands that clenched each other tightly before her.

"Go ahead," he said, "I suppose I'll have to listen before I can get any peace."

Mrs. Atkinson said in her crisp compulsive voice: "Now, Mamba, tell him exactly what happened."

When Mamba finished her recital she was sobbing into her apron, and her listener was sitting forward in his chair with his moustache bristling. "So he tried to rob her, did he?" he exclaimed. "When's the trial?"

"To-morruh mornin', suh. Ah ain't want foh bodder yuh 'til Ah can't wait no longer."

"Very well, we'll see what can be done."

Into his overcoat, then, and out of the door on his last word. He'd be ten minutes late at the office. Wouldn't do. Bad example. Loose morale. Rotten position he'd be in to-morrow, too. Tacitly backing up his wife in that absurd fiction about the plantation Atkinsons. They'd have a damned good right to laugh at him at the club now. Pretending himself a Carolina aristocrat. Pretence, of all things that he hated. But that poor old nigger and her story about her girl. Well, he was in for it.

*

When Atkinson entered the court room on the following morning he saw Mamba waiting for him just inside the door. Then he noticed that she was accompanied by a child—a mulatto girl about six years of age. It was the old woman's attitude toward her charge rather than the child herself that first caught his attention. The entrance was jammed with negroes who elbowed their way to the spectators' inclosure, and a bailiff was attempting to clear the doorway. In the confusion of opposing bodies Mamba was managing to keep the space about the child free. She was silent, but stood with the slender form held before her and gazed into the faces of the milling negroes with an expression of such cold ferocity that they instinctively drew back. Then he noticed the girl. He saw a slender, delicately made body, a small sentient face, and eyes that seemed to note everything that passed before them with that precosity which is characteristic of children with negro blood.

A trial was already in progress; a jury trial at that. It would be afternoon before they could get to Hagar's case. A whole day gone. Five perfectly good business hours. Well, he was in for it. He'd stick it out. Might pick up something that would be of use when the woman's time came. With characteristic economy of movement, he went straight to one of the swivel chairs behind the attorneys' table and motioned Mamba to a seat behind him. From under level brows his keen gray eyes appraised the room.

Against the rear wall of the courtroom were the two sections reserved for the public. There was a scattering of nondescripts behind the railing of the rectangle occupied by the whites. Across the aisle, the coloured space was packed to the walls. Black, brown, yellow, with intent faces and wide eyes, the crowd appeared as thought welded into a unit by its common and utter absorption. The overheated air was tinged with a faint exotic odour compounded of fertiliser dust, fish, and unwashed negro bodies inseparable from such a gathering. It offended the visitor at first, but soon he lost consciousness of it, for he followed the gaze of the crowd to the prisoner in the dock.

She was a big yahoo of a girl about sixteen years of age, very black, and with heavy negroid features. Her eyes set wide apart, and with the broad, flat nose between them, gave her an expression of bucolic calm. She was a creature for the simple rhythms of the country, and seemed out of place in the complex machinery of a city court.

Continuing his survey of the scene, Atkinson met the eyes of the prosecuting attorney, who was seated at a table directly in front of his own. He had a pleasant acquaintance with the young court official, but was unprepared for the informal and cordial reception that he received. The attorney was a man in the early thirties, blond, with that instinctive graciousness of manner toward a guest that Atkinson always admired, and secretly envied, in the men of his adopted city.

"Delighted to see you here, Mr. Atkinson," he said, extending his hand across the table. "Just looking us over, or are you interested in one of our cases?"

Atkinson explained that he was there to do what he could for Hagar.

"Splendid!" exclaimed the young lawyer. "One can't help liking the woman. She's not a criminal type. Do you know whether she is represented by counsel?"

"I think not. As a matter of fact, Mr. Dawson, the woman is guilty of the charge. I understand that the man is still in the hospital, and there is no doubt as to who put him there. But there are extenuating circumstances, and I'm here to vouch for them."

The prosecutor leaned forward and gave his instructions briefly: "You must make her plead guilty. Whatever you do, do not agree to a jury trial. We'll talk it over with the judge when her case is called and see what can be done."

The bailiff bawled for order in court, and the judge inquired formally if counsel for prosecution and defence were ready to proceed with their speeches in the case of the negro girl. Both men rose and bowed. The state's attorney traversed the ten feet of the space that separated him from the jury box and faced its occupants over the low railing. Instantly the suave and urbane individual who had been talking to Atkinson vanished, and in his place stood a tense, truculent figure. Swiftly, and with a deadly precision, he counted off the salient points of the case on his fingers. The woman had stolen clothing valued at forty dollars;

three competent white witnesses had nailed down the evidence; the clothing had been found in her room and identified by owner. A moment of dramatic silence ensued, then an abrupt transition. Leaving the damning facts hanging, as it were, in the air before the jurors, Dawson's body became electric with that facile violence which characterises the successful prosecutor and can always be depended upon to galvanise his auditors into attention. For ten minutes he poured out a vitriolic arraignment against the type of petty criminal who has the audacity to engage a lawyer to come and monopolise the valuable time of the court and the services of a "highly intelligent" jury. "Taking your time, gentlemen, I submit, to wade through the sordid details of a case upon the very face of which, I again submit, she is as guilty as Judas Iscariot." On then in the teeth of the jury itself, calling upon them to make a proper example of the case in question, that the culprit and those of her friends who were present might be impressed with the dignity and importance of the court. Turning away abruptly as from a finished task with a foregone conclusion, Dawson took his seat.

"Great Godamighty!" exclaimed a woman's voice in the negro section, and "Silence in court," bawled the bailiff.

Counsel for the defence got to his feet and commenced to speak. He was a big man with a heavy lethargic body and a stupid face. His lips were loose and crafty. He gave the immediate effect of one who was going through a familiar routine, saying the trite phrases with noise but without conviction. That tension which one expects to find at a criminal trial, and that Dawson had attained, was now wholly lacking, except in the tranced attention accorded by the tightly packed negro section. The jury lounged at ease in their chairs. The judge and clerk were busy with papers of other cases on the docket.

Atkinson transferred his attention to the prisoner in the dock. She was sitting forward following every gesture of the lawyer with

WINGS

Vol. 3   No. 2

The LITERARY GUILD

of AMERICA, Inc.

55 FIFTH AVE.

NEW YORK

In Memoriam

ELINOR WYLIE

This tribute to a celebrated poet and a lovely woman was written by Isabel Paterson of the New York Herald Tribune for December 18th, two days after the tragic death of Mrs. Wylie. The Literary Guild of America mourns the passing of its editor.

TO HAVE known Elinor Wylie at all, however briefly or slightly, made her death a personal loss. Brightness fell from the air when the news came. She died of a cerebral hemorrhage, about 8:30 Sunday evening, in her New York apartment. It was only about a week since she had returned from England; and her husband, William Rose Benet, was with her when death came without warning. It would seem that she sustained a more serious injury and shock from a fall downstairs last summer than her friends were allowed to realize. And her health had never been robust.

She was not much over forty, and looked younger. Before she made her name as a writer, she was reckoned the most beautiful girl in Washington society. Her tall slenderness added to her air of distinction. She had chestnut hair, hazel eyes, and a notably lovely throat. The eighteenth century word elegance, in its fine eighteenth century meaning, might have been minted for her. Elegance was the note of her mind as of her appearance. And her century was the eighteenth, but not the eighteenth century of powdered wigs and Alexander Pope. She belonged to the close of the eighteenth century, the Romantics, who revived the lyric spirit and the spiritual adventurousness of the Elizabethan singers. And she could talk like an angel.

Her career was stormily romantic; and being a poet, she lent herself easily to misunderstanding. For she had, surprisingly, a strong practical intelligence, the cool unswerving logic of the eighteenth century—the Age of Reason. If it

(Continued on page 5)

WHY THE EDITORIAL BOARD
SELECTED *MAMBA'S DAUGHTERS*

By CARL VAN DOREN

"MAMBA'S DAUGHTERS" by Du Bose Heyward belongs, with "The Happy Mountain" already issued to the subscribers of the Literary Guild, to a type of fiction which has long been common in the United States, but of which there are not, and cannot be, too many good examples. In a country so extensive, with such numerous differences in the modes of life from section to section, regional novels must long be depended upon to mirror a civilization at once too large and too diversified to be represented in any single book. Until the Great

American Novel has been written, as it never will be, a collection of novels must do its work. "Mamba's Daughters" is an important addition to such a collection.

Mr. Heyward has not hesitated to describe Charleston, South Carolina, where the scene of his story is laid, with all possible accuracy, even to the names of streets and neighborhoods and of some of the persons. He knows that a novelist must be precise to be convincing, that it is facts which give the sharp outlines and special colors to any truth. With the same exactness this novelist has studied the customs and idioms of his city, presenting them as he knows them and leaving it to his readers to recognize them as familiar or to be struck with them as novel.

When it comes to the men and women of the plot, Mr. Heyward has gone beyond historical or biographical description and has imagined his principal characters. Perhaps his white people are more local, more strictly typical of Charleston, than his blacks. At least the fortunes of the Wentworth family move on as the fortunes of

Southern white families often do in fiction. And perhaps the black people have the advantage of being more universal because, being primitive, they are less provincial. In any case, the three negro women, mother, daughter, and granddaughter, who live in Charleston in the flesh—since heroines, after all, have to live somewhere, are essentially citizens of the heroic world. Mamba the crafty, Hagar the mighty, Lissa the gifted—one after the other they rise from their low beginnings to eventual triumph each in her fashion. It is they who give tone and body and significance to the book. It is they who make a regional novel a work of art.

Mr. Heyward is already well known on account of his novel "Porgy," published in 1925 and put on the stage with great success by the Theatre Guild in 1927. "Mamba's Daughters" returns to the same scene, or nearly so, with even more power than was shown in the earlier work, and with a larger variety as regards types of character and phases of life in Charleston. Whereas "Porgy" concerned itself with a single savage drama enacted in Catfish Row, "Mamba's Daughters" reaches out to include three generations of negro life as they touch all the various conditions in which Charleston negroes live. In addition, there are many white people, shown not merely as they touch the personages of the black drama, but also as they carry on their own existences in passing from a traditional world of leisure, pride and poverty to the new industrial world which the South has lately entered.

In Memoriam
(*Continued from page 3*)
was not always applied, one must remember that to be a poet means not only wearing one's heart on one's sleeve but existing with nerves almost equally exposed. Unexpected audacities and shuddering avoidances are equally inevitable with such an endowment. In everyday affairs it is a cruel disadvantage; but it is an indispensable condition of art.

She was really erudite, but touched on her learning so gaily it was scarcely suspected. For she was also really and wholly an artist, one of the very few among contemporary writers. In her circumstances—that is, lacking the spur of necessity—even a fine talent may be dissipated in the poses of a dilettante. Nothing can save it but a veritable passion for literature, which Elinor Wylie had. She *worked*. She took endless pains, that her readers might be unaware of any. Her finest prose, as for instance the best pages of "Mr. Hodge and Mr. Hazard," comes near to the microcosmic crystalline perfection of a dewdrop.

IN announcing the incorporation of an exchange privilege in the Guild plan we feel that the Guild has scored another triumph in its brief but most interesting career.

This further guarantee of satisfaction to our subscribers removes the last possible reason for dissatisfaction with the Guild Plan. The encouraging response to our renewal subscription efforts this past year convinces us that we can count on even more of our membership continuing year after year. If we are correct there will be no reason for increasing the annual subscription fee above the present $21.00 rate. Last year we mailed our subscribers 611,000 books and saved them $1,150,000.00 in the purchase of these books. Such a service certainly promotes the reading of good books and we feel that our greatest contribution to the book reading public would be to increase this saving during 1929.

If you are dissatisfied with the current Guild selection it may be returned within one week after it is received and substituted for any book now in print. The Editorial Board has prepared a supplementary list of recommended books which appear on the next page. You are not limited to this list in making your exchange. It is only a guide for your convenience.

If you find it necessary to exchange a Guild book let us ask that you follow this procedure:

1. Return the current Guild book within one week after its receipt.

2. Send us your request for the exchange book with a check for the difference between the retail price of the book you wish and one-twelfth of the annual Guild subscription price ($1.75). As example:

Recommended Books	Retail Price	Aver. Guild Cost	Send Us
ORLANDO........	$3.00	$1.75	$1.25
ELIZABETH & ESSEX	3.75	1.75	2.00
WHITHER MANKIND	3.00	1.75	1.25

If you prefer a book other than those recommended by the Editors, and do not know the retail price, we will ship it to you C.O.D. Please do not ask us to open accounts on exchange books. We are operating this service at a loss for the convenience of our subscribers and consequently wish to eliminate the details of bookkeeping.

3. If you prefer a previous Guild selection we will exchange the current book at no additional cost, regardless of the retail price of the Guild book you wish. A few recent Guild selections which you can receive at no extra cost are:

TRADER HORN, VOL. 2 HAPPY MOUNTAIN
AN INDIAN JOURNEY FRANCOIS VILLON
MEET GENERAL GRANT
AN ANTHOLOGY OF WORLD POETRY

4. The Guild will also supply you with any other books you may desire to purchase. We do not solicit this business; but if you find it more convenient to pur-

chase through us, we will be glad to obtain books for you at the regular retail price.

The following books have each been recommended by at least one of the editors of the Literary Guild. Various reasons have made it impossible to include them among the twelve books regularly issued by the Guild during the past year. Some have seemed too close in subject or manner to other books recently issued. Some have been unavailable at a time when it was possible to make them Guild selections. Some have seemed too specialized for the general Guild public. Some of them have failed to win the approval of a majority of the editors. But all of them are recommended for this supplementary list with the assurance that they stand very close in merit and interest to the books chosen for the regular Guild list.

ELIZABETH AND ESSEX. By *Lytton Strachey*. $3.75.

A masterful account of the most important episode in the life of Queen Elizabeth by the master of the modern art of biography.

SHORTER NOVELS. By *Herman Melville*. $3.50.

Four remarkable short novels by the great American novelist whom Americans are only beginning to appreciate.

THE STRANGE NECESSITY. By *Rebecca West*. $3.50.

A brilliant book of literary criticism by a writer who can make criticism dramatic.

THE EARLY LIFE OF THOMAS HARDY. By *Florence Emily Hardy*. $5.00.

A sound biography of the last of the great Victorians, written by his wife.

BOSTON. By *Upton Sinclair*. 2 vols. $5.00.

A powerful novel based upon the Sacco-Vanzetti case.

ORLANDO. By *Virginia Woolf*. $3.00.

A highly original narrative of the life of a surprising imaginary character who sums up in himself the course of English civilization for three hundred years.

ZOLA. By *Matthew Josephson*. $5.00.

The striking life of a man who had a striking career.

THE CASE OF SERGEANT GRISHA. By *Arnold Zweig*. $2.50.

A German novel of the first rank and importance, dealing with the World War.

LEONARDO THE FLORENTINE. By *Rachel Annand Taylor*. $6.00.

A notable study of Leonardo da Vinci, probably the most gifted man who has ever lived.

MEXICO AND ITS HERITAGE. By *Ernest Gruening*. $6.00.

The best survey of Mexico as Americans ought to know it but do not.

THIS BOOK-COLLECTING GAME. By *A. Edward Newton*. $5.00.

The adventures and the advice of an expert.

WEST-RUNNING BROOK. By *Robert Frost*. $2.50.

New poems by a poet who needs no recommendation.

JOHN BROWN'S BODY. By *Stephen Vincent Benét*. $2.50.

A rousing epic of the Civil War, already known to most Americans who read.

As John Farrar Sees
Du Bose Heyward

THE author of Mamba's Daughters was born and has lived most of his life in Charleston, S. C. He has known all sides of the colorful life of that picturesque town. Of an old and aristocratic southern family, impoverished by the Civil War, he has both danced in ballrooms and worked on the docks, where he saw the life he immortalized in "Porgy." At one time he studied painting. Then he turned to poetry, and it was as a poet that Du Bose Heyward first gained recognition. When Harvey Allen was teaching in Charleston, they met, became interested in organizing the Poetry Society of South Carolina, and wrote together a book of ballads and verses called "Carolina Chansons". Having saved a little money Mr. Heyward decided to plunge, gave up his business, and took to lecturing and writing in earnest. Having spent many of his summers in the mountains of North Carolina he bought a small farm there, and began to divide his time between the South and The McDowell Colony at Peterboro. It was there that he met Dorothy Kuhns, a playwright. They were married and it was with her that he wrote the dramatic version of "Porgy", the success of which has made him internationally famous. The first book to carry his name alone was a slim volume of lovely lyrics "Skylines and Horizons". His second novel "Angel", deals with North Carolina whites.

Quite apart from his literary attainments, I know of no writer who has worn success so gracefully. He works long and hard over everything he writes. He re-wrote "Mamba's Daughters" several times. He has not taken the easy rewards that come to a writer in America with huge publicity; but works quietly ahead on the thing that is nearest his heart. When he finished this latest novel he told me he was going to write some more poetry before he tried another play or novel. He has the spirit of the artist. He is the honest creator.

JOHN FARRAR

How Literary Critics Received

AN ANTHOLOGY OF WORLD POETRY
The Guild's Choice for December

Those well-worn words, "a literary event," may well be pressed once more into service in the case of Mark Van Doren's "Anthology of World Poetry." This is a book, long needed, which reflects great credit upon its editor and its publishers. There can be no doubt that Mr. Van Doren's volume will make for itself a secure place among the few anthologies which really matter. He has given his work the widest possible scope; its extent may be gathered from the Table of Sections. This one has its flaws, but it deserves to rank with the best; and furthermore, it is the only thing of its kind. He is to be congratulated on the discernment shown in his choice of poems for the American section. Here, in less than seventy pages, he has succeeded in making a good anthology of American verse. As a piece of bookmaking the volume is a credit to its publishers.

J. Donald Adams, New York Times Book Review, 12/16/28.

* * *

And up until recently Edwin Markham's two volumes of poetry, compiled and edited after something like a lifetime of careful research, were supposed to head the list of comprehensive anthologies. But now it must take a back seat, remain very quiet, with its hands behind its back, for Mark Van Doren has won the triumph of editing "An Anthology of World Poetry," published in a single volume (very thin paper and 1,318 pages) by Albert and Charles Boni and elevated to still higher honors by being chosen by the Literary Guild for its December accolade.

Jo Ranson, Brooklyn Daily Eagle, 12/5/28.

* * *

If all poets attempting an anthology of this order entered upon their task with a learning and love for their art and for the deep centuries that have evolved it such as Mark Van Doren has shown, layman and poet alike would be better educated. Van Doren's greatest triumph lies in his selections from the Chinese, Japanese, Sanskrit,

Arabian, Egyptian, Greek and English. Here he has indeed found "everlastings."

Laura Benet, New York Post, 12/8/28.

* * *

It is an amazing symphony in our own accents. I doubt if Mr. Van Doren has missed much of importance. Certainly he has brought together something which previously has been scattered and unavailable. All of us are in his debt for his painstaking and spontaneous work. Let us praise this anthology to immoderation as a book libraries will need, and students; and as one that will give endless use and joy to youth and men and women generally.

Frank Ernest Hill, New York Herald Tribune, 12/16/28.

* * *

I've looked into many an anthology of poetry, but this is unquestionably the best I have ever encountered! It contains more genuine poetry per square inch, so to speak, than any other anthology I know of. And that it is superlatively good will be readily admitted by everyone whose interest in poetry is more than casual and who so much as glances through its table of contents. To the few anthologies that should be an integral part of every well-stocked library, public or private, "An Anthology of World Poetry" should be immediately added.

Stanley E. Babb, The Galveston Daily News, 12/23/29.

* * *

The poet that the editor is reveals himself anew in this large and faultless choosing. For me, now, fresh from days of sampling it, elated with the discovery, whole within it (not minced to anthology length), of rare books of poems, some of them unobtainable, the book takes first rank among anthologies. It is certain that this collection will become one of the best known and most necessary of books; the future perhaps will read it as a duty, fit reverence to a good book. But for us it is all discovery, and all the delight that goes with discovery.

Isidor Schneider, New York Sun, 12/15/28.

AMONG OUR SUBSCRIBERS

F ROM Charles A. Wright, the Managing Editor of the Lancaster Ave. News, Philadelphia, Pa. comes the following interesting letter:

"I have derived much pleasure not only from the Guild books, but also from the interesting comments contained in Wings.

"Which has led me to wonder if one of the improvements promised for 1929 might not be a further development of Wings. One suggestion which I would like to offer is that Wings, instead of being made in varying sizes to fit the different books, be made in one standard size, possibly that of the smallest book likely to be issued, in order that these may be preserved by the member, and perhaps bound uniformly.

"In reading the press comments on the books in Wings, I have been struck by the fact that only favorable ones have been used."

We wish to extend our thanks to Mr. Wright for his very sound criticism. The reason why we do not print "Wings" in a uniform size is that unless we made it very small indeed, it would not fit into all the various sizes of the Guild books. A magazine that could be slipped between the covers of "The Magic Island" would be far too big for a book the size of "Black Majesty," for instance.

———

And following Mr. Wright's second suggestion, we reprint a letter from Edith B. Meanley of Ruxton, Md. who has been for some time a Literary Guild subscriber. It contains comment both favorable and unfavorable, but interesting throughout:

"The Last Post: I never quite got into this book, somehow, though I did read it.

The Great American Band Wagon: Delicious. The author certainly 'has our number'.

Catherine-Paris: Interesting, but I couldn't read it twice.

Black Majesty: 'Majesty', in truth! What I would call a really great book.

Bad Girl: Except for one or two rather unnecessary (I thought) episodes, there is something very moving in this story.

Trader Horn, Vol. II: I am one of the very small minority who is not able to appreciate Mr. Horn's books.

An Indian Journey: Most entertaining. I can read this again and again.

The Happy Mountain: An appealing and very lovely story.

Francois Villon: An ACHIEVEMENT! It's perfectly fascinating.

Point Counter Point: This is where I am invited to take a back seat, but see if I care! I have never been fond of Huxley, though I could, heretofore, see how others could be. This time, however, I see no excuse at all. He delights in trying to make a farce of everything sacred or beautiful (how he would sneer at those 'mid-Victorian' words!). Mr. Huxley and I do not, apparently, agree that one of our chief aims in life (or so I thought) is to make other people happy.

MEET GENERAL GRANT: Very human and interesting.

ANTHOLOGY OF WORLD POETRY: A treasure—except that it has deprived me of my eight hours of sleep ever since it came! Please give us more poetry."

And this from Mrs. Marian Naylor Weidensee, County Librarian of the Potter County Free Public Library, Gettysburg, So. Dakota.

"While my Literary Guild subscription is a personal one I always loan the books to library patrons. I find that our sophisticated readers enjoy having an opportunity to use the books. One of them who is always more or less horrified at the books hoped I wouldn't drop the subscription for she says that as long as I get the books she hopes to get to read them. I think it's time that someone did just the thing you are doing, get away from the staples. As a matter of fact most people read too much along the same general line and thus get into a very deep rut. Literary

Guild books are varied and outstanding enough to be read. One woman who objects to "Point Counter Point" is nevertheless very glad that she has had an opportunity to read it. The university and college students like to have books of Literary Guild type and it doesn't hurt their opinion of the home library to find that we've been having books that they were discussing at school."

A NEW PREMIUM

The Wonder Fountain Pen Co. have just offered us the opportunity of obtaining a limited number of combination pen and pencils for distribution among our subscribers.

This pen-pencil retails for $4.50 and is guaranteed from the standpoint of both material and workmanship. We are planning to offer either the pen-pencil or 100 bookplates as a premium in our next member-get-a-member campaign. Won't you please help us decide by writing a note of your preference to our Mr. Weiner.

a hypnotic gaze. One got the impression that her interest in the proceedings was impersonal, detached. She was caught by the drama of it but had not succeeded in relating the obscure process that was under way to herself. She was in the grip of forces as remote from her comprehension as are the workings of destiny. Words, words, filling the air with strange, exciting sound. Later there would come a silence, then that fate which was approaching, and was already determined, would be revealed to her. It would make her happy or sad. It would have to be accepted as had other crises in her uncertain advance through life.

The lawyer ended his speech in a burst of noise, an oratorical invocation to the blind goddess who held the scales over the portal and who dispensed justice to rich and poor alike. He turned to his seat followed by such an admiring and unself-conscious gaze from his client that for a moment Atkinson feared that she might altogether forget herself and burst into applause.

The speech over, the court became animate. The judge charged briefly for conviction. The jury marched out and returned almost immediately with the verdict of guilty. The clerk ordered the prisoner to arise and receive sentence. The judge gave her a severe lecture, and, in the midst of a dramatic pause, seven years in the state reformatory.

A composite involuntary sound that was half wail, half moan, sounded from the negro section.

"Order in court," bawled the bailiff.

A deputy led the prisoner from the dock. She cast a final admiring glance toward her attorney. There could be no doubt about it; he had delivered a satisfactory performance.

Atkinson gasped at the severity of the sentence; then he went around and took an empty chair beside Dawson.

"Good God!" he exclaimed. "Seven years for a few dollars' worth of second-hand clothes. It's inhuman."

The younger man smiled into his earnest face. "I see you haven't got the hang of it yet," he said, "but don't be too scandalised at us. She is not going to do her full time. I'll keep a note of the case, and later she'll be let out on good behaviour. You see, there are a lot of shyster lawyers around here who take the nigger's money in advance and promise to clear them when they know there isn't a chance. The only way to convince the poor devils that they're being done is to throw it into them good and deep every time a case goes to a jury. But God! They learn slowly."

Hagar's case was called, and Atkinson saw her enter, dwarfing the deputy who led her to the dock. This was his first glimpse of his charge, and he was at once struck by the candour of the big, child-like face, and the questioning, live brown eyes that were so much like Mamba's. He was anything but an imaginative man, but in that moment he had a flash of divination. He saw the court, the officers, the jurymen, as these simple souls must see them; akin to the High Gods of Greek mythology, manipulating the vast mysterious force that was the law, looming suddenly and inexorably against the gaiety of life, to smash families—even to mark for death.

Dawson was speaking to him, and he turned with a start. "You had better have a talk with your client," he was saying. "Tell her to plead guilty when the clerk finishes reading the indictment and puts the question."

He beckoned to Mamba, and together they stepped to the prisoner's dock. There he commenced an involved explanation of the reasons why it would be best for her to plead guilty. Hagar did not take her eyes from his face, but he saw that her look was that of a drowning person who watches the shore rather than one of understanding. He stopped speaking. Then she said:

"What dat wo'd Ah's tuh say?"

"Guilty," Atkinson told her.

"Berry well, den. Yo' nod yo' head at de right time, an' Ah'll say um."

Mamba retired to her seat, and Atkinson joined the prosecutor. The clerk rose, read the indictment, and put the question. Atkinson nodded his head, and, in her deep contralto voice, Hagar said clearly, "Guilty."

The judge leaned over his desk and raised his eyebrows in interrogation. Dawson beckoned to Atkinson and stepped forward. "Your Honour," he said, "I would like to present Mr. George Atkinson of the Southeastern Cotton Seed Products Corporation, one of our leading citizens, who is interested in this case."

The judge shook hands warmly; then, leaning forward on his elbows, spoke in a leisurely conversational tone: "I am delighted to know you, sir. You are from the North, I understand."

Atkinson had been busy with plans for his client's defence, wondering whether he had not better bring Mamba forward and let her tell her story. The social turn taken by the court jarred him from his line of thought. He uttered a surprised affirmative to the comment. The judicial features above the desk smiled pleasantly down upon him, and the agreeable voice with its almost imperceptible drawl led the conversation among the amenities that usually preface an acquaintanceship.

Beyond the small circle of their talk the courtroom waited. Here and there a chair leg creaked or a foot shuffled. Beyond the window a huckster cried his fish in a deep baritone song. In the negroes' section the tension drew out until it became almost tangible in the air of the room. And at the desk the three men chatted of the relative merits of the Charleston and New York climates. They might have been in a club, or at a chance meeting after business hours. Finally the judge touched on the case.

"And so you are interested in this woman, Mr. Atkinson. Very good of you to assist us, I am sure. Perhaps you will tell me what you know of the affair."

Atkinson explained his connection with Mamba and Hagar. His interest seemed to be entirely understood by his hearers. The fact that he had espoused the woman's cause was taken as a matter of course. As briefly as possible he told the story as he had got it from Mamba.

When he had finished the judge looked inquiringly at the prosecutor, and asked: "And what do you know about her, Mr. Dawson?"

"She's been in the police court several times, Your Honour. Nothing serious: hot suppers, lodge meetings, and the like. There's nothing vicious about her."

His Honour pondered: "Still, she has a police record. That's got to be considered. Evidently the town is no place for her. Ought to get her out of it and give her another chance." He continued to speak, but now his glance took the other two into consultation: "A two-year suspended sentence ought to do. Give her six hours to get out of the city. Then put her on her good behaviour. If she is arrested anywhere in the county, or enters town again for any purpose whatever, the sentence will become immediately operative. Does that appeal to you as a fair adjustment, Mr. Atkinson?"

It had never occurred to that gentleman that he would be consulted in so important a matter as the actual measure of punishment, but he managed to say that he thought it not only very fair but decidedly generous.

"I am glad that you feel that way about it, sir," His Honour replied, then shook hands over the desk, expressed pleasure in the meeting, and nodded to the clerk.

An involuntary whisper lifted and died in the negro section. The bailiff bawled for order in court. The clerk called upon Hagar to arise and receive sentence.

Slowly and lucidly the judge made his pronouncement and explained its purport. Then he ordered court adjourned for the day.

The deputy who was to take charge of Hagar until she should leave the city led her from the room, and a bewildered George Atkinson got to his feet and made for the open.

When he was on the pavement again he found that Mamba had accompanied him. She had been so quiet during the proceedings that, in his absorption, he had forgotten her, and the presence of the child which she held tightly by the hand struck him with the impact of a fresh surprise. Mamba caught his hand, shook it, tried to speak, then turned suddenly and followed Hagar. He stood looking after the strange old figure. Age with its back to the wall, fighting for something against great odds. His heart contracted with an unfamiliar spasm of pity, then expanded with a desire to protect. All feeling of boredom had passed during the trial. He had espoused a cause. For the moment he had put his best into it. Now, with the fight behind him, he could not let it go. It kept tagging along beside him, plucking at the sleeve of his mind. It made him think about something that had nothing to do with cotton seed. It started something in his brain like the slow turning up of a light. This negro business; millions and millions of them. Race problem. What to do with the whole mass. You came up to that, and it was there before you like a wall without a gate. One either stood there battering his hands to pieces on it, or he walked away and made it his business to forget. But this old woman, now, and her great ungainly daughter, and that child that they had a way of speaking about with their voices lowered; this was something different. These three were not a race problem. They were individual entities battling with destiny, needing a leg up most terribly. The weak throwing themselves on the mercy of the strong. Mamba—Hagar—the child— not negroes now: but to his mind just isolated human beings driven by some obscure urge toward a vague elusive goal, as he was—his wife—his children. Was that the feeling behind the law as he had found it in the court that morning? Was it the key to the puzzling attitude of the men he knew who could be so callous to the mass, yet who responded with exaggerated generosity to the need of a known individual?

He came to a street crossing, and his alert mind leaped to grapple with actualities, suddenly and keenly cognisant of the world about him. Over the cobbles at his feet a low cart was being dragged by an aged goat. In it sat a crippled negro. His head was bare to the sun, and his face wore the vacuous look that is common to both dreamers and fools. His hat lay upward in his lap, and there were a few pennies in it. The sight was a familiar enough one to Atkinson. He had seen the beggar every day, and yet his existence had never impinged upon his consciousness. Now he saw him differently. "God!" he thought. "What a hell of a joke for life to play on a man." He fumbled in his pocket, drew out a dollar bill, and dropped it in the hat. The face below him became incredulous. Slow fingers picked the bill up and felt it, turning it over and over. Atkinson pulled himself together. "Can't stand here all day looking like Santa Claus," he told himself.

He turned on his heel and stepped briskly away, but his half-solved problem was not to be outdistanced; it was with him again, insinuating itself between his mind and the image of yesterday's quotation board. Individuals—human beings—that's the answer, perhaps. Can't lift the mass. No use to try, it's too vast. Can't get hold of the edges of it, and if one did it would probably drop and smash things to pieces. But when you know of one who is catching hell, got to be decent, human. And leave the race problem to God and the great-grandchildren.

He was at his office now. Squaring his shoulders, he took the steps two at a time, opened the door, and exclaimed briskly, "After-noon, Johnson. Got yesterday's reports ready?"

★

Saint Wentworth sat in the little room behind the camp com-missary, his brow furrowed with the intensity of his mental con-centration. Before him, propped upon a table, was a self-instruc-tion book of music, and his fingers were busy finding chords on the neck of a battered guitar. The open page showed diagrams of the strings with black dots where the fingers were to fall for each chord. Some of the combinations were awkward for his unac-customed hands, but he hung doggedly to each until he could find it with his eyes lifted from the page before he passed on to the next. At first glance one would have said that his three years at the phosphate mines had changed him but little in appearance. As he sat in the half light of the little room between the fading day against the small window and the flickering illumination of the open fire, he showed the same slightly stooping shoulders, the colour-less hair with its flaring cowlick, and the old lack of compression about the mouth which is to the conventional mind an infallible symbol of weakness. Only when he finally closed the book, laid the guitar aside, and, with hands jammed deep into trousers pockets, commenced to wander about the room, would one have noticed differences. Changes that became evident, not so much in the physical appearance of the man himself as in his interrelation with the room. He was one of those not uncommon people who find ex-pression in the things with which they surround themselves; people for whom no evaluation can serve that does not take the setting into account. There were books on a shelf, plays, biography, poetry, a modern novel or two; the astonishingly varied collection that in age may mean only the dilettante, but in youth the seeker. An etching was given one of the four walls to itself: an extremely well done piece of work by a young Charleston artist—the gateway of old St. Michael's with its wrought-iron urns and scrolls. A small but fine plaster of the Nike was given the mantel. A couch against one of the walls was covered with brown burlap, and had pillows of orange and lemon upon it. The draperies at the single window were the colour of sunlight. Now day was retreating rapidly behind the panes. The fluctuations of firelight grew more noticeable on walls and furnishings, thrusting mellow shafts under the table and into corners—possessing the room. Saturday night, and the negroes would soon be coming to do their shopping.

Wentworth cast a long look about him, sighed, and passed through the door into the commissary with its familiar odours— kerosene from the barrel in the corner, cabbages—the smells seeming stronger and more sour in the dusk. Then he caught a clean wholesome whiff from a pile of print cotton goods at his elbow. He threw some wood on the coals in the small open fireplace, lighted the lamps, and stepped through the outer door onto the little piazza. A cold red sunset burned low behind the serried pines, and over the eastern marshes the mists thickened and swirled, bringing night in from the Atlantic wrapped in their folds.

A group of negroes approached, their resonant voices preceding them. They were in high humour. To-night they could commence to buy on next week's wages. The exhaustion of credit that invariably pinched them during the latter half of each week was now happily at an end until next Wednesday, or even Thursday if one were careful. Maum Vina, with her kind, peering eyes, and Reverend Quintus Whaley, fat and unctuous, were the first to enter. Behind them groups of twos and threes gathered before the store, climbed the steps, and entered the building. Loud chaffing and banter filled the air. Most of the women were swinging bottles by strings to be filled with kerosene for their lamps, and some brought jugs for molasses. The men were covered with dust from the mining pits. This was the hour when labour was forgotten, friends met, and gossip was exchanged. The commissary building glowed hospitably. The open fire crackled on the hearth, and several oil lamps flickered in the draught and sent ribbons of smoke up among the rafters.

Wentworth waited on Ned first because he knew that he was in trouble and ought to hurry back to Dolly. His customer was a small black negro in late middle life, with a grizzled moustache, and large teeth between which was clenched a cheroot that added a smell like burning leather to the other odours in the room. He was pondering over a selection from several bolts of black and white cambrics and cotton flannels. He smoked steadily while he held the widths of cloth against a soap box, black for the outside and white for the lining, appraising the effect with his head cocked speculatively on one side. From time to time he would look up and speak to an acquaintance. It seemed to Saint that he was deliberately protracting his errand, enjoying the importance that it gave him. And there was a smugness about him that was annoying. Saint remembered the sounds of weeping that he had heard when he had passed his cabin, and the stricken face of Dolly as she looked from the door. Now he spoke sharply, "If you're sure the box is large enough, say what cloth you want and get through. I haven't all night to give you."

Ned produced a stick about eighteen inches in length and placed it in the box, where it fitted nicely. "Ain't yo' see, suh, dat he size? He ain't but a six mont' ole baby, an' he always been puny."

"Well, come along, then. Cambric or flannel?"

"Gib me dis"—and the man indicated the cambric—"two yahd black and two yahd white. Dat flannen cos' too much, anyhow." He added a package of tacks to his purchase. His gaze went long-

ingly to a glass jar filled with large candy balls of striped red and
white. "An' put in t'ree ob dem candy ball fuh sweeten my mout',"
he concluded. He spat the cheroot loudly into the fire and put one
of the candies in his cheek, where it looked like the symptom of an
acute toothache. Then around the obstruction he said, "Now, suh,
please gib me a cherry bounce an' I'll be gone," and he started opti-
mistically toward the keg which contained the sticky sweet drink
that the negroes loved.

"No, I don't," said Wentworth sternly. "Get on back to Dolly.
You ought to be ashamed to be hanging around the store and your
woman alone with your dead baby."

"Dolly tek on too much, Chief. Baby is plentiful. Dey comes
an' dey goes." And with this philosophical comment he took his
departure.

A young woman who was passing behind the speaker heard his
remark and sucked her teeth loudly at him. "Ole rooster wid
young pullet oughtn't to crow so loud," she flung after his retreating figure.

There was some laughter from the group at the fire, but an old
woman, Maum Vina, with the bright peering eyes, spoke soberly.
"Yo' hadn't ought to laugh at ole Ned like dat. Dat can't do no
good. What if Gilly Bluton is run after Dolly, he done de same by
plenty odder gal roun' here. When a man know dat anodder man
is runnin' after he 'oman, dat one t'ing. But when he know dat
odder people know, den he goin' fight. Yo' mus' want to hab killin'
in dis camp, enty?"

"Well, he ain't gots no right to strut so," the young woman said
defiantly. "An' Gilly ain't no gawd. He can bleed same as any
odder man. What de matter wid dese mens roun' here, anyhow,
dey 'fraid um so?" She cast a look of scorn around the circle which
the men chose to ignore. But old Vina was undaunted: "Yo' ain't

use' to talk like dat 'bout Gilly," she said. "Mus' be he done quit goin' to yo' house now."

Saint turned to wait on the next customer, then instinctively followed her gaze toward the door. A stranger had entered. In the small and intimate neighbourhood a new face was sure to claim attention, but this arrival was such a striking figure that her sudden appearance created a minor sensation. The noise around the fire seemed to recoil upon itself, leaving a poised question in the air. All eyes were fixed upon the open door, and the great bulk of the woman who filled it. She stood for a moment blinking in the light, then crossed with a heavy tread and faced Wentworth across the counter. In a deep, mellow voice, she said: "Is yo' know me, Mr. Saint?"

He shook his head in mystified denial.

"Well, Ah is hear lot 'bout yo'. Ah is Mamba' gal. Ma sen' me down here an' ax can yo' fin' me some work."

Saint had heard about the trouble during his last week-end in the city. It had only confirmed him in an antagonism that he had always felt toward Hagar. She was a thoroughly bad lot. Mamba's excuses for her delinquencies had never convinced him of her innocence. She would undoubtedly be a bad influence in the camp, and if he let her stay he would be answerable to the company for her behaviour. Mamba had no right to put her problem up to him in that fashion. Well, anyway, there was no work for a woman in the camp. He would only have to tell her so and send her on her way.

"That would be simple enough if you were a man," he said. "There's plenty of work in the pits, but we don't use female labour. You'll have to hunt somewhere else."

But his visitor did not take his dismissal. Instead, she drew a step closer and looked at him incredulously out of eyes that might have been Mamba's own. "Ma didn't tell me no other place to go," she explained. "All she say was for me to come to yo' an' tell yo' she done sen' me."

Saint thought: "Confound the old woman. Is there no limit to her audacity?" He met the singularly bright gaze that was bent upon him. In some uncanny way it seemed to evoke Mamba herself. It gave him the same melting twist in the pit of his stomach that he had felt when she had cozened those spurious letters of recommendation out of him three years before. "But I tell you we only employ men," he repeated in a voice that was weakly argumentative.

She unbuttoned her sleeve and jerked it back to the shoulder, then held out her arm, turning it slowly. Under the dark skin the muscle of the forearm rippled. She bent the arm upward at the elbow, and the biceps bunched. She gave a low, confident laugh. "Ain't dat all right?" she asked.

The negroes began to laugh and whisper. A woman in the pits —who ever heard of such a thing!

Saint regarded the demonstration of muscle and laughed. "It certainly is," he answered her. Then, quite to his own surprise he found himself adding: "If you want to try it, I don't see why you shouldn't." He took down an account book. "And while you're here you might as well give me your name."

The woman hesitated, biting her full lower lip with strong white teeth. Finally she asked: "Ain't yo' gots one in dere dat Ah can use?"

Saint wondered if she hadn't one of her own.

"Ah did hab one what Ma gib me, but it's done wore out."

He spun the pages of his book and stopped at one that showed an open account. There had been the usual purchases—rice, grits, molasses, candy, cheroots, amounting to perhaps a dollar, pleading mutely from the page for settlement. He read the name at the top of the sheet—"Baxter—how'll that do?" he inquired.

The woman repeated the word slowly as though to accustom her tongue to its use.

The negroes were regarding the performance with undisguised interest. Now Maum Vina spoke impulsively: "Do, Mr. Saint, don't gib she dat bad-luck name. Don't yo' 'member Baxter done got drownded loadin' a schooner?"

There was a moment of superstitious silence, while the negroes' eyes seemed to grow as they watched her, placing an absurd importance on the simple matter. The woman's voice broke the silence: "Ah guess Ah'll take it, anyhow. It gots a good sound to it, an', aftuh all, Ah ain't so lucky mahse'f." Then she seemed arrested by the drama of her predecessor. She reached across the counter and dropped a long index finger on the writing.

"When he buy dat bittle he been well an' hongry, an' he nebber lib long 'nough to pay for um. Ain't dat so?"

Saint nodded assent.

"Po' Baxter," she apostrophised. "Yo' ain't mean to cheat nobody. If Ah lib long 'nough Ah's goin' settle dat bill fuh yo'."

Saint had to leave her then to serve his customers. It was an interminable business—two cents' worth of grits, three cents for molasses, a penny invested in a herring, salt pork, kerosene—and so it went with each shopper. When he had time to notice Baxter again she had joined the group in the doorway and seemed already to have made her place among them.

Near closing time Gilly Bluton came in. They heard his buggy drive up and stop outside. Then he entered, elbowing his way through the crowd around the door, with a young woman clinging to his arm. "What make yo' don't stand back an' gib de lady room!" he demanded irritably.

They crowded back then, not breaking up and scattering, but opening for him in two closely standing divisions. There was a hostile significance in the way they massed, leaving the man and his partner more room than they needed, as though their touch were evil. But Bluton chose to ignore them and swaggered over to the show case where luxuries were exhibited. The man was a mulatto with negro predominating, but among the negroes of the camp, most of whom retained the sooty blackness indicative of undiluted Gullah blood, he seemed of a different race. The contrast was accentuated by the fact that he could read and write, and figure with great rapidity. Talents which, applied with energy and cunning and without conscience, resulted in his acquisition of most of the wages of the labourers that were not previously retained by the commissary or appropriated by the magistrate. He always wore store clothes of extreme cut, and never spent money unless he had an audience. The woman who accompanied him was not a resident of the camp, but lived at Red Top, a neighbouring hamlet. She glared her defiance and flaunted her triumph before the local belles.

With white people Bluton had an ingratiatingly confidential manner, and he now made the purchase of a highly coloured box of candy for the young woman appear as an especially intimate transaction between Saint and himself. Not that he presumed an equality, he was much too astute for that. But he always managed to give an impression to watching negroes that his basis of contact with the whites differed from theirs. Finally he purchased a real cigar from the solitary box which was housed under the cash till, lighted it, and turned leisurely to survey the group at the door.

Saint despised the man, and the necessity of serving him was the one real humiliation of his humble vocation. But Bluton was a person of importance and the one negro who had it in his power seriously to inconvenience the company if he were given a grievance. This had been intimated to Saint when he came to work at the mines. It had been pointed out that the negro's position as the confidential employé of Proc Baggart, the magistrate, would enable

him so to demoralise the labour that the operation of the camp
would be thrown decidedly out of gear. They would like to have
sent him packing, but he was too deeply entrenched, and he knew it,
and the power that it gave him.

He stood for a moment lolling against the counter and looking
disinterestedly at the group around the door that was now breaking up into pairs and individuals and straggling away toward the
cabins. The older ones left in silence. The younger women and
men told Bluton good-night, some boldly calling him Gilly, and
the timid ones Mr. Bluton. Some regarded him with fawning
wonder in their stupid eyes. The man nodded absently in response, then he shot after them: "What's the use yo' boys sayin'
good-night? I 'spec' I'll be seein' yo' all at de game 'bout nine
o'clock. Dis Saturday night, ain't it?"

Baxter had been sitting on a box beside Maum Vina, who had
promised to put her up for the night. Now she and the old woman
rose and called a good-night to Wentworth.

Bluton turned slowly and met her gaze. Without shifting his
eyes he removed the cigar from his mouth and crossed slowly until
he stood before her; then he looked her up and down.

"Whar did yo' come from, Big Gal?" he asked at length, his
large, facile mouth mocking her with its smile.

The woman was standing in the doorway, with the night behind
her, and the flickering lamps pointing up high lights in her boldly
modelled face, bringing out glints of dark amber in her wide eyes.
As the man approached, her body tensed defensively, and lifted
itself to its full height. There was nothing humorous about the
wrapped wool of her head—the shabby clothes. She was invested in
a sudden natural dignity.

"Ah come from Sabannah," she told him. "Ah come 'cause Ah
wants to. An' my name ain't Big Gal. It's Baxter." Her gaze
never wavered, the glints of amber giving it a strange lucence as it

held Bluton's eyes. For a moment they stood without movement. A sense of impending drama drew wire-tight through the room— twanged the nerves of susceptible onlookers.

Maum Vina's cackle, timid but urgent, jangled across it. "Come on, daughter. Time to go home," she said gently. She took Baxter's hand and drew it toward the door.

Bluton laughed shortly, uncomfortably, lowered his eyes, and folded his loose lips tightly over the cigar. The girl by the show case, who had been standing with a chocolate in her fingers, ran over and caught her man by the arm, glaring defiance at Baxter. The big woman regarded her with a look of supreme contempt, then turned without a word and went with Maum Vina. Behind her the tense atmosphere went suddenly slack.

Bluton collected his faculties and, stressing each word exaggeratedly, called after the disappearing figure: "All right, Sistuh, jus' as *you* say, ob course."

★

Saint experienced some difficulty in getting Baxter on the pay roll. No one could look at her and doubt her ability to perform even that gruelling labour. But this was the fatal objection: there was no precedent for it. Women worked in the fields, the home, bore children. But the mines were for the men. Then, too, the mining was done by gangs composed of two negroes each, and no man was willing to risk the ridicule of having a female partner. The prospect was becoming dark indeed when Saint discovered that an aged negro called Drayton was going to be laid off because he was becoming feeble and none of the younger negroes would take him on as pit partner. He arranged that Baxter should have a try-out with the old man. The woman had no idea what the work would be like, but she had superlative confidence in her muscle. And, too, the open country, the sense of space, and the cool yielding sand beneath her feet gave her a sense of harmony with her surroundings.

At the field's edge on that first morning she was joined by Drayton, a grizzled little man with a wisp of a moustache and old, stubborn eyes. There was a story that when he was in his prime and a schooner was being loaded with rock against time, he had wheeled and dumped five hundred barrow loads of four hundred pounds each without pausing even for food and had earned the record wage of seven dollars in a single day by his feat. Ever since this achievement he had strutted like a little cockerel, and the story was always on his lips. He would say to the big lazy bucks: "How much barrow can yo' load in a day?" When he got the answer he would always cluck his tongue in scorn and tell of his own record. He knew well that they would be glad to turn upon him when his hand grew feeble and his ultimate hour of humiliation arrived. But his worst fear had never conjured up the idea of having to work with a woman. To-day the sweet winter air was as wormwood on his tongue.

They stood in the open looking each other up and down, these strangely mated partners. Then, in a deep, bullying voice that no one had ever heard him use before, the old labourer took the offensive. "Spec' me tuh make mine han' out ob yo', enty! Well, Ah ain't gots no time fuh foolin'. Ah spec' yo' done heah 'bout dat time Ah done roll fibe hundred barrow in a day, enty? Well, dat de kin' ob a man yo' gots fuh partner. Ef yo' can't keep up wid me, Ah goin' quit, yo' onnerstan'!"

Baxter looked at the agitated little figure and saw the surrender masquerading behind bluster and noise, and her heart went out to him, but before she could reply the other negroes caught sight of them, and whoops of derision rent the air.

"Do look, Daddy Drayton gots he nurse wid um." "Whar dem fibe hundred barrows now, Daddy?" Hats were hurled into the air, and bodies bent double in spasms of laughter.

Baxter had been missing Lissa terribly, and now a flood of maternal yearning rose and overwhelmed her. She saw the old man turn on his tormentors and grimace fiercely at them, like an old and toothless dog who must seem so much fiercer than a young one because he is so uncertain of himself. She was full of tenderness for him. She would have debased herself if she could have propped up his toppling dignity thereby. She was sorry that her huge body made him seem all the smaller by comparison. She wished that she could shield him, help him over his bitter hour.

"Ah t'ank yo' fuh take me on," she said humbly. "Ah heah how yo' is de bes' man on de field. Ah ain't nuttin' but a 'oman, but Ah is goin' do de bes' Ah can." And so they turned their backs on the jeering crowd, and entered upon their strange partnership.

The field to be mined was a large one. The axe men had gone before them and cleared it of forest, and it waited, clean and bare, for the diggers. Presently the foreman came around and assigned a "task" to each pair of workers, or, if they were industrious, two together, while he was about it. A "task" was a rectangle four by six feet in size. The labour consisted in digging one's way slowly downward, throwing out the earth, which was called the overburden, and uncovering, at a depth of about six feet, the layer of phosphate rock deposit. Then the real labour commenced, for the rock, which lay in a stratum of about a foot in thickness, had to be broken into small pieces with a pick and thrown up out of the pit with a shovel by hand. This work was usually done by one of the partners, while the other had the far easier task of wheeling the rock in a barrow to the little railroad and dumping it in a pile for the cars.

Baxter spat upon her hands and closed them about the pick

handle. The first stroke drove the implement into the soil up to the handle socket. Drayton's eyes widened, and he could not restrain a grunt of admiration. The woman dug most of the day, and when they got to the rock, she elected to pick it out while he rolled it to the cars, telling him that she wanted to keep away from the men who were gathered at the tracks.

Once the foreman came up and looked into the pit. He was a gentleman, and his people had for generations been used to appraising negro labour. The hole had reached its depth of six feet, and the woman was standing on the bare floor of rock into which she was driving her pick. She paused and looked up. The pit had been full of sun all day, and the work terribly heavy. Baxter had thrown off her outer waist, and through her undershirt the man could see the swell of powerful shoulder and back muscles, the high lift of her chest as it rose and fell on long, unhurried breaths. He turned to Drayton with a wink. "You're not such a damned bad picker, after all," he observed.

The old man smiled; then, in the new, deep voice of authority, he ripped out some unnecessary instructions to the woman. She answered submissively: "Yas, suh. T'ank yo', suh." And he wheeled his barrow off toward the tracks.

She glanced up out of the pit full into the amused eyes of the white man, and a look of absolute comprehension passed between them. "You know men, Baxter, you'll do," he said with a grin as he turned away.

By the time that Saturday night came the jibes at Drayton's expense had ceased and he was the secret envy of most of the lazy young pit men in the field.

Baxter for her part had earned eight dollars for the week's labour. She had settled in old Maum Vina's cabin, and she owed half of her income to the commissary for supplies which she had contributed to their living. That first Saturday night she turned her back on the

allurement of gossip and laughter at the store, took her four dollars,
tied it up in a corner of her handkerchief, dropped it in her bosom,
and went home to bed. There would be a long journey to-morrow,
and she must be up and on her way in the early morning.

★

The next morning Baxter found that Maum Vina was going to
spend the day at Red Top, and, as their way would be the same for
several miles, they started off together. The day was flawless, and
the early sun sent its level radiance over the broad marshes, flooding
the barren winter wastes with gold until they looked like fields
of ripened grain. Down the tunnelled road under the live oaks the
light shot, edging the stalactites of Spanish moss with filaments of
fire. A red bird fell like a live coal out of the sky into a roadside
casena bush and whistled three confident notes up into the face of
the new day. The air had a tang to it and lifted the travellers into
a good stride. As Baxter strode along life throbbed upward
through the soles of her Sunday shoes and filled her with a sense
of well-being. This was reinforced when she lifted her hand to
her breast, where she could feel her four big silver dollars tied in
the corner of her bandana.

As the pair stepped briskly along Baxter stole a sidelong glance
at her companion, studying her in this first moment of leisure
that they had enjoyed together. The old woman had a strange
habit. In the house she was just like every one else, but as soon as
they were out upon the open road she walked with bent head. Her
large clay pipe clenched between her jaws wreathed her face in rank
tobacco smoke, and through it her eyes could be seen, bright and
eager, sliding from side to side of the road, missing no crevice or
rut in their scrutiny. Presently she referred to this unusual behaviour, and told her companion the cause.

Twenty years before, when her old man had died and left her penniless, a conjure woman had told her not to worry, that she would find money in the road before she was too old to look after herself, and that she would die in affluence. Since then the years had been cruel. She had seen her two children go into the little graveyard with the father. Age had stripped her down to that last pitiful hope. But there was not a shadow of a doubt in her mind that some day she would find her fortune lying at her foot. But already her sight was failing a little, the keen eyes missing things that they would have seen easily enough even a year ago. So she must hurry and cover many miles of road while she could, and she must be careful, too. Who knew but what the money would be there in the road right around the next corner? Once, in the excitement of the recital, she raised her eyes while she talked to Baxter, then, in a panic, she made her wait for her while she trotted back and returned, searching the ground.

The younger woman was impressed. "Ah wish tuh Gawd Ah had somet'ing like dat tuh look forward tuh," she said enviously. "Ah ain't gots nuttin' but bad luck gib tuh me when Ah talks tuh one ob dem cunjers."

Presently they approached a bend in the road and heard the rattle of a rapidly driven vehicle. Then a light buggy swung the curve into full view and raced toward them behind the finest span of trotters that Baxter had ever seen. Before her the fore legs flashed up and down with the precision of pistons, and she got a fleeting impression of broad muscular chests under glistening chestnut coats, eyes showing glints of white, and mouths quivering open to the relentless pull on the bits. The driver was pushing them hard, using the whip against tight lines, and they were upon the two pedestrians in a flash. As Maum Vina snatched Baxter's big, slow-moving body to the side of the road, the woman looked up in sudden anger at the man. Not personal resentment so much as a militant pity for the horses which were being so hardly used. The appraising of strangers was not a calculated business with her. She had always had instinctive first impressions, and experience had taught her that they were far more accurate than subsequent pondered judgments. Now, for the first time in her life, she was actually frightened at what she saw in a human face. The head was held straight on the rather spare shoulders, and a broad-brimmed felt hat shaded a long face that was shaped like a coffin—broadest at the high cheek bones, and tapering only slightly to an extravagantly long, square chin. The eyes were narrowed against the wind, and a broad, thin gash of a mouth was drawn in a tight, fixed smile. Under the shading hat brim the skin showed with a fungous-like pallor, most unusual in a country where the white men were used to working out under a subtropical summer sun. A shower of sand from the spurning hoofs stung the women's faces. They stood watching the vehicle diminish down the perspective of the avenue, take a far curve, disappear.

"Sweet Jedus!" ejaculated Baxter in a hushed voice. "Who dat rattlesnake, Mauma?"

Then, while they pursued their way, the old negress told her about Proc Baggart and the part that he played in the lives of the negroes of his section. She was an amazingly astute old creature. In the moments when her eyes were not employed upon their eternal quest they had looked into people's souls and minds and told her what they saw there. She knew much more about the operation of Baggart's magisterial office than a negro was supposed to know. She also knew enough to feign ignorance, which for one of her race is the ultimate in human wisdom. Baggart was the law for the mining district. First as constable, then as magistrate, he had killed six negroes. The last killing had been rather spectacular and had served well to put the fear of God into the onlookers. The victim had been drinking, and instead of scurrying to the roadside at the approach of the buggy had remained in the middle of the road. He shouted something unintelligible at the magistrate, who replied by shooting him dead from the buggy seat with a shotgun; then, with a Saturday night gang of fifty negroes about him, driving the vehicle over the body and proceeding deliberately upon his way to give himself up and go through the form of a trial.

The magistrate, it seemed, made more money than any man in the county. There were things called taxes that the negroes were supposed to pay, but they were afraid to go to the house in town to find out about them, because it looked like a jail. So the magistrate waited awhile until the taxes got penalties—a process which to Maum Vina's mind was similar to that by which an evil she-dog will eventually come home with a litter of still more evil puppies—then he sent for the negroes to come and pay him what he claimed. Sometimes he would send official-looking little blue papers by the constable. At other times he would just send word that such a negro was wanted. Once a new negro in the camp had asked for a receipt for his tax money, but after that he was hounded so that he had to go away. Then there were the dogs. That was where Gilly made most of his money, it was said. He would come slipping around when no one was looking, and if he saw a dog in a yard he'd report it to the magistrate. If the negro didn't have a license, and of course no one ever did, he'd have to raise ten dollars for Baggart, or sometimes twenty, if he wasn't civil. Gilly would get half of that as informer. That gave him mighty keen eyes. And Gilly also ran the big crap game just outside of the Company's land. Everybody knew that the building belonged to Baggart and that he must be in on the game, because it was never raided. They all knew that the dice were crooked, but it was the only safe place to play. An independent game out in the bushes always managed to leak out, and the offenders were given stiff fines or jail sentences. When the old woman finished her recital she was at her turn-off, and without lifting her glance from the white sand of the road she said good-bye and left Baxter to her meditations.

For the greater part of an hour the big woman's road led between woods, and she strode along with bowed head. Her thoughts were now upon her errand, and her darkly brooding expression gave place to a smile of happy anticipation. Abruptly the road left the woods, and her glance leaped free over the broad marshes and the silver ribbon of the Ashley to the city lying low along the horizon with the glamour of the morning sunlight upon it. Up the river, faint but very clear, came the familiar music of St. Michael's bells calling the white folks to service. An exquisite pang of nostalgia twisted the listener's heart. Now, in the crowded court on East Bay, in the long Sunday leisure, she would have been combing Lissa's hair out for her, trying to straighten it so that she could be in the new style and not have to wear it wrapped like the older negroes. And while she worked she would have been listening to the talk, and sharing the laughter. Then to-night there would have been church, and singing with her friends.

She came in sight of the bridge—a taut thread of white stretched between the city and her destination at the end of the road. Fear assailed her. Perhaps she was late. She quickened her pace to a lumbering trot.

When she reached the bridge two figures were waiting: Mamba in her Sunday black, and Lissa in a new cloth coat, a recent gift of her grandmother, and of which not even one of the Battery white folks need have felt ashamed.

Baxter panted up, huge, hot, and dusty. She greeted Mamba hastily, "Hello, Ma! How yo' been?" then fell on her knees in the dirt of the road and strained the child to her breast, drawing her finger tips along the soft cheek with her characteristic gesture. As always she was awed by the miracle that this fragile thing could be the fruit of her great crude body. After a moment, with gentle pushing movements, the child released herself from the enfolding arms and stood looking at her mother. Then, with the frank callousness of youth, she sidled over and leaned against Mamba's clean, stiff Sunday black. A little dashed in spirit, Baxter got to her feet and fumbled in her bosom for her handkerchief. Then she untied the knot, biting it free with her strong white teeth, and handed Mamba four silver dollars.

"If Ah is careful, Ma," she said, "Ah can count on dat each week, an' when Ah git hardened some more, maybe Ah can do better."

The old woman took the money and put it in a handbag that she carried. She was preoccupied with her calculations for the child, half forgetting the mother, who stood there waiting for a word of approval. But after a moment Mamba smiled her new smile, grim and rather terrifying with its big masculine teeth, and admitted: "Dat ain't so bad."

She stood pondering a moment longer, her lips moving silently to some thought, then she went on more brightly: "Now, if yo' can keep dat up steady, we can start dem music lessons for Lissa. Ah got her in the infant choir las' Sunday ebenin', an' de leader say she gots de bes' voice in de Sunday school. She say dat fuh three dolluh a week she can tek she right on up so she can earn a libbin' singin' out ob books an' teachin'."

They stayed for a while longer, sitting beside the road and saying the inconsequential things that always crowd up in the moments before a parting, while the real words that should be carried away to be remembered afterward elude the mind. For Baxter the glory had somehow gone out of the sunlight. The sight of Lissa leaning against her grandmother filled her with a new sort of loneliness that hurt her more than the past days of separation. Finally she rose to go. This time she did not take the child in her arms and kiss her, but patted the little head gently with her big hand. "Well, so long," she said, and turned abruptly away.

*

The winter passed slowly for Baxter that first year at the mines, for it was not merely a succession of days and weeks, but one of those periods in a human life when a new agony yields slowly to custom, and custom becomes a commonplace with which one can go on living without flinching.

Every Sunday brought Mamba to the bridge head, but Lissa was in the regular Sunday school now and did not want to miss the singing and companionship of the other children. So she came only occasionally to see her mother. When she did she was strange and diffident, preferring to sit by Mamba on the roadside embankment as they talked. The child's music teacher had got her into the Sunday school of the stylish mulatto church which was attended by only the most prosperous of the coloured citizens. Rumour in the negro quarter had it that there was a door at the entrance of the church painted tan and that, when an applicant for a pew passed through it, his complexion was observed by the vestry. If it showed darker than the door there were no pews for rent. Whether or not this was malicious humour on the part of the full-blooded negroes, there is no way of knowing, but the fact remained that, while they might scoff, it could not be denied that membership in the Reformed Church meant entrée to the coloured *haut société*. And so Mamba had gladly let Lissa go with her friend while she continued to attend her humble place of worship near the old East Bay tenement.

No better method could possibly have been devised in the old city, where the caste system among negroes went to exaggerated extremes, of making a colour snob of Lissa. The mother felt this instinctively, but her first definite impulse to try to prevent it was immediately suppressed by Mamba's inflexible determination to give the girl her chance to the new negro life that she felt to be so full of possibilities.

"Yo' an' me, Hagar—what de hell is we?—Nuttin'! But Ah ain't no fool at schemin', an' yo' gots de strength. Look like we ought fuh gib dat gal a chance 'tween us."

And so the spring wore away. The green and brown of the winter woods gave place to the spilled gold of jessamine, and the wood lilies marched in white battalions through the swamp proclaiming the Easter season. In the open, deciduous trees hung like puffs of yellow smoke against soft horizons, and in the swamps pollen spread a glaze coloured like verdigris over the pools.

Then came the hot days, with the sunlight trembling in waves over the denuded mining fields, and impounding its heat in the pits where Baxter laboured with her great body for her child and learned to spend her thwarted maternity on Maum Vina and old Drayton, who had to be humoured like a child while he was kept happy by her apparent submission to his authority. But the physical labours, at any rate, had not been without compensation. Her muscles were like iron and were no longer a vast half-directed force but a perfectly disciplined machine.

July came, and in its second week a spell of record-breaking heat. Baxter's pit was out in the centre of the field and would get no shade all day. Wednesday—and to-night there would be a church service, and after that a "love feast" under the auspices of the lodge. All over the fields the men were taking it at half speed. As they were paid by the output they were not pushed by the foremen, and when they carried a barrow to the cars they would sprawl for a few moments in the strip of shade. But Baxter could

not afford to lag. The sun had come up in a smother of red haze;
later it had climbed above it, but the moisture had flowed slug-
gishly along the earth and settled in the pits. Out of an intolerable
grey-blue dome the sun struck directly down into the humid ex-
cavations, making of each a veritable Turkish bath. Baxter had
stripped to the limit that her self-respect would allow and swung
along steadily, lifting ten pounds of rock with every hoist of the
shovel and hurling it out for old Drayton to barrow to the cars.

When knocking-off time came she was conscious of physical exhaustion for the first time since she had got her muscles hardened
to the work.

Church night, lodge meeting, and "love feast" all rolled into
one! What a night it was going to be! Everywhere the negroes
were beginning to show excitement, cutting pigeon wings and
shuffling. Mouth organs were coming from pockets and overwhelming the evening birds in the casenas and scrub oaks.

For two months the white men who worked at the plant had
been spending the nights on the high sandy ridge three miles away
where there was no fever in hot weather. They would scurry off
at sundown as though the devil were after them, and would not dare
to return until after sunup. But the negroes were immune to
malaria. They could stay. Unnumbered generations behind them
along the swarming Congo—in the swamps of Angola—had
tolerated the breed to the poison, had given them this heritage of
safety and these months of freedom from the surveillance of the
white man. What a God-given dispensation of nature! From
moonrise until to-morrow's sun—a negro country. Even Proc
Baggart, who feared neither god nor devil, wouldn't dare to prowl
in the malarial lowlands. When the white men were there no
liquor was sold on the mining company's property, and there was
comparatively little drinking among the negroes. But now! Negro
country! Who cared for rules with no one to enforce them!

Bluton appeared with a buggy load of half-pint dispensary flasks which he had brought from town and which he resold at double price, until every cent left of last week's wages in the camp went into his pockets. The negroes hated to patronise him—the yellow hound, the rattlesnake! Why hadn't one of them thought of going for it?—but they never did—and Bluton always remembered and had the jump on them every time. Now he got in his empty buggy and drove off with the money, telling them frankly that, if he came back later, he wasn't going to risk a pocketful of change in that gang.

In the air of celebration, with the spirits of every one about her vaulting, Baxter felt by contrast tired and depressed. She dawdled over to Bluton's rig. What a scramble there was for the flasks! She hadn't touched a drop since she came to the camp. Perhaps just a half pint might pick her up. She pulled the bandana out of her bosom and handed the mulatto fifty cents. The hot liquor was strong in her throat. It did not take long to saturate the system, like beer or wine. There was a great scramble for the last few bottles. Suddenly, as though animated by some overpowering force outside of herself, Baxter brushed the squabbling men aside, seized the last flask, and, flinging her bandana out, emptied it on the floor of the vehicle. Then everybody laughed as she shied the first flask, now empty, at a distant yellow pine. Near by half a dozen young bucks were skylarking, tussling with each other. A splendidly proportioned young black threw a larger one for a solid fall and turned to the onlookers with a shout of boastful laughter. Baxter sauntered amiably toward him, took him by the collar, snatched him suddenly across her knee and administered a resounding spank where his pants were stretched the tightest. She probably owed her easy success in some degree to the surprise of her attack, but it delighted the onlookers, who held their sides for laughter.

She felt her spirits soar. Life was glowing and singing for her again. What use were the lonesome blues, anyhow!

Time for meeting. The lodge members all wore their regalia—broad, flat blue sashes edged with silver fringe, crossing their breasts from shoulder to hip. The keeper of the great key arrived and elbowed her way through the crowd to the door of the building that served as both church and lodge room. Suspended about her neck on a silken rope was a silver key a foot in length. It was tremendously impressive. She fumbled beneath it in her bosom and finally brought out a small, rusty key with a dirty red string tied through its ring. Then with this she opened the ten-cent padlock that held the two panels of the sagging portal together. Ready hands opened the doors wide and placed props against them, and the crowd surged into the steaming room and seated themselves noisily on the unstable backless benches to await the coming of the preacher.

★

The Reverend Quintus Whaley let his large and cherished body through the door of his well-kept cabin and turned his steps toward the church. He had a broad sensual mouth and a pair of small cunning eyes that gleamed avidly under heavy eyelids. As he walked ponderously through the twilight the alternate advance of right and left thighs kept his pendulous belly swinging, not without a certain massive dignity, from side to side. He wore a new black tail-coat, a recent gift from the mining company, and the watch, which he presently hauled from a pocket in his alpaca vest, had come as a Christmas reminder of the fact that the white folks not only gave him his bread but buttered it as well. Astute as he was, he little realised the fact that, for the investment that he represented, he was the most valuable, though unproclaimed retainer of the corporation. The allowance at the commissary for supplies, the

best cabin in the village—these were good, but the coat and watch
that invested him with all the dignity of a city preacher—well,
they made it very easy for him to see the hand of God behind all of
the labour policies of the Company. He smiled now to himself as
he remembered the threatened exodus of labour during the past
autumn. One of the more intelligent and daring men had gone
North to work and had sent home such good reports that much
unrest resulted. A land with big wages—and no Proc Baggart.
Then, fortunately for the Company, the man had died of pneumonia.
Acting upon a brilliant inspiration, they had telegraphed instructions to have the body cremated before shipping. But it was the
Reverend Quintus whose magnificent rolling rhythms had pointed
to the hand of God in the fate that had befallen their brother.
And it was he who had exhibited to the awed negroes the ashes that
alone remained of the daring adventurer.

He entered the church, smiling and bowing from right to left.
The sisters greeted him effusively, craning forward to warm themselves in the light of his smiles. But the men sat unmoved and, for
the most part, silent. The reading desk was quite high, reaching to
the preacher's shoulders, and there was a shelf beneath the open
Bible to which the Reverend, with remarkable dexterity for so heavy
a man, now transferred a pint flask from beneath his coat.

A shrill leading soprano flung the first clear notes of a spiritual
into the close silence. A tenor rang in and chimed with it from
the last bench, then the full chorus lifted and beat against the thin
clapboarded walls in recurrent waves of melancholy beauty.

The Reverend Quintus dropped to his knees behind the high
reading desk and, safe from view, drew the cork from his bottle
and took a long preliminary pull. He was not always so lucky.
To-night he would speak with the tongue, not of men, but of
angels.

*

Baxter had not entered the building with the crowd. Her high spirits had not endured, and now she wanted to be alone. Maum Vina had lingered, watching her a little anxiously, but she sent the old woman in and promised to follow soon. The cool of evening was creeping up out of the swamp, sending low, flat layers of mist over the parched and tortured mining fields, banking up in the avenues under the live oaks, swimming out over the marsh to blur the horizon. As night grew heavy in the East, a gleam like phosphorus under dark water commenced to fringe the skyline, and the watcher knew that the lights were going on in the city. Mamba would be putting Lissa to bed.

Of late the pain of missing had become almost more than the mother could bear. She almost never saw the girl now. Mamba could only leave the Atkinsons on Sunday morning while the children were at Sunday school and church; and that was Lissa's opportunity to sing in the choir and meet the well-to-do members of her race. Mamba had pointed this out, and it had been accepted with that blind obedience that made Baxter still seem so much of a child. But the mother's spirit was the prisoner of a past from which it would not free itself because the present offered it no harbourage. And she could no longer visualise Lissa clearly—the child of even a few months ago was becoming confused with an imagined portrait of the young girl into which she was growing.

She dashed a hand across her eyes; she looked at the moisture streaked along the dark skin that she was holding before her face in the gloom. She forced a laugh, short and bitter, there by herself in the night. Deliberately she lifted her second flask, half emptied it, then set it mechanically beside her. Now the bitterness and the pain were ebbing. She let her memory go back into the old days, and, instead of the ache of longing, she experienced a warm sense of immediacy—an illusion of reality so intense that she almost felt the touch of soft skin against her hands. The image was quite clear now—no longer confused with physical change—the child that had been hers was hers to keep now, always, like this, near her.

She was happy now with her head bowed upon her lifted knees. Over the eastern marshes the moon pushed its flattened disk of copper, pulled free of the horizon, rounded out to a perfect sphere and brightened to polished brass. Then it sailed confidently up toward the zenith.

Maum Vina left the church building and came to hunt for Baxter. She was relieved to see her sitting so still. Touching her on the shoulder, she dispelled the reverie. There was a new peace in the big face with its features of a child that Baxter raised. The moon was well up now, pouring its light down on the cabins and church, arranging the little settlement rigidly in a cubist pattern of sharp blacks and whites, planes and angles. The church windows were three yellow slabs on a black rectangle. Baxter sighed heavily and got to her feet. Then she remembered the flask, picked it up with an odd detachment of manner, drained it, and threw it in a clump of bushes.

Maum Vina led her by the hand toward the church, and she went submissively, moving hugely behind the wiry little figure.

*

They entered the building at a dramatic moment. The Reverend Quintus was sending his mellifluous syllables against the walls in a call for confession and repentance, when a violent and misdirected gesture dislodged his nearly emptied flask from its snug retreat and sent it clattering, naked and blatant, down on the floor beneath fifty pairs of astonished eyes.

There was a moment of silence; then a crashing roar of laughter from the congregation. That was dangerous. The cloth could endure anything but ridicule. He leaned forward over the desk, and his tremendous voice rose over the babblement among the benches. In his extremity he relapsed into the thick Gullah dialect that he seldom employed in the pulpit.

"Onnah heah me condemn de hypocrite—enty? Onnah heah me say confess—enty? If onnah confess and repent when onnah ain't gots no sin, den onnah is hypocrite. An' God despise hypocrite worse dan rattlesnake. So now, in de presence ob dis congregation, I done t'row my licker down an' confess my sin. An' I calls on ebery nigger in deese walls fuh t'row he licker down! Yeah, verily, if dere be one among yo' what is widout de sin ob hypocracy, let him be de fus' to cas' he licker down!"

He paused for breath, and there was an uneasy fidgeting on the benches. He was quick to follow up his advantage.

"Remembuh what de hymn say: 'Hypocrite, hypocrite, God despise. He tongue so nimble an' he will tell lies.'"

He was glaring down at them now, and there was none to meet the condemnation in his eyes. He allowed the silence to grow for a full minute, then snapped the tension with a thundering blow on the desk and, without preface, flung his great, resonant voice into the opening line of a spiritual. Old tactics! But they could always be counted on in an emergency. Sitting protectively over their own flasks, his brethren were well content to let bygones be bygones and to hurry the present into the past with song.

*

It was time for the love feast. The committee had the refreshments ready—gaudy little factory-made cakes from the commissary, cherry bounce, thinned economically with lemonade. But the spirit of song had seized the bodies of the congregation, and the gross appetites of the stomach were forgotten. They passed the plates

to a few, but the singers would have none of them. Benches were
being thrown back and the floor cleared for a shout. Already
splay feet were slapping the loose boards of the floor. The spiritual
rang out:

> "Oh, mornin' star is in de West—
> Honour de Lamb, honour de Lamb!
> An' I wish dat star was in my breast.
> Honour de Lamb, honour de Lamb . . ."

Now the shouters were in full swing, bodies that could give
themselves utterly to a rhythm swayed and bent; here two facing
each other, the rest forgotten; there several together with a more
concerted interplay. But always the feet hit the same time, swaying and rattling the whole building.

> "Oh, way down yonder in de Harbes' Fiel'—
> Honour de Lamb, honour de Lamb!
> Angel workin' on de cha'iot wheel.
> Honour de Lamb, honour de Lamb!"

One of the larger groups started to circle, and a ring shout was
under way. The refreshment committee knew that this could last
until morning. They put their plates aside to be eaten by those
who would drop out later from exhaustion.

Shrill and piercing above the more measured rhythm of the
spiritual, with its worship of the new Christ, cut the voice of a
soprano in the Gullah shouting rhythm:

> "Simmi yubba leaba, simmi uyh,
> Ronda bohda simmi yuh . . ."

Only the two lines, but repeated interminably in a heavily
syncopated measure, with the concerted stamping of the feet
crashing through it like the thunder of a tribal tom-tom.

Some of the older people began to drop out and reach gratefully for the cooling drink. But, with the younger, the excitement mounted. Women screamed. Men emptied their flasks openly, their feet holding the rhythm the while.

Ned was there. He had tried to persuade Dolly to come, but she never went out with him now, and had said she was ill and would go to bed. They had a sort of understanding now. He did not ask much of her—except not to go around openly with Bluton. She was not to shame him before everybody. Now he looked up from his shouting and saw them in the door. Dolly was good-looking, the best-looking woman in the room. Her full figure was pressed close to the man to whose arm she clung. Gilly had been drinking, and the beast that he was looked unguarded out from his face. The cunning, bestiality, hypocrisy—there they were. His eyes were fixed on Ned, gloating with insolent amusement. The man and woman left the doorway and sauntered into the room. Then, with the rhythm of the shouters, who were so rapt that they were dazed, rushing it up to a swift dramatic climax, tragedy was upon them.

Ned had his razor out, holding it as the old razor fighters used to, the handle clenched lightly in his hand, and the blade with back resting against the closed fingers of his fist. Held so, it could not close on its owner and could be hurled downward with the full weight of the fist behind it. Some one snatched up one lamp and hurled it from a window, but one remained hanging from a beam and could not be reached. There was a rush for doors and windows. When the crowd gained the open and looked back, it was over. Ned had vanished as if by magic. Dolly was gone. Of the three principals in the drama Bluton alone remained. He lay under the lamp that was swinging slightly, casting his shadow eerily from side to side, creating a terrifying illusion of movement. He was not alone. Baxter loomed above him. She stood as though hypnotised, looking down at the dark venous blood that flowed out of the slashed clothing and sent the arc of its sinister circle rapidly toward her. Now it was under one of her great bare feet. She moved. A foot slid sickeningly and waked her suddenly from her trance.

"Sweet Jedus!" she ejaculated and dropped to her knees.

Knife wounds were nothing new to her. She opened a slashed sleeve and examined the cut. It was as clean and incisive as surgery—but, God! she didn't know a man had so much blood to spill. She hoisted her skirt, snatched off her petticoat and tore it into strips. She saw the windows and doors, then, filled with wide eyes and sullen faces.

"Gimme a han', somebody," she called. "Can't be yo' goin' stan' dere an' let a man dead!"

No one moved. Their hatred of Bluton seemed to make the air dark and thick about the kneeling woman. Ned had done it for them. They had only to go away and leave him. But no one could muster the courage to call her off. They could only watch and see which way the dice would fall—"Good Luck Gilly"—or the rest of them. He lay with his face toward her. There was a slash across the forehead close to the hair and, below it, the yellow skin had gone a ghastly grey. Alone—he was worse off than she, for all his money and his dubious good luck. His hand lay flung open beside her. It was long-fingered, sensual, soft, with that beauty of modelling so often found in the hand of a negro. The palm was scarcely lighter than the outer skin. She took it in both of hers, his plight forgotten for the moment. Her brain had been cloudy with liquor, but the excitement had charged across it like an electric storm and left it clear and ringing, but it was a thing separate from herself, working irresistibly from premises of its own choosing. The slender hand lying between her strong, dark ones held her fascinated gaze. It dissociated itself from the personality of Bluton. The touch of it made her flinch, but she could not release it. Then she knew why: it was an enlarged replica of

Lissa's, shaped and coloured the same. A warm smothering sensation took her suddenly, making her senses lurch and waver. Then her starved maternity took Bluton in. It was instinctive but it was utter. For that night, while he lay alone and near to death, she gave him all that she could have given to her own flesh and blood.

She worked with frantic haste. A band tied above a wound and drawn tight with her bare hands was as effectual as a tourniquet. He was deeply slashed in both arms as he had shielded his face with them, and there was that gash across the forehead. After the uproar in the room its poisoned atmosphere now hung in a dead and ominous quiet. The silent watchers at the window waited, their eyes following Baxter's every movement. No arteries had been cut, but the veins had poured out the man's life until he was in desperate straits. The ghastly visage thrown up toward the light showed that something must be done immediately. Baxter bound the wounds, staunching the bleeding. Then she stood up and met the eyes that were fixed on her.

"We gots to get um to town quick," she said. "If we can get um in de hospital, maybe dey can pull um t'rough."

Not a body moved. They kept on standing there staring at her inimically. She faced them desperately. Oh, if she only had Mamba now! Mamba who always made plans, pushed things through. She turned back on her own resources, and a plan began to form. She met old Drayton's eyes peering in a window, and in a second she had him by the arm.

"Listen!" she shot into his face. "Yo' go an' break in de commissary stable an' get de wagon here soon as yo' can. Ah'll fix it wid Mr. Saint." The old man hesitated. "If dat wagon ain't here in fibe minute I ain't nebber goin' dig anoder pit wid yo'. Onnerstan'!"

She loosed him and he started for the stable at an unsteady run.

A voice that was unable to conceal its satisfaction called out, "Dat ain't no use. Dey ain't le's nuthin' but city niggers free to de hospital. Country nigger gots to pay in exvance."

"Dat all right," Baxter answered. "Gilly always gots money."

She dropped on her knees and went through Bluton's pockets. Not a penny. Then they all remembered at once. The man had stripped the settlement of every cent on the whisky sale and had carried the money away to hide. The irony of the situation struck the negro humour and they began to laugh.

"Sarve um right," some one called. "Can't trus' we—now he can dead. Ain't nuttin' but a low white-folks nigger nohow."

The big woman glared at them.

"He ain't goin' dead. Yo' hear dat, yo' dirty passel ob yellow-liver nigger?—He ain't goin' dead. 'Cause Ah's goin' see um t'rough."

The wagon rattled up. Baxter heard it, stooped, lifted her charge in her arms, and, taking him from the building, lay him on the floor of the vehicle. There was an old tarpaulin on the seat. She spread it carefully over him and climbed in. Then she looked down at the sullen crowd about the wagon and lashed them with her parting words.

"Yo' gawd-damned low-livered niggers. Yo' fair mak' me 'shamed tuh be black."

No one answered, and the vehicle started off under the live oaks with the horse moving soundlessly between the deep sandy ruts and the passenger lying, awful in his immobility, under the tarpaulin.

*

Baxter brought all of her faculties to bear on the problem of getting him into the hospital. If she could only have Mamba here now—she would know what to do. Then, slowly, under the urge of necessity, her brain began to evolve a scheme. What if he were found near the hospital—lying unconscious in the street—who would know that he was not a town nigger? She had had friends who had been found so by the police and carried to the hospital, where they were cared for. She knew the city well. The police were few in the quiet part of the town. Perhaps she could slip through the darkened streets and leave Bluton on one of the beats.

They had covered several miles before she finally decided to risk the plan. She had been so intent upon it that no other consideration had entered her mind. Now she was aware of a menacing shadow— a prescience that all was not right. Then it came down upon her like a physical blow—what if she were caught? Two years in jail. Immediately the horror elaborated itself in her quickened imagination. What would Mamba say? Lissa!—All the young girl's toney friends—her music—and her ma in the jail! They would throw Lissa out—she knew it. Instantly it loomed insurmountable before her. But here was Bluton—she could not let him die now. Sweat burst out on her face, cold and clammy in the night air.

With the odd instinct of dumb animals, the horse had sensed her hesitation and stopped in the middle of the road. She mopped her streaming face. Then, with a decisive gesture, she slapped the animal's back with the slack lines. She'd have to gamble on her luck. Maybe it had changed. Anyway, she'd have to see it through.

She was on the main road now, and the going was good. In the distance she could see the taut thread of the bridge, white under the moonlight, and the red light at the draw glowing like a single ruby at its centre. Then came a short drive over the flats, with the marsh talking to her in its soft plopping monosyllables.

On the planking now, the loose timbers making a thunder of sound in her apprehensive ears as the shod hoofs fell rhythmically against them. The draw was closed. That made it final. She must go ahead now. Had it been left open to-night, as was sometimes done, fate would have turned her back. A high tide ran under the bridge, sweeping the moon's silver under it in a shining flood. Overhead the luminous disk—no longer brass, but a cold platinum—was so brilliant that its light had drowned out all of the lesser stars. The vehicle, with its silent passenger and the great hunched figure of its driver, moved toward the dark clustered buildings of the city as though it advanced beneath a vast flood light upon a gargantuan stage.

The toll office was closed for the night, but Baxter's approach had been heralded by the noise of the vehicle, and as she left the bridge she saw the night watchman waiting. He was a very old, bent man, and he stood swinging his stick and peering up in surprise.

"Where you goin' this hour of the night?" he called querulously, with the pettishness of one who has just been awakened. Then Baxter remembered that she had no money to pay toll.

"Jus' takin' some truck to town," she said lamely. "I'll pay comin' back when de office open."

But the persistent old creature would not let it go at that. She had stopped the wagon, and he now came up and peered over the side. He was standing there, undecided what to do. Baxter's mind was in panic. Should she risk bolting for it with the old horse and heavy wagon? They were both silent, trying to make up their minds. Bluton became the deciding factor. There was movement beneath the canvas and a low, agonized groan. With an instinctive reflex action, Baxter's foot shot out and caught the horse full on the rump. An astonished spring jerked the vehicle clear of the watchman. Then the animal gathered himself together and set off with the vehicle clattering and jouncing over the cobbles. The din would bring the whole town down about her ears if it continued, and so, as soon as the driver collected her wits, she threw her weight on the right line with the result that they were plunged into the immediate peace of an unpaved side street. She pulled the animal down to a walk and listened with her heart thumping heavily in her throat. There was no sound of pursuit. Evidently the watchman had gone back to his nap and the policeman had been at the remote end of his beat.

She waited a moment under a shade tree to quiet the trembling animal and to gather courage for the plunge from the pool of shadow into the relentless moonlight. Confidence that her luck had changed began to come. She had won the first break. The horse was quiet now. She must get on with it.

She moved out of the shadow, driving slowly and soundlessly in the soft deeply rutted earth. Now her whole being seemed concentrated in her sense of hearing. In the remote residential section through which she was passing the stillness was so absolute that she even heard faint snoring in one of the houses. Then, with a sudden intrusion of humour into tragedy, came a fretful female voice waking the offender and telling him to lie on his side. Then came footsteps on the pavement of a side street, indolent, heavy, maddening in their deliberation. Baxter pulled the wagon under the wide-flung branches of a tree and waited. Around the corner a half block away came a policeman. He was swinging his club by its thong, and his head was thrown back while he gazed up into the wonder of the night. Without looking down, he pursued his leisurely way down the street past where Baxter was waiting.

She saw his broad back receding ahead of her and knew that for the second time luck had been with her. Now she had only to wait until he was out of earshot, then follow, discharge her passenger near the hospital, and the officer would find him on his next round. Presently she was under way again and covered the three blocks to her destination without adventure.

She pulled the wagon into the shadow of a palmetto. A faint air was talking to the tree, and it was answering in its harsh gutturals, so different from the voices of other trees. The sound frightened Baxter, but she conquered her qualms. She climbed down and removed the canvas from Bluton's form. Then she saw that his eyes were open and fixed upon her.

"Oh, dat yo', Baxter?" he said in a weak voice. "What de hell is all dis about, anyhow?" Then he moved, became aware of his wounds, and groaned loudly.

"Shut yo' damn' mout'," she answered fiercely; then gathered him up, carried him into the light, and placed him on the pavement. Bending down, she spoke almost savagely into his face.

"Yo' want fuh dead?"

"Fuh Gawd's sake, no! You wouldn't——"

She cut him off. "Berry well, den. Listen! Keep yo' eye an' yo' mout' shet. Don't tell nobody who yo' is or whar yo' come from. Got dat straight?"

He nodded. Then she saw that the exertion had caused him to faint again.

She drove the rig down a side street, tied the horse beneath a tree, and crept back to watch. She had not long to wait. The deliberate steps were coming back. She saw the figure now, a black, solid bulk in the white light.

Now he was fairly on the supine form of Bluton. Had he gone blind? Then, "Well, I'll be god damned!"

He stooped, made a swift examination, then rose quickly, trotted to a box on the corner, and put in a call. Scarcely had he got back to the inert form before the wagon came. Two alert figures sprang out and lifted the wounded man in. Then, with a single clang of the bell, the vehicle lunged away toward the hospital.

*

Baxter slipped back around the corner of the fence that had been shielding her and returned to the wagon. There, suddenly, in her moment of triumph, she knew that she had lost. The bridge was the only way back, and the irate watchman would be waiting for her there. There would be no disguising her great body that always got her into trouble. She was caught in a trap. The realisation came with a numbing shock and paralysed her initiative. Mamba! She must get to her and ask her what to do. The recklessness generated by the whisky had gone from her blood; the maternal impulse that had driven her blindly into her danger was passing. She was suddenly terribly afraid; a little whimpering sound escaped her.

Then she heard a human voice, casually conversational, expressing amused surprise. "Well, if here ain't the big un back in town!"

She looked down and knew the man instantly. He had called for her more than once in the room on East Bay, and he had been the officer who had carried her off that last fateful night.

She was speechless, sitting massively above him, sobbing freely now into the crook of her arm. Down on the pavement the Celtic intuition in the big square body was beginning to put two and two together.

"So, it's you that just dumped the high yaller on Calhoun Street? Well, I got to hand it to you; you ain't fergot how to take 'em to pieces! Reckon you better drive back there to the box while I call a special to take you in."

"I swear to Gawd, chief, I ain't cut dat nigger up. Listen 'fore yo' call, fuh Gawd' sake! an' lemme tell yo' how 'tis!"

He led the horse out into the light where he could see the woman plainly and told her to go ahead. When she had finished her story he stood silent a moment. Then he said, "You know, Big Un, it's funny, but I don't believe you're lying. I think you're just about that damned a fool." Then he asked, "This the first time you been in town?"

"Yes, Boss. I swear tuh Gawd."

He fairly snapped his answer at her: "Well, git out o' it damn quick! An' I ain't seen no woman nor wagon since suppertime, I don't care what the hell anybody says."

He turned and walked briskly away. In a moment he had rounded the nearest corner, and his footfalls were fading into silence.

Hagar must get to Mamba now. That was the only thing to do. Her own mind had stopped working. She had to cross the city in a diagonal direction, and it was more instinct than conscious judgment that selected the deserted byways and alleys for her passage. But luck was with her—luck and a sharp retrenchment in the police department with a resultant cut in personnel—and she traversed the distance without being again in jeopardy. Finally, just before day, she drove the wagon into the court in East Bay Street.

She routed out a startled friend and sent her to wake and fetch Mamba; then sat waiting like a child who knows that she has done wrong and will be punished.

An hour after the old woman came cursing into the court arrangements were complete. The wagon had been washed down until it was scarcely recognisable as the mud-covered country vehicle; a half-grown boy had been engaged at an honorarium of two dollars to drive it over and deliver it to the commissary, and a fisherman had contracted, for the sum of three dollars, to row Baxter around the city and across the river where she would be within safe walking distance of the mines.

Mamba peered from the gateway and scanned the street. It was absolutely empty, its air astir with that indefinable thrill of expectancy which is the precursor of dawn. There was silence save for the far panting of a freight engine. Growling bitterly over the injustice of a fate that had imposed such a daughter upon her, the old woman conducted the culprit across the street and to the pier head. At the foot of a ladder a boat could be discerned, its rower waiting with oars ready.

Silently Baxter descended and took her seat. In the moment of departure, the old face, hanging above her against the thinning night, softened, and the deep-timbred voice said gently, "Good-bye, Daughter. Fuh Gawd' sake take care ob yo'self an' keep out ob trouble."

The oars dipped, and Baxter was once again out of the city. Behind her the night seemed to cower suddenly down into the narrow streets and beneath the dock. Far out beyond Fort Sumter a new day lifted, washed and shining, from the Atlantic. The oarsman pulled steadily ahead. Above the crouching woman, and looming fabulously into the morning skies, hung the great Battery mansions, their high-flung columns and façades showing rose and saffron in the young day. To her left the "mosquito fleet" was putting to sea for its day at the fishing banks, sailing straight into the eye of the rising sun, and, under Baxter's dazzled gaze, seeming to founder and vanish eastward in a flood of intolerable glory. Close by her now, where she could touch them with her hand, small, plangent waves sprang up and caught the light. She looked for a long moment, lifted out of herself by the splendour; then her large bullet head fell forward on her crossed arms.

"Sweet Jedus," she muttered, "in a worl' like dis, why Yo' gots to make me such a damn' fool!"

The oarsman pulled doggedly ahead toward the distant line of trees.

PART III

PART III

Mrs. George J. Atkinson dropped upon a Chinese Chippendale chair in the drawing room of the big house in Church Street, buried her face in her hands, and burst into tears. Before her, lying open on the Duncan Phyfe table, was a sheet of heavy cream-coloured notepaper. In the centre of the page a single paragraph had been inscribed in a small, delicate, but positive hand. It was the sixth "regret" for a luncheon party for eight to be given during the succeeding week. The High Gods—or, at least, Goddesses—of the social Olympus had decided that, if she was not impossible, she was at least highly improbable.

Of course it was George's fault. He never had held up her hands in the fight that she had been waging for years for their social recognition. There was nothing worth having that was not worth working for. And, by inverting cause and effect, there was nothing that could not eventually be won if you worked hard enough for it. A simple and pragmatical philosophy, and a proven one, for it had brought her well along toward middle life with an unbroken record of successes. Unfortunately for her, the methods took small account of the personal equation, and she was not attuned to the subtleties or skilled in the tactics of alternate advance and retreat by which conservative and observant strongholds are taken. She had made the fatal mistake in the beginning of assuming that wealth was, as a matter of course, an effective weapon, not realising that, with a number of the old families in straitened circumstances, simple living had become the criterion for good taste, and the ostentation had become, by contrast, mere vulgarity.

For several years now she had been entertaining with an industry that, taken merely as an example of unflagging effort, was little less than superb. Of course, she had had her snubs, but she had blanked her mind to them and concentrated on her more responsive acquaintances. Her parties had for the most part been well attended, and she had had many invitations to teas and large functions, but, as time passed and few acquaintanceships mellowed into friendship, she began to have misgivings. She consoled herself, however, with the knowledge that the old city was socially the most conservative in America and consequently, while the most difficult, the most desirable to claim as one's own. She had at last concluded that the time had arrived for the major movement. She knew well that there was no halfway ground in the society of the old town. Membership in the St. Cecilia Society and attendance at its balls was the one criterion. For a hundred and fifty years the managing board of the organisation had gathered annually, sipped their port, champagne, or Scotch, with the changing fashion, and decided whether any of the "new people" in town were eligible for recognition by their hereditary aristocracy. Within that charmed circle one belonged, one was a member of the family. Outside of the fatal line, one was always more or less a stranger stopping temporarily in the city. The fact that such a sojourn might be protracted for several generations was powerless to change the transitoriness of the visit or the chill and punctilious politeness with which an aspiring ineligible was received. He was relegated to the class the existence of which is admitted, but not encouraged. Yes, the time had arrived, she felt, when her husband might safely put his letter in for the St. Cecilia Society, and, in preparation for the event, she would put down a barrage that could be counted upon to blast out final obstructions.

Accordingly the misguided tactician had released a scourge of social activity upon the inner circle. It had been bridged, dined, tea'd—at first formally—and later with a certain creaking and ponderous informality that whispered over the teacups, "just among ourselves—you understand—" At first the attack, by reason of its surprise, seemed destined for success. But it had been launched too far in advance. There came a lull, and, as soon as the bewildered dowagers had time to draw sufficient breath, they laughed. Laughter—the most deliberately cruel sound that the human animal can make. Poor Mrs. Atkinson! Thumbs down.

In the meantime Atkinson had fought his way blindly through the turmoil. That fall he christened his evening clothes "the over-alls," and he climbed into them obediently every night and went on duty. He had not the vaguest idea what it was all about. At times he would become aware of his wife's eyes fixed stonily upon him; then he would pull himself together and turn wearily to his dinner partner and the weather. But he had a robust constitution, and the daylight was still kind to him. He manufactured his cotton-seed oil, did a stiff trick or two for the chamber of commerce, dropped into the Yacht Club for a cocktail and a word about nothing in particular with the men, and did not have a single social aspiration upon him.

Now he opened the door and stood gazing at his wife. He rubbed his eyes, blinked, and gazed again, incredulous of the evidence of his senses.

"The children!"

"No. They're all right. Read that."

Atkinson picked up the note, glanced at it, and patted his wife's shoulder consolingly.

"There, there!" he said. "I didn't know you were so fond of her. Grippe, eh? We'll send over some flowers."

She was always suspicious of George when he was as stupid as that. A man who was that great a fool could never have made such a success of his life. She had concluded once that because he never laughed aloud and had a way of smiling at things that any one could see were not in the least amusing, he had no sense of humour. Had it not been for this she might have suspected him of the supreme audacity of making fun of her. Now this suspicion fluttered in her mind, and she regarded him with a long, penetrating look. His mouth, which had been twitching at the corners, stiffened under the bristly moustache, and his eyes met hers with candour. While she gazed, they actually mirrored sympathetic distress.

Yes, George was devoid of perception, and she was an unfortunate woman, but she would not go into that now. She could tell him about his stupidity later. Now she could only say in a bleak voice, "She had grippe last month. She has been at three affairs this week."

"But she says, my dear, that she must save her strength."

She looked at him almost curiously. "Are you really as simple as that?" Then her voice went on in a wail of despair, "Oh, I ought to have known that it was no use trying with you around. You've never backed me up—you've never even understood what I was trying to do for your own children."

He kicked a gilt Louis Quinze chair out of the way, jerked up a substantial product of modern America, sat squarely upon it, and said:

"Right. I haven't understood. If there is a forest, I'm glad to hear it. I haven't been able to see it yet for the trees. Now try to tell me in words of not over two syllables exactly what it is you want."

"Very well," she answered. "I will. The point is that you simply have to get into the St. Cecilia Society this year because I have been counting on it; in fact, I was so sure that when I was in New York last summer I invited Valerie down to make her début with us. Now, if we don't get in, we'll be in the pleasant position of having to tell your sister that she can keep Valerie at home because we are not good enough to be acceptable socially. Now, do you understand?"

He was callous enough to smile. "Good God!" he said, "is it all really as simple as that? My dear, you have surprised me—and we have been married fifteen years. Tell me, please, who are some of the managers of the St. Cecilia Society."

She mentioned several names of the sort that the tourist might be seen any spring day deciphering from the oldest tombs in St. Michael's churchyard.

"It is sort of hopeless," she concluded, "because I never seem to see them at the teas and things that I go to."

His smile broadened into a laugh. "Those chaps—teas! I fancy not. Why, my dear, you have been tearing me away from them at the Club every evening to doll up and go to your accursed parties."

That night the House of Atkinson recalled invitations for two dinners, a tea, and a luncheon, and the following afternoon George settled his wife comfortably aboard the New York express. His parting words were:

"Better get several ball gowns—quiet ones. Outfit Valerie too. Bob's usually too strapped to give her nice things, you know."

During the succeeding weeks Atkinson had more time to spend with his friends. Two cocktails of an evening at the Club now, with plenty of time to talk markets and the economic aspect of the new city paving programme. Nice chaps, these, urbane, fastidious about rather unexpected things; not smart dressers; insular, yes— not too greatly concerned with the opinions and behaviour of the insignificant residue of the globe lying to the north of Magnolia Cemetery and the south of the Battery. Younger ones, who addressed him as "sir," secure in a breeding that kept the courtesy from appearing servile—older men, who knew a horse, a mint julep, and a gentleman when they met one—men who, like himself, were quite content to leave teas, the Sunday concerts, the Poetry Society, and the Episcopal ritual to their wives. Pleasant evenings those, with one's own kind and no fuss about it. And then, in the third week of his wife's absence, that flying trip to Washington to appear before the Interstate Commerce Commission on a rate hearing of vital importance to the old city. The Committee had asked Atkinson to act as spokesman. The clean, hard drive of his brain against a problem always brought concrete results. He could talk to the Yankees in their own language. Pleasant chats in the smoker. Nice chaps surely. No putrid smoking-room humour. And the homeward trip with the concessions in their pockets, a fight behind them, and a genial comradeship in the air.

It was during the last hour of that railroad journey, while the four of them were enjoying final cigars, that Atkinson spoke his first words bearing on the matter of the coveted membership. One of the men had been saying something to him—the fellow whose name always reminded him of an heroic phrase from early American history—"Damn the torpedoes—go ahead!"—not that—that was Farragut—oh, yes—"Millions for defence, and not one cent for tribute"—that was the chap! . . .

When the man had finished his question, Atkinson smiled and said, "Say, that's awfully hospitable of you fellows. Hadn't given the balls much thought before. Suppose there'll be a quiet corner of refuge for middle-aged knee joints?—Not much of a dancer, you know— Yes? Well, I'll send the letter over by messenger to-morrow."

Mrs. Atkinson returned from the North at an opportune moment. Mamba was receiving a thick, cream-coloured envelope from an elderly negro who had the bearing of an ambassador to the Court of St. James's. She lifted the missive from the tray and, with shaking fingers, removed it from its two envelopes—

"The Managers of the St. Cecilia Society request the pleasure . . ."

*

And while the social gods had been playing upon the hopes and fears of the Atkinsons, Saint Wentworth, having attained his majority, was journeying to Charleston in accordance with the family tradition to attend his first St. Cecilia ball and represent his generation of the line among his social peers.

But the years had wrought a change in the temporal, if not the spiritual, aspect of the pilgrimage. Two generations ago the Wentworth carriage, followed by a wagon for luggage and servants, would have driven down from the plantation and drawn up impressively before the hospitable Planters' Hotel. The tailor and an army of mantua makers would have been awaiting its arrival to put the finishing touches on the new broadcloths and brocades for the all-important début. To-day, Saint, with a week's vacation ahead of him, served his last negro, turned the store over to the malaria-bitten poor-white who was to take his place, washed up, and caught a lift on a wagon as far as the bridge. Over the ancient wooden planking he footed it to the city, caught a trolley, and finally arrived at the little brick house in Church Street.

The premises were deserted. Doubtless Mrs. Wentworth had gone out with Polly to purchase some consummating touch for the girl's costume. But the magnitude of the impending event had charged the inanimate walls of the building, and, as he let himself in, he caught the contagion of excitement in the air. He took the steps two at a time to his room—what a brick Mother was!—how absolutely invincible! His father's dress suit had been lifted from its long oblivion and made ready. He could see that the old broadcloth lapels had been faced with silk in the prevailing mode. The trousers lay beside the coat, beautifully pressed and folded. A new white vest, a shirt, a tie, and gloves were ranged beside the suit, and, under the edge of the bed, beside his old slippers, stood a pair of new patent-leather pumps with the light flowing and settling over them like some gleaming liquid.

Saint was caught by one of his rare waves of emotion. It choked him up, left him shaken. It meant so much to her—all this. His solitary life had given him leisure for thought, and he had developed a habit of passionate search into causes, a feeling that surfaces didn't matter; that behind every physical expression of a personality there lay the deep secret impulse. Now he lost sight of the makeshift wardrobe before him and stood abashed before the unswerving purpose of which it was an expression—the determination to hold a place for her children in the class to which they had been born. Out in the country he had not thought much about being a gentleman. It had seemed rather absurd in the only life in which he seemed capable of succeeding—of course, gentility was a state of being: you were born a Wentworth and you refrained from doing certain things because instinctively they put your teeth on edge. There you were—and that was all there was to it. But being a gentleman as a career—that was different. To be done properly it would involve so many things that were utterly beyond him: setting, education, attainments—what was the use! There were still things within reach—books, pictures, out of doors, and—yes—even the negroes there at the mines with their humour, tragedy, and the flattering respect and frank liking that they gave him. He was finding happiness there. What did clothes matter?—dances, girls, surfaces—what was the use of it all? And, God! what a lot of herself his mother had put into it—saving for years, sewing, taking boarders, catering—and his savings too, for he knew that a part of the money he sent home every week had gone into the bank for the "coming out." She could have taken things easier all of these years but for her determination to be ready when the time came to give Polly and himself these things—these—and, to her, the intangible, but incalculably valued significance that lay behind them.

He had things that he had wanted terribly to do with this week. The fossils that the negroes were always turning up in the mines had started him off on geology, and the director at the Museum had offered to show him books and specimens. Then there was the Art Gallery. A friend there had promised that he should meet some of the painters so that he could see how pictures were made. Now the precious week had to go in a round of entertainments—an ancient fetish. Of course he hadn't hesitated when his mother made the plans. In fact, he knew that he had been predestined from birth for this moment. But he felt that it was something to be done and—God willing—forgotten.

But the clothes, lying mutely before him, pulled against his mood and brought him back to his mother and the vague intangible thing that she was so determined to save from the wreckage of the past. He picked up the coat and carried it to the window. In the light he could see that the broadcloth was distinctly green in shade and shiny on the shoulder blades. Oh, well, it didn't matter. He had heard it said that many of the boys of his set went in their fathers' old suits, and the waiters—most of whom were family retainers—in their grandfathers'; that, in these lean years since the war, a dress suit was not worth the name that hadn't the vitality to see three generations of St. Cecilias. He slipped off his coat and tried the garment on. With the amazing adaptability of its kind the swallowtail fell snugly but easily over his shoulders. He surveyed himself in the glass and was surprised to see how broad it made his shoulders appear, how slender his waist. He had outgrown his adolescent stoop and ranginess of arms and legs, and the

boyish grace and co-ordination of body, that had made him a star
pupil in dancing school, had come back and waited unnoticed under
the cheap, poorly fitting clothing that he usually wore. Now, as
he surveyed himself, he became conscious of the change. Odd—
when he went to the country he had always been tortured by the
thought of his appearance—of how he looked to strangers; and yet,
in retrospect, he realised that, for those four years, he had forgotten
to think about himself one way or another. Now he was again
acutely conscious of the impression that he would make, and yet
no longer afraid. Perhaps it was the coat that had put a charm
upon him. Poor old Dad! He had had a terrible struggle of it,
but what a gentleman he must have been!—gentleman, no doubt of
that. . . .

He heard the front door open and the animated voices of his
mother and Polly, like two girls going to their first party—a great
night in the house of Wentworth. Well, he'd play up—give them
everything he had for this week. It was little enough, that.

They supped early; then, while they were waiting for the carriage, Mamba slipped over from the house next door to see them
dressed for the ball. She had retained calling acquaintance at the
little brick house. In fact, among these white folks who knew her
past, she rejoiced in a partial reversion to type, perpetrating outrageous audacities and assuming an intimacy that brought dignified
rebukes from Maum Netta down upon her unregenerate head.

She had brought Lissa with her to see the dresses, and the girl
entered the sitting room quietly and stood near the door, her hands
locked loosely against the front of her dress, her eyes taking everything in with a roving, eager glance. Saint had never seen the
child before, but his interest in Mamba and Baxter caused him to
notice her closely as she stood there. She must be about ten or
eleven, he thought, and her lack of embarrassment in the alien
setting struck him at once. Also she was beautiful. He knew

that it was in bad taste to think of beauty in a negro, but there was no other word that would serve. She was no more a pretty child than an ugly one. Beauty was the one word. Those eyes that were both Mamba's and Baxter's were like lamps in the small oval of her face. A moment of wild conjecture came to the boy—where would this child end?—what destiny did America hold for her?

Mamba stood surveying the three Wentworths—the mother in a black silk that fitted perfectly over her mature but beautifully modelled figure; Saint, wearing his swallowtail with an air; and Polly, radiant in the cloudy whiteness of her first ball gown.

"Yeah," the old woman ejaculated with emphasis, "dese is *my* buckras! Maum Netta now is jus' bawn wid um an' can't help sheself, but me—Ah is pick um fuh choice." She turned to Polly. "Goin' let Mamba carry dat slipper bag, ain't it?"

"Why, Mamba, I thought you'd be carrying Mrs. Atkinson's. I hear they are going to-night." Then she patted the old woman coaxingly on the arm and begged, "Do tell us how they got in. We're just dying to know."

Mrs. Wentworth spoke sharply: "Polly, I *am* surprised! Do you call *that* being a lady?"

But Mamba bent over in one of her silent spasms of laughter, and when she straightened up her eyes were snapping with mischief.

"Ah gots tuh tell," she said. "Ah jes gots tuh! Ah been fair bus' wid de inside laugh, an' Ah gots tuh let um out. De boss is fine," she said by way of preface. "But—well, Ah jes gots tuh say it straight—de missis, she's good tuh me, but she ain't one ob us, Miss Polly."

Mamba had memorised the words overheard in Atkinson's report to his wife upon her return to the city, and she gave them in a perfect reproduction of his crisp, incisive speech, bringing her narrative to a close just as a loud rap fell on the door and Maum Netta announced the carriage.

The driver, a grizzled veteran of many seasons, held the carriage door open, bowed them in, then banged it shut with that sound, at once loud, restrained, and almost ritualistic, which, heard up and down the silent downtown streets during the brief "season," denoted a St. Cecilia night.

"Oh, Mother," Polly gasped in ecstasy, "a slam-door carriage!— and me in it! Don't let anybody wake me up!"

Balls should always be given in buildings with high porticoes supported by Corinthian columns, and with wide pavements before them traversed by canvas canopies. There is something awe-inspiring, something out of Greek mythology about such a temple of Terpsichore, with the up-flung light accentuating height, and up above the soaring capitals the dark, pregnant with mystery. And the canopy that crawls like a striped canvas caterpillar down the steps and across the pavement to present its mouth to the carriage doors adds just the frivolous touch that bridges the gap between an ancient ecstasy and a modern one. It was before just such a building that a carriage presently drew up with a flourish and disgorged the family of Wentworth.

Up the wide stairway, with the covering of gleaming white, Kate Wentworth, on the arm of her son, led the way—then on through the soft glow of the ballroom and the warm cross-play of greetings and smiles, to the spot before the second fireplace where Wentworth mothers had chaperoned their broods for the greater part of a hundred and fifty years. Her cousins, the De Chatigny Ravenels, would be next to them, she remembered, and the Cooper River Heywards directly across the floor. Yes, there was Aunt Sarah Huger with her turkey-tail fan. She must be seventy now, but to see her to-night no one would believe it were it not for the fan, which dated her definitely with the débutantes of the late 'sixties.

There was constant visiting between the groups. Older cousins and family friends came to welcome Kate Wentworth back to her accustomed place and to cast an appraising eye over Polly and Saint. For the first time in the boy's life he was conscious of being regarded with popular approval. In the background of his mind there loomed a strange conviction that he had been there before. His usual diffidence was gone, and in its place he experienced an exhilarating sense of congruity, of measuring up to expectations.

Polly was immediately surrounded, her card taken from her fingers and scrutinised by eager eyes—"What, nothing saved for me, Miss Polly!"—"The sixteenth—no? Well, please—one for the next ball!"—"We can't let the season pass without one, now can we?"

Saint stood looking about him. Even the magnitude of the moment was forgotten in the beauty that surrounded him. The hall was large, with a high ceiling and tall, slender windows on both sides. An atmosphere of home, and traditional hospitality, was given by four open fires under Adam mantelpieces, two on each side of the apartment. About the fires groups were gathered, laughing and talking with hands spread to the glowing coals. But it was the colour that fascinated Wentworth. It trembled softly from shaded lights, glowed in only a slightly lower key from the women's costumes, and lay banked in a profusion of flowers on the mantelpieces and the musicians' dais. Last night he had been serving his negro labourers. A contrast. The sudden and unexpected beauty and colour of the room created a mood of unreality; yet an unreality in which he was intensely alive and in which he felt a glow of possessive pride.

He saw a broad, squarely planted back near him that looked familiar under the swallowtail coat—Mr. Atkinson. An awe that he had always felt for his successful neighbour was immediately forgotten in a sense of his individual responsibility as host. He stepped forward and held out his hand.

"It's a great pleasure to see you, Mr. Atkinson," he said. "But perhaps you don't remember me. I'm Wentworth."

The older man gave him a firm grip. "Why, thank you, Wentworth," he answered. "It is all rather new for us."

A kick on the ankle from Mrs. Atkinson's evening slipper brought the sentence to an abrupt end, and Saint replied quickly: "That's interesting. This is my début too. I hope that you will enjoy it as much as I intend to."

Atkinson smiled his thanks and turned toward his wife. "My dear, this is Mr. Wentworth. Surely you remember him."

"Indeed I do. But you hardly ever give us a glimpse of you now. You spend all your time at your—er—country place, don't you?"

"And this," interposed Mr. Atkinson, while Saint groped for an answer, "is my niece, Valerie Land. Valerie, let me present Mr. Wentworth."

The boy's first impression was one of eyes, dark brown and very intent, fixed upon his face with an earnest scrutiny. "Serious," he thought, "and at a dance, too. She won't be a go here." Then she smiled, and he knew that he had been wrong. Daring and mischief were there now. And beauty. And the swift fluctuations of a colour that could come and go. There was a distinct air of worldliness about her that was new to Saint in the women that he met. Even in that first casual moment of meeting, he knew that she was definitely motivated. That she would know quite well what she wanted. He responded to that with an instinctive masculine withdrawal. Then he met the mischief in her smile again and forgot to be afraid.

"May I see your card?" he asked. "I should like tremendously to have the pleasure."

He found a number of blanks. She had not met any one. Suddenly behind the smiles of the little group he saw actual distress. They did not know that rescue was sure to come, that guests on that ballroom floor were never left to their own resources. They were standing there smiling quite steadily without the least idea of what to do next.

A glance over his shoulder assured him that Polly was labouring amid an embarrassment of riches. He could catch glimpses of her bright young head through the milling circle of evening suits. Rapidly he scribbled his name twice on the card that he held, then asked if he might present some of his friends. His task was not a difficult one. Valerie Land was a light that, under no circumstances, could long have remained obscured. Soon she was having to smile her regrets and exhibit her completed card to new arrivals. The men who had secured dances thanked Saint. The Atkinsons beamed upon him. He had several dances for himself. Being a gentleman was becoming interesting after all. At least there was something to be said for it.

Behind its banked palms the band crashed into a Sousa march. Saint hastened to his mother and led her into the line that was forming for the cotillion. Everywhere about him couples were meeting, young men with white-haired women on their arms, gay old gentlemen playing the gallant to the débutantes—all of an age to-night, with the first-year boys and girls eyeing their seasoned partners for fear that they might miss some fine point in the old-world courtesy that still prevailed upon a St. Cecilia floor. There were things that ladies and gentlemen still refrained from doing and saying here that would be both done and said at to-morrow night's informal hop.

The dances—a sadly inhibited fox trot, a flapper dance tucked primly back into petticoats for the night. But the waltz! You could give your body to three-quarter time, it would seem, without violating the niceties. Saint took Valerie into the curve of his arm and launched her without a word upon the broad limpid tide of the

"Blue Danube." The floor was just crowded enough to require perfect guiding in the man and instinctive divination of his mood and tempo in his partner. The surge and lift of the peerless old waltz, and the girl in his arms, submissive to his slightest suggestion, yet so separate, so passionately individual, worked on Wentworth like a drug. The small brown head lay against his shoulder, and the girl never raised her face to his. Before his eyes colours swam and wove as they drifted between the couples. Colour always moved him deeply, and now the many-tinted dresses whirling and streaming across his vision blurred into one another, creating an effect like a rainbow with a frieze of faces sliding along its upper edge. When the music stopped it was as though the rainbow had fallen about them in a thousand gleaming fragments. They drew apart slowly. The girl pressed Saint's hand, then she raised her face and gave him a long and preternaturally solemn gaze. They did not join the promenade of couples, but turned away and found a corner under the palms by the band.

An old bent negro appeared in the doorway with a tray in his hand. Upon the tray gleamed a row of diminutive wedges of yellow fire. They looked rather like the illustration in Saint's old Bible story book of the coming of the Holy Ghost. He looked up and saw them there. Then he broke a tenet of the society by going and bringing one to a débutante on the ballroom floor. He felt that he must do something spectacular; substitute some memorable symbol for the inadequacy of speech. She took the glass by its slender stem and touched his own gravely with it, then they drained them without a word and put them down.

The touch of glass on wood seemed to break the spell. They laughed into each other's faces, the girl daringly, the boy a little shame-faced. "Silly, aren't we?" he said.

"Divinely."

"Well, if it is sentimental and all that, I don't care," he defended. "One does not have to apologise for being sentimental at a St. Cecilia ball. It is a part of the show, like the old silver, and the sixteenth dance. By the way, whom did you give the sixteenth to?"

She extended her programme, and her escort frowned heavily over it. "This will never do," he assured her. "Mr. Jervais is one of the managers, and every one will think that you were stranded and he had to come to your rescue. You must give it to me and let me tell him that there was a mistake."

"No," she told him firmly, "I understand that the sixteenth is saved for wives and sweethearts. I am not going to let you be gallant to a stranger and break some Charleston girl's heart."

Feeling very masterful, Saint wrote his name boldly down for the dance and handed the card back with a bow just as the band crashed into a march.

The couples were forming for the march, and Saint, who was unengaged, picked his way between them and returned to the great doorway, the old negro, and the little lambent flames. "To carry your liquor like a gentleman." The phrase was a commonplace worn thin by long usage. It did not really matter how much one got away with. It was knowing your limit and stopping just on the safe side of it. It meant becoming more and more and more of a gentleman with each drink until one emerged the supreme and effulgent personification of all gentility. But until to-night the question had been entirely a hypothetical one to the boy. In youth drinking is a habit of the gregarious, and Saint had always been a solitary soul. It had never occurred to him to go to the sideboard in the little Church Street house and help himself from the decanter that was always kept there. Now, as he downed his third sherry he experienced that expansion toward his own kind that comes from sharing a convivial glass. The bent old negro was an archangel of reverential persuasiveness. Other men were in the group around him. Barriers of reserve and restraint were crumbling. Now the low, habitual hum of life leaped to a higher, clearer note; lights went up; colours brightened, formed into beautiful accidental patterns, broke and fluttered out again among the dancers, hovered shimmering, in the corners. Roses heaped on the mantelpieces released perfume of an almost unbearable poignancy. Music was no longer an external delight. It had entered into his being and raced out in the pound of his arteries to sting exquisitely in his feet, so that waiting for his next dance to start was actual pain.

The hours rushed together and telescoped. The supper march formed, coiled about the hall like an iridescent serpent, and headed for the door. Saint, with his mother on his arm, stood near the end of the column, and as its head turned and moved toward him, he got a swift impression of the leading couple. Major Barker, the president of the society, was carrying his seventy years like a familiar jest to which he already knew the answer, but which was unfailingly amusing. He wore the red rosette of office on his lapel, and his face with its ruddy cheeks and white beard was bent smilingly toward his partner. She seemed scarcely more than a child, and her roving, mischievous glance passed from one girl to another with conscious triumph.

"Hello!" exclaimed Saint. "What is Betty LaGrange doing there?"

"Hadn't you heard?" his mother whispered. "It's the talk of the town. June Mayrant was married last week and expected to be the bride of the ball. But Betty has always hated her, so she ran off day before yesterday and married Herbert Deas. She returned this morning and, of course, as the newest bride, was asked by the Major. June was so furious that she stayed at home."

With incredible swiftness the supper march was followed by the ritual of the midnight repast—oysters, then boiled rice, duck, boned turkey. Champagne, and the rise and fall of talk that seemed gradually to become rhythmic, advancing and receding like surf. Champagne again, stinging the tongue deliciously, sending streams of tiny bubbles from the bottom of slender-stemmed glasses to burst soundlessly under your nose as you drank. Questions; and answers that you made from somewhere outside of yourself, while you sat apart and were amazed at their brilliance.

Dessert—and the moment when, according to the old custom, the men left their own partners to circle among the tables, drinking healths to old sweethearts, débutantes, visiting girls. Across the narrow table Saint could see his mother's face smiling at him through a faint, pink haze. Behind the smile he saw something that pulled him up. His glass was halfway to his mouth, but he replaced it carefully on the table. "Sure," he said as though she had spoken, "depend on me." Some one had stopped beside them. Saint looked up and saw his employer's big frame. Raymond held out his glass. "Twenty-three years ago to-night, Kate. Our last St. Cecilia together."

"Twenty-three years is a long time, Charles, but I still remember."

Saint saw the pink haze deepen over his mother's face. He experienced a shock of surprise, then a swift, clairvoyant moment of revelation. He remembered her reluctance to send him to Raymond for work, doubly strange he had thought at the time because of that gentleman's eagerness to do what he could for him, his almost paternal kindness during the interview. Now he saw his own father with a sudden intensity of visualisation. Usually he had remained in the memory only as a succession of impressions: a bafflement as keen as pain in the evenings when he would come from work—rare days when the child would be awakened in the dawn by the barking of dogs, smell of gun grease, old hunting togs, and those nights when his father would return bringing a sense of space and a shining joy with him from the woods. The house had seemed bigger on those evenings, there would be laughter and sometimes music with his mother at the old square piano. Then in a black wave he would sometimes be overwhelmed by the impressions clustered around that brief, sudden illness—whispers—darkened rooms—lilies—and the dramatic finality of death in its first impact against the child mind. But now, with his gaze resting on his mother's face, he was aware of his father standing there with them sharply etched against the retina. The picture faded, and in its stead he saw Raymond, his eyes upon Mrs. Wentworth's. In his highly attuned state Saint then became the possessor of certain knowledge—a fact that was there before him renascent in the thoughts of the other two. His mother could have married Raymond if she had wanted him. There would have been the big house on Meeting Street—ease. But she had taken his father, Dad, who had been born for the plantation and had been no better a fit in town than his son had proved to be.

In a flash it had come and gone. He saw that his mother's lifted glass was just meeting Raymond's and touching for the toast. The supper toast! The moment for old romances to be remembered. He rose and muttered his excuses, but the two who remained at the table were smiling into each other's eyes over their glasses, the woman with a flash of girlish coquetry that made her suddenly a stranger—the man with a flicker of an old pain about his mouth— romance. He turned slowly and surveyed the room. Where was the Atkinson table? he wondered—the Atkinsons—and Valerie Land.

While he searched, the dining room commenced to tilt slowly, like the saloon of a liner in a sea way. Finally, at the far upper edge of it he caught a glimpse of the face that he sought. The space between the tables was crowded with men going and coming, pausing to drink a health, then moving on. Heavy bodies jostled him from his balance, and the angle of the floor became more and more acute. Suddenly, when he had almost reached his goal that side of the room descended with a swoop, and carried him to the girl in a

headlong rush. She looked up and regarded him gravely, speculatively, waiting for him to speak. But now he encountered a new
difficulty. Something strange had happened to his lips. They were
alien to his face, like a circle of rubber, and when he bit them
cautiously he could not feel his teeth. He could still move them,
but they had lost their identity and could not be trusted with the
things that were clamouring to be said. Suddenly he saw a way
out. He placed his hand over his heart, as he had been taught to
do in dancing school, bowed from the waist, and touched the rim
of Valerie's glass with his own as he had done earlier in the evening
—just that—a silent toast—something too beautiful and significant
for words. She smiled and sipped her glass. He gave her a long
look heavily freighted with meaning, and executed a dignified retreat. Only, when he was safely back at his mother's table, his
exultation over his achievement commenced to give place to a vague
doubt. Why, at the last, had Valerie caught her lower lip under her
small white teeth, and why, as soon as his back was turned, had
there been that suddenly hushed burst of laughter at her table?

After supper—dances—one that impinged upon his consciousness
—the sixteenth. Out over the polished floor flowed the strains of
"Auf Wiedersehn," weaving their old, sentimental spell about the
feet of the callous new generation, deluging them with their flood
of associations. Mothers, grandmothers who had danced their six-
teenths to that air, and had in turn endowed it with their own
romances, watched with a happy mist in their eyes. Something
strange and new seemed to enter into the boy, clearing his brain,
sharpening his perceptions, infusing him with an illusion of
grandeur. He knew that he would speak clearly, that his thoughts
would be brilliant, his logic irrefutable. He went confidently in
search of his partner.

As she went into his arms, Valerie exclaimed: "What a perfectly
gorgeous orgy! Isn't it marvellous to throw shame to the winds

and revel in it once more with the old darlings? I never want to
be young again. I want to die a rank sentimentalist."

They plunged into the tide of music and movement. After the
first measure the boy was no longer conscious of the floor's solidity
beneath his feet. He circled through a rarefied ether, guided and
sustained by the music. Around him again flowed the rainbow with
its frieze of drifting faces. Now and then, out of the blur, eyes,
wide and eloquent, close to his own—poignantly intimate for a
moment—gone—the sixteenth!

*

Later, when Saint kissed his mother good-night in the hall of the
little brick house, he asked: "Well, dear, did I carry it off like a
gentleman?"

She answered with a shadowy smile: "By a very narrow margin,
dear boy; a shade too narrow, I would say. For a moment at supper
you frightened me a little, but that was silly of me."

He turned toward the stairs. Polly had said her good-nights and
had preceded them. Now for a moment mother and son were alone
together. He hesitated, turned, and saw her standing under the
hall lamp. The girlish look was still upon her face, she was smiling
faintly, and although her gaze rested upon him he realised that it
was unaware of his presence because of its projection into some far
place where her spirit had gone alone. He felt that shock of
strangeness which comes with a sudden glimpse of the familiar
from a new angle. In the down-flung light of the rose-hued lamp
he saw his mother as a stranger might have, dissociated from all
preconceptions; a woman still young, beautiful, and a thoroughbred
in every line of her figure, a woman who had fought a lone cause
with such dauntlessness of spirit that even the honourable scars of
the combat were hidden from prying eyes.

Saint harked back to the earlier moment of revelation, and almost unconscious of the fact that he was speaking aloud, said tentatively: "Mr. Raymond—at supper?"

She came back to him slowly as though returning by gradual stages from her far land. Finally she was there again under the rose lamp, beautiful still, but familiar. She did not answer the implied question that hung in the air between them, but beckoned the boy to her in silence. When he reached her side she took both of his hands in hers. Then she said: "Do you remember your father, Saint?"

"Sometimes, just barely—but to-night at supper——"

"Yes, I know. It was when Charles Raymond came to our table. I saw him then too. You're a strange boy. Sometimes I'm glad. Charles's son would never have gotten that."

She stood for a moment considering, her glance lowered, then she looked him full in the eyes and continued: "You'll be wondering why we had that flash. You'll be thinking it strange, maybe, but it's not strange at all, really. You see at the first ball of the season twenty-three years ago both Mr. Raymond and your father proposed to me. I loved your father—everybody did. To-night everywhere I looked I seemed to see him again. That's all—that's the story."

Saint said huskily: "And these things that mean so much to you —things that you could have had—you let them all go—for him?"

Kate Wentworth's form stiffened. Saint felt her fingers tense in his grasp. "Certainly I did not give them up. You could not have said that if you had known him well. We were both willing to wait awhile, that was all, until he had won them for me. We were gambling with all the odds in our favour—there was only one thing that we did not count on—it happened—and we lost—that was all."

His hands gripped so that she flinched. "Listen," he said, and his voice came in an odd constricted whisper, "I don't know whether you've lost or not. I've been wasting an awful lot of time with my silly head in the clouds, but I'm not old yet—I am going to try."

She drew him to her and kissed him, holding him close for a moment, but when she spoke it was with her usual serenity. "Now run along," she said. "You'll only want coffee in the morning, and you may have it in bed."

*

The next afternoon Saint came face to face with Valerie in an alcove of the Gibbs Art Gallery. Meeting any one there was a little surprising, as there were several teas in progress, and at that period art found it difficult to hold its own in competition with society in Charleston. He stopped short, his surprise and pleasure plainly evident. "You here!" he exclaimed.

"Of course," she smiled at him. "This is where I belong. But you! I did not gather from the men I met last night that they went in very much for art."

"They don't, and I suppose that is why I have always been rather lonely. After all, friends have to more or less like the same things, don't they?"

"They do nowadays, I am afraid. Life is so short, and being bored can kill so much of it."

They had drifted to a window and stood looking across the street into an old churchyard where great live oaks were bronzed by the late sun. "That's the sort of thing I like," he said—"funny old tombstones—pictures—music—books."

Valerie looked up quickly, and he closed his catalogue with "and brown eyes."

"And champagne," she supplemented.

He was immediately embarrassed. "That's unkind of you. Last night was an event, a sort of initiation. It won't happen again.

And now that I come to think of it, you were unkind last night too. You laughed when I toasted you at supper."

"God forbid," she replied piously. "A nobody from New York laugh at a Charleston gentleman!"

A suspicion caused Saint to bend and glance under her lowered lashes, then they laughed together in the quiet echoing room. "Oh," she gasped, "you were *such* a gentleman. I did not know that they made them like that any more. I suppose it takes lots of grandfathers to get away with a jag like that."

She swung him around and slipped her arm through his. "Come," she said. "It will soon be getting dark, and we must see what your local artists can do. I am out discovering Charleston to-day."

"You know pictures. What luck!"

"I ought to. I have starved for them long enough. There, those etchings are rather nice. Who is the artist?"

"Oh, she is a Charleston woman. Been plugging away mostly alone for several years, but she has taken several awards lately. I love her work, but I don't know enough about etchings to say why."

Valerie coolly removed the thumb tacks and carried the picture to the light. "Feel that surface. Get that texture? Good strong work. You know how they're made, don't you?"

Saint shook his head, and she gave him a brief account of the process—scratching the design on the protected plate, then biting the picture out with acid. "I wish I had you in Dad's studio for a while. I'd show you. And that group over there. That's interesting."

She hurried Saint across the gallery to a small collection of misty low-country landscapes. At a distance they gave the impression of pastel, but on close scrutiny they appeared to be treated by some process of colour wash.

"Say, here's something new," Valerie exclaimed. "Strong Japanese influence, and yet how individual, and how they have captured the mood of your country. It is local work, of course."

"Yes, and I know her quite well," Saint boasted. "You must meet her. And I don't think the Japanese influence is conscious. She is much too unspoiled for influences. Like most of us here, she has had to work out her own salvation. I've seen her out doing the marshes near the mines, sitting day after day like a tiny wren, painting away at a certain mood until she got it."

"We'll all be hearing of her some day," Valerie affirmed with conviction. "She's got something of her own."

Saint insisted on her seeing the permanent exhibit in the main gallery. They were portraits, for the most part, and the girl moved quickly along the big room. "These are interesting," she said after her inspection, "but not as art. I like them because they help to explain you. I suppose most of them were colonels, and I am sure they all carried their liquor like gentlemen."

For an hour they loitered through the pleasant rooms, and Saint got his first glimpse behind the surface of paper and canvas into processes and methods. He watched the girl avidly while she talked. Down the street St. Michael's flung out the quarter hours. He did not hear them strike. She had the thing that he had always wanted. She lived it, breathed it as naturally as air. He had waked that morning with a firm resolve to let the old dreams go, to find some solid terrain where he could plant his feet and renew his struggle, to give his mother and Polly their chance. But his motive had not been altogether unselfish. There had been something about his own experiences of the night before that had shifted values. Somehow the affair had assumed a greater significance than he could possibly have imagined. Now he stood as the recognised head of the family. There was a new and pleasurable sense of self-importance in the thought. His mother had accomplished, by being quietly and serenely exactly what she was, what no amount of argument could have brought to pass, and behind his mother that sharp invocation of his father. Then there had been the approval of the older people at the ball, an approval that tacitly assumed that he was being what was expected of him, that made him understand that measuring up to those expectations was after all a fulfilment. But now the cross current of Valerie's talk threw his mind into confusion. A longing that had nothing to do with reason twisted him with a pain that was almost physical. In a moment he had blurted out:

"I have always meant to go in for this some day. I am going to paint."

She turned and studied his face seriously, her own very grave. "I didn't know you felt that keenly about it," she said at length. "Tell me more about yourself, please. I really want to know."

He asked to escort her home, and they took their way through the crisp January evening around the Battery, where a winter sunset burned low across the Ashley and flooded the river with crimson lacquer. But now Valerie had turned from the contemplation of beauty to the more practical aspects of life. She asked bluntly: "What do you do for a living?"

Saint flushed. Her forthrightness challenged his own, but habit prevailed, and he gave the old, vague answer: "I am employed across the river in Phosphates."

"Phosphates," she wondered, "suggests something to do with soda water to my uninitiated mind, but I don't suppose a gentleman has anything to do with soda fountains."

"No," he said, too preoccupied with the threadbare deception to smile, "I have the management of the Phosphate Mining Company's commissary."

She gave him her wide gaze. "That sounds important. I am duly impressed."

Under her look his own eyes began to waver. Suddenly he blurted out: "No, that's all rot. It isn't important. In plain English I serve a gang of phosphate negroes all the week, then on

Sunday I wash up, come to town, sit in the family pew, and play the gentleman. So there you are."

She patted his arm in the gathering gloom. "I am so very glad you told me that," she confided. "Now we're going to be real friends."

"Not until you have told me something about yourself," he qualified.

"It's an awfully short story," she said, "and a grey little one. You see, Father is one of those artists who missed greatness. He even missed distinction. He thought that because he loved painting he could be a painter. Now he knows how little that has to do with it, and he is too old to start over at anything else. Mother—Uncle George's sister, you know—oh, she's such a brick. She works too, at lots of things, and helps, and when I get home I will have to turn in too and find something to do—not painting. Father says one artistic failure in the family is enough. But in spite of everything we do, we don't get anywhere. Father can't leave New York because he can get odd jobs there—something from the scenic studios, interior decorations, dribbling little things that keep us chained there yet won't give us enough to really live on. And New York is such a bitter place to be poor in."

Saint slipped his arm through hers, found her hand and pressed it. She let her fingers remain in his, and, after a moment of silence, looked up at him with her long scrutiny. "The two of us," she whispered. "Cinderellas at the ball. That was why I was so glad that you told me about your work too."

★

After his week in the rarefied air of the social world, Saint's descent to the earth of the mining camp had been a gradual one, during which he was still enveloped in trailing clouds of glory.

The events of the brief sojourn had remained so vividly in his mind that they seemed for those first few days more actual than the humdrum routine through which he moved by habit rather than thought. He measured cloth and weighed out provisions, but there was a shimmer over his tasks, as though an iridescent gauze floated between his hands and the things that they touched. It was not until the fifth day that he could actually be said to have arrived. He was dining as usual at the mess maintained by the white employés in a cottage near the washing shed. He was always silent at his meals, and the other men usually took him as a matter of course and discussed their poker and hunting across him as though he were a part of the room's furnishings. But to-day one of their number returned from town, where he, like Saint, had gone for the ball and a taste of the social season. He ragged the boy rather unmercifully, and the others joined in, with the result that when he stepped again through the commissary door the shimmering illusion was gone—salt pork, cabbages, and herrings were again salt pork, cabbages, and herrings. The swallowtail was definitely back in camphor, and his actual wage was twelve dollars and fifty cents a week.

He seldom had customers in the afternoon, as the negroes were still in the mining fields, and as the hours dragged by he came into a realisation of what the week had meant to him. Now, with the glamour gone, he could see quite plainly that its luminous centre had been Valerie Land. Sitting in his little sanctum behind the store, with his face buried in his hands, he looked for the first time into youth's keenest tragedy: a vast aspiration and the overwhelming conviction of his own inability to attain it. He tried to consider it impersonally and debated it as a purely academic question. Was it better to have caught a glimpse of the unattainable or to have stayed in ignorance of it all, sweating it out in the obscurity of the camp, finding escape only in his reading, music, pictures—

the sort of things that couldn't hit back? Now even the little
that he was sending home was desperately needed there. If Polly
was given this year, and perhaps next, she would probably marry,
and marry well. In the meantime she and his mother must have
the best possible background.

Looking back on his parting from Valerie, he realised that
some protective divination had been at work within him, for he
had made the farewell deliberately casual, as though they were
mere acquaintances parting after a week of festivities. She had
said that surely she would see him on the following Sunday when
he would come to town as usual. He had replied evasively, telling
her that there would be a lot of work to be made up, and he did
not know when he would be free again. He remembered that she
had looked surprised and hurt. Now he thought bitterly that even
that was best. There was no use to go ahead toward an agonising
smash. A clean break—and a memory—surely that was the wisest.
Now he must pull himself together—buck up—face it squarely.

Through the heavy stillness came the sound of an automobile
engine throbbing in the sand of the main road some little distance
away. It fretted the structure that the boy was commencing to
build—challenged its permanence. He dropped his face in his
hands. "A bunch of tourists on their way to see the Ashley River
gardens," he thought. They were commencing to discover them
now. Coming from way up North in their great new machines
that looked so out of place in the ancient solitudes of marsh and
forest. He wished they'd stay away. Their appearance stressed
differences so heavily, started absurd longings.

He heard a step in the store, got wearily to his feet, shook himself together, and went out. The large room was gloomy, and by
comparison the doorway seemed almost dazzling in the afternoon
sun. It framed a foreground of white sand road, and a towering

back drop of straight pine boles. In the centre of the picture, showing only in silhouette, stood Valerie.

She hesitated a moment, then advanced toward him. While he thought, "This isn't right. This will upset everything again," his quick perception of beauty caught the sinuous flow of the little body, carried now with a childish bravado. He said, "Oh, good God," and stood motionless. On his face was the old look that had counted so heavily against him when he was a child—the wide-eyed, almost vacuous gaze. Finally he broke into movement, holding out his hand—"Valerie."

"Yes," she said, laughing a little shakily, "right you are, but don't be so frightened. I haven't come to call. That wouldn't be proper. I have come on a mission. I have come to save you. Is there some place where we can talk?"

She had spoken in a light manner but with a serious undertone in her voice. Saint was mystified. He locked the store and opened the door into his own room. She entered, and he followed her in silence. He was bewildered by her sudden and unexpected appearance, and by the faint, exciting vibrations that her presence released in the familiar room. She did not look about her, saying at once: "Uncle George was taking the children to see the gardens, so I got him to drop me off here." Then with her characteristic directness, she came immediately to the point.

"You remember what I told you about Father and the bad time he has had?"

Saint nodded assent.

"Well, I have been thinking about him a lot since, and I couldn't help thinking about your saying that you were going in for painting. It made me see you in a new light, and it made me see your great danger. I thought maybe no one else would see it and tell you. You see, it struck me suddenly that Father must have been awfully

like you when he was young—his passion for beauty—for knowledge—reading—painting—confusing the love for a thing with the
ability to create it." She was talking now in short, rushing sentences, watching his face for any revelation that it might give her
of his response, but not giving him a chance to interrupt her. "And
Dad isn't the only one that made the mistake. I have seen lots
of others go the same way. You see, they are two such different
things. I knew a real artist once—he almost hated his art—it was
such a relentless taskmaster—he was a terribly lonely soul—but his
things are in the Metropolitan now. At first, at the gallery that
afternoon, you said you loved pictures. Then, after I had talked
to you about them, you said suddenly that you were going in for it.
That made me feel terribly responsible. I could not rest until I
could come to say *don't*. Hold on to the thing you have. Try to
make it pay the way. Then you can have beauty too. That's all.
Am I forgiven?"

She had been standing tensely before him while she spoke. Now
her body went slack. She sighed and let herself go into the depths
of Saint's big chair.

The boy stood looking down at her with preternatural solemnity.
"You are right to have come," he said, "but I don't know yet. I
can't think quickly, you know. There has always been a dream.
It seemed so far, so hard to get hold of. I kept doing all sorts of
things like those fossils there, hoping I would stumble on it and
see it clearly. Then came the ball. It changed values, made me see
other things as important, and on top of that, the day with you and
the pictures. Now here I am back on earth again. I see this job
for what it is. I am beginning to loathe it all—the ugliness—the
cheap hypocrisy. And yet I know now that I can't let it go. I am
even beginning to see some justification for the hypocrisy. Polly's
got to have her chance. I've got to play up for Mother. So there
we are!"

"But there's more than just that," she told him earnestly. "You see, I have been thinking terribly hard about it. It took a lot of courage to come, and I would not have dared if I had not had an idea."

She was so small and so desperately in earnest that Saint could not help smiling down at her.

"Oh, don't take this lightly," she begged. "It hasn't been easy for me, and I can't just waste it all. You must see it like this: Now you are in a job that you can do. I bet you can do it better than other men could, even not thinking about it. But you have lots of imagination that you have just been playing in this room with, keeping that door into the store closed all the time. Why can't you spend some of it on the job? Whatever it is, you can make it grow. Then when you have succeeded you will have time and money for Beauty too, and she won't disillusion you then as she has Dad."

Saint sat down opposite his guest and looked into the fire that crackled on the hearth between them. After a while he said: "Dreams are funny things. They had me mastered when I was a kid—shoulders right to the mat—but out here I have learned to keep them in their place a little. I only let them come into this room, and never across that threshold into the store. It was hard keeping them shut up at first, I can tell you. But now they behave. Then I started reading, playing a little, thinking things out, studying. It seemed that if I could only keep alive by what I got beyond that door, I could keep on finding my happiness alone in here. Then there was always the vague hope that sometime, somehow, a miracle would happen and I'd find myself writing, or painting, and would never have to open the door into the store again."

"But don't you see, you can't keep on that way. That's drifting. You must carry your imagination over that threshold—into life—and make it work for you. You are young, and no one can count on always meeting life alone." She blushed hotly, stole a sidelong glance at him that brought reassurance, then hurried on: "I mean life is something to be gone after—fought for—not just dreamed over."

She broke off suddenly, then mocked herself, "Here I am getting as intense as anything, positively preaching to you—and my pose in ruins. My nice casual little self gone moralist. Well, don't lie awake over what I have said. We've all got to think things out for ourselves, anyway."

She stood up, saying that the car would be back any minute and she had promised to be at the roadside to be picked up without delaying the homeward journey. She had an overdone air of indifference about her and held out her hand with impersonal coolness. Saint took it and held it for a moment. Then he said with the solemnity of youth, "Thank you, Valerie. I have to think this all out. But I'll never forget your coming."

"Oh, that's all right, quite all right," she replied in a deliberately passionless voice. "It is the sort of thing that my sort of meddling person can't help doing for a friend. You've taken it nicely. And now I feel better for having done it."

In the moment of departure she hesitated, turned slowly, and for the first time examined the room, noting the etchings, the books, the guitar; and on the table the rather absurd self-instruction book. She completed her survey in silence; then she came and took both of his hands impulsively. In the up-flung light of the fire her face was luminous.

"Oh," she said, "I am sorry for you and I'm proud of you. This little room—can't you feel it? It is not a playhouse, after all. It is your battle ground, and you're going to win." She dropped his hands suddenly and turned her back upon him, leaving him inarticulate and embarrassed. Then she looked over her shoulder and laughed audaciously.

"There's something else I came to say too, and I had almost forgotten. It's this: you need not be afraid to come and see me in town. I'll promise not to marry you unless you ask me."

The boy goggled at her, his face a mask of comedy. Finally he achieved a grin.

"Poor boy," she laughed. "The Wentworths have never had to contend with my sort before, but you're young. You'll learn."

He walked with her to the road, and they saw the Atkinson car approaching, a great, shining limousine, nosing its way along the winding sand road. Atkinson was at the wheel, and the children had a friend with them in the deep rear seat. Saint helped Valerie up beside him while he responded to the cheery greetings, then stood and watched the car diminish toward a far vanishing point. Instinctively he turned back into the old avenue of escape —the splendid abstract dreams that had pulled him through the bitter moments of his adolescence. He opened his mind to them, and suddenly they were upon him, bright and amazing, more actual than life. The great machine vanishing under the trees turned the trick—its incongruity in that primitive setting. Under the rubber tires, a scant six feet deep—carcases of dinosaurs, their great teeth and bone fragments waiting for the shovels of the negroes to show them the light again. They rose before him. In the dusk under the live oaks he saw vast moving shapes oddly balanced on hind legs while they reached to feed on treetops. They were so real, so marvellously convincing, he regarded them with a sort of detached pride akin to the thrill of creation. The last glimmer of a sanguine sunset, broken into long bars by the tree trunks, penetrated the dusk and burned faintly on the swaying forms. Then the swamp mists bellied in whitely and blurred the huge outlines.

Saint became conscious of the roughness of the bark against which he was leaning. "Yesterday and to-day," he thought, "and what does it all amount to, anyway?" He pulled himself up sharply.

What would Valerie say! She thought he had something in him, and she hadn't put him down as a quitter. He straightened up resolutely, and jammed his hands deep into his trousers pockets. Then he strode quickly across the road and entered the store.

★

One month had passed since Wentworth had been to the city for the St. Cecilia ball, four years since he had gone on the payroll of the mining company. Mr. Raymond had sent word that he would call at noon. There was an important matter to be threshed out. The two men had scarcely met since the morning when they had driven out together and Saint had been installed. Mr. Raymond belonged to a world of statistics, directors' meetings, and conferences, with his orbit definitely fixed in the big Broad Street offices and the surrounding financial district. Wentworth had been directly answerable to the commissary manager, an extremely low order of human being named Goodlow, to whom a trade was as the breath of life, and who naturally regarded his aristocratic subordinate with the traditional suspicion and dislike of the poor-white. Twenty years of penny-pinching had raised him from the keeper of one of the smallest branches to the position of purchasing and managerial head of the chain. Saint knew that the man disliked him intensely, but he also knew that, having come into the job over the manager's head, at the hands of the great Mr. Raymond, he enjoyed a certain mysterious prestige in the Goodlow mind, and that was why he was, at least, left largely to himself.

It was odd that Saint felt no nervous apprehension at the prospect of the visit of his chief. He wondered about this for a while. What had brought about the difference? Then he got the answer: the ball, not the event itself, but the things for which it stood, the odd feeling of importance that it left with him in spite of his disillusioning return to the realities of the camp. He remembered his panic that day when he had been given his job, and he smiled at his own expense.

When Mr. Raymond arrived he greeted his employé warmly, but there was a subtle something in the air that seemed to temper the extreme cordiality of his attitude toward him when they had driven out to the store that other morning four years ago. He stood silent while the outer door was locked, then, at a gesture of invitation, preceded Wentworth into his little sanctum. Strangely enough, the room seemed to impair the sense of superiority which an employer has every right to experience in an interview that deals with policies of the company. The room was less a part of the store building than it was of the man before him. It confused the issue, making him feel like a guest in his own house. Mr. Raymond stood looking about him in silence for a moment. There were many books, and his roving glance failed to discover a familiar title upon any of the neatly arranged bindings. There were several etchings, and odd bits of statuary. In a corner stood a glass case containing a small collection of fossils from the mines. His glance came back to Wentworth and rested on him questioningly. He had had him neatly catalogued. The boy had been hopelessly devoid of ability, personality, everything that could make for success. He had taken him on and buried him here because Kate Wentworth was one of the finest women God ever made, and he wanted to do what he could for her son. Now, reinforced by this inexplicable background, the boy was emerging as a mystery, and he was suspicious of mysteries, especially in business. His employé had changed physically too—filled out—and there was an ease and resilience about his carriage that denoted reserves of vigour.

Saint begged his guest to be seated and returned to the store for the box of cigars. When he re-entered the room Mr. Raymond was standing before the mantelpiece from which he was in the act of lifting a small curious object, holding it gingerly in his heavy, blunt fingers.

"What's this peculiar affair, Wentworth?" he inquired.

Saint took it and held it with a strange sort of deference. It was about six inches in height, made of some heavy, dark wood. Oddly out of proportion, it yet resembled a woman in a kneeling posture. The limbs were massive and primitively modelled, the eyes half closed, the nose broad and flat.

The answer came with diffidence. "Oh, that! Why, that's a piece of primitive African sculpture. It was almost a duplicate of a piece in a collection at the museum, and when it was offered the other day by the British Museum for sale or exchange, the director arranged for me to take it off their hands."

He hesitated a moment, while he studied the bit of wood, then he added impulsively: "Not often a fellow down here gets a chance like that, I can tell you."

"Ahem! no—I suppose not," Raymond replied. Then, seizing the opportunity offered by the topic, he sat down, relighted his cigar, and said with some sententiousness: "Negro, eh! Well, that brings us to the matter in hand. I thought, Wentworth, that we had rather given you an idea of the policy toward Baggart and his men out here. It's not the sort of thing that we issue orders about, you understand, but there is a general feeling among the men that it is for the good of all concerned not to interfere with his administration of the law in this district. Perhaps you haven't quite realised this?" And he looked at Saint with raised eyebrows.

"But I do understand, Mr. Raymond, and God knows I've minded my own business. Why, I even let that yellow skunk Bluton hang around the store, and keep my mouth shut while I wait on him."

"Oh, it's nothing about the store," said Mr. Raymond hastily. "It's this matter of Davy something-or-other. I gather that Baggart subpœnaed him for crap shooting Saturday night, and that you appeared for him and swore to his alibi."

"Oh, that!" exclaimed Saint, his face clearing. "Certainly. I see you don't understand. I had Davy here helping me take stock until midnight, then I saw him go home. When he told me about his summons I thought that there was some mistake, so I offered to go to the hearing and clear it up for him. That was all."

Raymond leaned forward with his elbows on the arms of the chair and regarded Saint intently. The boy was struck again, as he had been that first day, by the kindliness of his eyes, but when he spoke the bold, flexible voice had a decisive edge to it.

"I see that I have to be very plain-spoken with you, Wentworth. It is a hard matter to put into words, but I am going to try to get it over to you. We—that is, the Company, the labour, the magistrate, you—have all shaken down into a system that works. It may look unjust, it certainly is faulty, but I am not sure that it is such a bad arrangement after all. To begin with, the state put a magistrate here and requires him to maintain an office, a constable, and live like a white man on seventy-five dollars a month, and—here's the joker—such perquisites as the office may yield. The incumbent holds his office at the pleasure of the voters—not the mining interests with their few white votes, but the rank and file of the poor-white, small farmers, workingmen, who fear the negro in the mass worse than they do the devil. They give their man the job for what it is worth, requiring of him two things: to keep the negro, as they say, in his place, and, with almost no actual police at his command, to maintain order in the district. From their point of view Baggart is a success. He has absolute power to cause the arrest and fix the penalty of any man upon the knowledge and belief of his constable or the invaluable Bluton. Now you see what will happen to the mining company if it interferes. If we stand with a negro openly against the magistrate we are going back on our colour; according to his point of view, we are demoralising the negroes and putting unsafe notions in their heads. In reprisal, then, the magistrate has only to flood the village with warrants under perfectly valid statutes, crap shooting, delinquent road taxes, dog taxes, and God only knows what not, and in this way pauperise our negroes, and deprive us of labour. No, we are expected to extend co-operation, as it is called, and as long as we do we have a right to expect him not to be too excessive in his demands. At any rate, be the ethics what they may, we are powerless because Baggart is doing exactly what his constituency put him here to do."

"But," interrupted Saint, "all the money that the fines bring in, what becomes of that?"

Mr. Raymond inhaled a deep breath of tobacco smoke and blew it toward the ceiling. "That," he said with a cryptic smile, "is Proctor Baggart's little secret." After a moment he added: "I may say in the strictest secrecy that we are trying through an underground route to have all magistrates required to give receipts for fines. That may be some small restraint, but I doubt if we can get away with it."

"But, Mr. Raymond," Saint asked, "what would you have me do about Davy? Why, he was working under my eyes at the time. I had to take care of him."

"Certainly, take care of him, but in the proper way. What you've done is apt to lay him open for an ungodly disciplining now. It will be Baggart's indirect way of enlightening you. He has to come down hard on insubordination. He has to be invincible. That's what gives him his hold over them. Remember that last case? Time Bluton was ripped by that old fellow Ned? Baggart simply had to get that man. It cost him lots of money, private detective, and all that, but he put him up for ten years. Result: no more razor exercise since that night. But to get back to this specific case—here's how it stands: Everybody knows Davy's weakness for craps. He was due for a contribution, that's all. You had only to sit tight, and the next morning he'd have come to you for his fine. If his credit was strong on your books, you could have advanced him the ten dollars then and there; if not, you could have sent two down on account. Baggart makes terms, you know— two down, two a week. That way you would have been playing the game and everybody would have been happy."

Saint said, "I mind most getting Davy in wrong by it. What had I better do about it now?"

The employer gave the matter thought. At length he said, "I'll tell you what. Just go over to Baggart. He's not a bad sort to talk to. You'll have to handle it a little delicately. Compliment him on the way he keeps order. Tell him that you are just beginning to understand how he gets such fine results. That he can count on your co-operation in future. Fine word that—co-operation. Then say offhand that you have a special interest in Davy and that if he gets in trouble again to let you know."

"That's a nasty dose to stomach," Saint remarked, "but I can't have Davy persecuted. I suppose I'll end by going."

"That's right," Mr. Raymond approved. "Better take a bull by the horns and haul him out of the road. Only way to get ahead." He sat smoking for a moment or two, then touched on the subject in the abstract. "Strange tangle, this negro business. Had a talk with a neighbour of yours about it yesterday. Atkinson—fine chap —open mind. He's been thinking a lot about it and had it sized up pretty well. He said that the Yankee was all for the negro race, and hated him as an individual, but that in the South, we love the individual negro, while we hate, or at least fear, him as a race. I told him that if he had been South during reconstruction and had seen them making laws for us in Columbia, he'd know mighty well why, as a race, we have to hold him under control."

"But in the meantime," Saint argued, "they're not getting anywhere, are they?"

Mr. Raymond's voice was a little weary. "Oh, I don't know, I'm sure. Anyhow, there's always got to be labour, and they are the best for us. And you never saw one willing to work out here who had a dollar in his pocket. It isn't as though they were unhappy. Come, you have been working here four years. You keep your eyes open. Are they a miserable lot?"

"No, I can't say honestly that they are. They have enough to eat, and, to tell you the truth, when they actually cut loose for a good time they seem to get a lot more out of it than I do."

"Sure they do. The white man's burden," said Mr. Raymond, in dismissal of the subject. "Enough to eat, friends, more time than we have, the men have women, and the women have men. 'Sufficient unto the day,' as the Bible or somebody says. Now tell me how you're getting along yourself."

Saint said, "I'm glad you asked me that. There are some things that I want to talk over with you, and I want you to have a look at the books. I have been thinking a lot about the work here, and I believe it has possibilities. I have started some things already. Do you mind if I go ahead with suggestions?"

Raymond regarded him with a surprise that was not entirely free from amusement. He had never considered the commissary in the light of its business possibilities. "Go right ahead," he encouraged.

The boy began a little self-consciously, but soon lost all sense of himself in the telling of his plans. "There's quite a nice cash business now among the outside negroes who farm. We could make a small line of agricultural implements pay, I think. And I'd like to have Davy as a regular hand. He's quick at figures"—a wry smile tugged at the corner of his mouth—"quicker than I am, as a matter of fact, and he's the most popular boy for miles around. I could get him for five dollars a week, and, unless I'm mighty wrong, he'll pay for himself from the start."

Saint, watching intently, could almost visualise the new ideas sink slowly in, meet the dense wall of unquestioned preconceptions, and slowly rebound.

"Hmmm, not so sure about that last item. Never use negroes in the stores. Never thought of it. Can get a white boy just as cheap, and it has always been white man's work. Start now and it might put notions in their heads."

"Perhaps that's why the cash business has been going to the little negro shops over on the main road," put in Saint quietly.

"Well, I'll be damned." Then the big man laughed. "All right," he said at length. "Go ahead and try it out. Any more surprises for me?"

Half an hour later Mr. Raymond stood on the piazza of the store, blinking in the glare that the white sand road flung upward. "Well, good-bye, Wentworth," he said. "Remember to do your best by us in straightening out that damned awkward business with Baggart, and watch your step in future. And about the store: go ahead with your plans, and I'll stand back of you with Goodlow and the town office. If anything new occurs to you, you had better run over to town and take it up with me personally."

★

All that afternoon Saint was too filled with elation over the success of his plans to give thought to any other matter. But the next morning, plodding through the white sand on his way to Baggart's office, the unpleasant nature of the mission upon which he was engaged commenced to eclipse the brightness of his mood. He had locked the store and started off through the lemon-coloured winter sunshine whistling the air of the last waltz that he had danced with Valerie, and while his surface thought played lightly with that memory, plans for the store had been taking form in a substratum of his mind. But as he tramped along a shadow commenced to grow out of the Baggart business and cast a gloom over his mood. Finally he stopped whistling, then, almost defiantly, he faced the unpleasant issue.

No longer confronted by the powerful and persuasive personality of his employer, Saint now saw the incident for exactly what it was. He was on his way to apologise for having done a thing that, deep within his instinctive feeling for right and wrong, he knew to have been right. All of the arguments that he had listened to the day before could not change that. He remembered now how his simple and unpremeditated action had affected the magistrate's court when he had gone in and sworn to Davy's alibi. The negroes had regarded him with amazement. That had impressed him at the time and made him wonder. But Baggart had immediately suspended the case upon which he was engaged, received him with an exaggerated courtesy, at once removed the charge from the books, and thanked him cordially for coming. "The dirty hound," Saint thought. "He must have gone straight to the Company's office and whined about it." With that impulse to vent anger upon an inanimate object, he struck viciously at a wayside bush with the stick that he was carrying. Then his thoughts veered from the specific case to the ethics involved in the affair. What an intricate mess it all was. You could not go about righting a wrong in a perfectly direct and natural way because of appearances, because of the effect that it would produce upon a number of minds that had no concern with the actual incident. Everything had to be done upon such an absurdly personal basis. Davy was his employé, and so, for personal reasons, he would do what he could for Davy. Baggart, who was a state official, nevertheless managed to make everything that he did an obvious personal concession, and expected private and personal concessions in return. As long as a man looked after his own negroes in accordance with the customs prevailing in his particular locality, no one thought anything of it. But if he made an open move that carried the slightest suggestion of impersonal interest in the race, that was another matter, and he was due to be cozened gently back into line.

Well, now that he came to think of it, that was exactly where his grandfather had stood in 1861. He had enjoyed the reputation of taking better care of his slaves than any other man in the parish. He had positively pampered them. Yet he had died at Gettysburg in defence of certain principles, among which certainly must be numbered the institution of slavery. But no, that was not quite a fair comparison. In town, at any rate, there were now good schools. There was even a state college for negroes. There were coloured business and professional men who were earning tidy incomes and living comfortably. Saint's mind locked with this apparent inconsistency. Suddenly he saw an explanation—not a solution—there probably wasn't any—but at least the motivating principle. Expediency. In town, both numbers and power rested securely with the white, and so he could afford to appear in court for a negro, could educate him, give him a chance in business, indulge his own benign paternalism. Out in the agricultural region, staying on upon the same soil that had enslaved their grandfathers, they were held to the old code of behaviour by a tradition of servitude, reinforced in many cases by an actual affection to their landlords. There they were safe. Only here in the industrial belt, thronged as it was by the rag-tag and bob-tail of the race, ten, twenty, a hundred of them to a single white, the grip could not be allowed to slacken. White supremacy must remain absolute.

A dazzling idea struck the boy, an idea as fantastic, as improbable as the old grandiose and heroic dreams. Suppose he should openly abandon expediency for principle. Suppose he should turn back now, instead of going on and repudiating his attitude of three days ago. What would happen? He stopped dead in his tracks, trying to estimate the consequences. First, according to Mr. Raymond's reasoning, Davy would soon be apt to receive another summons. He would be fined, perhaps even given a term on the chain gang. It would be easy enough for Baggart to get him in a crap game if he just watched and waited. Then most certainly his own position would be jeopardised. He would no longer be one of a group bound together by a wordless, but absolute, understanding. He'd be out in a no-man's land of his own making. He would lose the chance that he was just beginning to realise in the store. Hunting for work again. Failure again. His mother—Polly—Valerie.

Out of a job, what good would he be to himself or anybody else? Supposing that he was really interested in the problems of the negroes and wanted to help, was it not best to stay here, observe the conventions, and give them a leg up one at a time? Yes, that seemed the practical thing to do. But if that was so, why was it so difficult to go on to Baggart's? It ought to be plain sailing if he had satisfied himself that he was right. He searched for a reason that would bring conviction to himself. Of course, it was his own pride. No gentleman would relish having to apologise to a man of Baggart's type. Well, then, he must make a personal sacrifice in the matter. For Valerie—his mother—Polly—for the assistance that he might be able to render to the negroes themselves, he must pocket his pride. He squared his shoulders, feeling not a little heroic. Before him the broad belt of white sand swung out to divide at a little distance into two roads, one cutting straight back between the pines into the vast loneliness of the black back country, the other swinging a sharp right angle toward the river and Baggart's office. Saint stood, his eyes before him, and tried to force the familiar, objective details of sand, forest, and sky in upon his mind. He must get out of himself and go ahead with the thing he had to do. But the picture-making faculty that had so often been his escape now turned upon him and endowed the way that he must choose, with its wide-flung alternatives, with a huge and momentous symbolism. His heroic pose collapsed. With a gesture of utter weariness he set his face in the direction of Baggart's office.

*

In Charleston the brief and intense social season had burned itself out, and the chimes of St. Michael's, that had carolled it brightly through its short career, were now, in their Lenten tolling, sounding its requiem. For Lent still made a sharp line of demarkation in the behaviour of the old city, with its deeply imbedded Church of England tradition. The imposing building, with its lofty façade and Grecian portico, where the St. Cecilia had held sway, had now about it an air of desertion and neglect. There seemed suddenly to be more old women in mourning, fewer girls in bright colours, for the visiting débutantes were packing for homeward journeys, and local belles were fluttering away on visits to more gala and less godly metropolises.

Saint was in the city for Sunday, but he did not attend church with his mother and sister. He had two engagements that morning. Mr. Raymond had made an appointment to talk with him at his home at eleven o'clock, and, after that, he had to tell Valerie good-bye before she caught a northbound train at two. Two such different engagements, each with its train of associations, had made the boy of two minds during a sleepless night and a preoccupied early morning. He was like a spirit that is trying to inhabit two separate planes of existence, and the way that his thoughts soared when Valerie brushed across them made it terribly hard to hold his feet down to the solid substance of the proposition that he was going to make to his employer.

It was almost three months since Valerie's call at the mines, when he had listened to her solemn warning. That event, and the visit of Mr. Raymond coming on top of it, had opened up a new phase of existence for him. Books, music, fossils, even painting had been forgotten for the time. He had plunged with the thrill of a fresh adventure into the problem of making the commissary a paying proposition. Once his interest had been aroused and he had looked over the records, he was amazed to see what had come to pass even without conscious effort. He had known that he enjoyed the confidence of the negroes, and that gradually they had started to bring their friends to shop at his commissary. But his mind had been absorbed with other matters, and he had not realised that, from zero, he had built up a very considerable cash business among non-employés of the mines.

Then had come the impulse that prompted him to ask for Davy as a helper. Immediately sales had boomed. At his own suggestion the boy had taken the slack hours in the afternoon to go out on advertising excursions among his friends, and the result had been that both Saint and himself were kept going at top speed during the hours when the negroes came to do their purchasing.

Saint was amazed at the ease with which results were accomplished. Always before business success had seemed to him a thing separate from life—a feat of legerdemain requiring a certain sort of person for its accomplishment. Now he saw it for the first time as the outgrowth of personality—a by-product of the man himself. He had discovered too that it brought a thrilling satisfaction entirely aside from the money that it yielded. It was a game to be played. His imagination was as busy as ever, only instead of being what he now considered a vague and demoralising agency, it was wedded to actuality and was building high dreams over the shabby little commissary.

Some of these dreams he had talked over with Davy, who knew

exactly what the negroes wanted and what they could afford to pay for it. Finally he had mapped out concrete plans and had asked Mr. Raymond for this interview, immediately after which he would have to go and tell Valerie good-bye.

Since the afternoon of Valerie's visit to the mines he had seen her as often as possible. At first they had spent their Sunday afternoons at the museum or art gallery. The pictures were not on exhibition on Sundays, but Saint had gained admission through the secretary, and he and the girl had the big echoing room with all of its splendours to themselves. They would look at the pictures for a while, then sit on a settee and let their talk drift where it would. Valerie told him about her father. "The sweetest, the gentlest man alive. Everything to make an artist but the little essential spark." Once she said passionately: "Only geniuses should be allowed to create. It's cruel to let others try and fail. You see the pitiful thing is that Father knows good work. He's his own judge. And the things that he has to do to keep alive! He will never go back to see them after they are done, and he won't let us go to see them. He has a creed, and he must break it to live."

Sometimes, in brighter moods, Valerie would tell of the other side of their life: the casual comings and goings of people who could sing, paint, act—New York, and the terrible splendour of its nights. Then Saint would momentarily revert to his old gods and exclaim: "I want that life, Val, I want it terribly," or, "That's the real thing. Can't you just feel that, Val?" and she would reassure him with, "But, don't you see, you can have all of that and more when you have succeeded at what you are doing. That's what I want for you, freedom—then beauty."

Then Mamba had taken a hand in their affairs. Employing her old tactics, she had insinuated herself into the good graces of Valerie and had attached herself to her as personal maid. Then one night, when Saint was telling Valerie good-night, she stumbled into them

at the front door and asked them with the excessive innocence of
manner that always masked some deep design if they would like to
accompany her to a special midnight service at her church. Saint
recognised the manner immediately and turned a knowing grin
upon her. "Old Machiavelli," he thought, "she has something up.
I wonder whether she is really doing it for love of us or starting
to run up an account against the next difficulty of one of her
precious daughters." He finally credited her with the double
motive. Valerie was thrilled at the prospect of the adventure.

Mamba led the way through an alley so narrow that both walls
could be touched at the same moment with the extended hands,
and on into the labyrinth of back-yard passageways of lower East
Bay, then suddenly through a side door into a darkened corner of
the large room that served as a meeting house. This was no ordi-
nary service subject to the occasional invasion of a white visitor in
search of local colour. It was a section of Africa transplanted to
new soil and, with the lapse of a century, still black with jungle
mystery, crimson with jungle passion. Mamba, seizing a moment
when the faculties of the swaying crowd were locked fast in the
grip of a chant, got them unobserved into a dark corner near the
door. Over them, like the crash of breakers, swept the terrific,
cumulative intensity of the worship, now throbbing with an old
terror of jungle gods, again lifting suddenly into rapt adoration of
the new Christ. This, and the pounding rhythms of the spirituals,
the amazing emotional release wrought by the music, so fascinated
and yet frightened the white girl that she sat huddled against Saint,
clinging to his hand with tense fingers, her head pressed against
his shoulder. While between them and the nearest group of
worshippers Mamba sat on guard with her rare and cryptic Mona
Lisa smile playing incongruously about her grim mouth and baring
the formidable teeth in a thin up-curving line.

It was in the art gallery on the following afternoon that the avowal had come. A silence had grown between them. The high, windowless walls muted the occasional street noises and surrounded them with a barrier of beauty against the importunate realities that waited for them out in the winter afternoon. The young lovers sat so quietly that a casual observer would have thought the room unoccupied, and in that deep silence there grew up between them so complete a communion that the final word seemed almost superfluous. Saint raised his eyes at last and found the girl's fixed upon him with their intent, reading look. He took her hands and said very softly, "I love you, Valerie." In the suddenly awakened silence, the words seemed to hover in the air about the girl, then she answered on a note that was almost one of sadness, "And I love you, Saint." They leaned forward then, like two children, and kissed, and presently took their way home through the darkening street, carrying their miraculous secret so carefully past the street windows of their friends that they scarcely spoke again until they said goodbye.

But gradually, as the weeks passed, they began to substitute long walks in the country for the hours spent in the art gallery. Saint began to see his old enthusiasms for his guitar and his pictures as just a little absurd. It was the store and its possibilities now, and Saint did most of the talking. The old flair was still there, making him forget himself in an idea, but the idea now concerned itself with a bigger store, more stock, perhaps a second store some day. Sometimes, for nearly an hour, Valerie would have scarcely a word to say, and she did not always follow the soaring flights of his reapplied imagination.

*

And now, on this momentous morning, Saint stood upon the doorstep of Mr. Raymond's colonial dwelling on lower Meeting

Street, and listened to St. Michael's measured announcement that the hour for his first interview had arrived. A step sounded beyond the closed door. He executed a tremendous effort of will, banished Valerie from his thoughts, and commenced to run over in his mind the things that he wanted from his employer: "more space—a line of fertilisers, and seed—new large piazza where visiting negroes could congregate—break all connection with Goodlow and do his own purchasing." At that point the door was opened by a maid.

"Yes, sir," she said in answer to his inquiry, "Mr. Raymond is expecting you in the library."

He passed in and the door closed softly behind him.

Half an hour later he was again on the doorstep, with the big form of his employer filling the opening behind him. Mr. Raymond placed a large firm hand on his shoulder.

"Well, you have what you want, haven't you?" he asked.

"I should say I have, sir."

"Good luck to you, then. I must confess that I am surprised as well as pleased with your results. But blood will tell. It will be fine working directly with you in future. My congratulations, and warm regards to your good mother, please."

Had he got what he wanted! Saint had to smile. A new wing for agricultural implements, fertilisers, and seed, a big piazza that would attract the negroes to idle and feel at home, authorisation to do his own buying and to be answerable to Mr. Raymond alone. Then, right on top of it all—right smack out of the blue—a salary raise to twenty-five dollars a week. The boy felt just a little intoxicated as he turned away from the big Meeting Street mansion.

When he arrived at Atkinsons' Mamba admitted him; then, as nobody was looking, she gave him a proprietary pat on the back, accompanied by a leer that was distinctly a throw-back to the East Bay epoch of her life.

"Ain't no use to hang back, Mr. Saint. Ah sho knows it when Ah sees it. She's in de parlour now waitin' for you, an' she's done all broke out wid it."

"You're a suspicious old devil," he told her with a grin, "and if I didn't have such a deep respect for the law I'd tell you to your teeth what I really think of you."

Yes, Valerie was waiting for him. The street windows were closed, as is the custom in the old city, and the light in the room was dim and chill. An open fire strove valiantly but only half-successfully to bring it to life.

The girl came toward him and gave him both of her hands, glancing up into his face with a new shyness in her own. But Saint, usually so quick to feel the mood of another, was bursting with his triumph. His eyes were shining with excitement, and his colour was high under the tan of his skin. He did not linger over her hands, but gave them a short, vehement grip and released them.

"I have come for your congratulations, Valerie," he exclaimed. "I have just been talking to Mr. Raymond, and he has given me everything I want. You can't guess how exciting it all really is."

"Oh," she said on a short indrawn breath, "you're happy to-day, aren't you? I am very glad. Sit down and tell me all about it."

With a new decisiveness of manner Saint led her to the sofa and sat beside her. He took her hand and held it between both of his, but his manner was abstracted, and his eyes gave her the odd impression of being focussed, not on her face, but on some remote point behind her. He talked rapidly, his enthusiasm vaulting minor details, hurdling obstacles, leaping at, and beyond, conclusions, so that she had very little idea what it was all about. Something very like egotism began to creep into his recital. The girl looked at him in dismayed wonder. She felt as though the sequence of their meeting—understanding—love had commenced to reel backward, and that presently she would find herself talking to a stranger.

She drew her hand away from between his relaxed fingers and saw that he was oblivious of the fact.

When his first gush had spent itself it was as though he came slowly back into the room from some far place, and his eyes became cognisant of her face. He stopped speaking and looked at her in surprise.

"Why, what's the matter?" he asked.

"Nothing, only I am wondering if I was wise when I went out to the store that day and tried to reform you."

Instantly he was his old self and very contrite. "I am an ass," he announced, "I have been babbling my head off. Please forgive me, dear. It's that silly single-track brain of mine." He took her hand again, and she let it lie cool and lax in his as he hurried on. "Why, how can you say that it might have been unwise? I can never tell you all that it has meant to me. See already what it has done. And I owe it all to you. I can never thank you enough—never."

"But you are happy to-day," she said with apparent irrelevance.

He was conscious of a note of accusation in her voice, and it mystified him. He said, "Why, yes, it's a big day. The biggest in my business career, I guess."

Her eyes rested searchingly on his face. "Yes, that's what counts with men," she said wearily. "We are different, after all. Well, I am glad for your success, but you must let me go and finish packing now. My train goes in an hour, you know."

"Good God, Val, I forgot. Can you ever forgive me?"

"I don't know," she told him. "It hurts."

"But I lay awake all last night thinking about you. And this business to-day—I wanted that for you."

She looked into his rueful face. Suddenly her own changed and softened. She answered slowly, translating an idea into speech as it grew in her own mind: "Yes, I can forgive you. I understand you now. I never guessed that you could lose yourself in an idea like that. It makes you different."

She stood with her face very close to his. Her eyes seemed to widen with the intensity of her gaze until at last Saint saw fright in them.

"What—what's the matter?" he stammered.

"Oh," she cried, "I was so sure that I was right until now. I was so certain I was saving you from defeat. But now I am frightened." Suddenly her arms were about his neck, her face strained to his breast. "Oh, my dear," she pleaded, "if you did have it in you to paint and I have blundered—please forgive me, please forgive me!"

Saint laughed softly, reassuringly. He was himself again, and vastly relieved that her fright was not the result of his neglect, but merely a fancied mistake on her own part.

"You funny, intense child," he said, "of course you were right. I was always meant for business, only I didn't have the sense to see it until this winter. And then you came and showed me how to go about it."

PART IV

PART IV

THE coming of the Reverend Thomas Grayson to the Phosphate Mining Camp created surprisingly little comment at the time. Later, when the man became an all-absorbing topic to both white and black, it was said that he had deliberately misled the Company, from whom he had rented the cabin in which he lived and the larger one near it that he converted into a church. He had come, it was then remembered, in rather shabby clothes, and had been civil-spoken enough, although reticent as to his plans. It is a more plausible theory, however, that he went about his business in a perfectly natural manner, having not the least suspicion that he would encounter any opposition. He attended to his affairs with his characteristic deliberation and persistence, and said very little about them, for the man was not a large talker. It is possible that the season might have contributed to the lack of questioning, for he arrived during that period that lies between summer and fall, when the long pressure of the sultry months had laid a lethargy upon both white and black, reducing their vitality to a point at which they did only what became absolutely necessary with the hands, and waited to reason until the bracing days should come to wake them for their season's work. Grayson had simply gone to the office and asked whether they had any vacant cabins. They had taken his money for six months' rent in advance, and, if the tide had been at flood, had continued to doze on the veranda, if at the ebb, to fish in a shady spot on the river bank.

It was not until well into October, when the scrub oaks were commencing to blaze against the dark green of the pines, that the new preacher finished the little belfry that he had erected over the gable end of the larger of his cabins, hung a cheap farm bell in it, installed some benches and a reading desk, donned his vestments, and opened for service.

The negroes, in the meantime, were becoming aware of his presence. He had been visiting quietly among them, talking his strange speech, like that of a white man, telling them of the new church that he was going to open, and inviting them to attend. Slowly their interest in him awakened. He was so utterly unlike any preacher, or negro for that matter, that they had ever seen, that the element of curiosity accomplished for him what no eloquence could have done.

It is likely that Saint Wentworth alone guessed the potentialities of his advent. Grayson had gone to the commissary immediately after his arrival, purchased some supplies, and asked Saint if he could recommend some good woman whom he could get to come and cook for him.

The hour of the visit was a quiet one at the store, and after he had waited on his customer Saint seated himself on the counter with his legs swinging and asked idly: "Going to settle here?"

"Yes," the man answered, and Saint noticed that he did not use the "sir" in addressing him, "yes, I think I am needed here, and, in God's name, I am going to do what I can."

The white man studied him intently from under half-closed lids. Grayson was rather under middle height, about thirty-five years old, and probably a shade darker than quadroon. His face was serious to the point of solemnity, and there were directness and sincerity in his gaze. He spoke with deliberation and with a careful choice of words, but neither then nor at any subsequent time did Saint detect so much as a single gleam of racial humour or imagination in the otherwise strongly marked negroid face.

"Preacher?" Wentworth inquired.

"Yes, but I hope to be a little more than just that. There are so many things that my people need here. I hope to do more than merely preach to them."

Saint's interest in the man extended to his attitude. It was different, strange. He was neither servile nor assertive. He seemed to take for granted a relationship that did not exist in the camp. He appeared to think it a matter of course that he and Saint should discuss on an equal basis. Neither respectful nor lacking in respect, he was merely himself. The white man was intrigued and continued his questioning.

"From the North, I suppose?"

"New York City, and I studied divinity in New England. But I don't like the big cities, I want to get started in the home mission field, and this is my first venture. You will realise that all of this is very new to me," and he swept his arm inclusively toward the settlement.

Saint felt a pang of pity for his customer, more acute because it was the last thing that he would have wanted of him. He spoke impulsively:

"Say, I'm not much of an advice giver, but you had better go slow around here. Take your good time and learn the lay of the land. There are lots of things you ought to know about. The magistrate, for instance—your rival, Reverend Whaley—the way your own people feel about certain things."

"That's very good of you, but, to be quite frank, I haven't a great deal of money. My mission is not backed by the board, and must get quick results. The people whom I have interested in the venture expect me to open for service in a month. They said up North that ought to be time enough."

"All right, only remember this isn't New York. Better watch your step."

Saint went to the back door and whooped for Davy. The young

negro entered smiling. He had a dark intelligent face quick with an irrepressible sense of humour.

"The Reverend wants a cook," Saint said. "Can't your ma go and look after him?"

"Ah reckon so, suh."

"Well, take him along with you and see. She's level-headed, as well as a good cook, and she knows how things stand around here. You better see something of the Reverend yourself, and, for God's sake, try to keep him out of mischief."

Saint smiled at his visitor. For the moment he had spoken in the usual offhand manner employed with the negroes that he knew, but he was now conscious of the fact that it had not been understood by Grayson. The man stood before him, trying in his deliberate way to decide how it had been meant—whether the white man was taking him and his mission trivially. Finally, without answering Saint's smile, he said briefly, "Thank you," and went out with his guide.

Saint thought, "He can't laugh—that's bad. No matter how bad a tangle things get in out here, if we can laugh together there's a chance. He can't get hold here without it— I wonder."

★

The first Sunday in October had the blue cleanness of a tempered blade. It clove the sluggish September vapours to ribbons and rang audibly against the straight, naked boles of the pines.

The new church stood at a little distance from the old meeting house. Brave in a coat of fresh whitewash and topped by its small sky-blue belfry, it stood sharply transfigured by the clear autumnal sunlight.

From a comfortable cabin at the end of the village, the heavy form of the Reverend Quintus Whaley lowered itself into the road, and proceeded ponderously toward the old meeting house. At the same time, Thomas Grayson arrived at the door of the new church. Presently the Sunday silence was sent clattering by the rival clamour of the two bells.

During the last month the Reverend Quintus had elected openly to ignore the presence of Grayson in the village, in private, however, poking sly fun at his speech and referring to him as "Dat Yankee nigger."

But now the gauge was fairly cast. There was the new church, and there was no denying that its bell had at least as loud a voice as the old one.

Presently the negroes began to leave the cabins and straggle toward the summoning bells. They gathered in little knots mid-way between the two buildings and discussed the situation. The talk grew in volume and bred excitement. Whaley was by no means a universally popular figure. The men especially distrusted him, and, with that play instinct that is so often their undoing, they now recognised in the situation a game of large possibilities. Eyes rolled toward the old meeting house, where the Reverend could be seen through a window peering hopefully toward them while he tugged away at the bell rope.

They hung on in the middle of the road deliberately, tantalisingly, and emitted explosive bursts of frank African laughter. The laughter increased in shrillness as the women became infected by the spirit of the occasion. No one thought of God now, and His gentle Son. Even the devil was a pallid figure of the imagination. They stood there deliberately baiting the two perspiring divines, and having the time of their lives in the doing of it. They knew what Whaley could give them, and even those who doubted his sincerity had always been proud of his ability to "slap it to them good and hot." There was no other preacher for miles around who could kick up such a lather in a sermon or shake the timbers as he could with a spiritual. But across the way hid the lure of the unknown.

A quarter of an hour passed, and the hilarity increased rather than diminished. Upon which one should they lay their bets? That was the all-absorbing question. Then a small negro boy came from behind the new church, his eyes showing white. He arrived at the group scarcely able to speak for excitement. Finally he managed to articulate: "Great Gawdamighty! De new preacher done all dress up in a long white shroud, same like uh corpse."

They had never seen a surplice, Whaley having always preached in his vaunted tail coat. Now a silence fell upon them. Here was a sensation indeed.

Davy seized the opportune moment and announced: "Ah goin' to de new church. Come on, folks." He took his mother by the arm and, followed closely by Maum Vina and Baxter, who had postponed her Sunday morning visit with Mamba in order to be present, started toward the new building. In a moment the whole crowd was stampeded. They jammed their way through the door and stood looking about them. They were impressed by what they saw. The benches had backs, and the reading desk was an imposing structure covered with fair white cloth. Behind the desk stood the preacher in his flowing robe, and at the side of the platform a small organ glistened in a shaft of sunlight.

Across the way the old bell gave up the fight slowly, dying, as it were, by inches—a clap—a wait—a clap—silence. A face was thrust from a window and regarded the new church with an expression that one would have scarcely expected to discover upon the visage of a man of God. Then, after a moment, Whaley emerged like a black and menacing cloud and set off in the direction of the Company's office.

In the new church Grayson stood face to face with a tremendous opportunity. The congregation was in a state of repressed excitement, and, had he possessed the touch of a true evangelist, he could have bound them to his cause then and there. His rival would have known so well how to go about it. He would have flung the coils of his mellifluous voice about them and released that excitement into the all-possessing rhythm of a spiritual.

But Grayson saw in the moment a miraculous turning to his God from the half-pagan, and wholly undignified, worship of the old church. He saw them as already converted, and asking merely that he lead them. Hymnals and prayer books had been placed in the pews, but as scarcely any of his flock could read they were useless. And so he read the full morning service through by himself. Strange words flowing out over the serried benches—a beautiful rhythm—a vague loveliness of sound—a thing utterly separate and apart from themselves. Slowly the excited faces went cold. Feet commenced to shuffle, benches to creak under shifting bodies. Now and then there was a brief recrudescence of life when Grayson seated himself at the organ and sang the hymns, but in this, no less than in the reading, he was alone, and after the brief animation of each hymn the congregation's interest went flat.

The sermon was long, for in it he told them of his plans and all that he hoped to mean to them. The collection followed, and was both a financial and social failure. Not that the congregation was stingy. Every one there had a coin for the occasion, but Grayson's system was new to them. In Whaley's church this was a moment replete with exquisite humour. It was during the collection time that the great man was truly at his best. A plate would be set before the reading desk, and the congregation would be cajoled, flattered, wheedled, twitted with sly personal allusions, told pointed jokes, until at last, in a gale of high spirits, they would disgorge the last penny and feel themselves well repaid.

Now, when Davy, who had been unwillingly commandeered for the occasion, passed a plate among them, they kept their pennies, hoping against hope that at last the new preacher would break through his restraint and give them the usual final run for their money.

When at long last the service was over, and the recessional hymn sung, it was after one o'clock. The exit was a hasty and a noisy one. They were anxious to escape in a hurry, and they did.

A strange sequel to Grayson's first Sunday morning service was the fact that he did not in the least realise what had happened. He had triumphed, but he was not vainglorious over it. It had been God's work. Now it remained for him to till the fertile field. He was up and out early on Monday morning, intent upon launching the first of his schemes for the village. By the merest luck, he hit upon the one thing that could possibly even temporarily have stemmed the tide that had started to ebb the day before, and that would have swept the entire congregation back to Whaley on the following Sunday.

This first inspired act was the installation of a vested choir. Robes for the ten best singers in the congregation! The men had gone to the fields when the new preacher set out to unfold his plan to the village, but the women gathered, and when they heard that the choir was to be given the robes and allowed to sit on the platform with the preacher, their flagging interest was immediately revived. Grayson set an hour during the afternoon for testing voices, and left them to talk it over among themselves.

That afternoon when he went to the church he found practically all the women in the camp present, dressed in their best, rolling their eyes, giggling, and nudging each other. But there was not a man to be seen, proving that his visit to the pits which had followed the talk with the women had been unproductive of results. Well, he would start without bass or tenor, and hope to bring them in later. In the meantime there was no lack of enthusiasm among the women. In fact, Grayson was a little at a loss how to cope with their lack of reverence, and decided that it would be wise to curb it at the start. He stood for a moment looking over the benches with their rows of laughing faces, their gorgeous accidental colour combinations wrought by head kerchiefs, hats, and dresses. Finally, the inevitable occurred, and his gaze was arrested by the vast magenta-clad bulk of Hagar.

"What is your name, my daughter?" he inquired.

She hesitated, then gave her adopted title of Baxter, her broad, ingenuous face wreathed in smiles. Immediately a chorus of giggles burst free among the benches.

Across the irreverent sound the pastor's voice fell chill and authoritative: "Sing something, please. I want to try your voice."

Baxter was undoubtedly enjoying the situation. She stood like a child at a party, deliberately hesitating for effect.

"Go on," he encouraged, "sing anything. I only want to test your voice."

Instantly from her silence, her deceptive air of embarrassment, she launched full-voiced into song. The voice might have been that of Mamba herself. It had the same depth and tenderness in the lower register, the same whimsical way of catching for an imperceptible beat on the high notes with the effect of laughter broken by a sob. But where Mamba's voice lacked volume Hagar's came from her great lungs with the magnitude of organ music. Unfortunately, in common with the other aspirants for robes, she had remained impervious to the reproof in the voice and manner of the pastor, and now her song, beating with the spirit of irrepressible and eternal youth, rolled forth and filled the building:

> "My mammy tell me long time ago,
>   'Gal, don't yo' marry no man yo' know.
> Take all yo' money, steal all yo' clo'es.
> What will become of yo' Gawd only knows.' "

The performance was greeted with whoops of delight from the floor, and cries of "Dat right, Baxter." "Tell um, Sistuh!" "Gawd know dat de trut'." And after the general laughter had died down a fresh outburst was provoked by an ancient Gullah negress who called in a high cackling voice: "Dat gal woice loud succa guinea hen."

Grayson stood regarding them in stern silence until the noise abated. Then he pointed out in a few brief but well-chosen words that the occasion was not one for ribaldry and that they were in the house of God. Down, down slid the mercurial spirits of the sisterhood. They sat in solemn rigid rows while one after another of their number was called forward to go through a constrained and self-conscious test on some familiar spiritual.

Finally Grayson singled out ten of the number, including Baxter, and dismissed the others. Then, seating himself at the organ, he commenced to whip the raw material into shape for the début on the following Sunday.

The week that followed was a busy one in the village. Grayson had purchased the entire stock of white longcloth from the commissary, as well as many yards of black cotton goods. He had engaged the services of several women who could sew, and himself supervised the designing and fitting of the vestments. Then, late every afternoon, he called a rehearsal at the church, thus dislocating the supper hours of a number of hungry and tired negro labourers.

But during those days of busy preparation Grayson was not the only energetic divine in the neighbourhood. The huge bulk of the Reverend Quintus could be seen at all hours visiting among the cabins, and to judge by the gales of laughter that attended him wherever he went he must have been in his most entertaining vein. Also he paid several visits to the office of the Company. These last, however, were not humorous in intention, to judge from the denunciatory exclamations that punctuated the conferences.

But when Sunday again dawned, victory returned to perch upon the little sky-blue belfry. Not one shroud now, but eleven! The lure was irresistible. Again the Reverend Quintus swung in vain upon his bell rope. Again the cheerful summons lost heart—clanged—waited—clanged—stopped. Once more an irate face glared from the window.

The service was more effective in holding attention than it had been the previous week. The choir was an unqualified success. It knew the hymns, and even a simple chant, and the presence of the vestments awakened a new awe in the worshippers that held them sitting quietly with solemn faces. When Grayson commenced the sermon they were ready to listen.

He preached upon "the powers of darkness." He had learned something during the week, and that was the necessity of plain speech. He had flown over their heads, perhaps, but now he would talk to them so simply that a child could understand. Accordingly, with directness and lucidity he struck at the hold of superstition upon the minds of his hearers. Fortune tellers and conjurers were children of hell, and their utterances were lies. Charms were devices of the devil, and those who believed in them were destined for destruction, unless they turned from their evil ways and prayed for forgiveness.

From where Baxter was sitting in the choir she saw a long shudder run through the frail old body of Maum Vina. She looked keenly at her friend and saw her eyes blur under a film of tears. Baxter had been listening to the sermon, but it had been a thing apart from her own needs. She had made no effort to personalise it, to relate it to herself. But Maum Vina, for all her years, took things in with remarkable clearness. What the new preacher was saying was meant for her. Had he not fixed her with his gaze while he talked? She made an heroic struggle to control herself. Baxter felt it, while only dimly beginning to grasp its cause. She got quickly to her feet and half carried her old friend into the open. Then she was shocked at what she saw in the ancient negress's face. It seemed to have been suddenly extinguished, and there was a sag to the whole body. Then Maum Vina commenced to shake violently, as with a palsy, and to sob in long, weak breaths.

"Yo' heah what he say, Baxter?" she asked between her sobs.

"Sho, but dat don't mean nuttin'. Le's we forget it an' get 'long home."

"Yes, it do mean somet'ing. Dat man ain't like Whaley. He tellin' de trut'. Ah know dat, an' Ah ain't nebber goin' fin' dat money in de road what de cunjer 'oman promise me."

They were joined by several other members of the congregation who had walked out and had been none too quiet in the manner of their going.

"Don't yo' b'liebe um, Aunt Viny," an old negro advised; "go ask Rev'rent Whaley. He know what he talkin' 'bout."

Baxter led her friend away, trying to console her with clumsy, tender pats, as though she were a child. Then she noticed that the eager light had gone out of the old eyes, and that they no longer searched the road with their incessant weaving motion.

"Better watch whar yo' goin'," Baxter cautioned. "Fus' t'ing yo' know, yo' goin' miss dat money."

" 'Tain't no use, gal," came the answer. "Ah's goin' be a care on strangers long as Ah las'. 'Tain't no use to s'arch no mo'."

*

During the ensuing week the new pastor was an industrious parochial visitor. There was something definitely wrong, some maladjustment between himself and his flock that pointed toward disaster if it were not quickly located and rectified. He reasoned that by adroit questioning he could draw his parishioners out and ascertain the trouble. But when he found the negroes at home he had encountered an attitude with which he was incapable of dealing. If they could not avoid him, they greeted him with a sort of negative cordiality. They would smile and ask him to sit, then disappear within themselves, speak only of abstractions, be deliberately vague and noncommittal. When he had touched on the subject of church or religion they had smiled again, and if it seemed the part of politeness to say something in reply, they had, still smiling, remarked that times were certainly hard for a country nigger, that last winter had been unusually cold, or that no food served so well to sweeten the mouth as hominy and a fat fried porgy.

There was nothing to lay hold upon. He began to experience a sense of vast futility. And his money was nearly exhausted. The experiment had been his own idea, and he had had to depend upon what he could raise from private sources. He had hoped to make an instantaneous success that would win full backing for the mission from the board. But now failure was staring him in the face.

Grayson was particularly puzzled by the behaviour of Cora, the mother of Davy, who served him as housekeeper. She had been a regular attendant at church, and when he had talked with her in her small, immaculately kept kitchen, she had a way of looking into his face with a candid and trustful gaze that seemed incapable of concealment or deception. But now, as the momentous week advanced, he noticed that there were long, unexplained absences, and that the dishes often stood unwashed after a meal. Finally, upon entering the kitchen silently, he found her with her face buried in her apron while her body shook with deep elemental sobs.

An overwhelming wave of pity rendered him suddenly speechless.

He had tried so hard and so unsuccessfully to be understood that his self-confidence was shaken. This was the sort of opportunity for which he had been hoping, when he might enter into the sorrows of his people and let his heart speak in actions as well as words. But now he experienced a feeling of utter impotence. It came to him that the words that he would speak would be mere empty symbols uttered in a foreign tongue. He crossed the room and dropped a hand gently on the heaving shoulder. The startled woman looked up into his face with an expression that changed from grief to sudden fright.

"Tell me, Cora," he urged, "what can I do for you?"

"Lemme go home," she sobbed. "Ah gots to go now."

"Certainly," he assured her, "go at once, and I'll go home with you. If you are in trouble I want to share it with you."

"No, no," she cried in panic. "Yo' stay here. Ah'll come back. Ain't nuttin' yo' can do." Then she was gone in a heavy lumbering run down the road in the direction of her cabin.

Two days passed and Cora failed to reappear. Now Grayson's visits seemed even more fruitless than early in the week, for the village was deserted. For the most part he found only children at the cabins, children and the ubiquitous yellow curs. The pickaninnies gaped at him when he questioned, but the curs with their singular instinct for sensing the moods of their owners followed him to the gates, hanging just out of reach, with their small sharp teeth bared. Finally, on Friday morning, he met Wentworth, who was swinging along the sandy road with a package under his arm.

"I suppose you're on your way to Cora's," hazarded the white man. "It's too bad about her trouble, and Davy's badly knocked out by it too. He was devoted to the little fellow, used to bring him to the store pretty much every afternoon."

"Cora's trouble?" inquired Grayson, and Saint was surprised by the agitation reflected in his face.

"Why, yes. She lost her youngest child last night. It has been in desperate shape for the week. The whole village has been sitting around out there with her. I thought you might have noticed. I am taking her along some mourning and a little money for the burial saucer."

While the two had been talking they had proceeded in the direction of the cabin, which lay well beyond the regular confines of the village, and now, through the clear, resonant air they caught the distant strains of a spiritual. Very distinctly the music sounded across the distance, not the robust shouting like that of a Sunday morning service, but the shrill, agonised voices of many women, each of whom had personalised the desolation of the mother and made it her own, and, tramping along an octave below them, the mellow, flexible beauty of a single tremendous bass.

Saint cast a sidelong glance at his companion and saw the broad benevolent face go ashen, the eyes light with a spurt of naked pain. He spoke impulsively: "I'm awfully sorry. I didn't think you cared so much, and I thought you would have known. They sent for Whaley three nights ago, and he hasn't left the house since. He is going to hold the funeral services to-morrow afternoon. They don't change quickly back here, you see, and he knows their ways."

There was silence except for the sound of singing that shook the air with its unearthly harmonies. Grayson had stopped in the road. Finally, in a shaken voice, he said: "I can't go on, Mr. Wentworth. My heart is breaking with that woman's sorrow, and if I went to her I'd only give her pain."

For a full minute he stood silently, his face working with emotion. Habit had carried his hand to a small gold cross that hung on a black cord from his neck, and he fingered it absently.

Saint could think of nothing to say but a trite, "I'm sorry." Then he saw the face that he had come to think of as being insensitive, almost stolid, quiver, and the eyes fill slowly with tears. At last, still fingering the little cross with an unconscious mechanical movement, Grayson turned slowly on his heel and commenced to retrace his steps toward his cabin.

From the house of mourning swept the music of the dirge. Shrill, monotonous, unvarying, it throbbed across the sunny afternoon with its burden of human desolation, and always under the shrill grief of the women marched the sustaining beauty and power of the single enormously vital bass.

★

Sunday morning was ushered in with a triumphant clanging from the old meeting house. Groups arrived, laughing and chattering, and filled the building to its doors. When the crowd had jammed its way in, Reverend Whaley started them off with a rousing spiritual. With one accord they flung themselves into it. It was good to be back with the old agreeable God again, the God who wanted them to sing and shout, to pour their sorrow out in a flood of song, who minded his own business most of the time and had a pleasant, laughing way with him when he touched upon theirs. Yes, they were foolish to have strayed for even a few misguided weeks.

In the new church Grayson sat alone, listening to the uproar with an expression of deep sadness upon his habitually solemn face. Yes, this was the end. They needed so much—and they would not let him give it to them. He had come full of confidence to bring enlightenment. His own people! Now he saw no use remaining in the empty building that was so eloquent a reminder of failure.

He rose to go, then he saw that a woman had entered silently and was sitting on the last bench, just inside the door. He walked down the aisle and stopped before her. Then he saw that it was the woman known as Baxter.

"Have you come to worship with me?" he asked.

Hagar nodded violently but said nothing.

Grayson's heavy face caught a fleeting gleam from an inner light. "Then we'll have our service just as though the church was full," he assured her.

He retired and donned his vestments, then asked her to come and sit just below the reading desk on the front bench while he held service. Vast and submissive, she went forward and took her seat before him.

While he went through the service, omitting only the sermon, she kept her eyes on his face with an expression of dumb, uncomprehending steadfastness.

Grayson pronounced the benediction, then came and sat beside her. Then he said, "I am very grateful to you for coming to-day. You have put new heart into me."

Baxter was overcome with embarrassment, but she managed to say, "T'ank yo', suh."

A silence followed during which the woman's embarrassment heightened to actual distress.

At last Grayson urged, "You do believe in the God that I preach about, do you not? A God of beauty and light and loving-kindness?"

Baxter's gaze was on the floor. She was absolutely still. Then suddenly she shook her head in a violent negative.

Grayson almost jumped, so unexpected was her answer.

"Then why did you come in to-day?" he asked.

She had trouble getting started. Words eluded her, and she was trying terribly hard to be honest and yet not hurt him. At last she said, "Ah been lonely a lot too. Ah ain't likes tuh be by myself in my trouble. Ah done set out fuh de ole church, and when Ah pass, Ah see yo' here, an' Ah can see yo' lookin' lonely. Den Ah come in. Dat's all."

The preacher got to his feet without a word and commenced to
close the windows. Baxter sat on, watching him, not knowing
what to do next. When finally the building was made fast and
only the door remained open he came back to her and held out his
hand. Then she saw that it contained a book.

"I want you to keep this to remember me by," he said. "It is
called the Book of Common Prayer. And see, here in the front is
my name and address. You must remember it always as that of
somebody who is grateful to you, who wants always to be your
friend. You have been a real Christian to-day. And now, good-
bye."

He held out his hand, and Baxter took the book; then she dropped
an awkward curtsy and said, "Good-bye, suh," and stepped over the
threshold into the bright autumn weather.

At the very moment when Baxter entered the new church, a
conference which also bore directly upon the destinies of the
Reverend Thomas Grayson was taking place upon the sunny piazza
of a bungalow near the Company's office. It had an appearance of
great casualness about it. Two white men had been sitting there
since breakfast, enjoying their pipes and the long Sunday quiet.
The rattle of a vehicle sounded in the distance, the rumble of hoofs
over a wooden bridge, and presently Proc Baggart turned into the
private road behind his span of trotters. He alighted, hitched his
horses, and stepped up on the piazza.

"Well, gentlemen," he said, "this is a mighty pretty spell of
weather we are having."

One of the white men motioned toward a chair. "Have a seat,
Cap'n, and make yourself at home. Yes, the weather's set fair, I

guess. When you can hear the town bells up here, it usually means a pretty spell."

Silence then for a moment, except for the far, faint throb of chimes that followed the river all the way from the city, and stirred the air about the men with a soft humming. Baggart lighted a cigar, gripped it in his strong, stained teeth, and smiled his mirthless, muscular smile.

"They tell me that the Reverend Quintus is having a nervous spell," he commented.

"Yes, and hard luck too," remarked the taller of his two companions. "The old fellow has put in the greater part of his life working among these niggers, and he ought not to be interfered with."

Baggart's eyes met those of the speaker, and his muscular smile broadened into a grin. "Yes, a nigger's a simple soul," he remarked, "and he's got simple ideas on religion. It would be a pity to have them upset. This crowd here's well behaved and an easy-going lot. They know what's good for 'em, and they ain't ready for new ideas yet." He puffed in silence for a moment, then asked casually:

"How'd that fellow Grayson get in here, anyway?"

The shorter white man flushed slightly under his tan as he explained: "Oh, he came in one day when we were just shutting up and said he wanted to work here. Looked straight enough and laid the money down for the empty shacks. I never thought much about it at the time."

"What sort of a lookin' cuss is he—how dark?"

"High yaller, I guess you'd call it. Comes from New York, I hear, and talks like a college president."

"Bad morals in New York, 'specially among the niggers. Can't have these God-fearing labourers perverted, as you might say."

Baggart permitted a moment to pass, and a glint in his eyes like the refraction of light from blue granite paid tribute to his humorous subtlety.

The two white men laughed softly, and Baggart's next question fell casually into the conversation: "Anybody told him yet that it's pretty unhealthy 'round here?"

One of the men said, "Well, to tell you the truth, Cap'n, we'd rather not mess up in the affairs of the labour. We make it our business to keep hands off in matters that are their own concern."

"Yes, very wise policy, I am sure, but some kind-hearted citizen ought to warn him. It's a mighty sickly country for a stranger, 'specially one with a touch of white blood, what with malaria and all that. If you gentlemen would like, I'll be passin' through the village to-night, and I could stop and give him a friendly word of advice as easy as not, or I could get Bluton to stop and see him."

The two white men were obviously relieved. The taller one said, "Well, that's mighty good of you, Cap'n. And don't forget, any time we can do any little thing for you, you know where to find us."

"Sure," Baggart answered, and his voice was almost hearty. "Always glad to co-operate in any way, and I know you gentlemen feel the same way about it."

Suddenly all three men sat forward in listening attitudes, then exchanged glances of satisfaction and understanding. From the direction of the village came the full-bodied music of a spiritual, swelling out across the marshes and ringing clear and sweet along the river.

"Hello!" ejaculated the short man who had rented the cabins to Grayson. "Sounds like old Quintus has 'em all back in the fold again."

Baggart got to his feet and threw away the stump of his cigar. "Sure he has," he said. "They know what they want better'n we do. Anyhow, I may just as well drop by to-night—never believe in leaving loose ends. Good-day. See you gentlemen again."

But that night when the trotters pulled up before the cottage in which Grayson had set up his simple housekeeping there was no one to answer Baggart's peremptory hullo. He got down from the rig and rapped smartly on the door with his whip. Inside the empty house there was a desolate momentary reverberation, then silence.

The trotters were feeling the chill night air and were pawing trenches in the soft sand with their fore feet. Baggart went to their heads and caught a muzzle in each hand with a sudden fierce affection. They whinnied, and he felt the brush of soft, warm velvet against his jaw. "We all know what we want," he thought. "Niggers—horses. You don't have to tell a horse to leave spaghetti alone and eat hay."

*

The spring of 1917, and half the world in fiery dissolution. America in at last. Money. Ships. Then, suddenly—man power. Up north at Washington the daily minting of beautiful illusory phrases—"A world made safe for democracy"—"Self-determination for all peoples"—"The war that will end war"—The mobilisation of a nation's advertising power—the press—Committee on Public Information—Four-Minute Men—Ministers of the Gospel gone militant—The flag and the cross side by side on Sunday morning. That indomitable good fellow, the community song leader, abroad in the land—febrile meetings—campaigns—campaigns—campaigns.

Atrocities. Handless children. Violated women. Nuns. "The mad dog of nations" loose, and the clamour of the hunt ringing around the globe. Charleston, the deliberate old city, deliberate no longer, separate and self-sufficient no longer. Fort Sumter forgotten at last, and the futile agonies of the 'sixties. All one people now. One flag.

Again and again, from the stage, the pulpit, the press, atrocities. The women. Smashing like a cannonade against the traditional sanctities. Suppose it were your mother. Your wife. Saint Wentworth's blood crawled cold to his heart, then flung back in a burning tide, leaving a red haze before his eyes and a taste like brass on his tongue. Now, if ever, he needed the heroic dreams to help him through. But they would not come to him. On the contrary, after the first flush of anger, there were hideous little tremors at the pit of his stomach. But he had certain knowledge of what he must do.

He turned the store over to Davy and went to town. In a week he was back. Crops were essential to victory—phosphates to crops—Saint, according to unanswerable departmental logic, was essential to phosphates. He was told to stick to the mines until he was called.

Back again into the quiet of black Carolina. He could scarcely believe that he inhabited the same planet as his friends a few miles away in town. Out in the wide solitudes of marsh and pine forest the shocks that were being delivered against the inertia of public opinion were muted to a far, faint murmur.

Then slowly the change commenced to come. Invading committees arrived. Groups of negroes from the coloured organisations in town, for the most part. Keen young mulattoes, very much in earnest, discovering their backwoods brethren for the first time, telling them that this was the great opportunity for the race—"A world made safe for democracy." "After this war—the Negro's chance"—getting pitiful little contributions to war funds. Then a young white lawyer from town with a gift for oratory, and two lovely girls in nurses' costumes. The Red Cross. Not vague abstractions now like bond issues and saving stamps, but suffering humanity—the welter of the battlefield—blood—agony—"The Good Samaritan"—Who was going to help? The realism of the

speaker was cut short by a piercing scream. A babblement of sobbing filled the room, punctuated by wails of agony. An unsteady
voice called, "De blood put he maak on me." The line was caught
up by the packed assemblage, and the spiritual crashed out in the
little meeting house.

In twos and threes the congregation commenced to slip out, while
those that remained kept the spiritual going. Finally there were
only a few left. The young lawyer was frankly disgusted. He
had been wasting his time on a bunch of crazy negroes, and they
had walked out on him without so much as a single donation. He
got into his overcoat, and called the two pretty nurses. There was
no use fooling around with this sort of thing.

Suddenly the chorus swelled up again, and he saw that they were
coming back. Into the church they packed and commenced to come
forward to the platform. Then he saw that they had money in
their hands, coppers, nickels, and here and there even a dollar bill.
They came and piled it before him. Every penny in the village.
They gave their tears, and the outpouring of human sympathy was
a presence in the room.

After that, in the black belt, there was the first glimmer of
realisation of the stupendous tragedy that was raging beyond the
city somewhere out in the void.

Then the draft: thirty prime boys from the camp, dressed in their
Sunday clothes, waiting in the road before Baggart's office, not
knowing a great deal about it all—very excited and self-important
—boasting inordinately. Women—lots of them, crowding about,
with the memory of the Red Cross speech in their minds, and an
old, dark jungle terror of the unknown stiffening their faces, widening their eyes, and here and there ripping free in a gust of hysteria.
An incredibly ancient crone, whose mind had slipped a cog and
snapped back seventy years, peering from half-blind eyes and wail-

ing: "Dey's goin' tuh sell um tuh de sugar-cane fields. Ah knows it. Dey's goin' sen' um tuh Louisiana, an' we ain't nebber goin' see um no mo'. Oh, Gawd hab a little pity."

A month since the men had gone; then, one bright day, Saint called the women to the commissary piazza and distributed envelopes from the government that contained the first separation allowances. Everybody rich now—excitement—laughter—and the dark fear forgotten. The thirty women who had been wept over when the men went away were now objects of envy in the village.

Strange talk in the air—something about "Gold Star mothers"— mystery. Then the spry little dentist who came and explained it all to everybody's satisfaction. So it was not "Gold Star" after all, but gold tooth mothers, and the government wanted the women to come to the dentist's office in town every month and get a gold tooth out of the check—one tooth a month to make them beautiful and to show how long their men had been away. After that, Midas moving through the village—smiles showing wide, and ever wider stretches of glittering yellow metal. And the spry little dentist happening by now and then to see how things were getting along, driving a twin-six that pulled up a great dust cloud wherever he went.

Now the commissary was getting its share of checks that seemed to vie with one another to see how soon they could vanish the day they arrived, and Gilly Bluton, who, strangely enough, had not been called, with his eyes everywhere, keener than ever at discovering unlicensed curs about the yards, and participants in hidden crap games.

Now labour was growing scarce and wages were soaring. The result was obvious: three days a week in the pits for the men who were left, instead of six. Why should a man in his good senses work a whole week when in half that time he could earn enough to keep alive and have a plenty of time to lie perfectly flat in warm sand, absorbing sun, or gossip on the store piazza? And so the camp developed a leisure class that loitered gloriously through the late summer and into the long autumnal quiet.

Letters came from the boys in concentration and training camps which were brought to Saint to read. They were having the time of their lives and sent photographs of themselves with chests straining at bronze buttons. Truly the war cloud that hung over half the world and cast its malign shadow across millions of hearts had nothing for this forgotten corner of black America but a gleam from its silver lining.

★

But over the old city across the narrow Ashley the shadow was widening. When Saint went to church now with his mother he saw the service flag with its fifty-five stars hanging in the vestibule, and, as the months passed, gold commenced to take the place of the white. Three of his boyhood friends gone now!

He went to headquarters and made another effort to be transferred to active service. He told them the whole truth about his job. But they were too busy now to listen to old stories with new twists to them, and he was sent back to the mines to wait.

Valerie Land wrote from her Red Cross unit in France:

"I wanted you to be in it, dear, until I got here and saw it. But now I am *glad, glad* that you were made to wait. It is not a bit like the posters. At first, in the canteen at Havre, it had the thrill of adventure about it, and I wished for you. But then the boys were going out. Now, here in the hospital, they are coming back, and my heart breaks into little pieces every day. If it were not for two of the old New York crowd who were wounded while serving in a camouflage unit and who are here in the hospital, I don't know what I would do. . . ."

Then another time she said:

"My boys are getting better, but their nerves are gone. Imagine sending an artist into it! Of course, camouflage is playing an important part in the war, but it is a terrible thing to keep the boys under fire. They are tremendously brave about it, but they have spent their lives learning to see clearly and feel keenly, and they can't protect themselves as well as the others, and they have to pay so dearly."

Saint's fingers closed over the insensate letter as though it were a part of the girl who had written it, and he felt her slipping out of his grasp. For the first time in his life he was furiously jealous. His blood seethed with rebellion. He strode about the little room with fists clenched and angry tears forcing themselves into his eyes, making him feel more useless and futile than ever.

He heard some one rapping on the counter to call him to the store. The sound came as the crowning and ultimate indignity. He flung open his door and stood glaring into the room.

Bluton was leaning against the counter. "Lemme have a coupla cigars," he called, and like an insult Wentworth heard the metallic ring of silver on wood.

Instead of going behind the counter he crossed the floor, his heels hitting hard, his fists clenched. When he was within two feet of Bluton the negro looked up and saw his face. His expression was one of ludicrous surprise. He backed away several steps, with the white man closing them in upon him. Then the surprise in his eyes gave place to a flicker of fear.

A wave of exultation swept over Wentworth. Exquisite tremors shook his muscles, then passed, leaving them pulled tight. He said in a hard, level voice: "Get out!"

The negro backed rapidly toward the door; then, with the opening at his back, he spoke: "What de matter? Ah ain't done nuttin'."

He was palpably afraid, and the knowledge of it flamed through Saint like an intoxicant. He closed the remaining distance that separated them and caught Bluton by the coat collar. The negro went slack in his grasp, waiting, terrified and inert, babbling softly and incoherently with loose lips. Saint swung him around, thrust him through the door, and kicked him squarely off the piazza.

Bluton lit and drew himself together for a bolt.

"Stop," Saint commanded.

The word brought the negro up like a tautened lariat, catching him in the very act of springing and pulling him about.

Saint looked him squarely in the eyes and said:

"I just want to tell you that I've got something on you that will put you up for ten years. It's all ready for you, and it's locked up in the office of a town lawyer. If you ever stick a leg in this store again I'll have you arrested. Get that? And if you take it out on any of my negroes, it's the same thing. Now, get to hell out of here."

There was an ashy tinge to Bluton's complexion. Without a word the man turned on his heel.

Wentworth opened and closed his fists several times, examining them in an impersonal and detached manner. Then he gave a short exultant laugh and put a question to the pines: "Now, where in the world did I get that from?" He stood pondering the question, his head bowed, his brow furrowed. Slowly the answer came to him. In the beginning he had unthinkingly taken the estimate of others on Bluton. The negroes feared him, and fear is contagious. The white men at the mines believed him dangerous on account of his connection with Baggart, and he had adopted their attitude of tactful and expedient handling. Now, suddenly, he had encountered the negro in a moment when his own rebellion had freed him from an habitual attitude of mind. He had been no one but himself. He had acted spontaneously on instinct, and the result had been electrifying. For the first time in his life he experienced that wonder and elation that comes from a successfully executed bluff. For the first time he realised the advantage that lies with the aggressor.

The two men who represented success to him came to his mind: Atkinson and Raymond. They did not sit waiting on the defensive. They had gone out and taken the world by the collar as he had done Bluton. Very well, he would do the same. If he couldn't go to France, he would at least get after the job here with hammer and tongs. He would go to town to-morrow and put himself at the service of the central committee for work in the mining district, and at the same time he would drop in and tell Mr. Raymond the straight story of the episode with Bluton.

The following morning, when Wentworth appeared at the general offices on Broad Street, he was shown at once into the sanctum of the manager. Mr. Raymond rose and shook hands warmly. His eyes were quizzical as he rested them on the face of his storekeeper. He never knew quite what to expect from Wentworth. He said: "I have just sent a message out to the mines asking you to come in. Something has happened out there that I want to discuss with you."

Saint reddened, but he said firmly: "I kicked him out of the store; that's all. I knew I would have to some day, and yesterday was the day. If you don't mind I'll tell you my story now, then leave it to you."

The employer regarded him with a grin. "Oh, so you kicked him out, did you? Go ahead. Who was he, and why?"

Saint told his story briefly, then sat back in his chair awaiting the verdict.

In a voice that gave no indication of his feelings Raymond remarked: "You have your own way of running things rather independently of the Company, haven't you?" Then, without waiting for a reply, he continued, "Well, I didn't know about the Bluton kicking. There was something else that I wanted to talk over with you. Yesterday Goodlow chucked his job. War pickings are too fat for him to resist. He's just the sort who would go in for them. Left us high and dry without a manager for the stores."

The completeness with which Saint had given himself to his new philosophy was demonstrated in his immediate response. He leaned across the desk, looked point-blank into his employer's eyes and said: "You've got to give me that job, Mr. Raymond. You've just got to."

"And have you kick my customers out of the front door?"

"You'll have to leave that to me, sir. You'll have to let me run things my own way. But if you do, I'll promise to give you everything I've got in me."

The big man got to his feet and held out his hand. "That's all that an employer can ask," he said with a smile. "Shake on it, and I'll be out to-morrow at ten to go over the details with you."

★

Nineteen hundred and eighteen—a hectic year. Stupendous energies were hurled into colossal tasks and accomplished miracles over night. Winter—spring—summer trod on each other's heels in their haste to finish the job. But out in the mining camp dew was still unshaken from the morning grass, sun still poured gracious warmth on laxed bodies, full moons lifted over vast marshes, pulled their flood tides high into salt creeks, then released them to dwindle seaward again. Nothing was changed deeply. It was as though the fossils beneath the feet of the living spoke to them out of their long death, telling them of the transitoriness of human existence, the futility of all human effort in the changeless face of time. The great pines towered above the scattered villages. The broad marshes rimmed their world with silence.

The men who had gone from that district were in a labour battalion. Their letters told of a world full of wonders but little of the horror of war. And, in the meantime, wages were mounting to still higher levels, separation allowances continued to arrive monthly with unfailing regularity, and the smiles of the "gold-tooth mothers" grew always broader and more effulgent. And why not indeed! In the last war had not Mr. Lincoln come South and smitten the chains from their legs with his own hands, as shown in pictures upon many cabin walls? And now, was this war not making them rich? Why then should one be stingy in the dispensing of golden smiles?

Then suddenly a new word crossed the Ashley and made its début in the camp. The word was "Armistice." It had a ringing sound like smitten brass; it filled the mouth, and it mated well with other fine reverberant words. The Reverend Quintus Whaley heard it first in the office of the mining company, memorised it then and there, and the following Sunday employed it three times with great effect. The first occasion was: "Ah say unto yo' sebenty time seben, button on yo' sword an' armistice, an' battle wid de debil." Ten minutes later a subtle change of meaning was revealed in this usage: "An' dere war t'ree angel singin' at de golden gate, an' one been name' Gabriel, an' one been name' Philadelphy, an' de las' one, an' de greates' ob all been name' Armistice." But the final appearance of the glittering new acquisition was at the same time the most audacious and mystifying, for it popped suddenly into the benediction and associated itself upon terms of such intimacy with the Trinity that, had an orthodox believer been present, the result must certainly have been a heresy trial for the Reverend Quintus.

It was a great word. There was no gainsaying that. But later, when its meaning became definitely associated with the cessation of hostilities, there was general disappointment at its obvious temporal limitations.

The Armistice! To not only the Reverend Quintus Whaley did the word reverberate with varied and significant shades of meaning.

From the Atlantic to the Pacific it rang from a hundred million throats, clanged from frantic bells, and bellowed from a continent's factory whistles. Peace. An end to the slaughter. Then, like a starting gun in a stupendous race, it thundered back and launched the country upon its brief and preposterous epoch of post-war extravagance, expansion, and inflation.

Across the Atlantic the masks were off at Versailles. The Fourteen Points, impractical, perhaps, but born of the agonies and aspirations of a people who would have done with war, were being manipulated cleverly as decoys, then, when the exhausted game had fluttered to hand, forgotten. Everywhere nations, business, individuals, in a mad stampede for the spoils. On the exchanges stocks were rocketing, dazzling unaccustomed eyes, piling up illusory fortunes. Over mountains and across the plains the rails were humming beneath vast movements of freight. Wages were soaring. Every one had something to sell—something to buy.

In the little room behind the store at the mining camp sat a very different Saint Wentworth from the self-effacing boy who had entered the employ of the Company as its commissary keeper. The flaring cowlick still played havoc with all attempts at a disciplined part, and gave his hair an appearance of sprouting in various directions from a given point over his left forehead. But the brow seemed to have heightened with his greater maturity, and the old daydreams that had filled his slate-coloured eyes with a vague chaos had made way for a purposefulness that rendered them intensely aware of the physical world upon which they rested. His figure was slender but muscular and lent an air to the sombre and rather undistinguished suit that he wore.

He had just completed the final reports on his various war work committees—the draft board—the work for the Committee on Public Information—food conservation—agriculture. He had done his best by it all, but now he was glad that it was over. Glad, with the exception, perhaps, of the last. That had been largely his own

idea. He had realised the uselessness of attempting to educate the
local negroes in the vast abstraction of the European conflict. He
had cast around for some one concrete and logical use to which they
could be put, and had hit upon the scheme of encouraging them
to farm. He had gone to town with his plan and had made
arrangements for the financing of a number of small tracts that
had been put in truck by negro families. He had become tremendously interested in the experiment, and now that they had been
given a start he intended to keep behind the movement for the
benefit of the negroes themselves, and to prove to his financial
backers that the proposition could be made to pay on its own
account.

He glanced around the little room with a rather grim smile.
As it had reflected the boy, with its books, guitar, specimens, so
now it offered dumb but eloquent testimony upon the man. The
centre table had given place to a large flat-top desk, and a filing
cabinet stood in the corner once occupied by the bookcase. The
guitar, the collection of fossils, the treasured bit of African sculpture, the etchings, had vanished. Valerie had once said that the
room was his battlefield. Well, here it was after the first engagement, and, as Saint surveyed it on the day of casting up accounts,
there was in his own mind not the least doubt that the fight had
gone well. He smiled a little indulgently as he remembered the
doubts, the vague gropings, the boyish passion that he had put into
the quest for something that always eluded him, something that
glimmered now and then from a printed page, that throbbed in a
chord of music, that took him sharply when autumn rang against
the pines. He was done with abstractions now. He was face to
face with something actual, something that yielded results that
could be computed upon an adding machine.

He was living in town now, back in the little brick house.
Polly had fulfilled her destiny and had done very well for herself.

Her husband, already out of olive drab, was back in his substantial law practice in Richmond; and Richmond was one of the very few other cities in America in which a Charleston girl could contemplate existence without an instinctive shudder of repulsion. Then there had been another change in the little house, a sad one from which Saint's mind still winced when his thoughts touched it. Maum Netta had gone. Almost a year before, when the carnage had been at its height, unknown, except in her tiny orbit, the old woman had joined in the vast migration and answered the call of the only voice that could proclaim her emancipation from the Wentworth family. Now, try as he might, Saint could not become accustomed to the crisp mulatto maid who had come to take her place.

But there were pleasant things to think about. There was the car to be exhibited as a symbol of success and to serve when he went the rounds of the several stores under his control. There also was his desk in the main downtown office. These things meant the realisation of his mother's definitely patterned dream, and it was also beginning to mean a great deal to him. He was now a gentleman with a Broad Street address and an adequate income. Now he could think seriously about marriage, and next week Valerie's unit was due to sail from France.

★

Mamba sat in her window over the old carriage house in the rear of the Atkinsons' garden. About her everywhere the spring was busy with its splendid occupation of the old city. At the pavement's edge it had captured a gnarled oak that had not yet waked from its winter sleep, and had buried it beneath the headlong rush of a wistaria vine. Now, from this vantage point, flying columns were being flung to right and left to whelm the chrome and madder of a winter wall beneath invading mauve and purple. During the night the wind had changed. It no longer lashed in from the sea with its wintry tang of salt, but swept across the city from the southwest in a broad languorous tide, heavy with earthy smells from the waking sea islands. It was the season when youth strains forward with racing pulses; when age, disturbed and saddened, takes stock of the past and draws solace from such philosophy as the years may have brought. With elbows on the sill and her face propped between her palms, Mamba looked upon the alarming visage of spring with an expression in which the spirit was still un-vanquished but in which fear was held at bay only by her old indomitable look of determination.

Under her feet the years were gathering speed alarmingly now. There were black moments when she would wonder whether she had it in her to hold on until Lissa could take care of herself and make her own way in that strange new world of hers. The Atkinson children were growing too, and no longer needed her care. But she had made no mistake when she had elected the family as her white folk and bound them to herself by an illusory mutual past. As the boy and girl achieved emancipation from her watchful eyes and became absorbed by school, athletics, and the social diversion of the ultra-social old city, she felt herself gradually taking rank as a pensioner of the family. Now the thousand-and-one odd jobs that had engaged her time when she first insinuated herself into the lives of the Wentworths were again her lot. She no longer carried the slipper bag to dances, for Jack, now a breezy lad of seventeen, resplendent in his first dinner jacket, and his sister, who was be-ing beautifully finished at an expensive school, went rolling out of the gate in the big new car that had come to live under Mamba's room in the old carriage house. But there were still shoes to be shined, flowers to be found, and the front door to be tended on Mrs. Atkinson's afternoons. She knew that as long as she could hold on, could successfully substitute the illusion of being valuable for actual value, Lissa would fare well. Her large clean room over the garage gave the girl a good home, and her white folks fed her, just as they did Mamba, in their kitchen. But if she failed, now at this most critical of all times for her grandchild, the girl would have no claim on the Atkinsons—and her mother would be less than useless as a guiding hand. Sometimes now on Sundays, after the long hot walk to meet Hagar, there would be moments when she would forget names and faces and the steady light of her purpose would be obscured by blowing mists. Then she would summon her forces and pull her faculties together again, but it was an effort that always left her shaken.

Had she spared herself in any particular in her sacrifices for Lissa, her hardness to Hagar would have been quite without justification, but she had given everything that she had looked forward to in her old age for the girl, and so, as a matter of course, should the mother. When Lissa reached the age of seventeen, so long had it been since she had seen her mother that the figure had first grown vague and then been remodelled in her imagination into at least partial conformity with her new standards. To her friends Ma, who was now "Mamma," was employed "up state" and sent her the money for clothes, music, and all of the things that enabled her to hold her head up in the Reformed Church set. The girl's voice was beginning to attract attention. She was doing solos in church, and in programmes given at the new coloured Y. W. C. A. rooms. In appearance she was unforgettable. A large girl for her age, her figure was well developed and straight as an Indian's, and that almost obscured strain of Indian in Mamba had flared up in the grandchild, as it so often will, and given her a skin of pale lustred bronze through which the colour beat in her cheeks and her full-lipped small mouth. Her hair, fine and straight, was worn after the fashion of the Mona Lisa, and beneath it she held in reserve small close-set ears, which, like her beautifully modelled hands, were a heritage from her mother's people. But her glory lay in her eyes, which under stress of emotion would deepen and brighten until they glowed like dark amber in sunlight. She had the negro's faculty of giving her whole being to an emotion, so that under stress every gesture became a graphic interpretation, but her years of hard drilling in music, and her teacher's directions for posture and platform presence were in danger of overdisciplining the emotions as well as the body. Her early natural charm was becoming a studied attitude. Now, only when she was singing for fun, as she would say, could she let herself go and forget herself in music. But the cultivated air of well-bred restraint was the charm that presently admitted her to the most exclusive circle of negro society in the city.

Among the girls that she knew it was said by many that she was hard—that what she wanted she took regardless of others. But in a set rife with jealousies, and with her conspicuous attainments, talk of this sort was no more than was to be expected.

In the old city that was so strong in its class consciousness among the whites it was singular that there was so little realisation of the fact, that, across the colour line, there existed much the same state of affairs. There were, in the opinion of most of the white residents, two general classes of negroes—those who knew their place, and those who did not—and of late years the latter class was drawing upon the former in lamentably large numbers. If they thought at all of the innumerable distinct segments that comprised negro society it was apt to be with mild and, on the whole, indulgent amusement. For it was well known that the sharp cleavages between full-blooded negroes and mulattoes, between the waning power of the ministerial union and the new secular leaders, the labour element and the young but powerful business class, all served to make any dangerous concerted negro movement improbable.

In the set in which Lissa moved she seldom met a full-blooded negro—the barrier of mistrust and prejudice that rose between her fellow members of the Reformed Church and Mamba's friends on East Bay was scarcely less formidable than that separating white from black. The atmosphere that she breathed was that of the Victorian drawing room. Music, which had always found a spontaneous outlet in the spiritual and work chant, colour which was flung with a lavish hand over house fronts and clashed and rang in the women's dresses down in the waterfront district, had, in that rarer air, become "culture," and found expression in the Monday Night Music Club, and exhibitions of paintings. The untrammelled hilarity and broad humour of Mamba's friends was here muted to the restrained mirth of the late 'nineties. The pendulum had swung with a vengeance and was then at the limit of its range. Far above, in the life of the aristocracy, the new freedom was beginning to be manifest, smashing conventional usage; talking its Freud and Jung—rearranging moral standards, and explaining lapses in its pat psychoanalytical jargon. But in the Monday Night Music Club ladies were ladies, those who were pale enough blushed, a leg was still a limb—and gentlemen asked permission to smoke cigarettes.

It was all a little absurd, one might say—copybook gentility with its middle-class taboos and reticences. Neither the one thing nor the other in the amazing old city of colourful extremes on the one hand and interesting tradition on the other. But it must always be remembered as a beginning. It was establishing standards, putting a premium on chastity. Drawing-room pioneers, perhaps, but adventurers none the less, and leading the way into a terrain that was new and strange.

★

The Monday Night Club held its meeting at the home of Thomas Broaden, a fine old frame building of the conventional Charleston type with piazzas along its south façade, overlooking a square of garden on upper Coming Street.

Seen about the street Broaden was an inconspicuous figure, of middle height and age and light in colour. He habitually wore a soft felt hat pulled well down over his eyes, and always walked, although he was known to be exceedingly well-to-do, and a number of his friends now owned machines. In his office of the new negro bank, however, and facing a caller across his desk, he emerged as an individual. Immediately one would notice the high broad structure of the forehead and the deep thoughtful eyes. Mrs. Broaden was a perfect partner—small and delicately made, she carried her fifty years as though they were thirty and managed the home with that consummate skill which conceals itself in its work and gives an effect of effortlessness and ease. Both Mary and Thomas Broaden had taken degrees, but his was from Tuskegee, while she was a graduate of Howard University.

On the first night that Lissa attended a meeting of the club, such was her eagerness that she was the first member to arrive at the Broaden residence. Her hostess greeted her affectionately. "I am so glad that you have come early," she exclaimed. "Now I'll have a chance to make you feel at home before the others arrive." Explaining that her husband had been detained at the bank, she took the girl by the hand and led her over the lower floor of the house, through large, high-ceilinged rooms in which periods gave the impression of being superimposed upon each other like geological strata —red plush—horsehair—down to several pieces of beautiful old Hepplewhite and Chippendale—for the Broadens had always been free negroes, and some of the furniture had been in the family for more than a century. Lissa was amazed at all that she saw and heard. Here was a life among her own people that she never knew existed. Finally her hostess stopped before a picture. It exhibited a group of mansions on East Battery at the time of the earthquake, porticos down, and great fissures zigzagging across the walls. She spoke of it sadly as one might of a friend who has received a hurt.

"Say," said Lissa with a note of surprise, "you really love this old town, don't you?"

"Why not?" she replied with a smile. "It's home."

"That's funny: most of the crowd in the choir and at the Y. talk of nothing now but a chance to go to New York. That's where the money is these days—that's where coloured people have a chance."

"I wonder," said Mary Broaden wistfully; then, with a kind earnestness, added, "You mustn't say coloured people, my dear—that doesn't mean anything—Japanese, Indian—all are coloured. You are a negro—doesn't it make you proud to say it?"

Lissa looked at her closely to see whether she was serious.

"No," she replied; "my friends don't like that word. It's a new idea, being proud of it."

Her hostess gave a light indulgent laugh and patted her on the shoulder. "I am glad that you didn't wait to say that when the others are here. Frank North, for one, would have withered you with a look."

"Frank North?"

"Yes; he's the painter, you know—and he plays the violin too."

There was a sharp ring at the bell. Mrs. Broaden stepped to the door and opened it. From the drawing room Lissa heard several voices pleasantly blended in a composite greeting. Then they drew apart and she distinguished a suave low-pitched man's voice, a higher one with a bright vital quality that she decided must belong to the artist, and several women's voices still interwoven in talk.

When they entered, the owner of the higher man's voice was at once presented, confirming her guess as to his identity. He was pale and slender, with an eager look in his sensitive face. Not more than twenty, Lissa thought as he held out his hand. Bowing slightly from the hips, he said, "I am delighted to make your acquaintance, Miss Atkinson."

Nella Taylor, her music teacher, was there, and she put her arm around the girl's waist and faced the others. "This is my star pupil," she said, "and we're going to give you a treat this evening —aren't we, Lissa?"

She felt by the sudden stiffening of the girl that she was embarrassed, and she hurried on with the introductions. They proved to be an interesting group. There was Dr. Vincent, a short motherly woman in late middle life, a graduate of a Northern university who had turned her back on a promising practice in a large city above the line and had come back home to the old town to work at a minimum income among the women and children of her own race.

The owner of the deep, suave voice proved to be Frederick Gerideau, a contractor and builder who was an authority on colonial architecture and who had restored most of the old dwellings in the lower part of the city. He placed a 'cello on the sofa and greeted the girl warmly.

Gardinia Whitmore Lissa already knew—she was the soprano in the Reformed Church choir, a large girl with a magnificent voice and a bold mulatto beauty that she flaunted like a battle flag. Lissa liked Gardinia, and her youth and obvious good-fellowship helped her to feel at ease in an atmosphere that was commencing to have an overpowering effect upon her.

They fell into groups, standing about in the large rooms. Others entered: the secretary of the Y. W. C. A. and a young social worker from the new civic bureau; both were young mulatto women, and both exhibited the flawless approach of the trained worker.

In spite of the fact that Lissa was standing with her teacher, to whom she was devoted, and young North, who was obviously interested in her, she found herself talking in a constrained half whisper. She felt as though they were all playing parts and that she alone was not letter perfect.

North said, "I heard you sing the aria the other night at the Y. concert and have been wanting to congratulate you. The performance was entrancing."

She could only manage an embarrassed "Thank you very much." Then was relieved to see that the performers were gathering at the piano. One of the young women was playing first violin, North second. Gerideau seated himself with his 'cello against his knee, and Miss Taylor was at the piano.

"Shall we start with Beethoven?" she inquired with a crisp professional accent. "How about the 'Moonlight Sonata'?"

There was a turning of sheets on the stands—silence—then they launched into an excellent rendition of the piece. Lissa could see that they were all highly trained musicians, and that technically the performance was of a very high order. But they played with their eyes on the notes, and instead of releasing the music that was prisoned there to fill the room with its magic, they seemed to hold the performance down to a technical demonstration.

Some one asked for Chopin, and Miss Taylor beckoned to Lissa. The girl rose unhesitatingly and crossed the room. Her teacher had been drilling her in the fifth nocturne, and she felt confident of her ability to acquit herself well. The piece was open, ready. She made a striking picture seated before the grand piano.

"Ready?" she asked, then, after a moment, commenced to play. She knew the nocturne by heart, and she loved it, but there was something in the air about her that kept her from throwing herself into it. This wasn't playing for fun. There was a weighty seriousness about it. She found herself, like the others, reading the page, desperately intent on a finished technical performance, thinking with an intensity that almost hurt, conscious of notes—notes. Bound together by the relentless exactitude of the score they advanced toward its conclusion with a precision that evoked a round of applause. Later Lissa sang Gounod's "Serenade," and although it was enthusiastically received she knew that the restraint under which she laboured had rendered it a colourless performance.

Mrs. Broaden called the girl to her and made a place on the sofa beside her.

"We shall be very proud of you some day, my dear," she said. "You have genius, and we will all be telling that we knew you when you were a young girl."

Some one suggested spirituals. Lissa had learned dozens of them from Mamba, and still sang them with the old woman in their room. She saw the ice breaking at last and rose impulsively. "Oh, do let's sing them," she cried. "Do you know 'Play On Your Harp, Little David'?"

"You will find the Burleigh arrangements at the back of the piano, Nella," Mrs. Broaden called. "There is a quartette of 'Swing Low, Sweet Chariot' that is quite charming."

North, Gerideau, and two of the young women took the parts, and Miss Taylor accompanied.

Lissa took a seat beside her hostess and told herself quite positively that she was realising a cherished ambition, that this life was the thing that she most greatly desired, and, finally, almost argumentatively, that she was enjoying the evening immensely. She wondered about the others. They were so different from her childhood associates. What were they thinking, feeling, behind their drawing-room reserve? North, for instance. She raised her eyes and met his singularly intense, bright gaze. It gave her a faint pleasurable shock, and for a moment they sat with the breadth of the room between them, and a tingling sense of each other's presence bridging the distance, drawing them subtly together. Then he smiled and dropped his eyes to the music. Lissa's face grew hot, she looked quickly away and noticed Gardinia Whitmore observing her with open and mocking amusement. Gardinia was seated alone in a shadowed corner and with her full, dark body held in forced inertia seemed literally to smoulder in the gloom. But her smile was not only for Lissa, the girl noticed. From her retreat it took in all of them one by one. There could be no doubt about it—she was deliberately laughing at them all. The eyes of the two girls met, Gardinia's openly inviting Lissa to share her amusement. For a fraction of a second there was an instinctive response, then Lissa's look changed. It became deliberately unresponsive, obtuse, ranging her definitely on the defensive and with the club. What right had Gardinia Whitmore to be pretending a superiority? she thought angrily. She was lucky to have been taken up by them. She ought to be thanking her stars.

When the music ceased Mrs. Broaden smiled upon Lissa.

"You see, my dear," she said, "what our race is accomplishing artistically—when we have Burleigh, a poet like Paul Laurence Dunbar, and in painting, Tanner, to speak for us, we have something to be proud of; and, by the way, you must ask Frank to tell you about Tanner. He has some photographic reproductions of his pictures, I believe."

They lingered awhile over ice cream and cakes, and then, to her relief, the girl found herself out under soft spring stars with the April night cool against her face. North had asked to see her home, and they took their way downtown through the deserted streets. Lissa sighed and stretched her arms in a wide and deliberately undignified gesture. Then she stole a glance at her companion. He seemed to have brought the atmosphere of the room with him, and was regarding her with polite inquiry in his face.

She said, "If I ask you a straight question, will you give me a straight answer?"

"Why, of course," he assured her.

"This evening—was that your idea of a good time?"

North was mildly shocked. "I thought the evening was a great success," he said on a note of reproof. "What's your idea of a good time?"

"Oh, I don't know—I thought I'd rather sing than anything else, but it doesn't seem to be the fun that it used to. Don't let's talk about it any more. Tell me about yourself and who was it?— oh, yes, Tanner."

"You know his work?" he said eagerly, taking up the end of her request first. Then, without waiting for an affirmative, he plunged into a description of the artist's triumphs and methods.

Lissa was sorry that she had started him, it kept the drawing-room atmosphere tagging along with them. When he paused she asked, "Now tell me about yourself."

"Oh, there isn't much to tell," and she was relieved to notice that he was embarrassed. "Graduated from Avery here in town and Dad gave me two years in an art school in New York. Now I am going in for portraiture. I want to paint my own people, and they are good about sitting for me."

Their way had led them through wide unpaved back streets under large shade trees. A faint air smelling of the sea moved through the young leaves and made them whisper. At a far street intersection a big double-truck trolley passed. Lissa heard the clank-clank —clank-clank and the hum of the motors as it drew away in the distance. Then she became cognizant of another sound: the unmistakable rhythm of a spiritual. "Where is that coming from?" she asked.

"I believe I heard that a church near the jail was having a revival this week," he said without interest. "We can go that way if you want," and he turned into a dark and rather forbidding byway

Beyond her Lissa saw the menacing battlemented tower of the

jail against the soft stars. Soon they arrived at the church, a small frame building behind a fence of whitewashed palings. The door and windows were wide to the spring night, and the building was jammed with black humanity. The service was well advanced, and the congregation was swaying to "Swing Low, Sweet Chariot." This was not the Burleigh arrangement. Thought had little to do with this performance. The air rocked to a deep solid chorus, yet a chorus of individuals each creating his own part—shaving harmonies with fractional notes so fine and so spontaneous that no written page could ever capture and prison the sound.

Lissa gripped the palings with her hands. She was trembling with excitement. "There," she said, "that's what I mean. They're having fun when they sing. They don't care whether the notes are right or not. They are just naturally cutting loose, can't you feel the difference?"

The rhythm beat in waves against the soft spring night—the air was heady with the faint, indefinable, yet intoxicating odour of untamed bodies rocking in a close mass, one with the song that they were creating.

North's voice, held on a deliberately casual note, cut across the music. "Oh, that's all right for these ignorant negroes, I suppose, but where'd we be if we stopped at that? We've got to go beyond it. We've living in a civilised community."

"Oh, hell!" the girl cried, "forget it, will you?" She caught him by the arm and urged him forward. He was so amazed at the change in her that he went a step before he collected himself. Then he stopped and looked at her. But she kept on tugging at his arm and pleaded, "Oh, let's step in and cut loose just once—listen to that," and she started to hum the tune. "How can you stand there like a dummy with a chance to sing like that?"

She felt his arm relax for a moment in her fingers. "Good boy," she said, "here we go."

Suddenly he pulled back sharply. "No," he said sternly. "It won't do—we've got to get away from here. I must get you home. This isn't our sort of crowd, and we must stand for something, you know. Think what Mrs. Broaden would say if she heard that we were seen at a revival—shouting our heads off with a lot of dirty negroes."

He took her firmly by the arm and was surprised at her sudden and complete capitulation. She turned away and walked without a word by his side. Only a few more steps and they were passing the jail. Above them the high buttressed wall soared, cutting the sky away almost to the zenith, and above the wall the loom of the battlemented tower hanging dizzily in sharp outline against the milky way.

Lissa looked up, and the black wall seemed to swoop forward and hang poised above them. The night was suddenly dank with the suffering of the thousands who had lain there in the cages— slaves, freemen, her own people. Her mother's face sprang vividly up before her, and she thought that she must go to see her with Mamba next Sunday morning.

Then they were under a bleary gas lamp. She had not said a word since leaving the church, and now North looked at her curiously. "Why, you're crying," he exclaimed. "What in the world's the matter?"

"I am lonely," she said in a trembling voice. "I'm the loneliest girl in the world, I reckon. Just let's hurry, please: I want to get home."

★

But the following Sunday found Lissa at church as usual, where she had a small solo part in the offertory selection. She had forgotten all about it that night when she had that strange brainstorm near the jail and had decided to cut church and go to see her mother. She would go some time, of course, but this was her career. Mamba said that her mother would be the last person to want her to miss an opportunity to sing.

The solo went well, she did not feel the restraint in church that she had experienced at the Broadens, and she let herself go into the music. Everybody spoke about it when service was over and the congregation went streaming out into the spring sunshine. Absurd, that fancy of hers that she was lonely. Why, no girl ever had more friends.

North came and asked her to join a party that was going to his studio to see his pictures, and she found herself stepping into a closed car with several well-dressed men and women. North introduced her to Mrs. Prescott, and then, with punctilious observance of the social code, presented Mr. Prescott to her. His introductions were always ceremonious.

The Prescotts occupied the front seat, and the man's large, faultlessly gloved hands lay in an attitude of easy familiarity upon the wheel.

Lissa had never touched such luxury before. The handsomely dressed woman gave her a welcoming smile over a cloudy fur collar. The car exhaled a faint but pervasive violet perfume.

North and Lissa crowded into the rear seat with another young couple, and while the car glided smoothly over the asphalt he told her how their hosts had made their money. Prescott had started out as a carpenter, then climbed into a small contracting business, and now owned several blocks of negro tenant houses which yielded him a handsome income. They had just returned from a visit to New York where they had heard Roland Hayes in a recital, and had seen Paul Robeson in an O'Neill play, and North asked Mrs. Prescott to tell them about it. Lissa listened greedily while she told of the successes of the new negro artists, and the life in Harlem with the theatres and concert halls, its dances, and its emerging intellectual group.

"Some day I am going there to have my try," the girl said with flashing eyes.

"Of course you are, my dear," Mrs. Prescott assured her; "you can't bury a voice like yours here forever, you know."

North pressed her arm and smiled. "That's what I've been telling her," he said, "but she wouldn't believe me."

The studio was a large airy second-story room, and a number of portraits were already hung, while many more were stacked against the walls. The group scattered, examining the paintings and exclaiming over them. Lissa was left standing alone before two portraits, a man and a woman in middle life. Then she recognised them as the Broadens. She wondered why she had been so slow in knowing them. The likenesses were good, she could see that the features were those of her host and hostess of a few nights ago. What was the difference? She turned and examined other portraits that hung near, puzzling out the problem as she looked from one to another. Then in a swift revealing moment she had the answer. In spite of the fact that the drawing was well done and the features characteristically negro, they gave an effect of not being negroes at all, but white people painted in darker shades—some subtle racial element was lacking. While she pondered, this inexplicable lack commenced to associate itself with other impressions in her mind—the Broadens' drawing room, the music that she had heard there that night.

North came and stood beside her, looking eagerly at her face for her verdict. She tried to find words for her inchoate impressions.

"I can see you know a heap about painting. Those pictures are just like Mr. and Mrs. Broaden, only they don't look just like coloured people and the Broadens do." North was slightly dashed in spirit. "That's a matter of artistic technique," he explained. "You learn to paint in the academy by a certain method, a method that has been used by great artists, then you apply that technique to your own subjects. After all, if the pictures look like them, that's about all that we can do, isn't it?"

The girl noticed a defensive tone in his voice and hastened to reassure him. "Oh, I think they're fine. And I know what you mean about technique. It's the same with music. You are awfully smart to catch them so well."

They were joined by Mrs. Prescott, and the girl returned at once to the subject of New York.

"I wish you'd tell me some more about the coloured people up North," she begged.

"Certainly, my dear. And Frank must listen too. Things have changed a lot even in the three years since he has been there." She stepped between the young people and slipped her arms through theirs. "Come and sit down," she said. "Frank can leave his pictures to entertain his guests for him. That's the good of being a painter."

"Those men you told me about. Do white people go to hear them sing?" Lissa asked.

The older woman laughed. "Do they? Why, my dear child, if a negro wants to hear one of his own colour he has to get a seat in the gallery. We are not good enough to sit in the orchestra yet, but they will pay three dollars a piece to hear us sing or act."

North said, "When I was there Charles Gilpin was about the only one. I saw him in *Emperor Jones*."

"That's ancient history," she asserted. "Why, there are a dozen or more top-liners now, and lots of capable artists earning handsome incomes."

"I suppose it would take an awful lot of money to go on and study?" Lissa queried.

"Yes, that's the big trouble with us here in the South. It takes so much to even reach a starting point, and there is so little to do it with."

Lissa hesitated on the edge of a vital question, then framed it, with her wide warm gaze on the woman's sympathetic face:

"How much money do you think it would take?"

Mrs. Prescott considered a moment. "Oh, I suppose it would take at least a couple of years to do it properly—even to get a good start, and living is high up there, somewhere between two and three thousand dollars, I imagine."

Lissa received the information in blank silence. The older woman saw the disappointment in her face and patted her hand sympathetically. "But don't you worry about that. Something is sure to turn up sooner or later."

They were joined by several others, and the talk turned on North's paintings. Presently the party commenced to break up and leave, and Lissa's new acquaintance asked if she would like to be dropped at home, as they were driving downtown and would pass near the Atkinsons'.

In the privacy of the comfortable sedan the girl seemed wrapped around with an atmosphere of security and luxury. Looking out upon the familiar streets from such a vantage point anything seemed possible, even a New York career, even two thousand dollars. She talked to the others, a light answer here, an inconsequent question there, but beneath the surface, her mind hung blinded in a dazzle of radiance, possessed by a dream and deluded by a dreamer's illusion of actuality.

The car came to a standstill at the curb, and Lissa met the questioning eyes of her friend. "Yes, this is the house," she said, "and thank you so very much for bringing me home."

She stepped out and closed the door behind her, then stood for a moment waving farewell as the car drew away. Across the street a group of white people were standing before a handsome Georgian dwelling. Lissa looked up and caught their gaze fixed upon her with that frank amusement which in the old city is always provoked by the sight of a negro attempting what they would have described as putting on airs. There was nothing inimical in their regard. The girl was merely very amusing.

The effect on Lissa was actually physical, like that produced by the violent awakening of a hypnotic subject. She swayed slightly, pulled herself together with an effort, and climbed the stairs to the room over the garage.

Mamba was sitting on a large chair, her eyes fixed on a sun-drenched roof across the way upon which pigeons were strutting and making soft drowsy talk. Her hands lay in her lap, and between the thumb and forefinger of her right hand, much as a reader might pause and rest, spectacles on lap, she held Judge Harkness's large gleaming teeth.

Lissa flung herself down beside the old woman, buried her face in her lap, and burst into a storm of weeping. The paroxysm was so violent and so unexpected from the habitually self-restrained girl that Mamba was frightened. She patted Lissa's head with her gnarled brown hands and begged her with tremulous urgency to tell her of her trouble.

Finally Lissa looked up into the familiar face that was dimming a little now with the advancing years. The girl was getting herself in hand again. The sobs ceased, and a bitter little smile thinned and stiffened her full lips.

"It's no use, Grandma," she said, and there was a new hard tone in the low-timbred voice. "I've just been wanting something like hell that I'm never going to get. There's no use breaking our hearts over it. You better forget it, and not let it fret you."

"But all dem new frien' yo' got—ain't dey yo' kind? What's de matter wid dem?"

"Oh, I don't know," Lissa said wearily. "They seem to spend all their time saying how glad they are to be negroes and all the time they're trying their damnedest to be white."

"Hush yo' mout', chile," Mamba chided. "Ain't yo' knows swearin' ain't fuh ladies?"

"I'm not so sure I want to be a lady, after all," Lissa exclaimed. She got to her feet and strode to the open window, then turned and faced Mamba again. Her body was drawn taut against the brilliance of the Southern noon, her fists were clenched at her sides and shaking slightly from their muscular tension.

"Oh, I don't know what the hell I want," she flung out in a reckless voice, "but if I don't find out soon and get it I'm going crazy."

*

Lissa had never been on intimate terms with Gardinia Whitmore. This was strange, because their music had thrown them together constantly, and as their voices were perfectly suited to each other's they were always in demand for duets at recitals and concerts. The explanation probably lay in Lissa's instinctive good taste. She was not herself aware that she possessed such a characteristic. But she realised that, while she was attracted by the flamboyant personality of the popular soprano, she experienced an involuntary withdrawal into herself at the other's frank advances. She knew also that Gardinia did not hold the same position in society that she did, for while Gardinia was accepted everywhere on account of her voice, it was obvious that she did not belong.

Seen in the Broadens' drawing room Gardinia immediately made one think of a Bengal tigress in a zoo. She was magnificently proportioned, with a slack sinuousness of body and dark, heavy-lidded eyes in which the banked fires of desire smouldered and glowed. She seemed at times to move among the furniture with a desperate and scarcely veiled hostility. By turns she would be seized by a gaiety so reckless that it seemed almost violent; or sit watching the others with her sardonic and sultry gaze. But over her lay, like a transparent gauze, a surface sleekness which, while it did not in the least disguise her essential self, gave her hostesses something upon which to fix their attention while they introduced her to their friends. But when Gardinia sang, everything was forgotten, and people ceased explaining her even to themselves.

It would have been difficult to find a more interesting contrast than that which the two girls presented in one of their appearances in a duet. They were of the same height, but Lissa was more slender and showed a greater refinement of form and feature. She gave the impression of holding her powers in reserve, and there was behind her art an indefinable suggestion of tragedy that made even her lighter numbers poignant. Gardinia, on the other hand, was an emotional geyser, and except when she was under the rigid discipline of the Monday Night Musical Club, she captured her listeners with a power that was almost physical.

The Sunday following Lissa's outburst to Mamba she found herself on the pavement before the Reformed Church, with the congregation from the morning service streaming past her. The week had increased rather than diminished her feeling of unrest. In spite of Mamba's entreaties, she had not confided in her. In the first place her own feelings were too vague to put into words. There was no use to tell her grandmother that she wanted two thousand dollars with which to go away. She knew that the old woman had been putting something aside for her every week, every cent that she could spare, in fact. It was to be hers to help her along when she no longer had the loving care of the shrewd old head and busy hands. She had never let herself think of it, for to do so brought the tragic prescience of the human loss that it would imply. And what would that pitiful sum amount to, anyway? No, she could not ask Mamba for money, and what the other things were that she wanted she did not know.

Overhead, the portico of the church hung against a soft gray-blue sky, and the air was voluptuous with the warmth of early summer. About her many feet shuffled on the pavement, friendly greetings filled the air. A girl slipped an arm through hers—"Going my way?" Lissa shook her head, and the girl moved on.

The crowd was thinning, breaking away in ones and twos, laughing in the bright summer weather that the negroes loved, bound for Sunday dinner, or long idle walks through the quiet street. Lissa saw the Prescotts getting into their car. North was with them again, and Nella Taylor, her music teacher. They all saw her together and beckoned and waved. Lissa shook her head and watched them drive off with a feeling akin to relief. Then she heard Gardinia's voice behind her. She had a heavy, rather husky speaking voice. "What's the kid waiting for?" she asked. "Got a date?"

"No, I am going home. Just waiting for the crowd to scatter. I hate crowds." Then she gave Gardinia a faint smile and added, "But I am surprised not to see you with a feller. Thought you always had one on a string."

"Did, but I forgot my umbrella and had to go back for it. Now he's gone. I bet that yeller cat Lila snitched him while I was inside."

"Well, I guess I'll be going," Lissa opined.

"Say, you ain't so chummy, are you?—regular chilly sister. But I'm going downtown too, and I just as lief trot along with you."

"Sure, glad to have you."

They walked in silence for a while, then Gardinia turned and looked with frank curiosity into Lissa's face.

"Do you know," she said, "I can't somehow make you out. You look just like a human bein'—got hands and feet 'neverything, but you don't seem to get no kick out o' life. All bus' out with the blues all the time. Say, what do you do nights, anyway?"

Thus challenged Lissa gave the matter thought. "Oh, I don't know," she answered. "Of course, there's the Monday Night Musical——"

"Good Gawd!" her companion exploded. "You don't call that life, do you?"

"Well, most nights, when I am not singing, I just sit round with Grandma and talk."

"You little hell-raiser," Gardinia mocked. "Aren't you 'fraid the cops'll get you?"

"Sometimes Frank North comes around, and we walk out."

"Frank North—so that's it! Don't you know, bright eyes, if you keep that up you'll end highbrow?"

Lissa drew away and regarded her companion coldly. "Look here," she challenged. "You've a great way of throwing off on my friends. Frank's the only boy I know who's got something to talk about. You could learn a lot from him yourself."

Gardinia refused to accept the challenge. She remained silent for a moment, then yielded to an impulse.

"Say, kid, wouldn't you like to try just one real party? You think you're gettin' life with that highbrow crowd, just because you don't know what life's like. What you say I fix up a date for a dance with a coupla fellows for next Saturday night? What you say? You jus' try it once, life with a red lining, and night turned on bright——"

Gardinia shocked Lissa's sensibilities, as she always did when she let herself go, but the girl was conscious of a vague excitement over the idea. Also she was acutely aware of the physical attraction of the girl at her side, whose sheer animal spirits called to something hidden deep within herself.

"I wonder," she whispered.

"Oh, hell, don't wonder, come along. Nothin' ain't goin' to happen that you can't get over. Meet us on the corner by the post office at half-past eight, and we'll be ready to pick you up and highball up the road."

"All right. I guess I'll go. What'll I wear?"

"The best you got, kid, and your dancin' shoes. And maybe you better not say anythin' 'round at the Broadens' to-morrow night. It ain't their stuff. But, believe me, it's got class of its own."

At the next corner Gardinia bid Lissa a breezy farewell and left her to continue on her way with a chaos of contending emotions as an accompaniment to her thoughts.

*

Saturday night found Lissa pacing slowly back and forth before the post office. All day she had vacillated between an overwhelming desire to go, and a deep premonitory fear that prompted her to stay with Mamba. When the late dark finally gathered she had dressed with a desperate speed and without telling her grandmother where she was going had kissed her passionately, then rushed out, leaving the old woman's questions unanswered.

After all, she had arrived at the rendezvous ahead of time, for she had been standing several minutes when St. Michael's chimed the half hour. About her the streets were quiet, and high over her head mellow tones of the old bells ran their double trill and left the air singing. Lissa caught the faintly throbbing note and held it until the last vibrations fluttered out and died. The corner on which the girl was waiting was one of the most beautiful and significant in the old town. Opposite her the church lifted its straight white spire out of the yellow glow of the street lamps into the cool faint glimmer of the early stars. Diagonally across the way the clusters of lamps were aglow on the City Hall steps, with the building darkling above them like frowning brows over watchful eyes. Behind the City Hall lay the dim quietude of the park, with its stained marble busts and shafts ghost-like under the spreading trees.

Under the spell of the familiar beauty the reckless mood that had finally decided Lissa to come commenced to pass. Her gaze followed the pointing finger of the steeple into the vast serenity of the summer night, and she gave an involuntary start. She was standing out at the pavement's edge, at the intersection of the two broad thoroughfares, and now, as she gazed up, she realised that they marked the sky off above her into a gigantic cross, its head and foot pointing north and south and its arms dipping east and west into the two rivers.

A fear that was neither superstition nor religion but a little of both assailed her, making her suddenly long to be safely at home with Mamba. What if she cut Gardinia and her crowd now and ran home? They were late, anyway, and that would give her a good excuse.

Then abruptly the moment of quiet was broken and with it the spell that it had woven upon the girl. Several automobiles approached the corner, sounding their claxons. Down the rails from the north a great double-truck trolley hummed and rattled, then passed with a series of deafening jars over the switch.

Two white men came out of the post office and passed close to her, smoking and talking together. One glanced at her curiously in the half light. They sauntered on, and she heard laughter and, very distinctly, the words "high yellow."

A moment later a dilapidated Ford came to an abrupt and noisy stop before her, and she heard Gardinia's husky, voluptuous voice.

"Here's th' lady friend—all dressed up and bells on, eh, Lissa? Good girl. Meet my friends. This here's Charlie, and that's Slim in the back seat. Boys, this is Lissa. No Miss and Mister in this gang. Hop in there with Slim. He's going to be your feller for to-night. Look him over and see if he ain't got class."

Charlie called "Hello, Lissa" from the driver's seat. Slim jumped out and shook hands. "Glad to know you," he said, and he held the door open for her to get in. Then they were seated. The machine seemed to crouch for a moment, took a spasmodic leap, then settled down into a brisk steady gait.

The couple on the front seat paid no further attention to their companions but sat close together talking in low voices that were absorbed in the rattle of the vehicle.

At first Lissa could think of nothing to say, and Slim seemed to experience the same difficulty, for he sat well over on his side of the car and let the moments pass in silence. When they drove under the arc lights Lissa took advantage of the transient illumination to appraise her partner. He was dark, a full-blooded negro, with a receding forehead, a broad flat nose, and a very large mouth. Once he looked up, met her scrutiny, and broke into a broad, friendly grin. She saw the whiteness of his teeth spring out against the black, and his eyes laughing shyly into her face. She was reassured and began to feel that they would get along together. There was nothing about him to make a girl afraid. Then the lights were behind them, and ahead the road, a broad grey band of concrete, plunged straight out between dense patches of woodland and nebulous distances of open field.

The car, like a wild creature that has broken long captivity, flung the city behind it and leaped for the open. Gardinia's voice came back with the whistling wind to the silent couple behind her.

"Hey, there, you two—what do you think this is—a funeral?

What's the matter with you, Slim, you don't hold that gal in—don't you know she ain't use' to country ridin'?"

Thus encouraged, Slim allowed himself to be bounced over to Lissa's side of the car and put his arm around her shoulder. For a moment the girl's body remained rigid. Then, on another bounce, the man's arm fell lower and closed firmly about her waist. A tremor shook the girl. Then suddenly she relaxed into Slim's arms and closed her eyes.

"Don't you worry," he said in a low husky voice. "Ah ain't goin' to let you get thrown out."

For half an hour the car drove steadily northward; then from the dense shadows of massed live oaks a row of lights leaped out. Charlie jerked the machine hard over. It left the concrete for a rough side road, executed a series of jackrabbit bounds, and brought up short before the door of a dance hall. A rush of talk, laughter, song, and instrument-tuning greeted them, shattering the peace of the night and challenging the new arrivals with a mood of wild gaiety. Slim waited with the girls while Charlie parked the car.

The wide doorway was swarming like a hive; couples came and went between the tawdry brilliance of the room and the piled blackness of night under the live oaks. A group of young bucks lounged near the door, smoking and passing a flask from mouth to mouth.

Charlie rejoined the party just as the music flung its unifying rhythm into the discordant babel. They elbowed their way through the press and entered the hall. The room was a-flutter with tissue-paper streamers of every shade that depended from the rafters and responded with an agitated waving to the sound and motion beneath. There were eight men in the orchestra, and Lissa noted immediately with the colour snobbery of the Broaden set that they were all full-blooded negroes. There were two guitars, two banjos, a fiddle, a cornet, and trombone, and a man with drum and traps. The sound was unlike anything that the girl had ever heard. Strive as she might, she could not recognise the tune. As a matter of fact, it was not an orchestra in a strict interpretation of the term, but merely a collection of eight individuals who had taken some simple melody as a theme and were creating rhythm and harmony around it as they played. Her immediate sensation was one of shock at the crude and almost deafening uproar. Then, as she stood listening, a strange excitement commenced to possess her. Music had never moved her like this before. It had made her cry—and it had shaken her with delight, but this seemed to be breaking something loose deep within her—something that seethed hot through her veins and set her muscles jumping.

The crowd came jamming into the room, black girls with short knappy hair, tall long-limbed negroes from the wharves, sailors from the Navy Yard, dark and heavy, with here and there the pallor and passivity of a Filipino. There were many couples out from town who, like themselves, had the mark of the city on them in their straightened hair and well-made clothes.

Slim caught Lissa closely to him. His shyness had vanished, but to the girl that did not matter, for she was no longer afraid. The music snatched them up, and they were off into the thick of it. It is unlikely that anywhere else in America at that moment there were more and different steps being trod on a dance floor. The old fundamental rhythm of the turkey trot prevailed, but the more sophisticated were dancing a one-step or fox trot. In a corner out of the jam a group of country negroes were dancing singly. The dance was a strange, fascinating, and wildly individual affair. They stood two and two, facing each other, as though dancing in competition rather than together, and the basic step consisted of rising on alternate feet while the free leg was hurled outward and backward, knees touching, and toes turned in, parrot fashion.

Lissa made Slim stop with her to watch, and immediately the desire to dance it possessed her. Slim laughed. "Come along," he urged, pulling at her arm. "That's nothin' but a ole country nigger dance."

She would not listen. Presently she had the step and started in at the edge of the circle. When the music stopped she was angry. "Oh, I almost had it, Slim," she exclaimed. "One more try and I'll get it pat. Why did they have to stop just then?"

Her partner led her out of doors, then slipped his arm around her and guided her toward the automobile. Gardinia and Charlie were there already, and when the four of them were together, Gardinia handed Lissa a flask. "Hit her up, Sister," she invited.

Lissa hesitated. "What's it—whisky?"

"Sure—go ahead, ain't goin' do you no harm."

The girl lifted the flask and took a swallow, with the result that she choked and coughed.

They all burst into laughter.

"My Gawd," Gardinia mocked, "can't you even take a drink o' hooch?"

Lissa snatched the bottle back from Slim. "Can't, eh? I'll show you." She wasn't going to be laughed at by Gardinia, that was certain.

What a night! Life with a red lining. The orchestra was at it again. That new dance. Lissa must master that if she kicked the floor boards loose.

★

During an intermission, when they crowded to the door for air, a wicked-looking stripped Ford, painted scarlet, jerked itself into the light and stopped. Gardinia grabbed Lissa by the arm. "Here's Prince," she cried. "You got to meet him. Hello, Prince, here's a lady friend I want you to know."

The new arrival was evidently a favourite, especially with women, for a number ran forward and crowded about the car. He got languidly out and, with casual greetings to right and left, came forward and joined the girls. They met where the shaft of light from the open door stabbed the darkness and splayed out on the gravel. "Lissa, this is the Prince I been tellin' you about," Gardinia introduced.

"Glad to know you," he said, and took her hand, while he slid his glance over her in deliberate and frank appraisal. Then he raised his eyes to her face, and the grip on her fingers tightened. He gave a low whistle and, still gripping Lissa's hand, addressed Gardinia—"*Some class,* baby; where'd you find her?"

A shudder of repulsion started under the man's hot, moist clasp, flashed up the girl's arm, and communicated itself to her whole being. The man sensed it with evident satisfaction, his loose sensuous lips parted, and he gave a low, confident laugh. He bent forward, and Lissa got an impression of a light muddy complexion, heavy-lidded eyes, and a long scar across the forehead close under the hair. The air was heavy with its warning of danger; she felt her skin creep under it. And yet, in spite of the repulsion that she felt at his touch, there was a compelling power that drew her toward him and made her pulses race. She summoned all her strength and snatched her hand away.

Prince laughed again and turned toward the hall. "Me an' you's goin' to be buddies," he said. "Come on in an' let's have a drink on it."

His glance included Lissa's party in the invitation, and the four of them followed him across the hall to the gaily decorated booth in the corner where soft drinks were being served.

"What'll you take?" he asked largely.

They made it "dopes," and when the glasses stood before them their host produced a silver flask and poured a generous drink in each tumbler.

Charlie exclaimed, "Hot damn! None of dat moonshine rot-gut for Prince. Nuttin' but de bes'."

Lissa noticed that Slim's bashfulness had descended upon him again and that he accepted the drink from Prince with reluctance.

The music crashed out, smiting the air with the flat impact of a blow, causing the fluid in the tumblers to quiver. They emptied their glasses in gulps.

Prince drew his hand across his mouth and said, "All right, girlie, le's go."

Slim seemed to have suffered a sort of paralysis. When Lissa looked toward him, he said nothing, but stood looking at her with wide mournful eyes. Prince put his arm around her, and she looked into his face with a shaken, reckless little laugh. "I'm on," she said, and was snatched from the corner into the maelstrom of the dance floor.

They danced three dances together. Prince looked older than the boys with whom they had come, but he could dance circles around them. Lissa was delighted to find that he was an expert in the step that she had just discovered, and she made him go to a corner near the band and teach it to her.

It was while they were there that the musicians broke into a medley of old jazz tunes, launching from their wild syncopated improvisations into that early ragtime classic of the Johnson brothers, "Under the Bamboo Tree." In Lissa the music ceased to be a thing external, apart. It became a fire in her body taking her suddenly like sheeting flame about a sapling, cutting her off from the others, possessing her, swaying her irresistibly forward toward the players. She did not realise that she was singing until her gaze rested on the face of the leader, and over his fiddle she saw the white flash of his grin and the surprised delight in his eyes. He waved his bow in invitation and called, "Come up, Sistuh. Up here's whar yo' b'longs." Then she was among the swaying bodies, the smashing harmonies of the band. Her muscles twitched to the rhythm, moving her feet and legs in the intricacies of the new dance, her arms were thrown wide with fingers snapping the time. She forgot that there would be a solo in church to-morrow and that her voice needed saving. She remembered nothing except the words and music that came in a rush out of an old forgotten memory, beating out from lungs and throat in a torrent of song.

> "If you lika me lika I lika you,
> An' we lika both the same,
> I'd lika say this very day
> I'd lika change your name . . ."

On the floor couples were still dancing, whirling more wildly under the added excitement of the song. The drive of the music through the girl wrought in her for the first time the almost miraculous duality which is the gift of only the true artist. It seemed mysteriously to divide her into two separate entities, one of which floated over the heads of the dancers through the wide doorway to go blundering inconsequently about among the soft summer stars. This part of her was concerned only with beauty—with far thrilling things—Mamba's love—the harbour at dawn—Battery gardens under summer moons—all of these things it must capture and prison in the music that she was making. The quest seemed suddenly more holy than her prayers. It lifted her to the point of exaltation that trembles on the brink of tears. Then there was the other part of her that followed her gaze here and there across the dance floor, cool, deliberate, detached, arresting first one couple, then another, holding them tranced and gaping where they stood. This Lissa was egotistical, supremely self-confident. "I will make them all stop and listen," it boasted. "I shall possess them all before I let them go. I can. I will." It was the personification of this second self that stood there on the dais, clad in close-fitting red silk, her sinuous body a fluid medium through which the maddening reiteration of the rhythm beat out to the listeners and forced them to respond, her voice with its deep contralto beauty the very spirit of youth, yet shading the edges of laughter with a shadow of a sob.

When the song ended the leader merged it without an appreciable break into "Yip I aidy I ai I ai." The choice was an inspiration. Lissa had them all now. Out under the fluttering paper streamers the crowd stood motionless except for those who, while they held their eyes fixed upon the singer, swayed their bodies unconsciously in unison with her own. She had made good her boast. She had captured the last one. The new song with its devil-may-care note of triumph lifted over the weaving accompaniment of the band and beat against the flimsy walls like a living thing. It said: "You are all mine—mine." It flung it at them arrogantly with a trace of indulgent contempt, then it wavered, softened, and said it again in a torrent of passionate gratitude and love. Her very own—her first audience.

> "Sing of joy, sing of bliss,
> Home was never like this.
> Yip I aidy I ai. . . ."

With an intoxicating thunder of applause sounding in her ears, Lissa stepped down from the platform. Charlie was waiting there for her, and before Prince could reach her side he slipped an arm about her and elbowed a way for her through the stamping, shouting crowd. When they were finally out of doors they were joined by Gardinia, who flung her arms about Lissa in a hug that left her breathless. "Where did you get it, kid?" she asked in wonder.

"Heaven knows! I guess I was as surprised as you."

Gardinia gave her a second embrace, then turning to Charlie dismissed him with: "Run along. I got something to say to this sister."

When he had passed out of earshot she said to the girl: "Look here, bright eyes, you want to watch your step with that feller they call Prince. Did he ask to drive you home?"

"Yes, he did say something about it."

"Well, I hope you told him no. After all, Slim's settin' you up to the party to-night, and he's got some rights coming to him."

"All right," Lissa replied obediently. "I'll turn Prince down."

"An' look here," the big girl said seriously, "don't you go losin' your head over that nigger. He's free with his money, and he's always good for a swell time, but the sky's his limit—watch your step. I ain't so sure you're his sort, anyhow. Now, me—that's a different matter."

Lissa gave a confident laugh. "Don't you let that worry you, Sister," she replied. "I'm a pretty good hand at taking care of myself."

Charlie and Slim came up and joined them.

"All right," Gardinia warned, "just watch your step—that's all."

It was well after midnight when the Ford bounced out onto the concrete road and headed south with the four revellers. Slim sat in his corner glum and silent. He evidently felt that he had been rather hardly used. Lissa made several attempts to draw him out and finally yielded to a growing exasperation. If he thought that she was going to apologise and eat humble pie, he had another think coming. Her anger rose. He ought to thank his stars that she had even gone with him, she, a member of the Reformed Church, a friend of the Broadens. She did not need to worry. There was Prince, now, ready to show her a good time. The premonition of danger that she had felt toward him at first had abated until it had left only an exciting element of mystery and adventure. She smiled at the memory of Gardinia's warning. As if she couldn't take care of herself. No. She was out on her own now, and she didn't have to ask favours of anybody.

When Lissa entered her room she found Mamba sitting just as she had left her; the lamp was turned low, and the old woman was slouched deep in her big chair, her gaze fixed beyond the open window to where the late fragment of a moon was climbing over the housetops. She did not scold as the girl had expected. Instead she turned her eyes, which had a slight film of weariness over them, in mute questioning toward the door.

Lissa exclaimed, "Why, you ought to be ashamed, Grandma, sitting up at this hour. How come you didn't go to bed?"

The old figure drew itself together in the chair and spoke. "Turn up dat lamp so Ah can see yo' an' come here."

Lissa did as she was bidden, and Mamba took her hand and drew her down upon her lap, then peered searchingly into her face.

She said, "Yo' been drinkin', chile."

"Oh, nothing much, Grandma, just a couple."

"Yo' ain't been bad?"

The girl laughed and patted the old face lightly.

"Not on your life, Grandma. You needn't worry about me. I had a swell time dancing, but I'm nobody's fool."

"Well, go 'long to bed, an' in de mornin' yo' got to tell me all 'bout it."

"Sure thing," Lissa replied, "but you mustn't wait up for me like this. You need your sleep, you know. I got to take care of this old lady. I can't get along without her."

She caught the old woman for a moment in her strong young arms, then got to her feet and commenced to undress.

"Ain't no use to say dat, chile," Mamba replied. "When you gone out nights Ah all de time gots a feelin' you might need me, an' Ah ain't likes to take off my clo'es till yo' gets back home."

★

Lissa brought Gardinia to meet Mamba with some trepidation. She feared the impression that her now constant companion would make on the astute old woman. She thought that her grandmother would be easier in her mind if she had only her account of the dances and late motor rides that were becoming more and more frequent as the summer passed.

But one Sunday after morning service the girls were walking together on the Battery and Gardinia came as far as the gate of the Atkinson garden. Suddenly she was seized by one of her characteristic impulses.

"Say," she exclaimed, "I believe I'll go in and meet that old grandma of yours you're always talking about. She must be a rare old dame. I want to know her."

There was nothing to be done but to accede, and after an imperceptible moment of hesitation Lissa said, "Sure, come on in. I reckon she's in the room now."

Gardinia's glance was busy as they passed through the well-kept garden and to the neat two-storied building in the rear, with the garage below, and a glimpse of clean white curtains showing in the windows above.

"Pretty swell dump," she admired. "Pretty soft thing you've got here, I'll say."

"Grandma," Lissa said on entering the room, "this is my friend Gardinia; she wanted to meet you, so I brought her in."

Mamba came forward and took the younger woman's hand. From their network of wrinkles the old eyes looked searchingly into her face. Then she smiled, showing her big white teeth.

"The kid's been telling me so much about you," Gardinia explained, "that I just wanted to come in and get acquainted. Guess you think I'm a funny sort of friend for that highbrow gal of yours, eh?"

Mamba murmured something about being glad to meet her.

But as is so often the case with first remarks, her words meant little or nothing, serving merely as a screen from behind which each of the women was exploring for the real ego that lay secreted behind words, eyes, lips.

Lissa, watching closely, realised that they liked each other. That in spite of the differences of age and outlook there was a hidden bond of intimacy to which they both responded. It mystified her. She was still too unknowing to recognise it as the sisterhood of the unchaste. It was something that needed no words. There it was in each. In Mamba a thin echo from an incredibly vanished past; in the girl, only yesterday, and perhaps again to-morrow, but across the years it sent its spark of understanding and was tacitly accepted by each. Strange to say, it was not prejudicial. It was a phase of their world, and it was a phase that belonged to the generous, the kind, as well as to the penny-grabbing, the depraved.

Gardinia burst through the reserve that she had been wearing like a strait-jacket. She laughed heartily, her eyes looking into the old woman's and sparkling mischievously.

"I bet you were a gay one yourself once," she said. "I'll bet you knew what it was like to hit the ceiling on a big night—eh, Mauma?"

Lissa was shocked. Mamba had taught her to treat age with great respect. But to her amazement she saw that Mamba was pleased.

She answered with her surprisingly young, vital laugh:

"T'ings was diff'ent in dem days, an' if Ah is broke loose den dere ain't nobody libin' to tell on me now. But nowadays gals gots to behabe."

"Sure," Gardinia agreed, as she took a seat and let her admiring gaze take in the cozy and tastefully furnished room, with the sunny garden showing beyond the window. "Sure, and don't you worry about Lissa. If she'll just listen to me she'll have a good time and she won't get into no trouble."

She looked around for her friend, but Lissa had gone into the next room to change from her Sunday dress. At the same moment Mamba also noticed that they were alone and immediately took advantage of the opportunity.

"Tell me," she begged in a lowered voice, "who dis yaller nigger Lissa goin' roun' wid? She won't tell me nuttin' 'bout um, but Ah seen um t'other day when he come by for she, an' Ah wouldn't trus' um far as Ah could t'row um."

Gardinia said, "Prince ain't so bad. He's too mashed on himself to last long with anybody else. But he flings the long green high and far, and he'll show her a good time."

Mamba leaned forward and said confidentially, "Ah 'fraid for my gal. She ain't like yo' an' me, Sistuh—she ain't seen nuttin' ob mens, an' dat yaller nigger gots woman-chaser wrote all ober um."

"Don't you worry, Mauma," Gardinia said reassuringly, "the first thing I did was to put Lissa wise, and besides, she's one of them cool sisters. Ain't no danger of her losing her head."

"Well, all Ah asks is dat yo' keep an eye on she for me, an' ef trouble breaks any time let me know. Ah is ole but Ah ain't no fool at takin' care ob my chillun."

"That's right, old lady, I just bet you ain't no fool. But there ain't goin' be no trouble."

Lissa came in then, and the three chatted for a few moments. Then Gardinia took her departure.

"Dat's a good gal yo' gots fuh friend," Mamba said when the girl had gone. And Lissa stood wondering just what the definition for good could be in Mamba's lexicon.

*

Labor Day—steaming and hot, with an opaque sky and a red sun burning through it. Underfoot the pavements streaming with

condensed moisture and flinging back reflections of houses, shop
windows, sky, in colours soft and wonderful to see. Summer's fag
end, with its spent ardours behind it, and autumn around the next
corner. And for to-day nothing for the negroes to do but to be
glad, to leave the wharves, the bakeries, the buildings of the houses,
the stoking of furnaces, and tell the world how good a thing it is
to be alive, to have laboured, and now to claim a respite.

September weather.

Down in the white residential streets, block after block of closed
mansions sleeping away the hot hours in gardens where nature spent
her beauty with open hands, and still had more each day to fling
over deserted piazzas in a foam of climbing roses, to pour in pools
of oleander bloom between moss-hung live oaks. On King Street
the fashionable stores dozing behind their drawn blinds. Here was
a town that the winter tourist would not recognise, a town claimed
for the day by its darker half. Its pavements swarming with noisy
ragamuffin black children watching eagerly for the parade. Bands
passing across street ends blaring for a moment, then gone. Down
on Broad Street the massed trombones and horns of the Jenkins
orphanage, assailing the offices of the morning *News and Courier*
with a blast of good will that temporarily paralysed the editorial
brains within and traffic without. The parade: all of the unions in
line. The dignity of labour might be well enough for the white
brotherhoods, but among the negroes the pompous old institution
was finding it difficult to maintain its pose. Hand saws, carried
over shoulders, fluttered incongruously with coloured ribbons, and
hammers were wearing gaudy streamers. The bakers, attired in
white aprons and starched chef's caps, bore aloft a gigantic loaf
of bread that was dressed for Mardi Gras. Bands kept the steamy
air vibrating, and the crowds sweated and cheered with complete
abandon. The afternoon would see an exodus to all of the negro
parks, and along the wharves several dilapidated excursion steamers

waited in nervous and asthmatic expectancy for their gala freight.

Lissa was awakened early by the laughter and talk in the street. For a while she lay luxuriously in her bed and through the morning haze watched pigeons strut and gossip on the wet purple of a slate roof. How different the day was from the usual workdays. She felt a pleasurable excitement in the air. Everybody would be having fun to-day—cutting loose—forgetting troubles—just living.

Mamba lay in her bed across the clean airy room with heavy sleep still upon her. With her eyes closed and her alert spirit off guard, how different, how shrunken and old, she seemed. Why, she wasn't Mamba at all. Lissa wouldn't look at her like this. It made her feel suddenly alone and unprotected—out of key with the day. Soon that strange, quiet figure would open its eyes again, and then the person Lissa knew would return, watchful and sure, to see that nothing could harm her.

The girl stretched lazily, got out of bed, and went to the window. Outside the lawn lay wet and sweet with dew. The sunlight was a faint pink now, and the shadows purple. It was going to be a hot day, a mild sea air moved the curtains and fanned her skin through her sheer nightdress. She conquered a sudden impulse to strip off the garment and yield her body to its seductiveness: to let its soft fingers stroke her breasts and follow the curves of hip and thigh. No, Mamba wouldn't like that. It was the sort of thing that she mustn't do.

Well, she had a lot to be thankful for, more than most of the girls she knew. The Atkinsons were away at Flat Rock cooling their heels in the mountains for the month and had left Mamba to look after the house. It was almost like their own now, with the kitchen to prepare their meals in, and the lovely things in the big dim rooms to be looked at and enjoyed at leisure.

She had a full day ahead of her. Dinner at two with the Broadens, and after dinner the other members of the Club would come in for some music. Then at night a party up the road with

Prince. They would dance that exciting dance together. Funny—that story she heard, that they were taking it up now in New York—calling it the Charleston. White folks going wild over a black folks' dance. Well, she for one could understand that. Then home when the night was late and cool—splitting the air in Prince's red racer—"Life," as Gardinia would say, "with a red lining." But she mustn't talk too much about that. Mamba had a way of worrying when she went to a dance, and she didn't want to fret her.

And yet, for all of its bright prospects, when Lissa came in to supper she had the feeling that, so far, at any rate, the day had been disappointing. She had set out early for her dinner engagement, planning a long leisurely walk through the more shady of the streets, but at the intersection of one of the main thoroughfares she had run foul of the parade. At first she was annoyed. The jostling crowds of negroes, the impact of small black, sweating, bodies offended her senses. Why couldn't they enjoy themselves quietly and decently, anyway—why did they have to be so dirty. But it was impossible to cross the street, and she was forced to be an onlooker. She supposed, after all, that people had a right to enjoy themselves in their own way. But what a racket they made. The carpenters passed, with their absurd ribbons fluttering from work-scarred tools, grinning and calling to friends in the crowd. Then a band went crashing by, giving her a funny twist inside and plucking at the muscles of her legs and feet. She started to mark time and unconsciously to drift in unison with the crowd. When the masons came abreast of her she looked up and met the eyes of a bright-faced young negro. He had a large trowel in one hand and a small one in the other, and he was beating time in rhythm with the band. "Hello dere, Sistuh," he called with a grin. There was something infectious about that grin with its gleaming teeth and full dark lips. She laughed back with sudden camaraderie, "Hello yourself!"

He stopped for a second before her and said boldly: "What boat

yo' goin' on dis ebenin'? De *Planter*, de *Pilot Boy*? Le's make it
de same."

Still laughing, she shook her head, and the marchers swept him
away while he looked back with a rueful glance.

She came to herself and glanced around sharply. Had any one
she knew seen her? But what fun they did have! A sudden pang
of envy assailed her. She wrenched herself out of their holiday
mood and stemmed the tide in the direction of the Broaden home.

Later, all through the eminently polite conversations, the excel-
lently rendered music of the club, the artistic pronouncements of
North, she kept seeing the face of the young mason, and pictur-
ing him dancing on the deck of the excursion boat—eating watermelon and spitting seeds over the rail, grinning boldly at the girls.
"Hello dere, Sistuh, what boat yo' goin' on dis ebenin'?" and his
comical, rueful face as he passed out of sight.

*

During supper Lissa was silent and preoccupied. Mamba studied
her closely with anxiety showing in her keen old eyes. At last she
asked, "Yo' goin' out wid dat nigger Prince to-night, chile?"

"Yes, Grandma."

"How come yo' nebber bring him to meet me like yo' done
promise long ago?"

"Oh, that's so—you did ask me to, 'way back in July. I've been
meaning to bring him, but I keep forgetting."

Mamba spoke sadly: "Yo' ain't forget, chile. Ah ask yo' in July,
an' Ah ask yo' in August—an' yo' ain't de forgettin' kin'. Why yo'
don't want fo' me to see um?"

Lissa looked up into the old woman's face. "All right, Grandma," she answered, "since you put it that way, it's because you
wouldn't like him and he wouldn't like you. He's different. He's

new time—you're old time. You'd be thinking things about him that aren't so. I've known him three months now—I know just where he begins and just where he leaves off. We had a good talking out, and since then we haven't had any fooling—just a good time—dancing, riding in his car—that's all."

"Ah saw um at de gate once," Mamba told her. "It been half daak, but Ah could see woman-chaser writ all over um. Ah ain't want yo' fuh know dem kin'."

The girl sprang up impulsively, ran around the table, flung herself into Mamba's lap, and gave her a hug.

"Oh, quit worryin', Grandma," she begged. "I'm just as hard as nails, I tell you. I never saw a man yet who could keep me from coming back home to you. But I'm not an old woman—I've got to play a little bit—I've got to dance and cut loose now and then, and Prince is the swellest sport between Savannah and Norfolk—and he sure can show a girl a time. Now, you leave him to me."

Mamba said nothing more then, only patting the head that was buried against her breast, and swaying a little in her chair, as though she were rocking a small child in her arms. But an hour later, when Lissa left the room attired in her red party frock, the old woman lock-stepped her down the stairs and out to the car that stood at the curb beyond the Atkinsons' garden. She was going to have a look for herself.

What she saw was a small evil-looking scarlet roadster with two low seats side by side, and in one of them, with his legs extended indolently before him, a man who looked as though he had lived about forty years and had lived them hard. In the faint glow of a street lamp she could see that there were pouches under his eyes. The eyes were shadowed beneath the visor of a checked cap where they could tell no secrets, but when he turned toward Mamba she felt that they were laughing at her from their safe retreat.

Lissa must have sensed it too, for her body stiffened, and she pressed defensively against the old woman.

Mamba and Prince looked at each other for a moment of silence, then Mamba said: "Yo' been seein' a lot ob my gal."

She was answered by a low confident laugh, and: "A lot's a big word, ole lady. Ah ain't seen nuttin' of her yet."

That the sinister implication of the reply was not lost on Mamba was evidenced by a tremor of the hand that she closed upon the side of the car as she leaned over and spoke directly into his face.

"Ah ain't expectin' no hahm to come to she, an' Ah ain't tryin' to baby my gal. Ah trus' she anywhere wid anybody any time. But when she go away from here wid yo', yo's 'sponsible for she. Ef enyt'ing happen to she yo' gots me—Mamba—to settle wid. Yo' gets dat?"

The man looked her up and down. It was not in him to feel the spiritual power that animated the fragile old creature who hung to the side of his car. He could only see a rather comic little figure with great false teeth gleaming in the lamplight against the black of her face, and a hand that trembled absurdly and impotently on his car. He laughed at her frankly, throwing his head back so that she saw the insolent challenge in his eyes, and a livid scar that crossed his forehead like a long centipede.

Lissa put her arm around the old woman and drew her close to her side. "Here, cut that out," she cried sharply to the man. "Nobody's going to laugh at Grandma and take me out—you can just get that straight now."

Prince's change of front was almost comical in its suddenness.

"Me laugh at de ole lady?—Honey, yo' don't know me. Ah jes laugh because she think anything can happen while Ah takin' care of yo'."

He reached over and patted Mamba's hand reassuringly. "Don't yo' worry, Gran'ma. Make your min' easy. Your gal ain't never been so well fix' befo'."

During the brief parley the engine had been running slowly. Now he advanced the accelerator, and the sound swelled suddenly and ominously in Mamba's ears.

"Get in, Lissa," he called. "We's late enough already."

But there was no disguising the fact that he had laughed at Mamba. He had not supposed that Lissa would care, and he had taken the chance. Now the girl stood with her arm tight about the old woman and hesitated, looking at him with anger and distrust in her eyes. For a moment it seemed as though she would let him drive away alone. But she had longed so for the night to come. The mason in the parade that morning had started a hunger in her for youth that could forget itself and send worries flying—and she had been such a lady all afternoon—and there, half an hour away, were waiting music—dancing—throbbing young bodies—"Life with a red lining."

She caught Mamba to her, half smothered her with kisses, and sprang into the machine beside Prince. There was a hoarse triumphant cry of metal as the gears meshed, and the red car lunged northward.

Mamba stood and watched it go, first a crimson blotch that came and went as it passed under successive arc lights, then only a tiny red spark that zigzagged around other cars and went out slowly like a star in blowing smoke.

★

Mamba sat at the open window. There was a tensity about her attitude as though she were waiting by prearrangement for a certain occurrence and that she was unsure only of the hour. St. Michael's chimes had spoken to her every quarter hour, and each time at the first mellow note she had sat forward, counted with an inaudible movement of the lips, then, in the ensuing silence, let herself go slowly back in her chair to wait for the next. She was fully clad, even to the sedate black straw bonnet which was an emblem of respectability without which she was never seen upon the street.

Midnight had passed, heavy-footed and weary, then, almost staccato by comparison, came the single clear note announcing the new day.

A ramshackle automobile rattled noisily up the quiet street and stopped with a sigh before the Atkinsons' gate. At the same moment that Mamba's form strained from her window, Gardinia Whitmore arrived breathless on the grass below.

"Lissa home yet?" she asked.

Mamba disappeared immediately and a moment later stood beside the young woman, her fingers closed in a grip that was almost painful about Gardinia's arm.

"No," she said briefly; then: "Ah been waitin' fer yo' to come fo' me. Whar yo' t'ink she gone?"

Gardinia's voice was edged with hysteria. She had been drinking, and exhaled an effluvium of corn whisky.

"I swear to Gawd I didn't have nothin' to do with it, Gran'ma," she began. "I did just like I promised, I kept an eye on her, but there was something about that licker of Prince's. It knocked me out, an' it knocked out Slim, an' we ain't no babies. When I come 'round, the first thing I looked for was Lissa and Prince, and when I ain't seen them I made Slim burn it down here to you, just like I promised."

Mamba's voice came urgent, steadying: "Where dat nigger Prince lib? Tell me all yo' know 'bout um, gal."

"Nobody don't know much about him, and he's such a liar, you can't count on what he says about himself. All I know is he lives across the bridge. He says he runs a big truck farm and a lot of stores over there."

"What he name? He mus' hab more ob a name dan jus' Prince."

Gardinia stood silent, trying to remember. Then she called Slim. With maddening deliberation he detached himself from the car and slouched indolently forward.

"What's Prince's real name?" the girl demanded.

The man stood shuffling one foot backward and forward on the grass, his mouth sagging open, while he pursued the glimmer of a memory through the labyrinth of his befuddled brain. At last he announced, "Ah got it. Ah done heard some of the mens call him Bluton—Gilly Bluton."

The word shocked Mamba into instant activity. She spun around and re-entered the house, emerging a moment later with a big old-fashioned pocketbook in her hand. She took each of the young people by an arm and propelled them toward the gate, her body rocking with her speed and the intensity of her purpose. At the car she stuffed a bill into Slim's hand. "Ober de bridge, boy," she ordered, "an' fuh Gawd' sake hurry."

Then, while he was obediently cranking the car, she turned and laid a hand on Gardinia's shoulder. "Go home an' sleep it off, gal," she said in a gentle voice. "Yo' ain't a bad gal, an' yo' done what yo' can."

Slim sat silent, giving his whole attention to the task of getting the utmost out of his dilapidated machine. Mamba's thoughts wrestled with the problem that confronted her. It was useless to plan. She would have to depend on Hagar, who knew the ground. But she had an almost superstitious fear of the consequences that might result from such a dependence. Always it had been the well-meant bungling of her great awkward daughter that had precipitated trouble. She remembered vividly the summer dawn when Hagar had sent for her to come to the East Bay tenement after she had jeopardised all of her hopes for Lissa by rescuing Bluton and bringing him to the city to be found and cared for by the police. The malign and ironical fate that prompted Hagar's good impulses had never played a more cruel joke on her than that. She had risked everything to save Bluton—for what? To attempt the ruin of her own daughter. The thought stabbed the old woman like a blade, and she broke her silence, urging Slim to greater speed.

It must have been between two and three o'clock when Mamba reached the cabin in which Hagar lived with old Vina. Overhead the great void of sky was filled with drifting mist, dark to the east, and showing a luminous area over the western treetops where the moon was tilting toward the horizon. In the faint light the cabin had a ghostly, deserted look. Mamba sprang from the car, and knocked upon the door, calling urgently, "Hagar—Hagar!"

Almost instantly the door was opened, and the woman stood in her white nightdress, looming huge against the dark.

"Lissa's ober here with dat damn' nigger Bluton," Mamba shot at her; then she strove by repetition to drive the idea into the sleep-dulled brain. "Here—here—do yo' unnerstan'?—wid Bluton."

"Can't be, Ma—not Lissa."

"Ah tell yo' she is. We got to find her quick. Where'd he take her? Yo' knows him, yo' know his ways wid women."

Hagar was awake now, and she responded to Mamba's old power over her. It was almost as though the older brain had assumed control of nerve and muscle in the big body, telling them what to do. Hagar reached into the room and caught up a cloak that she flung over her nightdress; then, with Mamba, she sprang for the car.

*

Over the uneven road the machine bounded, plunging through tunnels of blackness under live-oak avenues, racing between broom-straw fields under a wide emptiness of sky. And always Hagar, sitting on the rear seat and leaning forward with her face at Slim's shoulder, told him which turnings to take. About them the night, under its shroud of mist, lay as quiet, as indifferent to human urgency, as death. The steady pulsing of the motor and the rattle of the vehicle served only to accentuate the awful loneliness of the country.

They rocketed past the huddled cabins of a settlement and struck a narrow dirt road that led out through a stand of yellow pine toward the swamp that lay black and solid against the horizon. Hagar's fingers clamped down on Slim's shoulder.

"Stop," she whispered.

Under her hand the machine seemed to die in midair, gasping, and settling suddenly to earth. The trees that had been rushing past them stopped in their tracks, crowded close, and looked down on the three intruders.

"We got to get out here an' walk," Hagar said. "Come on, we ain't got no time to lose now."

But the man did not leave his seat. Mamba turned back and asked why he waited.

He settled forward in the seat, his body relaxed, his head propped against the back.

"Nuttin' doin', Gran'ma," he drawled. "Ah's a hired driver. Ah ain't got nuttin' against Prince. Ah ain't see nuttin'. Ah ain't hear nuttin'. When yo's ready to go home, yo' can wake me up."

But now the initiative had passed to Hagar. She caught Mamba by the arm and urged. "Come on, Ma, we ain't need no man to help."

They would soon be there now, Hagar explained as she hurried the old woman forward. This was the place where Bluton ran his crap game. A little farther, at the swamp's edge, they would find the cabin. Then they were upon it. There was a small opening in the trees, and through it the sky let down a dim grey light. The cabin was a black cube with one candlelit window. Before the door in spidery outline stood the red racer.

Not until the women were at the door did they hear the first sound. Lissa's voice in a sort of desperate monotony: "Not that, Prince—not that—not that."

Hagar kicked the door open, and they entered together. Lissa was seated on the floor with her back to the wall, her knees drawn up, and her chin on them. Her arms were locked about her legs below the knees. The candlelight flickered upon the golden brown of her shoulder and upper arm where her dress had been torn. Bluton was hanging over her in a threatening attitude.

At the entrance of the women both faces were flung toward the door.

With a shrill cry Lissa was up and in Mamba's arms. Between them and Prince stood Hagar, her feet planted wide apart. Her arms held akimbo under the full coat exaggerated her already massive bulk to a preposterous breadth, and her head, held low and thrust menacingly forward, was scarcely visible to the women who stood in the shadows behind her. No word had been spoken. There had been no sound except Lissa's cry, and the waiting silence of the night had seemed to suck the shrill note from her lips and leave the four occupants of the room suspended as though in a vacuum. From the swamp came the demoniac scream of a cat— a struggle—a strangling death wail—and again silence. A subtle change became manifest in the appearance of the girl. She ceased trembling. Her form drew to its full height. A ripple of tautened muscle stirred under the smooth bronze of her skin where the shoulder rose above her tattered clothing. Then in a flash she was out of Mamba's arms, past the gigantic form of her mother, and upon the cowering man. Words that rose to her lips were broken there into strange, savage utterance unintelligible as speech, but more eloquent—more terrifying. One slender hand clawed downward and four livid streaks followed the flensing nails from forehead to chin. Hagar reached out an arm and caught the girl in its curve, pressed her to her side for a moment, then passed her back to Mamba.

As suddenly as it had come, the girl's passion left her. Her head went down on the old shoulder. "Oh, Grandma, he tried to—he tried to——" and her voice broke into uncontrollable sobbing.

The deep compassionate voice soothed her: "Ah know, chile, Ah know—but dat all done now, yo' wid Mamba now." She drew the shaking girl from the room and into the heavy stillness of the night. There was something terribly complete about those two, about their entire sufficiency to each other. The enfolding devotion of the old woman covering the girl and isolating her from every evil, every alien touch—Mamba and Lissa—no one else.

Hagar stood for a moment like one who has been blinded by sudden intense light. Her eyes still held the image, quiveringly alive, of the splendid thing that was her child. The dream pattern that she had treasured of the slender little girl was shattered, and as yet she could not take in this new and marvellous being. She was dizzy from the revelation. She was also vaguely conscious of a loneliness deeper than any that had gone before.

The chaos of her mind was shot through by an instinctive warning. Suddenly her brain cleared, her body tensed. She spun around and faced Bluton. The naked fear in his face gave her an exquisite pang. Something deep and elemental broke free inside of her. She stood watching him, catlike, as he moved along the wall in the direction of the crap table which stood at the farther end of the room.

She knew what he wanted now. She let him get almost to the drawer with its brass knobs, her eyes and his locked all the time. She saw his face change, glimmer with hope, relief. Then she was before him, with the table at her back. As he had advanced slowly, with his studied attempt at casualness, so now he retreated before her, while she closed the distance between them. It was like some ghastly rehearsal, carried out with utter absorption, for some momentous event that was set for the future. It was so deliberate, so mechanical in its studied advance and retreat. Then at last the wall was against the man's shoulder blades.

The touch of the unyielding timber seemed to turn his limbs to water. His knees gave, and he had difficulty propping his body upright. He raised his arms before his face in a weak defensive gesture.

Hagar said, "Yo' rattlesnake! Yo' would be dead now 'cept fuh me—an' now—my own gal Lissa——" Then, after a pause, "*You!*"

The man found voice in a screech. It was so weak that it scarcely filled the little room—at its peak it plunged suddenly into silence.

★

Mamba wanted to be going. She wanted to get Lissa away from that horrible place, back into the ordered peace of streets and houses. But Hagar did not come. Why couldn't the woman hurry and let them get to the automobile and away? She put the girl, who was quiet at last, out of her arms and started back to the shack. The door was open, and the draught played with the candle flame, peopling the room with lurching shadows and half lights.

The old woman entered, with Lissa peering fearfully over her shoulder. Hagar stood with her back to them, her arms hanging straight and long at her sides, her bullet head thrust forward. Her huge shoulders flung a black arch of shadow over half of the wall before her. Bluton lay in a huddle at her feet. His head was twisted at a preposterous angle. The yellow of his face had gone a dark purple, and the candle flame was flung back in two cold high lights from his wide, unblinking eyes.

Lissa screamed. Hagar turned heavily in her tracks and looked at them dully from raised eyes under lowered brows.

Mamba advanced toward her. In her extremity her voice seemed heavy with hatred for her big bungling daughter.

"Yo' damned fool," she said. "See what yo' done now, eberybody at dat dance know Lissa been wid Prince. People seen me come out here. Ah ought to ha' known if Ah turned my back on yo', yo'd play hell——"

Hagar buried her face in the crook of an arm and commenced to sob. "Oh, Gawd, Ma, Ah ain't stop to t'ink. Ah only know he been hurt Lissa."

Mamba wasted no sentimental pity on the broken thing upon the floor. Her whole being was focussed on the staggering predicament that confronted her.

"Get outside," she ordered. "Ah got to t'ink." She blew out the candle and followed them into the open, thinking aloud: "Ah got to sen' Lissa away quick, an' she got to go far. But Ah can't let she go alone, an' she ain't got no frien' to go to."

Between broken sobs Hagar said surprisingly, "Ah got a frien'."

Mamba looked at her skeptically. "Yo' has? Where?"

"Ah got a frien' what's a Reverent, an' he lib in Noo Yo'k."

"Yo' know whar he house is?"

Hagar was getting herself in hand now and had stopped crying. "Ah got it writ in a book he gib me. He a good man—yo' needn't be 'fraid to sen' Lissa to he."

"Oh, he dat Yankee nigger what use' to be down here?"

Hagar nodded assent.

"Come, den," Mamba commanded. "We ain't got no time to lose."

They waked Slim, who grinned sleepily and leered when he saw the girl, and started him back to the village. When they reached Hagar's cabin she ran inside and returned in a moment with a small black book in her hand. She pressed it on Mamba, who had followed her to the door.

"De name an' number is writ inside," she said. "Lissa can tell he dat she Baxter gal—an' to 'member what he say 'bout always bein' my frien'."

Then Mamba handed Hagar a ten-dollar bill from her pocket-book and gave her instructions: "Listen! Ah been t'inkin' hard. Now yo' hit it out an' hide. Dat's bad, but if yo' stay roun' here, you'll be gibbin' yo'self away by mornin'; so dere ain't nuttin' fo' it. If Baggart catch yo', keep yo' mout' shet. Don't say so much as yes or no 'til Ah sen' my boss or Mr. Saint to talk for yo'. Ef yo' open dat fool mout' ob yourn, nottin' Ah can do'll sabe Lissa. Now you unnerstan'?"

Full of her plan-making, Mamba turned to leave her daughter. She felt a gentle tug at her sleeve and faced Hagar again, impatient at the delay.

"Well," she snapped, "what yo' want now?"

Hagar made one of her gauche childish gestures toward the automobile. "She wouldn't care so much—ef Ah go an' tell she good-bye?"

Mamba caught her breath sharply, and suddenly she was no longer merely the fierce intelligence that drove that inarticulate, powerful machine in the service of the grandchild, but Hagar's own mother, feeling her child's loneliness and sorrow in her own spirit.

She took one of the big, beautifully made hands and drew Hagar forward, speaking gently as they plodded through the heavy white sand: "Ah sorry, Daughter, Ah mighty sorry—Ah get t'inkin' so hahd Ah fuhget. Ah say hahd t'ings Ah ain't mean. It ain't fuh me—Ah jes study all de time 'bout dat gal, an' my mind seem like it dry up on odder t'ing."

Hagar stopped beside the car. The girl sitting alone on the rear seat looked up, and the eyes of the two met. For a moment they stood so in a silence that was eloquent with emotions that speech could only have cheapened and tarnished. So long since the cord had been severed. Centuries lay between them now—and yet, in that fractional part of a minute life beat out again from the heart of the big black woman, throbbed in her child, and coursed refluent and warm back through her own being. Hagar lifted one of Lissa's hands and humbly, yet with a certain possessive pride, kissed it upon the open palm. But in a sudden tumult of emotion the girl snatched her hand away, flung her arms around her mother's neck, and kissed her again and again.

The car gave a warning shudder, and the women separated. Hagar said, "Good-bye, chile. Don't be 'fraid. Nuttin' goin' hahm yo'." And the next moment they were gone among the mists and shadows.

★

Saint Wentworth sat in the lobby of the Pennsylvania Hotel and impatiently watched the hands of a clock that seemed to have been stricken with creeping paralysis. At noon he was to meet Valerie over on the Avenue and select the ring. It was a terribly complicated business, getting married in New York. Saturday they had got the license. Simple enough, he had been told—a few minutes at the Municipal Building—that was all. They had gone together, blinded by a new glamour in the air, and feeling themselves marked for public notice by the magnitude and unusual nature of the step that they contemplated. But upon their arrival at the vast downtown structure, they had been both reassured and chagrined to find themselves in a queue half a block long, sandwiched between a frankly infatuated negro couple and a pair who made love in foreign liquid syllables. It was odd how many people had the same idea. Then there was the big room with long tables where couples sat, while Eros, in the guise of an officious elderly man, leaned between them and explained in lucid and complete detail the meaning of certain perfectly obvious and embarrassingly personal questions. Saint, very red, tried to forestall him by explaining that they both understood. It was no use. The man was filled with the zeal of a public servant who glories in doing well and conspicuously work that occasions no effort.

And now to-day there were more details—more complications. The minister had to be seen again, and forms prepared. Saint had telegraphed home for a copy of his birth certificate and had not received a reply. It seemed that you could not be married in New York without documentary evidence that you had been born. The fact that you could be seen, touched, even separated from a fee, were inconclusive evidences of existence. Only eleven-twenty. No use to start yet and have to cool his heels on the Avenue.

His thoughts drifted to another matter.

He was brought to earth by the sound of his own name droned in a loud monotonous voice. Good: that would be the wire about the certificate. He signalled the boy and tore open the envelope. The telegram was from his mother. It said:

Mamba's granddaughter Lissa in trouble arrives New York noon train. Mamba begs you to meet and assist her.

Good God: Couldn't he even be safe from the old responsibilities here, and at the one time in life when a man should be free? And Val—just about their biggest moment—buying the ring—then blissful hours at the stores and decorators, planning for the new furnishings. And now at the exact hour when she would be awaiting him he was expected to respond to this unreasonable and insane summons. Well, he'd be damned if he would. Mamba, yes—but not to the third generation.

Perhaps he could still catch Val by 'phone and postpone the engagement. But why think of that when he had decided against going? He tore the yellow slip, balled it up, and volleyed it at a waste-paper basket. Then he went through an instinctive hand-washing gesture. Well, that was that.

He got up and strode restlessly about the vast lobby. When he came to a standstill he found to his dismay and anger that he had paused before a telephone booth. "Go to hell!" he apostrophised it fiercely under his breath, and turned away. But a power that he was at a loss to explain kept dragging him back, filling him with a deep and inexplicable misery as long as he moved away. Mamba out of the long past with the funny string-wrapped hair, the solitary fang—her savagery—her understanding tenderness. Mamba with her one idea and her everlasting persistence. What did she care if it upset his plans?—Lissa—Lissa! He was reminded of the time she had made him take Hagar in at the mines. Would he never be free of Mamba's daughters? What was there about her that could hound a man across the miles and make him feel like a cur until he did her bidding? A comical old negress a thousand miles away, and yet, somehow, he felt that he dare not go back and meet her eyes unless he had responded to her summons for help.

He found himself calling a familiar number. Valerie's voice—even over the 'phone, that dewy early morning quality that made his heart hang a beat. Good God! he hadn't thought yet what to say. How could he put it?

"Val, I'm desolated, broken-hearted. Promise you'll forgive me for what I am going to say. No. Not that—not that—I am sorry I scared you. It's that I can't meet you at noon. There's something else I have to do. . . . Well, it's awfully hard to explain over the 'phone. There's a girl coming up from Charleston I've got to go and meet. . . . Mamba's granddaughter Lissa. You remember her, don't you? . . . Yes, she's in some sort of trouble, and Mamba has gotten Mother to telegraph asking me to meet her at the noon train. . . . Jove, you're a dear. Three o'clock, then—at Tiffany's. You're an angel, Val."

Wentworth did not at once recognise his protégée when she came up the stair from the lower level in the stream of passengers. He had been looking for the girl whom he remembered vaguely as being slender and pretty with eyes like those of Mamba and Hagar, and who, alas, would now be in trouble. It was not until he could have touched her with his hand that he recognised her. Taken from her familiar matrix and placed before Saint against the novel setting of the vast station, she stood out for the first time, not as Mamba's grandchild to be taken as a matter of course, but as Lissa Atkinson, with an individuality of her own. Wentworth was startled. It was as though he saw her for the first time.

She was clad in a modish tailored suit of dark blue with a flash of bright embroidery on collar and cuffs, and carried a small blue silk umbrella suspended from her wrist by a loop. Wentworth's glance took in the slender, superbly carried figure and the expressive face with its small full-lipped mouth and Mamba's eyes.

She met his gaze and flashed him a look of surprised, almost incredulous, recognition. "Why, Mr. Saint!" she exclaimed. "What on earth are you doing here?"

"Hello, Lissa," he answered. "Didn't you know that Mamba sent me a message to meet you and help you get settled?"

"Why, no. You see I left in a hurry. She must have heard of your being here after she told me good-bye. That's just like Grandma. She thinks of everything."

The girl's self-possession was colossal, almost disconcerting. Saint took her small valise. There was something at once flattering and embarrassing about the unquestioning way that she put herself in his hands.

They stood under the vast dome, with scurrying humanity brushing past them, and Wentworth wondered what to do next.

"Have you any place to go?" he asked.

Lissa opened her hand bag and produced a Book of Common Prayer. Then she opened it at the flyleaf and presented it to Saint. He studied the inscription for a moment. Of course—the Reverend Thomas Grayson. In his mind's eye arose a picture of a broad imaginative face with heavy earnestness of purpose.

"What luck!" he exclaimed, his expression clearing. "We'll hop in a taxi and go right up."

Safely in the cab, which was threading its way toward Harlem, Wentworth was free to give his whole attention to the problem of his travelling companion.

"What's the trouble, Lissa?" he asked.

She sat back in her corner and with that complete faith in his willingness to assume her responsibilities that had embarrassed him in the station, told him simply and with complete self-possession what had occurred.

When she had finished he gave a low expressive whistle.

"Well, I must say," he commented, "you don't seem to be afraid of the consequences as far as you are concerned."

"I am not," she replied confidently. "Grandma and Mamma'll fix it at home; there's nothing they can't fix. And I have you to look after me here."

This alarming surrender to his care provoked a very pertinent question.

"How are you fixed for money?" he asked bluntly.

She opened her handbag and gave him a roll of bills and a pass book on a Charleston bank. He counted the money—three hundred dollars. Then he opened the pass book. It showed an account in the name of Lissa Atkinson that had been opened nineteen years previously. He spun the pages that exhibited columns of deposits of one dollar—sometimes two—here and there a week was skipped. That was when Hagar was up for a fine, he thought. After each of these eloquent breaks the amounts would run to one fifty or even two fifty until the deficit had been made good. He came to the final page and found the balance: fourteen hundred and twenty-five dollars. For a moment he sat struck dumb by the utter beauty of the thing that lay behind the prosaic columns of figures. Mamba—a maker of bricks without straw, a disciple of a single transcendent ideal, in the name of which she had worked her obscure miracles, with none to know, none to applaud.

Wentworth turned with a new curiosity to examine the girl who had been the cause of such devotion. The very magnitude of the sacrifices which she represented endowed her with an importance out of proportion to herself as an individual. She was a symbol into which had gone the blind upward urges, the stumbling aspirations, the great fantastically conceived dreams of the old woman, and behind Mamba, of millions of her inarticulate kin.

During the brief space of time that he had been with the girl Wentworth had been conscious of a growing annoyance at her calm acceptance of the sacrifices that were being made for her, at the coolness with which she had precipitated a wreck, then left the débris for others to clear away. Mamba, Hagar, Grayson, himself, would attend to details. Why should she worry? Now the little book that he held suddenly explained her attitude. It went farther and convinced him in some inexplicable fashion that her assumption was justified.

Lissa would attain her goal because she, like her grandmother, had never once removed her gaze from it. He knew, of course, of the girl's reputation in coloured circles as a singer, and of Mamba's faith in her future. Now he saw that this faith was the only thing that mattered in their lives. It had been born and bred into the girl. Her own belief in herself was supreme. Of the great faith that she and Mamba held in common there were certain articles that she must perform. Mamba had others. It was their job to carry through together: the job of believing in a thing so intensely, so single-mindedly, that the day would come when that belief should become an accomplished fact. If Lissa hesitated now, if she removed her gaze from the steady light to which it had become accustomed, and turned back, dazzled and blundering, she would have broken faith with Mamba. She would be guilty of unpardonable weakness. She must look only forward, and leave the road that she had travelled to the watchful eyes of the old woman.

A pang of envy assailed Wentworth. Of late he had been enormously pleased with himself. He was a success. Charleston said so, and, as it had watched him from boyhood, it ought to know. The symbols of conquest were his. Next week he would return to town with Valerie; then comfort—love—probably children—an ordered and beautifully complete existence. Yet there he sat envying an unknown mulatto girl, and seeing with a sudden and terrible clarity a seedy youth in a country store hunched over a guitar, groping for the unattainable with eager, clumsy fingers. But the past had reached dead hands after him, guiding him imperceptibly this way and that. Forces that had driven forward in grooves for generations had pulled against his amorphous longings, his only half-realised dreams—had held him true to form and tradition. Behind Lissa there had been nothing; before her, Mamba's one immovable idea. An old loneliness that he had known in that far-gone time stabbed up through his complacence, and now he knew that it had been a singular and beautiful thing, and that there exists for certain solitary spirits a loneliness that holds more ecstasy than the delight of any human companionship. And so to-morrow was to be his wedding day. And there was Lissa following her dream.

He realised that his hands were trembling, and he tensed them savagely. He was a sentimental fool. His mother had been right. Val had been right. Life would still be an adventure.

He stole a glance at his companion and realised that she was no longer conscious of his presence. She was sitting forward with her gaze fastened upon the crowds, the towering buildings, the surging traffic. Over their heads the Elevated hurled its mechanical thunders. From a yawning excavation almost directly under their hurrying wheels thudded the heavy detonations of blasting. Faces hurtled by in taxis. Faces intent and watchful swept in full tide along the pavements. After a while the girl turned toward Saint, and in her first remark showed that already she had sensed a thing that the Southern white man had never felt, that in the vast unconcern of this city there was escape; that in the very heart of this crowd there was a strange and private hiding place where no one had time to wonder who you were or what you were doing.

"This is where I belong, Mr. Saint," she said. "Nobody here has time to wonder whether I am even white or coloured."

Presently they were on Lenox Avenue north of the line, and the white faces were behind them. Lissa saw the change instantly, and her composure vanished. She clapped her hands with a delight like that of a child. "Here are my folks, Mr. Saint," she exclaimed. "See, everywhere—and such big houses."

The taxi swerved to the right, and they were in a street that showed a glimpse of the East River under the high-flung bridge of the Elevated. Then they drew to the curb and stopped.

Wentworth awakened to the realisation that he was sitting with Lissa's money and bank book still in his hands. He put them hastily back into her bag, took the valise, got out, and discharged the driver.

They found themselves on the pavement before a three-story

brownstone building. Over a push button beside the door was a brass plate which stated: "Rectory of St. John's Episcopal Church."

The mulatto maid who admitted them said that the Reverend Thomas Grayson lived there, was at home, and would be with them presently.

In the few minutes during which they sat in the quietly furnished room Saint was again impressed by Lissa's ease and appearance of belonging. Once their eyes met, and she gave him the bright transfiguring smile that linked her with Mamba and Hagar, but, except in that moment, he felt she was already at home in the alien metropolis and that he was the provincial visitor.

Grayson entered, holding Saint's card in his hand. He was older than as Wentworth remembered him, and his expression of seriousness had deepened almost to one of solemnity. His shoulders and chest had grown heavy with his greater maturity. The large head set firmly on his short neck gave an impression of rock-like solidity to the figure. His ears were small and close-set, and the closely clipped graying hair revealed the lines of his skull and stressed the negroid formation. The years that had passed since his residence in the South had produced in some subtle way an appearance more characteristically negro, a race consciousness that had become definitely assertive. He conveyed a sense of power, but it was the power of one who moves slowly, predicating action upon a laborious logic, not to be swayed by an appeal to the emotions until the matter had been thoroughly weighed. Knowing his history, one would have said that his experience in the South had taught him to fear and distrust emotional hysteria, and had swung him to pure reason as a basis for behaviour. As a result his position in Harlem was one of unique importance, for his church had attracted the rising intellectual element, and through them he was in contact with the leaders of advanced thought among the white people of the metropolis, thus profiting by this first opportunity of the race in America to meet the Caucasian upon an equal basis of give and take.

Grayson showed no surprise at the visit, and sat in an attitude of easy attention while Lissa told him her story. Then the girl drew the little prayer book from her bag, opened it at the flyleaf, and handed it to him.

"My mother said to show you this," she said simply, "and ask you to look out for me."

He sat looking at the page for a moment, then he raised his eyes to Saint's. "The mills of the gods, Mr. Wentworth," he said; "perhaps my venture into the mission field has borne fruit after all."

He turned to Lissa. "And you will stay here for a while, at any rate, with my wife and me. We have no children of our own. She will be glad."

Saint thanked him and, feeling an enormous relief from the burden of responsibility, took his departure.

The maid appeared to show him out, and while she was handing him stick and hat he caught from the drawing room a fragment of conversation that he was never to forget: the deep voice of Grayson said, "And you, my child, have you any plans? Is there anything that you can do?" And immediately into the ensuing hush like the cry of a bird at dawn came the answer:

"I can sing."

PART V

For several minutes after the departure of Lissa and Mamba, Hagar stood in the road. Her eyes, still resting on the spot where the car had stood when Lissa had embraced her, were wide and intent, like those of a sleep-walker, and a faint, fixed smile was upon her lips.

In a scrawny cedar close by there sounded a drowsy flapping of wings, then Maum Vina's big rooster stood erect on a limb, arched his neck eastward, and flung a ringing challenge into the teeth of the advancing day.

With a start Hagar recovered herself and looked about her. She was quite alone now, and there was something to be faced there in the dark without Mamba, without any one; all by herself now she must make plans and carry them out. She thought of Bluton lying in the shack, but with neither regret nor terror at what she had done. Only out of that thought there seemed to grow a blackness that menaced Lissa and that was unendurable.

She turned and entered the cabin, and with a clumsy meticulousness, as though every simple movement was the result of an elaborate mental process, she made her preparations for departure. In the faint glow of the lowered kerosene lamp that stood beside Maum Vina's bed, she dressed herself and made up a small package of cornbread and cold meat that she found in a closet. For a moment she stood looking down at the old woman who had been first her guide, then her charge for so many years; then she slipped quietly out and closed the door behind her.

The fowls had quieted down again after the first cock-crow, and

271

she saw them, misty blobs of darkness, ranged along a limb against the sky—that meant a good hour of darkness ahead of her. She drew her skirt up and tucked it high like a field hand's, leaving her long legs bare to the knees and unimpeded. Then she set off with a free stride in the direction of Bluton's shack.

The moon had set, withdrawing its diffused radiance from the misty west, so that now even the solid mass of the swamp toward which she journeyed was invisible against the horizon. But the tides of life had definitely set toward the new day, faint as yet, but stirring along the earth in little exhilarating waves, filling the air with those subtle vibrations that are the precursors of light. Through the gloom the big free-striding figure of the woman advanced. The movement about her quickened. She threw a glance behind her, and, high in the east, she saw a finger of light touch the mist. Then suddenly she was upon that hour of the twenty-four when Earth recapitulates her creation, when in a brief cosmic atavism she slips back to her wild beginnings.

The void through which Hagar moved no longer hung poised in inertia. Free-running tides of life set it swinging and pulsing. The mist lifted and divided itself into vast slow-moving bodies that hung close to the ground and hesitated until some unseen force seized them and whirled them together in silent chaos. The woman stopped in the road, touched by the magic of it, and stood gazing about her. She saw vague inchoate masses heaped upon the dim earth. She saw these masses obliterated by the mist, and when she looked again, the curtains were withdrawn and the young day had modelled them into forests, fields, and cabins. The light gathered speed. It poured along the ground, dividing tree from tree. It lifted into the branches that still clutched at retreating mists and peopled them with separate leaves. Then, as at a given signal, the world burst into sound. Birds shrilled from the casena bushes, and like an ominous call Hagar heard the teeming life of the swamp awake and lift its composite voice. She had been tricked by beauty, and day had taken her unawares.

She broke into a dog trot. It was imperative that she reach the shack before people were up and about. The voice of the swamp grew louder, and now, against its gloom, she saw the squat ugly bulk of the shack.

Bluton was lying where she had left him. Quickly she bent over, gathered him up and flung him upon her shoulder. Then, casting a hasty glance around, she went out and closed the door. She had only a hundred yards to travel for cover, and this was fortunate, for, as she left the shack, the sun pierced the mist and drenched the clearing with light. It outlined the huge figure of the woman with fire, and cast a gargantuan shadow before her as she laboured forward beneath her rigid and grotesquely posturing burden.

She extended an arm and parted a curtain of vines, then she passed through into welcoming gloom. Black ooze squirted between her toes and covered her feet. She heaved a deep sigh of relief and paused to take her bearings.

First she must dispose of the body, and to do this most effectively she must penetrate to the heart of the swamp where no one would be likely to find it. She bent forward and shifted the burden from her shoulder to her arched back. Then she set off as briskly as possible, tearing a way through the matted growth with her right hand while she steadied the body with her left. But this position caused her to advance with lowered head, and eyes fixed on the pools of shallow water through which she waded. At first this pleased her, for the little mirrors flung back pictures of sky seen through swaying cypresses, with small white clouds tangled in their branches. But presently she became aware of the reflection of an object that projected over her shoulder and looked down into the water, as she was doing. She paused, and the reflection did likewise. Then she recognised its cause as the head of the corpse which hung over her shoulder close to her own.

With the first sense of uneasiness that her deed had brought to her she shifted her load so that it would no longer gaze downward and started forward again. But with an almost animate persistence the body moved with each stride, and gradually the round, blank silhouette again eclipsed the miniature skies through which she waded. Now her anger rose, and she splashed heavily through the water, shattering and dispersing its reflections.

An hour passed, and the sun, now well over the treetops, commenced to draw a thin steam out of the swamp. The din of voices that had heralded day commenced to abate, settling in drowsy diminuendo into an almost complete silence. Then, as Hagar reached the dense growth that clogged the central area of the morass and made progress difficult, the air about her broke into a shrill ominous whine, and a black cloud of mosquitoes enveloped her, settling like dust on head, shoulders, and legs. Involuntarily she struck out with both hands. With a heavy splash her burden fell from her back and commenced to settle slowly into the semi-fluid ooze. Slapping wildly at the maddening cloud, and with her skin on fire from the poison, Hagar turned her back on the body and broke savagely through the tangle in search of one of the little islands that rise through the water of the swamp and offer a slight harbourage from the pest.

At last she found it, a knoll of high ground, lifting out of the cypress knees, and having above it an irregular circle of opaque blue-grey sky. Crouched over almost on all fours, with prehensile hands tearing her way through the undergrowth, the great woman emerged like a prehistoric creature quitting its primal slime, and climbed out upon the knoll.

For a moment she sat panting heavily, her face and arms streaming with sweat and blood from stings and thorn lacerations. Then from her pocket she drew a bandana handkerchief, a clay pipe, tobacco, and matches. She mopped her face, filled the pipe and lighted it, then sat gulping the acrid smoke in great draughts and blowing it in a cloud about her. The last of the mosquitoes took reluctant flight, and with a long sigh she lay back on the tough swamp grass to think things out.

She realised with relief that there was no occasion for speed. Beyond the swamp lay a broad belt of open and populous land planted in truck farms, and this must be crossed at night if she would escape detection. She need not resume her journey, then, for several hours, and this was the best place to wait.

She ate breakfast from her package of provisions, and refilled her pipe. Already her fatigue was passing, and her mind commenced to turn over her problem, dwelling upon its various aspects. Usually, when Mamba had told her what to do, that ended it, and she gave the matter no further thought. But now, with the realisation that the guiding genius of that intelligence had gone from her, perhaps forever, a sense of individual responsibility bore down upon her and forced her to study and reason on her own account. Mamba had had to think mighty quickly there in the dark with Lissa waiting to hurry away to safety. And Mamba did not know this country as she did. Did not know Proc Baggart, for one thing. Mamba's plan depended for success entirely upon her escape; her ability to traverse the mainland and reach one of the Sea Islands where there were almost no white folks, and where the negroes would hide that big clumsy body of hers from the police so that she could not be caught and questioned.

Her train of thought broke off, and for a moment her mind was a clean blank; then vividly the image of Bluton intruded itself. She saw his limbs jutting woodenly from the water, and black ooze creeping toward his open eyes. Poor Gilly—she couldn't hate him now. Then she wondered if he would hate her. If he would forget that she had saved him once and remember only that she had strangled him and left him to rot in the black mud of the swamp.

Well, what was done was done, and there was no use to worry about it. Now, if she reached the outer edge of the swamp by sundown and waited an hour, then set out to the southward—— *But Gilly hated the dark. "Bright lights," he would say, "gimme de bright lights."* Yes, to the southward, that was what she must think about—thirty miles to Edisto Island. By fast travel she could do that by sunrise. Her thoughts came slowly, they made short rushes, stumbled, brought up against obstacles, like a child learning to walk. By sunrise . . . She'd not risk the bridge—but swim across below it . . . *Perhaps if Gilly hated the dark so he wouldn't stay where she had left him.* "Saint Helena Island," she said suddenly, out loud. She had heard lots of talk about Saint Helena—two nights farther away—maybe three—thousands of niggers there—lodge members—if she could get there and tell a lodge sister that she was a "Vestal Virgin" they'd hide her sure. The "Virgins" always stood together—even their own men couldn't find out their secrets. . . . *When dark came on and Gilly couldn't see the stars—only black water—what then . . .* Yes, the "Virgins" always stuck up for each other. She remembered once when— *He'd be so frightened maybe he'd break loose.* In the hot sunlight Hagar's blood was suddenly chill. She mopped her face with the bandana. Then she refilled and lighted her pipe. The Reverend Grayson knew what he was talking about. He had said right out in church that spirits couldn't walk. Even old Maum Vina believed that—and she had been almost a conjure woman herself with her herbs, and her money in the road. She would think about the Reverend awhile. . . . He always wore that shroud. . . . *Yes, Gilly would forget that she had saved his life once. . . . He'd only remember that she had strangled him and left him with his eyes full of black water.*

The Reverend—the Reverend—— Hagar made a desperate effort to visualise him, but his face eluded her—he was only a column of whiteness against a wall that had a cross painted on it. What had he said that day when he took Maum Vina's hope away from her? . . . Spirits only lived in heaven or hell. . . . That was it. The terror that had been pressing in upon her was suddenly dissipated. Again her mind was a clean blank. She got to her feet and moved about the island, stretched her limbs, and again became conscious of the hazy sunlight that beat down upon her.

She saw that the sun was directly overhead, and she realised that she was hungry. Opening her lunch she ate heartily of her corn bread and cold meat, then lay on her belly and drank a few swallows from the side of the island where the water was clearest. A sense of well-being pervaded her body. Why worry? She'd be on Edisto by to-morrow morning. Likely as not they would never find Bluton and think he had gone away. Then Lissa would always be safe. Some day, a long time off, she might even get back and see Mamba again and hear all about Lissa from her. She stretched her length on the grass, and presently, in the steamy narcotic noon heat, she dropped into sleep.

She saw Bluton turn slowly over in the mud. She saw the rigid knee and elbow joints give and the man stand upright. Then she saw him following her path through the swamp, but without effort, and this was strange, for his eyes were blind with swamp ooze. Briars that had impeded her did not detain him. He parted the vines and thrust his face into the clearing. She opened her eyes in a stare. *And there he was.* After the passage of an indeterminable space of time, the apparition faded.

Hagar was terrified, but she knew what she would have to do before she proceeded on her way. Fighting mosquitoes with tobacco smoke and flailing arms, she retraced her steps and with incredible labour of body and agony of spirit dragged the corpse to the island. Rigor mortis was passing, and Hagar composed the limbs decently, and bathed the face and eyes with her handkerchief. Then, leaving it gazing up into the open sky, she set off for the outer edge of the swamp.

★

Her spirit soared, her step became light and sure. It seemed that only now was she free of the actual physical incubus. She stretched her arms wide and straightened her broad shoulders. Gilly would rest easy now with the sun in his face all day and the stars keeping him company at night. She was shed of him at last—free.

She made surprisingly good time, and it was still afternoon when she noticed that the trees before her were no longer a solid wall but showed thin places where the light filtered through from the open fields beyond. She was in splendid trim for the journey, her senses keen, her muscles vigorous. In contrast to the depression of the morning she waited in excited anticipation for the coming of night.

Out beyond the trees, where the sun still lay heavy and warm, an abominable mongrel hound rolled over in a broom-straw field, yawned, lifted a fretful hind leg and scratched his mangy ribs. Twenty feet away a cottontail took alarm, hoisted its white ensign astern, and sailed silently away toward the cover of the swamp. A vagrant air caught the scent of the rabbit and trailed it past the nostrils of the somnolent cur. The animal raised its muzzle and tongued, long and quaveringly. From a neighbouring hamlet half a dozen answers sounded, bell-like in the heavy silence, and the broom straw commenced to sway to the threshing of excited tails.

With her confidence at its height, Hagar heard them coming. An icy hand seized her heart, contracted about it, and her blood crawled frozen through her veins. *Dogs!* A primal terror that was proof against argument and reason silenced both and paralysed her brain. The clear, high unceasing rhythm of the tonguing shook along her nerves in waves of exquisite terror. A strange guiding force broke the inertia of her body and worked a subtle change in her appearance. Her nostrils quivered. Her hearing became more acute. She faced the sound and commenced to retreat silently, warily. Her back touched the trunk of a great live oak. She spun around. Then she found herself climbing, reaching always for higher limbs, swinging herself up, panting—trembling. When she reached the top branches she crouched in the heavy foliage and peered down through the leaves and moss.

They were nearer now, and the cry had accelerated until it was a taut rope of sound that had one end in her body and that shortened with every second.

The dogs had gotten Ned. He had been loose for two weeks after he had cut Bluton. He would have got clean away but for the dogs.

The pack passed almost directly beneath her perch. She could scarce retain her hold upon the branches as she peered down. Then she saw it for what it was: the flash of a small tawny body with a bobbing white spot, and the parcel of yelping mongrels.

Slowly reason returned. They could not have found Gilly yet. Nobody knew he had been killed. She took herself in hand and fought the weakness of fear. She became conscious of sunlight about her, sky above, and, just below, the plateau of treetops.

A shadow swept over her, and she raised her eyes. Scarcely twenty feet away she saw a buzzard, the rondure of his belly—the blue-black wings—the baleful, questing eyes. He was not sailing idly, but winging purposefully eastward. Then another and another flashed past with a soft purring sound of wings against air.

A black premonition caused her to turn her head and follow

their flight to its destination. She knew in that moment that she had lost. To the eastward, over the spot where the island lay among the trees, the air was black with flying shapes. They sailed in the formation of a waterspout, wide and slow moving at the top, but narrowing and whirling faster and faster as it descended until the base disappeared among the treetops like a pointing finger. She looked westward again and saw the air lanes dotted with still other shapes winging steadily down from the rookery at the western extremity of the swamp.

So Gilly had won. He hadn't been afraid of the dark after all. What he had in his mind was that she must bring him out into the open where the buzzards could find him and tell Proc Baggart.

Now she knew that it was useless to proceed. The strength of her muscles that could carry her through a race with the living would be unavailing against the cunning of the dead. Gilly had proved that Grayson was wrong.

Her gaze was drawn back to the eastern skyline and the whirling column of wings. In the great emptiness of sky it would be visible for miles. Perhaps already Gilly had been missed and searching parties were hurrying along the trail that she had broken that morning.

Suddenly, there, in the moment of acceptance of the inevitable, a miracle occurred. Somewhere in the inner depths of the woman's soul, in some remote and secret abiding place, a bolt snapped back, a door opened, and a new courage flooded her being. This was not merely the old force that had always fortified her against physical suffering. It was something radiant that shook through her body in a swift, clean ecstasy. It made her suddenly and astonishingly glad to be there; to wait expectant for a supreme moment of revelation that she knew was coming. All feeling of urgency left her. No need for speed now. No need even for Mamba. She herself would be sufficient for the event. A strange and beautiful

sanity lay across her mind like a shaft of light. She turned it this
way and that, and many dark and obscure things were made plain
to her. She knew that Mamba had been right about Lissa all the
time, that she did not matter of herself, except that now, at last,
she was going to give her child something of value; something that
she could always remember.

Squatting on her limb, with only sky above her and tree tops
below, her mind turned on Mamba's plan for her, and she saw its
great flaw. The white men would take her, and they would want
to know everything in her mind. She might try to hide Lissa
away in some dark corner where they could not find her, but she
knew that would not avail. She had seen other negroes try concealment, but Baggart and the others had so many ways. Their
minds could dig and dance and circle until, at last, out it came.
Then suddenly she was upon the answer. Her mind seized upon
the idea, turned it over, discarded nonessentials, built logically,
beautifully, completely. The moment had come. She was ready.

★

It was past ten o'clock, and Davy wanted to shut up shop and go
home. He was the commissary manager now and he frequently kept
open until late hours, especially in fever season, when there were no
white folks around and the negroes would gather and talk. Wentworth had agreed to the plan, and Davy had showed with pride that,
like most of his ideas, it had a sound commercial value, the sales on
"bounce" and candy during the social hour amounting to a tidy sum.

Now the commissary manager commenced to clear his premises
by the simple process of moving among the boxes, stools, and barrels
upon which his customers were seated and dislodging them forcibly
from their perches.

"Git on home, yo' lazy niggers," he ordered. "What yo' t'inks dis is, anyhow—a white gentlemen club?" He called to a negro who was standing in the doorway: "Hang up dem outside shutters, Ben, den come an' gib me a han' wid dese no' 'count niggers."

But some one was about to enter, and Ben stepped aside to allow her to pass. With one accord the negroes looked up, and there stood Baxter, very dishevelled and appallingly muddy, with bare legs and her skirts tucked up above the knees.

Keen observers all, they were immediately aware of a change in the woman. They had known her as a rather silent person who upon occasions, such as lodge meetings, passed suddenly to the other extreme of temperament and indulged in almost violent bursts of animal spirits. Now, looking into her face, they sensed something new and disturbing. Her heavy features were in repose, but she conveyed an impression of smiling down upon them from a height. Her eyes were wide and unusually bright, and as she crossed the room toward Davy there was immediately evident a new co-ordination of movement that invested her great bulk with a sort of massive dignity and made her appear almost majestic to the mystified onlookers.

When she reached the high counter, she turned her back to it, rested her elbows on it, and stood looking out over the heads of the negroes, who had resumed their seats and were regarding her in watchful silence.

For a long moment she stood so. She did not seem to realise that it was time to shut up the store and go home. She seemed to think that she had all the time in the world. Finally, as though she were not speaking to them at all but to some one who stood at their backs, she put her first, inexplicable question:

"Any ob yo' folks eber hear ob a nigger killin' heself by what de white folks calls committin' suicide?"

Before her, eyes showed white glints here and there. Heads turned as by a common impulse, then faced her quickly again.

A woman's voice said, "Fuh Gawd' sake, Baxter, don't talk dat talk!"

Silence.

Then a man said, "Everybody know nigger nebber kill heself."

"Why dat is?" Baxter persisted in her strangely impersonal catechism.

" 'Cause nigger ain't worry heself dat much," came the answer.

"Tain't always goin' be like dat," Baxter said in a slow musing voice, as though she were thinking aloud. "Time comin' when nigger goin' worry jes like white folks, an' den Gawd goin' show 'em what to do when he trouble get too deep fur he to wade t'rough."

The fixed attention of the group broke before a wave of uneasiness. Bodies shifted, and some one started to speak. But now Baxter looked down, and her glance travelled from face to face.

"Anybody seen anyt'ing ob Gilly to-day?" she asked in a matter-of-fact voice.

The tension broke. Several of the negroes laughed nervously. A number of voices were raised in negative answers. But her next question alarmed them again by its irrelevance.

"Anybody seen any buzzard roun' here to-day?"

Yes, they had all noticed buzzards over the swamp. Somebody had lost a hog, no doubt, or maybe a dead mule had been dragged out there.

Hagar stood apparently debating the matter, her gaze again fixed upon the air over the heads of the negroes. Then with a faint smile she turned to Davy and motioned to a shelf where several dusty account books lay.

"Get down dat oldes' book, Davy, an' bring um here."

The man obeyed and placed it on the counter before her, studying her the while with his bright disturbed eyes.

"Now turn back twelve year 'til yo' comes to a man by de name Baxter. Ah gots a promise to keep."

Davy spun the yellow pages, found what he sought, then raised his eyes interrogatively.

"How much he owe when he done get drownded?"

The man peered at the fading pencil scrawl. It was a dollar and a quarter, he informed her.

Hagar drew a ten-dollar bill from her pocket. The yellow-back was an unusual sight in the commissary, and the negroes, their curiosity getting the better of their alarm, crowded forward to see.

Still holding the money, she indicated the large glass jar of "jaw-breakers" on the counter. "An' how much for dat bottle ob candy?"

"De whole t'ing?" he asked in amazement.

"Sure, de whole t'ing."

"Well, dere mus' be two hundred in dere. Dat'll be two dollar."

With a broad gesture Hagar lifted the jar, withdrew the stopper, and poured the contents in a cataract of red and white out over the counter.

"Help yo'selves," she invited.

"An' now dat keg ob bounce. How much dat?"

Davy, in an incredulous voice, opined that three dollars would pay for it.

"You niggers get to dat keg and fill yo'selves up," she commanded. "Ah all de time been wanting to gib yo' a party, but Ah ain't had no free money till now."

Slowly they withdrew in the direction of the keg, and Hagar stood looking after them with something of her old childlike wonder in her smile.

She turned back toward Davy. "Poor ole Baxter," she mused. "Ah done keep yo' waitin' a long time, but we's quits now. An' Ah ain't done so bad by yo' name." Then she spoke directly to Davy: "What he all come to, Son?"

He computed the account at six dollars and a quarter.

She handed him the bill, and, as he took it, she said with a spurt of fierce and uncontrollable exultation in her voice: "Don't gimme de change, Son. Take um to de do' an' t'row um far an' high. Ah's done wid money. Ah's free now," then after an almost imperceptible hesitation, added, "free as Gawd."

The amazed youth looked up, but already the mood had passed. It was as though the Baxter whom he had known, and even the strange creature who had been there a moment before, had gone quietly out and another woman had entered.

She said in an incisive tone of command, "Now get a pen 'n' paper, an' take down what Ah say. Time's passin', an' Ah got to be gettin' along soon." She raised her voice and called, "Come here, all yo' niggers. Ah want yo' to swear to dis writin' Ah's goin' to gib Davy."

When he was ready she dictated in a clear steady voice, never hesitating for a word, retarded only by the deliberation of the writer.

"Las' night Ah strangle Gilly Bluton to deat' wid my two han'. Ah kill um 'cause he use' always tuh be my man, an' he git sick ob me an' t'row me 'way. Dere ain't nobody dere but me when Ah kill um. Dere ain't nobody know nuttin' 'bout um 'cep' me. Dat's all. Now sign um Baxter an' gimme de pen so's Ah can make de mark."

The negroes stood goggling at her, petrified into attitudes of incredulity, horror, fear. Davy leaned over the paper like an automaton that had run down, its motive power ceasing while the pen point hovered over the sheet.

Hagar stamped her foot impatiently. "Get on and sign um," she commanded. "De time's close now, an' Ah got to go."

A woman broke through the circle, pushing the paralysed negroes to right and left. It was old Vina. She was as frightened as any one, but she had courage. She laid hold upon Baxter's arm and pulled her around.

"Wake up, gal, wake up an' talk de trut'," she pleaded. "Dere ain't been a night sence yo' come here dat yo' ain't slep' all night in my room." She turned to the gaping crowd. "Don't yo' b'liebe she. Yo' niggers—ain't yo' see she ain't right in she head?"

Baxter brushed the old woman away like a fly. She was shaken by a storm of passion that flung the circle from her like physical force. They backed away, knowing at last that their first impression when she had entered was right. Baxter had lost her wits. She glared at them and stamped thunderously upon the floor.

"Ah's talkin' trut'," she shouted, "an' ef any pusson in dis shop say Ah ain't, Ah's goin' make um sorry 'til he done dead."

She spun around again on Davy and shocked him into action. "Write Baxter." The pen descended upon the paper and the letters fell from its point in jerky succession: "BAXTER." Hagar took the pen from Davy's fingers and made a firm black cross.

"Now," she said, "to-morrow yo' take dat to Proc Baggart an' tell him Ah sen' it."

She dropped the pen, and in the dead silence of the room, it rang a sharp clear note as it struck the counter. Then she turned, and the watchers saw that her passion had passed and she again wore the odd aloofness of expression with which she had entered. She turned her gaze to the door with its square of misty, moonlit night.

"De time's come," she said. "So long, eberybody."

For a moment they saw her, a huge black silhouette set on frosted silver; then she was gone.

Maum Vina's scream cut the silence and loosed the negroes from their trance. "For Gawd' sake, stop dat gal," she shrilled. "She out she head, an' she goin' do sheself hahm."

They jammed through the doorway and scattered out on the piazza.

Only the night was out there; vast and tranquil it lay upon the square of white sand, the pine forests. Above them it was an infinitude of moonstruck mist, its utter silence not even broken by the far whisper of a star. They waited bewildered, not knowing what to do next.

Suddenly from the river came the loud bark of a dog, a single shout, then a confused babel of voices. The negroes broke into a run, and presently they crowded out on the narrow wharf.

Beside the pier, seeming to strain its spars upward, lay a schooner that had been moored there the day before. Its crew were already at the pier head gesticulating and pointing downward.

All afternoon the September spring tide had been pumping its vast burden of water into the low flat river lands, saturating porous marshes and setting the grass tops awash, piling incalculable tons of brine into salt creeks, brimming secret lagoons. Now the great heart that lay somewhere out beyond the moon turned from systole to diastole and called its tide home.

On the pier head the negroes stood in silence and looked down. There was nothing to do—nothing to say. Below them, so close they could have reached down and touched it, the river drummed against the piles. Beneath its surface sleekness the currents writhed and turned like giant muscles under a velvet skin. So fast it sped. An hour, and its crest would be free of the little rivers and out again into the open sea.

*

Above the metallic roar of the subway a brassy voice shouted "One Hundred and Twenty-fifth Street," and, like a succession of enormous exclamation points flung for emphasis after the words,

a series of posts flickered across Lissa's vision. Gradually the per-
pendicular bars lessened their speed until finally each exhibited the
numerals 125 in black against glaring white. Behind the girl the
hurtling darkness fell away. The train shot out into a pool of
light and came to rest with a jerk that precipitated her through
a newspaper and against a hostile breast. Doors sprang open with
mechanical precision, and with a sigh of relief packed white and
black broke their enforced common imprisonment, the negroes
pouring out on the platform, the whites appropriating their places
and regarding their retreating backs with resentment and relief. On
the platform the dark mass hesitated for a moment, drew deep
breaths, stretched limbs, then, like a breaker that has found the
shore, it lifted, caught Lissa up on its crest, hurled her before it up
the stairway, and deposited her breathless, but triumphant, on the
pavement. Saturday afternoon—her first thrilling week of study
under Salinski behind her—his grudging word of praise singing in
her ears.

The day was warm, but the sun lacked the torrid pressure that
had enervated Lissa during the Southern summers. Over her head
the sky was no longer the throbbing cobalt of a Charleston noon,
but a thin ultramarine that seemed to lessen the power of gravita-
tion and lift her along with a new buoyance. She swung east in
the direction of her home. In her new liberating environment an
inherent elegance in her carriage and manner that had impressed
her Charleston neighbours as merely amusing lent her distinction
and gave her that air of self-assurance which in Harlem differ-
entiates the cosmopolite from the newly arrived provincial. She
was clad briefly in dark blue tailored silk. The colour was a concession to Mamba, the brevity to Harlem. A scarf of flamingo
red was knotted loosely about her throat, and a small jaunty hat
of the same shade fitted closely about her head. Below the dress
a rather astonishing length of champagne silk stocking was evident,

and, symbolic of her complete emancipation, these terminated in a pair of red high-heeled pumps. She carried a modish vanity case, and a small umbrella in the accenting colour was pendent from one elbow.

With that power to evoke memory which contrast possesses to an even greater extent than similarity, the alien setting switched the girl's thoughts back to her last eventful night in Charleston. She had been a member of the Grayson family for ten days, and with her faculty for expelling from her mind all that caused her discomfort, the tragedy of Bluton's death and her hurried departure were already as completely dissociated from her life as a printed story in a book that has been replaced upon its shelf. Out of the experience only one impression remained sharp and actual—Hagar, who in that hour had suddenly materialised out of the characterless parent that it had pleased her to imagine, had taken matters into her own hands, and at the last had surprised her into that overwhelming surrender to maternal love. It was strange that she could feel no horror over her mother's act. On the contrary, a latent savagery in her own nature caused her to feel a curious pride, a deep sense of sympathy with her mother, and a realisation of a kinship closer even than that which existed between Mamba and herself. Out of the sheltered life that Mamba had provided for her with its dependence upon the protection that civilisation throws about the weaker individual, she had crashed suddenly into conflict with life in the raw, and she had been helpless. During that hour when Bluton had held her captive, and behind the shack the swamp voices had shrilled and wailed in implacable nocturnal conflict, she had had it in her heart to kill, and only the man's preponderance of strength had kept her fingers from tearing at his throat. Then Hagar had come, terrible in her direct and unfettered simplicity, and had put Bluton beyond the power ever to harm her again. After the years of separation Hagar had stood forth in that one illuminating hour more real, more vividly alive, than Mamba, for all of the old woman's shrewd planning and untiring devotion. Then, in the moment of parting, had come the climax when the big, inarticulate woman had kissed her hand and she had found herself in her arms. Her reason told her that here was a specific act for which she should be ashamed of her mother, yet by some strange paradox the thought of her was a swift infusion of warmth—a feeling of completeness where before there had been a sense of want—a sudden and inexplicable pride of birth. For the first time in her life she quickened to the realisation of all that Hagar had done for her—the money that she had sent each week for her music—her clothes. And she had never even gone to see her. It made her feel ashamed. "Well," she told herself, "I'll be able to make it up to her before long." Now that Salinski had undertaken her training, and with the money that could be made in New York.

She took the brownstone steps of her new home two at a time. In a vivid flash she saw Mamba's face wearing its mask of ferocious disapproval. Do you call that being a lady? What the hell! Now she was free—neither a lady of the Broaden set nor a waterfront nigger. Lissa Atkinson with at last a will of her own—nothing behind her, and everything that she wanted from life waiting for her around the next corner.

She let herself into the dim coolness of the hall. In the drawing room a song stopped in the middle of a bar, and Ada Grayson parted the portières and kissed the girl affectionately. With her glasses, her slow, kind smile, she was ridiculously like her husband in appearance. Lissa had liked her from the moment when the three of them had sat together after Saint had left her in the drawing room, and Ada had watched her husband's face with divining intensity; then, realising that under his words he had really wanted the girl to stay and was not merely submitting to a command of conscience, had taken her into her affections without reservation.

"Now, I sha'n't detain you, my dear," Ada told her smilingly. "You'll find a letter from home on your dresser, and I know you're anxious for news."

Her new buoyance lifted Lissa up the stairs with the effortless spring that had brought her down the street and up the front steps. It shot her breezily into the room and across to the dresser, where the letter lay with her name staring boldly up into her face. Then her mood went slack. The air of the room seemed suddenly chill, inhospitable. She picked the letter up gingerly between a slender thumb and index finger. Whose was the bold, disjointed handwriting? It startled her like the shouting of her name by an unfamiliar voice. Slowly, reluctantly, a slender flexible index finger slid beneath the flap. She paused and examined her hand with an impersonal admiration, deliberately putting off the opening of the letter. The colour, neither black nor white, had never before interested her. Now, in contrast with the dead white of the paper against which it lay, it seemed rather lovely to her with its warm bronze tint, its pointed and polished nails that glittered like little blades in the light. Finally she rolled her finger beneath the flap and pried it gently open. She turned the envelope over and shook out a number of newspaper cuttings and a brief note. Her gaze focussed on the signature: Saint Julien de C. Wentworth. It was a moment before she identified the august name with Mamba's Mr. Saint. Then she read:

"These clippings will pain you, but you ought to know what they say. In no other way can you realise the sacrifice that Hagar has made for you. To the few of us who know the whole story, she has revealed herself as heroic, a mother of whom you should be proud as long as you live. The body has not been recovered and was probably carried far out to sea. It took Hagar's death to show us what she really was, and I for one am proud to have known her."

The body—sacrifice—the awful clippings with their sharp and uncompromising black type . . . The room where she stood had gone chill with warning. Mr. Saint shouldn't have done that to her. Mamba wouldn't have let him if she had known. She wasn't used to pain. *Hagar dead.* She felt the warmth that had infused her being from her mother's last kiss slowly ebbing, while a strange numbness took its place. She had a premonition that if she read the clippings she would find herself to blame—would have to accept the responsibility—be answerable for the event. Why not simply accept the facts—death—loss—and destroy the papers that lay defenceless before her, yet which menaced her peace of mind? She should save herself for the sake of her art—Mamba had wanted that —Hagar herself. How could she be expected to sing and be gay with her mind full of trouble?

Still undecided, she lifted the printed strips. One of them dropped face up on the dresser. NEGRESS MURDERS LOVER THEN TAKES OWN LIFE. But that wasn't so. Her mother had never loved Prince. Now she was impelled to proceed. She commenced to read, her eyes taking in the words and transmitting them to her brain, and all the while her old self in utter panic, flinging the words of a silly song at her, trying to distract her, to get her away to the old protected plane of consciousness. "If you lika me lik I lika you an' we lika both the same . . . *Unusual case. A search of old files reveals no other case of suicide in a local negro—had saved Bluton's life ten years before*—I'd like to say, this very day, I'd like to change your name— *Evidently the result of a jealous rage followed by remorse* . . . Under the bamboo tree. A great night that, when she had first realised that she could take an audience—knock them cold—smash of the band—the air full of paper streamers— and, far away, stars out of the open door—Prince!! *Las' night I strangle Gilly Bluton to deat' wid my two han'. I kill um 'cause he use' always tuh be my man, an' he git sick ob me an' t'row me*

away. Dere ain't nobody dere but me when I kill um. Dere ain't
nobody know nuttin' 'bout um 'cep' me. (Signed) Baxter. I'd
lika to say . . .

In a sudden violent synthesis the story before her rushed to com-
pletion—assumed form—unity—silencing the indecent irrelevance
of the song, confronting her with its tremendous implication: if it
hadn't been for her, Hagar would be alive to-day. After a while,
with a conscious physical effort she wrenched her gaze from the
words of the confession; then, with deliberate thoroughness, read the
clippings one by one and piled them with mechanical exactness before her. The papers had given an unusual amount of space to the
commonplace of a negro murder. In spite of its colour, it held the
elements of excellent copy—human interest—passion—jealousy—
and the culminating touch of the confession, superb in its stark
simplicity.

Lissa folded the last strip, placed it upon the others, and stood
gazing out over them at nothing that the room contained. Her
brain, busy in estimating the cost to herself, told her that she was
safe, that so beautifully had Hagar built her plan that at no point
could danger touch her. Her mother was known only as Baxter, a
vagrant negress who had come to the mines ten years before, had
once saved Bluton's life, and had later, presumably in a fit of jealous
rage, destroyed him. But while her mind assimilated these facts,
coolly felicitating her upon her escape, upon the final complete
erasure of the record of her own origin, an inexplicable tremor seized
upon her body, shaking her so that she fell into a chair, seized the
arms with her sallow expressive hands, and gripped desperately
while the tremor possessed her like the sustained tension of a galvanic
current. Presently the seizure abated. Then came weakness as
from a protracted illness, and a pang of loneliness and longing that
swelled, mounted, and overwhelmed her, flinging her head down
upon her arms, and blinding her with a gush of tears.

With every one there is some picture etched into the child mind by the bite of some early and penetrating emotion. It stands there always, isolated, marking the beginning of memory, obscuring lesser subsequent impressions. Up now from under the drifted years this picture flashed into Lissa's consciousness—a great bruised figure standing in a doorway with a policeman beside it—a strange salty taste upon her child lips where her mother had pressed a farewell kiss. The girl sat waiting. Her tranced gaze had found the window and had escaped the confines of the room into an infinity of sky. Then another picture began to brighten, assume colour, form —a gigantic black woman kneeling in the dirt of the public road, patting her with great clumsy hands, while her body mingled a tang of sweat and phosphate dust with the druggy perfume of roadside honeysuckle. This memory held a poison that she could not at once identify. Then it came—the beginning of a fastidiousness in herself that had turned her away from the great creature who might soil her dress to the cleanness of Mamba's arms. A gap. A time of things wanted because of a strange loneliness that needed assuaging—a fire in her blood that had driven her in a half-desperate search for the unattainable to the Broadens—the roadhouse dances— the last night with Prince. Her last picture of Hagar, the dominant figure of that insane night looming like destiny over the body of Bluton, taking her in her arms and giving her for one brief moment a sense of refuge, of sudden arrival at some remote and illusory goal. It was strange now that she could not remember a word that her mother had ever said. She imagined her as vast inarticulate power —encompassing love, possessing her all the more now because of her silence.

She saw now with agonising clarity all that Hagar had given, and now that she had gone there would never be anything that she could offer in return. She felt an impulse to wound herself in some way, believing vaguely that pain would expiate her thoughtlessness, her indifference. She closed her hands in a muscular spasm that drove the nails into her tender palms, and imagined a slackening of the grip upon her heart. Now she was fiercely glad that she was alone. For the first time in her life she was glad to be free of Mamba and her indomitable will. The old woman would tell her to look ahead and forget what had happened. Now her only comfort came from sending her thoughts back to the three impressions of her mother, and in a blind search for some way in which she could punish herself for her selfish neglect.

Beyond the window the shortening September day dwindled into twilight. In the street the cooling pavements called the dark children from the serried houses. They swarmed down, noisy as blackbirds, and flung a gay chattering sound up to Lissa's room. From the two adjacent Elevated lines sounded roar and answering roar as the trains hurtled with mechanical punctuality over the darkening streets. To Lissa they seemed like the tick-tock of a titanic clock dividing the present into minute segments and hurling it into the limbo of the past. On the Avenue the windows of an apartment house lost the red of the sunset, stared blank for a moment, then winked to life again, restless in the blue dusk. But these things that Lissa had loved as symbols of her new life had lost their magic. She sat staring through them into the Carolina Low Country. Once she rose from her chair, got from a bureau drawer the prayer book that Hagar had given her, opened it at the flyleaf with its inscription, then sat again with the volume in her hands.

*

It was not until after breakfast the following morning that Lissa left her room. She wore the clothes that she had had on when she came from her music lesson the preceding afternoon, and she went directly to the study of Thomas Grayson, opened the door without knocking, and entered.

He sat at a large square desk in the middle of the room looking over the notes for the sermon that he would deliver at the morning service. The massive severity of the desk made a fitting base for the bust and head of the man who sat there.

Lissa closed the door behind her, and stood with her back against it as though taking refuge from some pursuer. Grayson looked up and saw her face. The live bronze had gone a lustreless brown, except where it had darkened to violet under the eyes. From swollen lids the eyes looked with a hard brilliance. The hint of tragedy that had been latent in her expression was suddenly all that he saw there, rendering the face drawn and haggard. Her hair was dishevelled, her dress looked as though it had been slept in. There was a shocking incongruity in the pair of frivolous red pumps on her feet.

His response was characteristic. He said in a deliberately matter-of-fact voice: "Don't be afraid, Lissa. Come here and tell me your trouble."

Without rising, he motioned to a chair that faced him across the polished mahogany with its piles of meticulously arranged papers. The girl hesitated. He seemed unsympathetic—more rock-like than ever in his unyielding power. Then she saw his face soften. He leaned forward and extended a hand across the desk. "Sit down, daughter, and tell me," he urged. "Ada and I have been fearful that your letter brought bad news."

She sank into the chair, then she placed the letter, clippings, and prayer book before him. "Read that letter and those papers please," she begged. "They're about Ma."

She watched him take the papers in his heavy, well-kept, hairless hands, and read them through with his habitual thoroughness. Now that she was close to him her feeling toward him changed. Out of his massive silence strong emanations of sympathy flowed toward her. She felt his power now, not as opposition, but as a sustaining force. She was glad that he had not spent it in easy volubility.

He finished the last clipping, then folded them all carefully and returned them. When he spoke his voice seemed stilted, inadequate in contrast with his unspoken sympathy. "Your mother was a truly great woman, Lissa. The just God who knows everything will forgive her. She has given her life for you. You should be proud of your parentage—your race."

She did not comment upon this tribute. Her reply struck out at a tangent, as though she had waited for him to finish speaking to say what had long been on her mind. She leaned forward, swaying slightly in her chair. Her speaking voice had caught the tragic timbre of her low singing notes. Her short sentences were spoken in unconscious rhythm. "I can't stay here now. I can't let it stand like that. See what she says—that he was her lover. She despised him—it took me to put up with his kind—I've got to go home and tell them the truth—I've got to face the Broadens and their crowd with it—I've got to claim her now before everybody. It's all I can do."

Grayson sat heavy, solid, his arms resting on the desk before him, his eyes on her face. Without speaking he made Lissa feel his attitude as it changed from the sympathetic to the coolly judicial.

"You're emotionally upset to-day, Lissa," he said at last. "You're in no condition to arrive at such an important decision. You must wait a day or two."

Her form stiffened. She eyed Grayson with distrust. Immediately she was on the defensive. "I thought I could count on you," she said. "I thought you'd see it as my Christian duty and help me, or I wouldn't have told you. But you can't stop me now—nobody can—not even Grandma. I always did what other people thought. Now I am going to think for myself, and I know I'm right. I'm going."

Grayson made no reply; then Lissa realised that he had not been listening to what she had said. He had not moved, but sat gazing past her, his eyes intent behind their glasses, his brow deeply furrowed. In one of her violent reversions she sprang to her feet.

"A hell of a lot you care for other people's troubles!" she flung at him; then she turned to go.

"Wait!"

She was arrested by the impact of the single word and faced him again, her beautiful expressive body fixed in an attitude of fear like that of an animal at bay.

"Now sit down and keep quiet," he commanded.

For a moment longer her defiance lasted; then suddenly she bent her head and commenced to cry softly into the crook of her arm in the manner characteristic of Hagar when faced by overwhelming difficulties. Then obediently she resumed her seat.

When Grayson broke his portentous silence his voice was compassionate but firm. He said: "I've thought it all out now, daughter. Look at it this way": he picked up the clippings and selected the one which contained Hagar's confession. Lissa raised her tear-stained face, and he pointed to the words. "That," he said, "is your mother's last will and testament. In it she has left you something that she has conceived to be of inestimable value. It was all that she had to give. You cannot repudiate it. You must give her silence in return."

"But it's a lie. I can't go on always living a lie. What am I to do?"

"You must carry on. Make your life worth the price that has been paid for it. There's no turning back now without breaking faith with your mother. There's nowhere for you to go but ahead; no way to praise her but in your works."

"I won't go on," she rebelled. "I hate music. If it hadn't been for that Ma'd be alive to-day. I didn't know until that night how much I was missing her. I was always lonely, and I didn't know why. Grandma never gave me time to think. Now she's gone, an' I'm sick of everything. I'm the loneliest girl in the world."

"I know," said Grayson gently, "you think now that it is this great loss that makes you so. It isn't. Like Ishmael, you were born for loneliness. But you have this to be thankful for—you were also born for success. I had a talk with Salinski yesterday. He's extravagant in his praise of your voice. He has never taken a negro before, and it took all of the influence that I could bring to bear to interest him in giving you a trial. It's a great chance for you. It's more than that. It's a great chance for the negro race. If you drop it now, go South and perhaps run the risk of being arrested as an accessory to the murder, certainly, at the least, returning to start over again handicapped by a scandal, you will have thrown that chance away. For Hagar—Mamba—all of us— you've got to carry on."

He picked up the little prayer book that he had given Hagar, opened it at the flyleaf, and let his gaze rest upon the inscription. "Strange," he said, "that this should be here with us now. When I gave it to your mother I was face to face with my great disillusionment. I had thought that the fight should start at the bottom. I had put everything that I had in me into it, and I had failed. I have learned since that the battle is on here—not in the South. Not that we receive more kindness here. There is a certain kind of cruelty that we meet in New York that is not known in South Carolina. We have been taught to expect things here, and then when we come we find these things denied us. But here we find a market for our own peculiar gifts—talents that are our heritage, and of these yours is the greatest—the gift of song. Nothing can take that from you. You must put the past behind you as I did —as all of our people must do. You must succeed."

Lissa's tears had ceased. She sat with her eyes fixed upon the desk before her. The room bore inward upon her, exerting an invisible force against her body—holding it powerless in the chair. Even Mamba had never been so implacable as this will that had assumed magistracy over her destinies. She knew that the moment when she met Grayson's eyes would see her complete and ultimate surrender. And yet through sheer weakness she longed to turn to that power for support.

She knew that Grayson had risen. She heard him moving behind her, then softly the door closed, leaving her alone. Through the open window came stray notes from the complicated symphony of human existence—the shrill ecstasy of a child—deep, careless negro laughter—a piano lingering over a sentimental song in a neighbouring apartment—slow, rambling talk in two women's voices on the pavement—Harlem obstinately opposing its lazy rhythms to the headlong theme of the metropolis—flinging an alien syncopation of laughter and song against the measured reiteration of the Elevated, the sustained monotone of hurtling traffic on the avenues. Her own people about her everywhere. But different. Singing for fun—just cutting loose—crying when they wanted to—living up to the limit and never thinking about it. Why couldn't they let her be like that? Why couldn't they let her alone?

★

Saint Julien de Chatigny Wentworth, up from Charleston with his wife and his mother for a fortnight of music and the theatre, settled the ladies of his party in the third orchestra row of the new Metropolitan Opera House, and, appropriating the vacant seat between them, abandoned himself to the mood of the unique performance. Individual as he appeared in the heterogeneous audience, he yet had upon him the mark of a type. Upon him a dinner jacket seemed a more formal garment than it did when worn by the men who were seated near him, and his tie, too wide for the prevailing mode, had about it the quaint suggestion of a stock. Already, while only in the middle thirties, his figure was com-

mencing to show the comfortable outlines of one who appreciates
the pleasant things of life at their full value and who has learned
to meet the unpleasant ones with an amiable acquiescence. Yet the
face, with its high forehead and thoughtful slate-coloured eyes,
showed evidences of having passed through some spiritual conflict.
The strong line of the chin indicated sufficient courage for an individual course of action, but the sensitive mouth suggested that
when this course violated the standard of good taste of his class its
pursuit would be at a cost that would amount to a minor heroism.

It was now seven years since his marriage. Seven years since he
had responded to Mamba's summons and had placed Lissa in the
care of Thomas Grayson. That this should occur to him now was
natural enough, for the performance, which had already commenced,
was the occasion of Lissa Atkinson's début. Presently, with that
faculty of submergence of self in the contemplation of a work of
art, which is in itself an art, he became a disembodied presence
moving in a realm of illusion upon the darkened stage, and, by the
stage's magical power of projection, beyond that again into a pine
barren of the coastal South.

Beyond the pines glimmered a faint red dawn that cast a vague
radiance over the bent or recumbent figures of a number of people.
From the figures came a chant, hypnotic in its interminable reiteration of a single strongly syncopated phrase. A limpid mezzo-
soprano drew upward from the monotonous level of the chant. Instantly Wentworth recognised the voice—Lissa's—Hagar's—Mamba's. The song lifted and hovered above the shadowed figures in a
repressed agony of yearning and supplication. Wentworth's emotions attained that height at which delight and pain are fused into
one and become pure ecstasy. Then the curtain descended in a
swift obliterating rush and stilled the voice. But in the wide
silence of the auditorium its vibrations kept beating on like a pulse.

High in the dome constellations of incandescents commenced to glow faintly. A stir went over the audience. Saint felt sudden anger. Why couldn't they leave him alone in the actuality of the music? Why drag him back into the make-believe of people, walls, lights? The glow brightened and flooded the auditorium, calling him back into full possession of his faculties, and he became aware of the well-dressed audience that seemed to be pressing in upon him. For a moment longer they hung breathless, then shattered the silence with a spontaneous thunder of applause.

From the people near Wentworth stray ejaculations and comments leaped clear of the clamour and impinged upon his consciousness. "Good God, where'd she come from?" some one queried. "What's it anyway, a play—an opera—a pageant?" And the rejoinder, "For Heaven's sake, don't label it. That's the trouble with us. What we can't label we damn. Can't you see it's new—different? Can't you feel that it's something of our own—American—something that Stallings and Harley got a glimmer of in 'Deep River'—that the Theatre Guild caught the pictorial side of in *Porgy*; that Gershwin actually got his hands on in spots of his 'Rhapsody in Blue'? It's epoch-making, I tell you." Behind Wentworth a man said in a tone of finality: "Well, they've done it. It's native from the dirt up—it's art—and it's ours." "Ours?" a voice inquired. "Do you mean negro?" "Negro, if you will, yes, but first, American."

The auditorium was aglare now, and the fused single entity of the audience had melted back into its component atoms. The ugly blur of confused talk swelled suddenly and drowned individual voices. Wentworth let himself go back into his chair. The experience had left him shaken. He hoped that Valerie and his mother wouldn't talk. Sometimes they didn't seem to understand that there were moments when silence can be richer than speech. His emotion had broken his thoughts free from their habitual moorings. Now he'd like just to let them drift. With relief he saw that his companions remained silent, evidently lost in their own thoughts; Valerie with a bright, forward look in her eyes; his mother's lost in reverie. He returned to himself: "God! What music!" he thought. "Primitive? — Sophisticated? — Neither — both. Savage, tender, reckless. Something saved whole from a race's beginnings and raised to the nth degree by Twentieth Century magic—a blues gone grand opera. . . . Not a bad idea that. Make a note of it and use it when I start to write. . . . No, it's too late now—Mother—Valerie—the *boy*. . . . By God, he'll have his chance—painting—music—literature—it's up to him now. . . . Three generations to make a gentleman. Rot. Five. Ten. Then, war. Two more generations to gather up the pieces—to carry on until the tide turns. Well, those two can't expect everything. . . . Lissa! What a voice—power—beauty—everything, and that heart-breaking pure negro quality—Hagar—Mamba. Rotten time of it, like as not, for all the laughter and singing—climbing up out of the mud—making a gallant fight of it. . . . Others too—back at home—different kinds with different sorts of trouble. That banker Broaden, for instance—good citizen—hoeing a hard row and not bellyaching about it—precious little recognition. . . . What would he think if I addressed him as Mister? . . . What would my white friends think? That's easy: 'Turn their heads,' 'Black menace.' Absurd, looking from this distance. . . . 'Good morning, *Mister Broaden*,' saying it like that—meaning it. . . . Why not? . . . Little enough, God knows! . . ."

And Kate Wentworth, sitting close to her son, where she could feel the warmth of his arm touching her own, not understanding his mood, but sensing its existence, feeling him asking to be let alone. "What in the world is opera coming to!" she is thinking. "This mania to be different is at the bottom of it, I suppose. . . . Verdi—now he gave us music. . . . Or if one wants to be modern, there is Puccini. But this—outlandish, I call it. . . . Libel on the South—nothing less than plain libel. . . . Who, in pity's name, from a section which is famous for its aristocracy, elected to go and hunt up negroes to be sung about? . . . Mamba's Lissa! Hagar's! Still more incredible. The girl's air of distinction—style—they must have come from somewhere. . . . I wonder who could have been her —No, don't say it—don't *think* it. Shame upon you, Kate Wentworth. You are forgetting yourself. To a lady, the ———'s of mulattoes do not exist. . . . But if it had to be negro music, why not, at least, the beautiful old spirituals? . . . Lissa—what a remarkable looking child she was, with her speaking eyes and that air of being at ease in the drawing room when Mamba brought her in. . . . Now a famous person. . . . 'Practically born in my back yard.' . . . Well, then, '*raised* in my back yard.' . . . Well, then, 'the grandchild of *our* dear old Mamba.' . . . Now that song of hers at the end of the act—no, I wouldn't call that outlandish— strange and different. . . . Perhaps after all they did suffer at times on the plantations. . . . But not at the hands of the aristocracy— overseers—poor-whites—and, of course, traders. . . . Saint—how distinguished he is looking now—so like his father—a Wentworth! Silly of me to sit here crying when I'm so happy—when the fight is all over—when my children have won. . . . What a sensitive profile he has—a thoroughbred—a success—a manager of the St. Cecilia Society—youngest on the board. . . . Valerie—a fitting mate for my boy—lovely now with that smile on her lips—living in the memory of the music, no doubt—well, she's of the new generation, perhaps she gets more out of it than I do. . . . A good mother to my boy's son—a good daughter to me. . . . Shall I go behind the scenes with Saint afterward? Shall I take Valerie instead right after the curtain and leave him to follow? . . . These new negroes—so different—wouldn't understand who I am—something awkward might happen—expect to be addressed as Mr. and

Mrs. no doubt—No, I couldn't manage that. . . . Now, Lissa, she would understand with her Southern raising. . . . But the others! No, it would not be wise to stay. Saint can wait if he wants to and join us later. It is different, less complicated, with a man."

And on Wentworth's left, with the smooth ivory of her shoulder brushing his broadcloth sleeve, sits Valerie, lost in her own reverie. "The boy," she is wondering. "Is Miss Jones taking proper care of him? He's such a restless sleeper—needs watching. . . . He's so absurdly like Saint. . . . It is good to know that once, at an important turning, you thought straight, acted for the best, threw your weight on the right side. . . . Good to know that your child will have every comfort—every chance—that your husband is happy —respected—successful. . . . Lissa! What a strange upside-down place the world is. . . . Mamba! That night when she took Saint and me to her church. . . . I knew then that I had to have him. . . . Funny old thing, Mamba—knew my heart before I did— wanted to help us along. . . . The wedding. . . . The boy! Is he missing me? Wish I knew more about Miss Jones—still she *was* well recommended—looked competent. . . . Will he sing, I wonder, or paint—or write?—It means so much to his father. . . . But I'm not so sure. . . . Dad's failure! Yes, but money makes such a difference—gives talent its chance. We're secure now—Saint— *the boy* . . ."

*

Slowly the light in the big auditorium commenced to ebb, dimming the modern decorations and endowing them with a mysterious beauty, then plunging the audience into interstellar night. The slow throb of music filled the dark, then the curtain of the final act drew up on a stage of swirling mists and vague half-lights.

Instantly the mood of the play was re-established, fixing the watchers in attitudes of rigid expectancy.

Dawn again, but no longer the red of an old despair. A thin essential radiance breathed upward behind the massed towers of a metropolis. It gathered strength, spraying out like the corona of an aurora, gilding the towers, then dominating them. The music caught the mood of the sky. The arresting dissonances, the sharp syncopations of the early acts, were no longer individually evident but seemed to merge into a broader irresistible current of sound. The rhythm, too, was no longer a thing separate. It became a force as indistinguishable and pervasive as the life current. It was a fundamental law that moved light, music, the sway of the crowd, the passage of time, in a concerted and inevitable progression. The artificial declamations of operatic convention were gone. The cast was reduced to two elemental forces. The crowd with its heavy mass rhythms and reiterated choruses was the body, and the single transcendent mezzo-soprano that soared above it was the spirit, aspiring, daring, despairing, lifting again. The movement became faster. The voice commenced to lift the chorus from its inertia and carry it along on short, daring flights. Then, in a final acceleration, the scene soared toward its tremendous climax. The light, the movement, the music, merged into a sweeping crescendo, the chorus sprang from its lethargy, while the voice of the woman climbed triumphantly above it until it shook the air like a storm of beating wings. Then the curtain shot downward.

When Wentworth recovered from his trancelike absorption the house was applauding; the large negro chorus was taking a curtain call. The demands of the audience became deafening. Lissa's great hour! She advanced to the footlights and bowed. Now, in the full light she was plainly visible for the first time, a mulatto, a little above medium height, and of superb proportions. Wentworth noticed that she wore no make-up except a slight darkening of the lips that made them seem fuller, more deliberately negroid. This struck him as significant. From the light bronze of her face her eyes looked out, large, expressive, and extraordinarily brilliant— Mamba's eyes—yes, and Hagar's. Now, for the first time, he noticed that she appeared self-conscious, anxious to be away. She bowed for the second time, and without waiting for the curtain, withdrew among the chorus.

But the audience would not let it rest at that. They got to their feet and cheered. They kept the clamour going with a sort of mad persistence. After five minutes of it the curtain was seen to move, rising slowly on a bright vacant stage.

Lissa stepped from the wings, and the clamour plunged into silence. The trace of embarrassed self-consciousness was gone. She seemed detached, oblivious of both herself and her audience. The conductor rose and looked up to her for his cue. Apparently she did not see him, for she gave no sign. Instead she stopped where she was just out of the wings, and unaccompanied commenced to sing the National Anthem of the American Negro.

Apparently most of the audience had never heard of it. Wentworth never had. From the first note he was aware of an absolutely new sensation. Against his perception beat the words of James Weldon Johnson's inspiring poem swept forward in the marching rhythm of Rosamond Johnson's music:

"Lift every voice and sing
  Till earth and heaven ring,
  Ring with the harmonies of Liberty;
  Let our rejoicing rise
  High as the list'ning skies,
  Let it resound loud as the rolling sea.
  Sing a song full of faith that the dark past has taught us,
  Sing a song full of the hope that the present has brought us:
  Facing the rising sun of our new day begun,
  Let us march on till victory is won."

Wentworth, listening, felt suddenly the impact of something tremendously and self-consciously racial; something that had done with apologies for being itself, done with imitations, reaching back into its own origin, claiming its heritage of beauty from the past.

On the stage, as the song progressed toward its conclusion, the singer commenced to sway—sway as Mamba always did toward the end of a spiritual. Only in this young voice to which art had brought discipline there was a difference. It wasted nothing in hysteria, but released the full torrent of its pent emotion into the words and music. Now she was singing the final stanza:

"God of our weary years,
 God of our silent tears,
 Thou who hast brought us thus far on the way;
 Thou who hast by Thy might
 Led us into the light,
 Keep us ever in the path, we pray.
 Lest our feet stray from the places, our God, where we met Thee,
 Lest our hearts, drunk with the wine of the world, we forget Thee;
 Shadowed beneath Thy hand,
 May we forever stand.
 True to our God,
 True to our native land."

The song ceased, and the curtain descended. In the auditorium the audience paid it the tribute of a breathless silence. Then they rose quietly and filed out into the street.

*

It is a Saturday in late May, and Mamba, happy in the gifts that the gods have left her, sits upon the doorstep of her crumbling mansion and lets the new and altogether mad world go hurtling past. Beneath her feet the multi-coloured flagstones have given

place to a cement pavement. Before her eyes the old cobbles have
been superseded by an asphalt roadway from which the heat quivers
visibly upward, shaking the geometric perfection of lines that con-
verge toward vanishing points northward and southward. Upon
the buildings to her right and left the restorers have been at work.
It is now several years since this army of invasion appeared, determined and zealous, to restore the district to its ancient high
estate. Strangely enough, Mamba recognises among the invaders
faces of those who, earlier in the century, came to tear the cobbles
from their century-old beds, to smash the flagstones to atoms and
haul them away. But now they are bent upon a frenzied quest for
the antique, buying the ruined mansions, banishing the negroes,
and preparing the street for white occupancy. Only the great
four-story structure where Mamba sits and suns herself, and which
is said to contain some of the finest Georgian panelling and ironwork
in the city, is impregnable, for its title stands in the name of one
Lissa Atkinson, and Saint Julien Wentworth, who manages the
property, states definitely that it is not for sale.

Unmindful of the direct rays of the morning sun, Mamba is
sitting, as is her custom, to watch the New York steamer put to
sea. As though in mute protest against the invasion of law and
order, she is attired in an old wrapperlike garment, faded and far
from immaculate. Her legs, thrust straight out before her, are
stockingless, and her feet disappear into disreputable-looking men's
shoes. An old clay pipe juts at a rakish angle from between her
toothless jaws, and from it smoke fumes in a lazy cloud about her
face and drifts away to offend the sensitive nostrils of the white
passers-by, who are becoming more and more numerous as the
houses fall one by one into the hands of the restorers. Her age is a
matter for speculation, as it is a subject upon which there is no
one left to speak with authority. Her body is shrunken with the
actual physical contraction of age. Under the tired flesh the bones

are commencing to assume undue prominence, foreshadowing their grim survival. Through gaps in the sparse gray hair the skull shows in sharp outline, and the brows are ridges beneath which the eyes are lost when the head is lowered. But this inevitable physical mutation which in another would denote senility has, instead of diminishing the force of her personality, in some strange way intensified it, so that those who speak to the old woman as she sits there feel it in the air about her like an aura. The negro children who come and go sense it and grin delightedly at her word of affectionate abuse. The cur now lying beneath her knees with only his muzzle showing under the folds of the wrapper knows it, and has gone there for refuge from a world that has no pity upon an unlicensed mongrel.

Mamba has at last accomplished what she believes to be her final adjustment to the changing exigencies of life, and she has no complaint with Fate. The old room one flight up where Lissa was born, and from which Hagar was led to her banishment, is again her stronghold. But now how different in appearance! Papered with pictures of Lissa—Lissa at a steamer's rail, off to Europe—Lissa smiling from the centre of a rotogravure page in the costume of her latest opera—Lissa in a hundred poses, a hundred settings.

But Mamba, scorner of limitations, has at last learned the necessity of their acceptance, for only by so doing can she project her memory back into a past shared by her daughters. Across the way, where the muddy beach once lay, where the mosquito fleet was wont to dock, and where the negroes would swarm and chaffer; where the smacks, when they were sea-weary, would leave their bones awash in the warm tides, all is now quiet—barren—orderly. If she moves her gaze ever so slightly to the north it encounters the long line of a modern pier; to the south, and her happiness is ambushed by the spectacle of a dozen gleaming yachts belonging to rich Yankees who have invaded her familiar precincts. And so she has schooled her eyes to span the distance and dwell unimpeded upon a rectangle of sunny harbour. Beautiful, familiar, unchangeable, it lies as always mirroring the first dim fires of dawn or sparkling in the bright windy afternoons. And across it, as they used to do when Lissa was a baby, the New York steamers come and go, bellowing their deep hails and farewells.

Over the hot roofs come the measured tones of St. Michael's chimes announcing the hour of ten. From behind the pier sound shouts and commands. Mamba sits forward, tense, expectant. Then, majestically, across her rectangle of harbour moves the lofty cut-water of the New York steamer, folding back the flat blue into a thin green line lipped with white, drawing after it the steep, black wall of the hull, the high, gleaming superstructure.

This is the moment for which Mamba has been waiting. Now that the vessel has drawn its full length into her sphere of vision she sees in it more than the form of a familiar friend out of a loved past. It is no longer a great and mysterious adventurer putting forth from her little world into a vast unknown. No. To-day she is watching a sure voyager of that fabulous distance which lies between the wish and the rainbow's end—between her first fantastic dream for Lissa and the consummation of that dream.

Now from the whistle a plume of steam is blown against the stark blue of the sky, and a hoarse, baying note wakes the echoes along the waterfront. Far below the crowded decks, the soaring funnel, on her own private doorstep, Mamba draws herself together, and her eyes light with a gleam of her old impudent spirit. "Git along, den," she says patronisingly. "Git along. Ah ain't holdin' yo'. An' when yo' get whar yo' is goin', 'member what Ah tol' you' an' gib my gal huddy fuh me."

THE END